Finding Ruth

ROXANNE HENKE

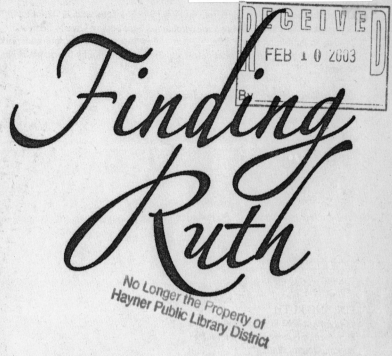

HARVEST HOUSE PUBLISHERS

EUGENE, OREGON

Cover by Koechel Peterson & Associates, Inc., Minneapolis, Minnesota

FINDING RUTH
Copyright © 2003 Roxanne Sayler Henke
Published by Harvest House Publishers
Eugene, Oregon 97402

Library of Congress Cataloging-in-Publication Data

Henke, Roxanne, 1953–
    Finding Ruth / Roxanne Henke.
       p. cm. — (Coming home to Brewster; 2)
      ISBN 0-7369-0968-0 (pbk.)
       1. North Dakota—Fiction. 2. First loves—Fiction. I. Title.
PS3608.E55 F56 2003
813'.6—dc21

                                       2002009430

Printed in the United States of America.

03 04 05 06 07 08 09 10 11 / BC-KB / 10 9 8 7 6 5 4 3 2 1

Philippians 4:12-13

I have learned the secret of being content
in any and every situation…
I can do everything through him who gives me strength.

To the people of Wishek, North Dakota,
my Brewster,
the somewhere I call *home*.

Acknowledgments

Thanks to:

The many readers who wrote to me after reading my first novel, *After Anne*. Your letters are the reward for all the lonely hours at my computer. Thank you for sharing your thoughts and encouragement. The meek might inherit the earth, but I hope letter writers get first place in the checkout line in heaven's library.

My editor, Nick Harrison, whose eagle eye and heart for fiction made this a MUCH better book. And to the wonderful staff at Harvest House, who held the hand of this new-kid-on-the-block this past year as I waded through the "new author" landscape. You made my journey joyful! Thank you.

Dean Mastel of Cumulus Broadcasting in Bismarck, North Dakota. Everything I know about the radio business, you taught me. Anything I got wrong is purely my imagination run wild. You are a gem in station manager's clothing.

Jenel Looney, my writing friend (whom I *still* haven't met), and my sister Kim, both early readers. Your feedback gave me the courage to keep writing. Many thanks.

Debbie Turner, the only other member in our Book Club for Two. Who else would understand the "need to read" (and write) like you do?

My Mt. Hermon friends Cathy Elliott, Bob Russell, Henriet Schapelhouman, Dee, and B.J. Your e-mail friendship has meant the world.

Jackie Baumgarten and Yvonne Engelhart. Whenever I need an ear, or a boost, you're there. How do you say thanks for that?

My mom, Jean Klein, who has embraced my writing career with enthusiasm only a mother could muster, and my sisters, Kim Anderson and Ann Jensen, who offer unconditional love and unfailing support, for which I am beyond grateful.

My husband, Lorren, and my daughters, Rachael and Tegan…you hold my heart. Always. Thank you from the bottom of it.

Brewster, North Dakota. Middle America, USA. The kind of town where everybody knows your name. Where everybody knows what everyone else is doing…or thinking of doing. A place where neighbors run cookies over with the latest gossip. Where the waitress at the café is your next-door neighbor. Nine-man football. A twenty-bed hospital. A grocery store that offers home delivery on Thursdays. All these things can be found in Brewster.

What else can be found there? People with hopes and dreams. People in love and people with broken hearts. Friends and foes. Families and faith. When you get to know the people of Brewster, you'll find it isn't all that different from where you live.

Welcome to Brewster…it's a good place to call home.

Prologue

Ruthie

For Jack, it was always about the music. He'd walk around listening to his own drummer, drumming his way down the school hallways, thumping on desks with his fingertips, tapping his feet in a syncopated rhythm that even had the band teacher yelling, "Jack, stop it!" I didn't know him then, but I knew who he was. "Musicman," we called him. For Jack, it was always about the music.

Not for me.

For me, music was my way out. Out of my boring life. Out of my confining small town. Out from under my parents' control. Out of Brewster and on to somewhere else. Anywhere. If I turned up the music loud enough, it was even my ticket away from me.

All I ever wanted was a chance to dream. A chance to live my dream somewhere besides in my imagination. I wanted a chance to find somewhere where I belonged, and I just knew that place was somewhere beyond Brewster, North Dakota.

Ironically, it was the music, and Jack, that brought me to that place. To the place I could truly, finally, call home.

But that makes it sound so simple. It wasn't. It took me a long time to find that place. Very long.

You see, I've taken the "Detroit Route." A saying in my family that means going completely out of your way to get to where you intended to be in the first place. That's me, Ruthie Hammond, finally home, via "Detroit."

It may be clearer if I start at the beginning. Well, not exactly the beginning. More like somewhere in the middle, but by the time I'm done you should know the whole story, via Detroit.

Somewhere in the Middle

Ruthie

It would have been easier to turn off the radio, but Jack was driving and I knew he'd give me one of those *what's the deal?* looks and make a federal case about me turning off the radio midsong. One of his many pet peeves. I knew because I'd been counting lately. It seemed I couldn't stop. I was up to eleven this week. Instead, I sat there and silently wrestled the memories that came washing back when I heard our old song. Not mine and Jack's. Mine and Paul's.

Without even closing my eyes I could remember Paul holding his fist to his mouth like a microphone, mouthing Van Morrison's plaintive words to "Brown Eyed Girl." Singing them to me. Sometimes I hated memories. I'd thought I had gotten pretty good at dealing with them, but I was wrong. The song made me think about the life I could have had, not the one I got. My heart started feeling all squished up and achy, and I could feel tears stinging my eyes. I knew better than to let them fall. That was another one of Jack's pet peeves. Me crying. Not that I'd done much of it lately. It was easier not to.

Sometimes.

I pretended my ears were itchy and rubbed at them like a dog with fleas. Luck was with me.

"I never did like this station." Jack punched the button for me, switching from the oldies to heavy-metal and cranking up the volume. He started thumping his hands against the steering wheel. "Now that's what I call *sound*." He looked at me to see if I agreed.

I forced a smile, glad to hear anything but the song that had been playing.

"That's the kind of music I want to play on our station someday." He popped the dashboard as if it were a cymbal.

"Not going to happen as long as we stay in Brewster," I responded.

"You got that right, babe." He snapped his fingers until the song ended, then turned down the volume. "I don't know how much more of that country twang I can take. You'd think people would be getting tired of that stuff by now, but noooo, every day someone calls in…" He added a hillbilly sound to his flat Midwest tone, "'Could y'all play that "People in Low Places" song? Ya know, the one by Garth?' Well, golly, gee whiz, ma'am, I surely can." Jack laughed at his imitation and then added, "I'm so sick of Garth I could puke. Just you wait, babe. We're going to get to the big markets yet."

I'd heard that promise for years and knew better. Jack always promised we were going to computerize the station "next month." Next month never came; the bills did. I knew enough to keep quiet— the subject was a sore spot between us. I leaned forward and adjusted the volume. "I like this song." I'd said the words before I heard what was playing. It was a metal-version remake of another old song that reminded me of Paul. What was it with the radio tonight? Everything reminded me of him.

Of course, at first, almost everything in Brewster had. The city park where we'd first held hands. The movie theater where we'd sat in the seventh row from the back almost every Sunday night for four years. The school where we'd met the first day of first grade. I could hardly remember a time in my life when Paul hadn't been there. Until… I certainly wasn't going to think about that now. Not with Jack jiving in the seat right next to me.

"What're you thinking about, babe?"

Jack's habit of asking me what I was thinking about was getting to be one of *my* pet peeves. Along with his habit of calling me "babe." I had a name. Just in case he'd forgotten, I reminded him. "*Ruthie.*"

"You're thinking about yourself?" Jack tossed his chin and rolled his eyes, amused with himself. He knew very well what I meant.

I took a deep breath, trying to keep my growing irritation under wraps. "I'm wondering how much longer the bank is going to keep sending us overdue notices. I thought you said you transferred five hundred dollars from our savings account, but we got another notice yesterday."

"Don't worry, *Ruthie.* I've got it all under control." Jack reached out and patted my knee before turning up the radio so loud that the music vibrated inside the car.

I knew bringing up our growing financial problems would silence him. Now I could think all I wanted. We had at least an hour to drive before we'd hit Brewster's city limits. An hour for me to put my head back and imagine what my life should have been like. What it could have been like if I hadn't ever hooked up with Jack. If I hadn't agreed to move back to Brewster all those years ago and start a radio station.

Even with the vibration of the heavy-metal music pounding through the car, I had no trouble at all conjuring up the memory that had come to mind minutes ago. A memory I'd tried to erase for years. A memory I'd replayed in my mind hundreds of times, imagining how different life would have been if only I'd said yes when Paul had asked.

Had it really been almost twenty years…

⁓

Thump. Thump. Thump. Superintendent Baumiller thumped the microphone three ear-shattering times to make sure he had our complete attention. "Can I have your attention?"

Paul and I exchanged an isn't-he-weird look.

"Can I have your attention, please? The grand march is about to begin for this year's junior-senior prom. As soon as everyone settles down, we'll begin."

The disc jockey the juniors had hired for the night turned up his music. I suppose he thought it would let everyone know things were about to begin and he'd be on his way to getting his paycheck.

I'd been waiting for this night almost as long as I could remember. When I was younger I had come to this same decorated gymnasium with my mother and gazed at the older girls in their gowns through the stars in my eyes. In junior high I'd come with my friends and dreamed of the day I'd be part of a night like this. Then I'd gone home and dreamed of the day it would be my turn to walk down that crepe paper-lined path. But this year I'd dreamed of the prom because it represented the last big night before graduation. The last big night before freedom. I was going to leave this Podunk little school in three weeks and I couldn't wait. The sooner the grand march started, the better.

"Shhhhh!" I motioned to the couples behind me. "It's time to start."

I could see my sister, Vicky, tug at the arm of her date, Dave Johnson, pulling him into their spot near the middle of the line. She was a sophomore and wouldn't even be here if Paul hadn't matched up his best friend with her at the last minute. "Every guy should go to his senior prom," Paul had told me when he asked if I thought my folks would let Vicky go with Dave.

Personally, I thought Paul didn't want to be at the prom without Dave. The two of them had been friends as long as Paul and I had. Minus the kissing part, of course.

"The first couple in tonight's grand march is Paul Bennett, senior class president, and Ruth Hammond, senior class student council representative."

Music filled the gym as Paul took my arm and guided me through the vine-covered archway and down the pale blue paper walkway. I could see my mom and dad sitting in the bleachers, Dad looking slightly bored, Mom checking the camera to see why it hadn't flashed. From the look on her face I knew she had forgotten to open the shutter. She always forgot to open the shutter. It was a family joke. "You don't have to smile for the first picture. Mom's just practicing."

I paused, holding Paul in place until the flash blinded us, then we parted to form two lines, the boys on one side of the gym, the girls on the other. Soon Mr. Baumiller was motioning Paul and me back together, telling us to form an arch with our arms so the other couples could duck their way through. I knew exactly what to do; after all, I'd had years of practice watching this orchestrated march. Paul and I linked hands, lifting them high, forming the start of the Tunnel of

Love. At least that's what I'd always secretly called it. Tonight it seemed more like the Pathway to Freedom. One more gauntlet to pass through until graduation.

As Dave and Vicky came near, Paul lifted an eyebrow at me. Our arms came down, capturing the two of them. Vicky turned beet red, her face clashing horribly with her fuchsia dress. Dave didn't look a shade lighter. The kids around us started chanting, "Kiss! Kiss!"

Dave looked as if he were a deer caught in headlights. Vicky looked everywhere but at Dave. There was no way out but for him to comply. Shooting Paul and me a look that would have killed if it could, Dave leaned down and kissed Vicky on the cheek. The crowd hooted, booing their opinion of his chickenhearted kiss. Of course, when Paul and I made our way through the tunnel Dave and Vicky stopped us, Dave whispering loudly, "Payback!"

Paul flashed him a Romeo-style smile. "Watch. This is how it's done." Paul gathered me in his arms and placed his lips firmly on mine, not at all bashful to be kissing me in front of our classmates, teachers, and parents. The crowd hooted its approval. Through my closed eyes I could see the flash of several cameras, and I remember wondering if one of them was my mother's.

"Way to go, Paul!"

"My turn next!"

The voices of our classmates filtered through his kiss, the music, and the clapping.

"When're you two getting married?"

Paul released me with a flourish and bowed to me as if I were Cinderella at the ball. He turned to Dave. "Practice makes perfect."

As Paul grabbed my hand and pulled me along the tunnel I could hear Vicky saying, "They must practice a lot."

We did. But we hadn't always kissed so easily. I could remember our first kiss as if it were—

"Hey, babe, can you drive? I'm fading here."

Jack's voice startled me out of my memory. I sat up and shook my head. It took me a moment to remember where I was. Oh, that's right, we were driving back to Brewster from Carlton. Jack had insisted we check out a radio station there he'd heard was for sale, even after I reminded him we couldn't pay the bills for the station we already had.

"Nice setup," Jack had said to the station manager, who showed us around. Jack had acted as though he knew exactly what each computer was for. I knew better. He eyed the dedicated weather monitor hanging from the wall. "Beats looking out the window," he joked. The station manager laughed, clueless to the fact that at KBRS we used our thermometer regularly.

I knew it was a waste of time touring that station, but Jack insisted he had a plan. Why I believed him was beyond me. Why I'd believed him all these years was even more incredulous. But then, I'd come to see that without an education, without some kind of plan, following the path I was on was simply what made me feel safe. Not happy. Just safe.

Jack slowed the car, pulling it onto the shoulder of the road, the gravel there crunching under the wheels. "I'm whipped. You gotta take over for a minute."

I rubbed my eyes, wondering if I'd been thinking of the prom or dreaming. "Only if I can choose the station I want."

"Go at it." Jack got out of the car, stretched, then walked around to my side.

I slid into his seat, lifting myself over the gearshift. I'd rather do interior gymnastics than get out into the cold night. I turned down the volume on the radio, fastened my seat belt, and shifted into gear, remembering that it was Paul who'd taught me how to drive his beat-up old Volkswagen, a four-speed floor shift. The only car he could afford at the time. From what I'd heard, beat-up old Volkswagens were a thing of the past in Paul's current life. Jack was asleep before I shifted into third. I hit the scan button on the radio, stopping it at the oldies station we could only pick up on cold, clear nights such as tonight.

Within seconds I was back inside my memory, at the very spot where Jack had interrupted...

I could remember that first kiss as if it were yesterday. Third grade.

"I'm going to catch you. You'd better run fast!" Paul screamed his daily challenge to my back as our class burst through the school doors for recess.

We were playing our ongoing game of boys-after-girls. It was a given Paul would chase me. Everyone knew that. Paul had managed to tag me a few times, but with a quick curve of my back I would always elude his grasp. He'd never actually caught me, and I didn't intend for it to happen today.

"Slowpoke," I taunted, keeping one step ahead of him. I was a fast runner. Faster than Paul, anyway, which was all that mattered.

Usually Paul tired of the chase long before I was winded. He'd run off to join a kick ball game, and I'd join the group of jump ropers, one eye peeled toward him just in case he decided to take up the chase again before the bell rang.

But this day he wouldn't give up, and I was getting tired. My eyes watered with the effort of trying to stay an arm's length away. "Time out!" I panted, forming a "T" with my hands.

"No deal!" I could hear his tennis shoes pounding the ground behind me.

How close was he? I tossed my head, trying to gauge his distance. Maybe a quick sidestep would send him flying past me and I could catch my breath. Instead, my shoe caught on an indentation in the ground and I stumbled. My arms flailed at the air as my feet searched for stable footing. I was desperately trying to maintain my balance when Paul grabbed me.

To this day I'm not sure if he was still chasing me or trying to help me stay upright. Either way, we ended up face-to-face, his arms around me in a vice grip. We stared into each other's eyes; I was as tall as he was then, and our breath mingled as we huffed and puffed from our race. Time seemed to stop. Neither one of us knew what we were supposed to do. And then, as quick as a bird pecking at a seed, Paul kissed me. It wasn't right on the lips, but close enough that it counted. Before I had a chance to comprehend what had happened, he'd released me and run off to join the other boys who had long ago given up the chase.

It was six years before we kissed again. But that's the only kiss I clearly remembered. Well, the only one until the last one, the night of our senior prom—

"There's a deer! Stop!"

Jack's cry startled me out of my memory. I slammed on the clutch and brake, only to find the road clear and my seat belt gripping me in place.

Jack, however, was cussing. "Ouch!" He rubbed his left wrist where he'd hit it against the dashboard. "What was that all about?"

I looked at him, flabbergasted. "You were the one who yelled there was a deer on the road."

"Oh, sorry." He sounded sheepish. "I must have been dreaming." He settled back against the seat, cradling his wrist. "Keep driving, babe. You're doing fine."

My heart was pounding. I clenched my teeth and muttered, "Jack…"

"I'll be fine. It didn't really hurt, anyway." He leaned into the space between the seat and the door, bracing his head against the window, acting as if he were already sleeping.

I noticed he was holding his wrist as if it hurt. Good! I shifted into first, then second, getting the car back to cruising speed in no time. My memories of Paul faded as my irritation with Jack rose. I glanced over at Jack. His mouth hung open and an irritating snore filled the air. What had I ever seen in this man?

Fame.

Fortune.

My ticket to the big time.

Those were just some of the answers. Those reasons seemed awfully foolish when I considered the reality of our tiny radio station in Brewster, but at the time I'd hooked up with Jack I had thought destiny was just around the corner and he was the one to lead me to it.

There was a time when I'd thought Jack and I would get married. Not a love match, exactly. More a match of convenience. But he said we didn't need a piece of paper to tie us together. In reality I didn't think he wanted a reason to be tied to anything. So the loosely tied slipknot between us stayed in place as the radio station we owned together unraveled.

Sometimes, in the dark of night when shadows helped hide the truth, I'd try to imagine what my life could have been like if I'd had the courage to follow my dreams. If I'd had the chance to. What if I'd backpacked through Europe? What if I'd finished college? What if I'd moved to New York? What if…? Tears always came before answers. And, like now, I'd blink them away, shake my head, and think of something else.

It was hard to think of anything with Jack loudly snoring on his side of the car. I jabbed him in the side with my finger, harder than I would have had to. He changed position. The dim light of night emphasized the shadows under his eyes and around his nose, making him seem old and worn in an unattractive way. He was getting older. So was I. High school had been nearly twenty years ago and here I was, still hoping for some sort of miracle that would make my life different. Make it fun and exciting. A world filled with possibilities instead of bills. I sighed, gripping the steering wheel tightly for a minute before finally releasing more than I'd grasped.

Part of getting older was facing reality. And reality was that my dream of leaving Brewster might never happen. Tears pushed at my throat. I wasn't ready to give that up. I looked up at the half-moon, as if seeking an answer. What was I going to do? The moon was silent, unlike Jack, who continued to snore. I turned up the radio. I knew from experience it was better to try and drown him out than to make him stop.

From the crest of a hill I could see the lights of Brewster blinking on the horizon, which meant four more miles and we'd be home. I shifted down a gear, not anxious to get back to my life there. The first of many hills leading toward town blocked my view of the lights. Fine by me; I didn't need any reminders to know just how small

Brewster still was. The thought made me slow down even more. No one was going to stop me for speeding tonight. There was nothing waiting for me in Brewster but a broken dream.

As we neared the edge of town I could see the spot where Highway Three met up with Highway Thirteen. Even at high noon there was never much traffic through Brewster, so it was hard to miss the only other car on the road heading into town this time of night. One of those new-style Beetles turned onto the highway in front of me. No one in Brewster drove a car like that. I was already practically coasting, so there was no need to even tap the brake. I gladly bided my time behind the strange car. Let whoever it was in their shiny silver Bug get to Brewster before me. They were welcome to it.

Paul

The lights from the car behind me glared in my eyes. I adjusted the rearview mirror, wondering how far I'd driven without seeing any other cars. It had to have been since I'd passed through the last small town, nineteen miles back. That sort of thing never happened in Chicago.

My eyes searched for the sign on the south side of the street. It was tough to read in the near-darkness, but there it was. "*If you lived here, you'd be home now.*"

Home.

Brewster.

I hadn't lived here in almost twenty years, not since I'd left for college right after high school graduation, but Brewster was still home to me. It never mattered how long I'd been gone. Every time I drove into Brewster I felt the same, as if I were shedding the burdens of the world and coming home.

Home.

And to think maybe this time I'd be staying.

Ruthie

Where was Jack? For the fourth time in thirty seconds I glanced at the large clock on the wall. Six-fifty-nine. A.M. He knew full well he was supposed to be on-air this morning. I'd arrived home from Carlton at the exact same time he had last night, and I was here. Where was he? I shot one more look down the hall, sighed, swiveled my chair, and flipped the switch. "Good morning!"

I tried my hardest to keep my irritation at Jack from my voice. "It's looking to be a beautiful day here at KBRS, your voice in the country. Coming to you live from our studio in downtown Brewster, North Dakota. As we in Brewster like to say, 'The town that's miles from anywhere. You gotta wanna live here.'"

Yeah, right.

Grabbing a tape from the stack near the mike, I read the label as I said, "I'll have the weather for all you folks right after this new song from Claaaaay Walker. It's a good one."

I punched the tape into the machine and sat back, running my hands through my hair. If we had that computer system Jack always talked about getting, I wouldn't have to be so tied to the microphone. Half this stuff would be preprogrammed. As it was, I had exactly two minutes and fifty-two seconds to figure out how I'd gotten myself into this mess.

Sometimes I blamed the whole situation on my high school speech coach, Mrs. Webb. She was the one who had told me to try radio broadcasting as an event. "You're a natural," she'd encouraged when I'd protested I didn't know how to do it. "Come to practice. Listen to Jack. He's a natural too. He makes it look easy. You'll have fun. It'll be good for you."

She'd been right on three counts. Jack did make it look easy. I was a natural, and I did have fun. But good for me? There she'd been wrong. Way wrong.

Well, okay, I imagine Mrs. Webb didn't think she was pairing Jack and me for life when she asked us to team up for the Humorous Duo event saying, "You'd be good together." Who knew we'd win the state competition our first year? When Jack won the radio broadcasting contest our junior year and I took second, at the award banquet Mrs. Webb said, "Watch these two kids; they've got a future in radio." And then senior year, when we flip-flopped the honors and she stated, "Look out world, here they come!" I don't think she meant we had to buy a radio station together.

If it hadn't been for Mrs. Webb, I would have never had the idea that being on the radio was a way out. *My* way out. I would have gone off to college with Paul as planned. Probably gotten married shortly after college graduation and lived my life happily as a…? As a what?

Housewife?

No! Back then becoming that word was exactly what I'd feared. I was going to *be* somebody. Travel the world. *Do* something with my life. Something more than my classmates had in mind for themselves. Funny, how pairing up with Jack had seemed like the opening of a door, when in reality it had caused the door to my dreams to slam shut instead. What would have happened to me if it hadn't been for Mrs. Webb and radio broadcasting? Who knew? Certainly not me.

Paul had never minded Jack and me as speech partners. After all, Jack was just Musicman and Paul was everything else. Football captain. Basketball standout. "A" student. My boyfriend. It was a given Paul and I would get married. Everyone thought so. Even me.

Until Mrs. Webb assigned me to radio broadcasting.

I was good at it and I knew it. I could feel it. It had nothing to do with music. It had to do with words. Suddenly, I knew that words from my mouth could open doors. Doors that held more exciting things than a town like Brewster could offer. More than what my small-town boyfriend had planned. I was going to go places.

Alone.

Speaking of alone, that's exactly how I was at this moment. Jack was supposed to be doing the morning show, not me. But it would be my reputation on the line as soon as the song ended. Where was he?

With both hands I flipped my hair off the back of my neck, the cool shot of air calming me a bit. This wasn't the first time a no-show Jack had put me in a sweat. I'd have to figure my way out of the mess my life had become another time; in the meantime, I had a show to do. Think. What should I be talking about next? I glared over the console holding the tape machine and boom mike, through the glass window separating the broadcast studio from the hall, and into Jack's office.

Empty.

Staring daggers into an empty room wasn't going to produce Jack or this show. I didn't have time to think about anything; I had to get moving. I grabbed my sunglasses, jumped up from the chair, and ran into Jack's office. Pushing aside the curtains covering the window, I tried to focus on the thermometer hanging just outside. The sun blinded me for a moment, but finally I saw what I needed. Racing across the hall, I slid into the chair as the last notes of the song ended.

"You heard it here folks, Clay Walker's latest." Quickly I turned my mouth from the mike, expelling a breath of air and grabbing another one away from the earshot of listeners. If anyone was listening. "Now here's that weather I promised you. It's a bright sunny day out there today." I rolled my eyes. Any fool could see that for themselves. "That old mercury is creeping up on fifty degrees. You moms out there might want to get out the sprinkler. Those kiddies are going to want to cool off by noon. You farmers are going to have a great day to make hay. You know what they say, 'You gotta make hay while the sun shines.'" I rolled my eyes at myself. Someday soon I could do the whole show in clichés. The way the people around Brewster were, no one would notice but me. Unless Mrs. Webb decided to tune in from the nursing home.

Palming the next cassette with my right hand, I removed the Clay Walker tape and inserted the new one in an easy motion. "To give you a little inspiration, here's Faith Hill to kick-start your day."

I leaned back in the chair, stretching my chin towards the ceiling. I let Faith's voice wash over me, doing what she was singing, just breathing. *Calm down.* I'd done this before without Jack; I could do it one more time. I breathed deeply, then sat back up, elbows on the desk, my right hand wandering automatically to the miniature Statue of Liberty I'd placed there when Jack and I had started the station. The figurine had been a talisman, of sorts. A symbol. Coming back to Brewster to start this station wasn't a step backward; it symbolized only the start of my path to something bigger. That idea seemed almost laughable now, this station almost as small, in terms of radio stations, as the knickknack.

I rubbed the small torch with my thumb, the gold paint long ago worn off from my dreaming. Appropriate now that my dream had all but disappeared. It had been this tiny souvenir that sparked my dream.

"Ruthie, come here." My Aunt Lillian crooked her finger at me. I had been seven and fascinated by the soft purple felt hat she wore. Inside our house, no less. No woman I knew in Brewster wore hats inside. Much less purple. "I brought you something." She reached into her handbag and pulled out a small box. "It's from New York." She could have just as well said Istanbul. Wherever New York was, I knew it was far away. A place exotic and mysterious.

I pulled the small figure from the box. A lady in a long flowing robe held a torch tipped in metallic gold that sparkled when it hit the light. Suddenly New York was a place I wanted to see. Badly. I placed the small statue of Lady Liberty on the coffee table, marching my fingers around it as if I were walking at her feet myself, my dreams already marching ahead of me. Aunt Lillian's clear laugh filled the air as she leaned forward and ruffled my hair. "I wonder where in the world we'll find Ruth someday?"

Find Ruth? Was I going to be lost? I'd been lost once before, in the tall aisles of Magner's Grocery store. It was scary, until my mother wrapped her soft arms around me. Getting found felt good. I climbed on the couch and snuggled next to my aunt, rubbing my thumb over the souvenir as I listened to her travelogue. There was a whole world beyond Brewster. A world bigger than Captain-May-I and freeze tag. A world I was going to see someday in a purple hat of my very own. And if I got lost, someone would find me, that I knew. The next year she brought me a miniature replica of the Eiffel Tower, but by then my imagination had already taken wing.

"…just breeee—eeeee—eathe." There was a small hiss as the song died out and dead air played.

Just breathe? How about just get back to work? I jumped for the mike. "That song was so pretty it left me speechless," I said, covering my tracks. Just like I was covering Jack's. Where *was* he? "Here's another song, back-to-back." I hit the play button. The first strains of music played over the air. I spoke over them, "Stay right here, I'll have the specials from Magner's Grocery for you right after we hear from Bonnie Raitt."

The strong beat of the song fueled my irritation at Jack. My foot practically stomped as I rummaged through a stack of papers looking for the grocery flyer. Mr. Magner's ad package called for three, thirty-second spots each morning featuring his weekly specials. Where was the flyer? With a hard shove I slid my chair to the other side of the studio where another stack of papers rested. Here it was. No, that was last week's. My foot quit stomping. Where was it?

"Hey, babe." Jack poked his head around the doorframe. "You sounded real good reading the livestock report this morning."

I didn't answer. If he'd been listening, he'd already know I hadn't read it. I'd had enough to cover for him as it was. Jack knew darn well that was one of his duties, along with pulling the weather reports from the wire service. The fact that this was the fifth time in the past two weeks he'd come in late didn't seem to faze him one bit. If he thought his compliment served as an apology, he could think again. Not glancing up, I continued searching. Bonnie was on the last verse. Where was it?

"Here it is." Jack dangled the colored flyer between two fingers. I noticed he had an elastic bandage wrapped around his wrist. The one that *didn't hurt* last night. I wasn't about to give him any sympathy. Sore wrist or not, it was no excuse for missing signing on this morning. "Looking for this?"

"Yes." I grabbed for the flyer as he pulled it out of my reach. "Ja-ack, give it to me. I need it now." Bonnie held the final notes as the band repeated the last refrain of the song.

"Give me a kiss first." Jack puckered his lips. If this was his idea of apologizing, not only was his wrist going to be aching, but so was his head if he didn't hand it over. "Jack." My voice held a warning. "Now."

"Kiss." Jack thrust his face forward, eyes closed, the flyer dangling above his head as if it were a flat piece of mistletoe.

In one quick motion I reached up and tickled Jack under his arm. One advantage of living with someone is that you learn where their vulnerable spots are. His eyes popped open as he dropped the flyer and pulled his arm to his side. I grabbed the flyer in midair.

"Now that's the way to start a day." My radio voice held no trace of my emotion toward Jack. I was getting good at hiding my feelings when I was around him. Smoothly, I went on, "When you're out and about today, stop in at Magner's Grocery, where they have tomato soup on sale this week." I pressed on a fold in the flyer and read, "Five cans for two dollars."

I could see Jack saunter into his office. I continued to scan the flyer, reading into the microphone the deals of the week, keeping one eye on the clock. Inside, I seethed. Closing the flyer I announced, "I've got a special treat for all my listeners today. I don't do this often, but it's such a gorgeous day I've just got to step outside and see it for myself, so I've got ten solid minutes of music coming your way. Listen up folks." In two seconds I had the music playing and was heading toward Jack's office.

He must have seen me coming, must have known I had it in for him, because before I could walk through the door he was on the phone, motioning to me that it would take a while. I didn't have a while. I was going to talk to him *now*. I folded my arms across my chest and waited, tapping my foot to let him know I wasn't going anywhere. He took his good, sweet time, but finally couldn't drag the conversation out any longer. "Thanks for taking over for me this morning, babe," he said as he hung up the phone.

Oh, he was quick, acting as though I'd done him a favor instead of him not showing up.

"Really, I was going to get up as soon as I smelled the coffee, but guess what? I never smelled it." An overeager smile played on his lips.

If his remark was supposed to make me smile, it didn't.

"Hey, but you did a great job on the market report. I might have to turn that over to you full—"

"Cut it out, Jack. I didn't read the market report this morning. Someone forgot to call for it yesterday."

"And that would be me, I suppose?" Jack pointed a thumb at his Tommy Hilfiger sweater.

I noticed him wince as he cocked his wrist. Poor thing.

"I was just going to call the livestock barn yesterday when the phone rang and then we had to take off for Carlton and—"

"Listen." I didn't have time for his excuses. "You were late. I covered for you. Again. End of story. I've got an appointment at the bank at ten-thirty and before that I've got to call on four ad accounts. I expect you to be on-air the rest of the morning. I've got paperwork to do before my meeting at the bank." I turned on my heel.

"Aye aye, Captain." It was whispered but I heard him loud and clear.

Slowly I turned to face him. "Maybe you have a better plan as to how we can bail this sinking ship out of the water? Or do you intend for me to go down with the ship alone? I don't see you volunteering to go talk to the loan officer today. Wayne Jorgenson has called repeatedly for either one of us to come in. Unfortunately, I've been so busy filling in for you I haven't been able to return his calls."

"Come on, Ruthie, give me a break. I've been on the air plenty."

"Oh, yes, I forgot." My voice rose in anger. "I guess it was because I was running all over town during the few minutes you showed up, trying to sell ads to pay our bills—"

"You've got thirty-seconds before your ten minutes of music runs out."

I raced across the hall. How could he do that? He didn't even glance at the clock and he knew, he just *knew*, time was up. Through my anger I couldn't help but marvel at Jack's innate flair for radio. It was one of the traits that had attracted me to him in the first place. He definitely had a gift. Not only had he talked me into bed, he'd also talked me into moving back to Brewster, the town I'd thought I had left behind, convincing me it would be the start of our radio empire. Our flagship station.

Instead it was turning into my own personal Titanic.

Paul

"Paul, you might want to get up now." Mom poked her head around the door. "I wish you could sleep in today, but you said you were meeting Dave at nine and it's after eight."

I tossed back the covers and swung my legs over the side of the bed. "Thanks." I scrubbed at my face, the scratchy stubble surprising me. For some reason sleeping in my childhood bed made me feel as though I should wake up and be twelve again.

Holding on to the doorframe, Mom slowly backed out of my room. "Will you be home for lunch?"

"I should be."

"Could you stop by Magner's and pick up a loaf of whole wheat? I'll make tuna sandwiches and I won't toast the bread."

My favorite. She remembered.

"You got it."

Shedding my T-shirt and gym trunks, I stepped into the combination tub and shower. Not the water pressure I had in my condo, but at this point any hot water would do. Not moving, I let the water pour over my body for a minute. The warm stream felt as if it were washing away layers of the city. Layers of me. Defenses I kept in place in order to compete in the business world. Fences I'd put up to protect my heart. I was hoping I wouldn't need any of those if I moved back to Brewster.

I grabbed the soap and lathered up. It had been late when I'd arrived at Mom's last night, and then we'd sat up another hour talking. Maybe I should have flown from Chicago; it certainly would have been faster, even including the almost hour-long drive from the airport in Carlton. But I'd wanted the driving time to think, at least that's what I'd told myself. I hadn't been on a plane in two years. What Dave had asked was a big decision. I'd thought about it all the way from Chicago. I'd been thinking about it for two weeks. I was still thinking.

Dave's call had come as a complete surprise.

"Hey, buddy!"

I had recognized my old friend's voice instantly. "Hey, yourself. Hold one second." I buzzed my assistant. "No calls, please." Then I was back. "We still on for hunting this fall?"

"You bet! I've got some CRP land lined up that's primo for grouse…pheasant too." Dave's early-season hunting report was a bit too early and a bit too enthusiastic. The fact that he'd called me at work was odd too. Dave and I talked often, but always from my condo. He'd never called me at work before. I knew something had to be brewing. I swiveled my chair, looking down on Rush Street. Downtown Chicago was busy, as always. I wasn't looking forward to the after-work crush of people. Of course, by the time I left work, the streets had usually cleared out. The thought of Dave sitting in his office in Brewster, miles from any place larger, instantly uncluttered my mindscape. I could almost feel the breeze on my face, imagining our annual hunting trip.

"Wish I could do some scouting with you. The only wildlife around here—" An image of a spike-haired young man—or had it been a woman?—I'd passed on the way to work came to mind. "Well, let's put it this way, you wouldn't want to eat the wildlife around here." I changed the subject. "How's Vicky? The kids?"

"Good. Good. Kids are ready for school to start. Angie told me last night, 'Summer's kind of boring.'" Dave chuckled. "Can you imagine? We never got bored, did we?"

"Not that I can recall." My early summer memories were filled with baseball, riding our bikes on old Buck Trail, and meetings of our secret PDR Club. Paul, Dave, and Ruthie. At the thought of Ruth, I had one of those odd blips in my chest. Funny, her name could still do that to me after all this time.

Dave kept talking. "Vicky's having trouble finding help for the café. But that's old news. We sure can't complain about the unemployment rate here in Brewster. Say, speaking of employment…"

Dave was trying so hard to sound casual it was almost comical. I wanted to tell him, "Just say it, whatever it is," but I could detect something deeper in his tone and bided my time.

Dave cleared his throat, something he did when he was nervous. "They made you president yet?"

I'd been in investment banking since I'd graduated from college. The field had been good to me, and Dave knew it. At times I'd worried my profession might get in the way of our friendship. After all, an investment banker in downtown Chicago made far more change than an insurance agent in Brewster, North Dakota. But Dave was one of those true friends who was as pleased with my success as I was. He'd been the first person I'd told when I was hired right out of college interviews, blurting out a salary we'd never have thought to dream of in our PDR Club fantasies. I could still almost feel his bear hug and hear his heartfelt words, "Here you go, buddy. Here you go."

I would have called it the luck of the Irish, if I'd been Irish. Instead I had nothing to credit but hard work and God's grace. I'd climbed the ladder so fast even I had to sit back and marvel at times. How a small-town guy like me had ever ended up as Vice President of Securefunds was anybody's guess. Growing up, my dreams had been to marry Ruthie and take over my dad's hardware store. I'd found out that sometimes God has other plans. When Dad died my second year of college—

"Paul? You still there?" Dave's voice cut into my thoughts.

"Yeah, I'm here. Sorry, got distracted for a second."

"Thought we were cut off. Well, uh, the reason I called…"

Here it was.

My intercom buzzed. "Hold on one second, Dave." Annoyed, I punched the intercom, "No calls." A moment later, "Okay, bud, I'm back."

"Hey, I know you're pretty busy. Maybe I'll catch you another time." Dave's voice was fading, as if he was hanging up on himself.

"What's up?" Now I *was* curious.

"You know, I think this is the sort of thing I should talk to you about in person." He cleared his throat again. "You aren't planning a trip home anytime soon, are you?"

"No...not until hunting season." I'd never heard Dave sound so nervous, except for the time we'd found two whole cigarettes and had been in his basement trying to get up the nerve to light them when his dad came down the steps. Within three questions we'd fessed up and had never been tempted to try the vice again.

"Ummmm," I could hear Dave flipping pages of some sort, "what are you doing say, Tuesday, next week? I could come then."

"Come here? To Chicago?" Now I was the one sounding odd. I'd invited Dave numerous times, but he'd only visited once, shortly after I'd started my job. Long enough to take in a Cubs game, eat five slices of Chicago pizza, and sleep nine hours on my couch. The next morning he'd stretched, packed his duffel bag, and headed back to Brewster. Something was definitely up.

I checked my calendar. Clear. "Well, sure, you're welcome here anytime." I tried not to sound like I was screaming, *what is going on?*

"I'll let you know what time I'll be there. Tuesday, then." He hung up.

I had hardly removed my hand from the phone when my assistant buzzed. "Mr. Bennett, while you were taking that phone call Councilman Bradford called to reconfirm the fund-raising reception on Tuesday. I told him you'd be there."

Tuesday. The day Dave would be in town. I wondered how Dave felt about attending a fund-raiser? I guessed I was going to find out. I punched the intercom. "Judy, please send directions to the Marriott to Dave Johnson. In Brewster. Tell him to meet me there on Tuesday."

⌒

The next few days passed slowly as I tried to imagine what would prompt Dave to visit a city I knew he had no use for. Finally Tuesday arrived and from across the room I caught a glimpse of him as he walked into the Marriott ballroom. He was too far away for me to do anything but try to maneuver in his direction through the crowd. I knew I'd reach him eventually; I just hoped he'd stay put long enough for me to get there.

After the usual hug and handshake, I introduced Dave to a few professional acquaintances and touched base with some of my clients. Every so often I glanced over at my friend, who looked clearly out of his league. Uncomfortable.

⁓

Later that night back at my condo, I laughed until I had to cough for breath as Dave described his version of the fund-raiser.

"A hayseed in a bowl of pearls, that was me. Out of place with nowhere to hide." Dave pulled the tie from his shirt collar, unbuttoned the top button, and stretched his neck like a dog freed from a choke chain. "First thing I see is a waiter dressed better than me looking down his nose at my blue sport coat and offering me a tray of mystery morsels. I took three. Hey, they weren't bad. I snagged him again and took three more." Dave grabbed a handful of peanuts, then leaned back on the couch, toeing his shoes off his feet. "I was beginning to worry that if I didn't find you I might have to fill in as a waiter to get the leftovers. I didn't think I could afford to buy a meal in that place."

Leave it to Dave to put a funny spin on his insecurities. I wondered what his real impression was of my life in Chicago. It was a far cry from what I knew his life was like in Brewster. Dave had hurried through his four years of college, anxious only to get back to Brewster and marry Vicky. His job in his uncle's insurance agency was a perfect match for his outgoing personality. Five years ago, when his uncle had retired, Dave had bought the business. "Investing in Brewster," is what he'd told me. Small-town life suited Dave to a T. I didn't have to wait long to find out what he thought about life in the city of Chicago. One thing I had always appreciated about Dave was his honesty.

"You know," he went on, "I stood there looking at that fancy room, and I wondered what I was doing there. If I hadn't already paid a bellboy five bucks to keep my suitcase until I found you, I would have been tempted to hop the next plane out. It felt like I was in a foreign country. Between the mystery food and the velvet kind of wallpaper and the chandeliers, it wasn't the banquet room in our café back home, that's for sure. Those brown Formica tables and vinyl chairs at Vicky's café look kinda plain next to white linen tablecloths and upholstered chairs." Dave tossed the last of the nuts in his hand into his mouth, lifted his feet onto the coffee table, and laced his fingers together behind his head, relaxing. "Even the women looked different than the ones in Brewster." His eyes widened at the memory. "They were more...more...well, they wear more makeup, that's for sure. And tighter dresses. Right about then I would have given anything to be home with Vicky and the kids. You know what I mean, Paul? It's a different kind of life here."

I knew just what Dave meant. I'd grown so accustomed to hotel fund-raisers I'd forgotten all the trappings that went along with them. Caterers trying to outdo the last guy with some new concoction of food. Women trying to outdo each other in what they wore. I had no trouble putting myself in Dave's shoes. I'd noticed all the glitz myself the first few years I'd been here, but it had all become part of the background as I concentrated on the only thing I seemed to have left. My career.

It was only in the past year that I'd taken time to take stock of what my life held. A year that had at times seemed more nightmare than waking reality. Without Mia or Jenny, my condo seemed more of a shell of protection than a home. I wasn't sure if it was a shell of protection or more of a shield, keeping emotions outside the walls, where I was safe from feeling them. Either way recently I'd felt restless with myself. Ready to move on to something more than the emptiness I'd been living in. Ready to risk my heart again. I'd been praying for direction. Answers had been slow in coming.

Listening to Dave I realized part of my restlessness might be due to the superficial way I'd been living my life, doing my job. Part of that was my fault; I'd shut myself away from most everyone the past two years. Part of it was simply climbing the corporate ladder. A guy had to play the game to move ahead. I wasn't so sure I wanted to do that anymore. Or needed to. Whatever Dave had come to tell me, I was all ears.

Unlike me, curling up in a past I had no control to change, Dave didn't dwell on his lonesomeness for home; he continued relating his version of the evening. "Just when I was ready to bolt from the room, someone sidled up behind me and said, *'Bet these folks have never tasted deer steaks cooked over a campfire by the lake.'*" Dave waved a hand in the air. "Why am I telling you that? You know what you said." He tucked his hand back behind his head. "I tell you, Paul, I was never so glad to see that mug of yours in my life. After I recognized you in that tuxedo, that is."

I recalled the hearty pounding Dave had given me earlier that evening. He'd clapped me on the back as though I was his long-lost buddy, and in a sense I was. While I'd always thought of Dave as the next thing to a brother, I knew the miles between us, and our differing lifestyles, set up a distance that took some time to overcome each time we got together. I'd felt that distance at the fund-raiser, but now that we were back at my condo, it was as though time and distance had disappeared.

I was still waiting to hear the reason for his visit, but he didn't seem in any hurry to get to the point. I shrugged out of my jacket, undid my bowtie, and threw my feet on the coffee table across from Dave's. I was enjoying seeing my world in Chicago through his eyes. He made it look different in a way that seemed amusing even as it revealed the falseness of much of it. A view I was more than ready to take a hard look at. Maybe God was answering my prayers in this unexpected visit. I crossed my arms, resting them on my chest. I was listening.

He shook his head as if still trying to take it all in. "When I heard that jazz band tuning up across the room, well, I don't know if I've ever heard a live jazz band. Heck, I haven't even heard all that many jazz recordings! You hang out in classy places these days, buddy."

I tried to get a word in, but Dave was on a roll.

"And then you introduced me to...how do you say her name?"

"It's Corinne. Like the 'core' of an apple and then, 'in.' Core-in. Corinne."

"Fancy name for a fancy gal, I'd say." He wiggled his eyebrows. "Wipe that grin off your face, Bennett. I saw the way she was looking at you."

"The only thing I'm laughing at is you. Did you know Corinne is the account rep for the advertising agency that handles our firm's account?"

"Oh, *account rep.* Is that what you call her?" Dave slid his feet off the coffee table and onto the floor. He leaned forward, resting his forearms on his knees. The way his mouth curved up at the side I could almost guess what was coming next. "The way those long red fingernails curled around your arm sure didn't look like a business deal to me."

I threw a cashew at him. Quick as ever, he caught it and popped it in his mouth. Talking around it, he continued, "Hey, don't get me wrong, I think it's about time you start seeing someone. I mean, uh, it's been almost two years now, and—"

Go on, say her name, I silently urged, leaning forward. *Say both their names. I won't fall apart. I want to know you remember them.*

Dave glanced at the photos on my mantle. I felt the familiar jolt shoot through my chest as I also looked toward the pictures. Two years and I still couldn't believe they were gone. Mia and Jenny, my wife and child. When they died in the plane crash I thought my world had died too. I found life did go on, even when I didn't want it to. God was there whether I railed at Him or turned to Him. And I did a lot of both. Lately, though, I hadn't had time to do much of either. Business had been booming in the investment banking field, and I found immersing myself in work was a good buffer for pain.

"Sorry, Paul." Dave interrupted my thoughts. "I know you've been through some rough times, buddy, but you need to look to the future." He straightened his back and cleared his throat. "Which is why I'm here." He cleared his throat again.

I put my feet on the floor and sat up to face him. "I've been wondering when you were going to get around to it. Beating around the bush isn't your style. What's up?"

Dave took a deep breath and began slowly. "Okay, here goes. I know you've got a great life here in Chicago, Paul." He swung his right arm in a half circle as if encompassing my condo and all of Chicago in his grasp. "To anyone in Brewster it looks like you've got everything you've ever wanted. Great job. Beautiful women. Life in a city that offers anything you could want to do." His eyes shot to the photos again and he said, "So, I hope you don't think I'm nuts when I say what I'm going to."

"I'm going to *go* nuts if you don't hurry up and say it." Our past conversations consisted of hunting, sports, or Vicky and the kids. I couldn't imagine what he was getting at. "Spit it out," I urged.

"Well, uh, I've been authorized by the bank in Brewster to make you an offer to—" he coughed nervously, "to...well, to be president of the bank."

"The bank in Brewster?"

"Uh-huh." As if he were afraid I'd say an immediate no, he rushed to explain, "The Brewster bank recently acquired another bank...in Carlton. Since that's the bigger town, Bob Marsden is going to transfer over there. Run that office. So we need someone to run the Brewster bank." He sat back, the purpose of his long trip finally out.

In all my wondering I had never thought Dave was coming to me with a job offer. I'd imagined he might have a proposal to go in on some hunting land, or at the very outside maybe he needed to borrow some money, even though I knew his insurance agency did a good business. But a job offer? I already had a great job. Didn't I?

My mind raced back to the fund-raiser we'd been at a couple hours ago...

"Corinne," I'd said, "could you introduce Dave to a few people? I need to speak with Councilman Bradford before too many others get to him."

"You go on. Dave and I will be just fine." Corinne wiggled her long nails at me as she threaded her other fingers around Dave's arm.

It felt as though the entire governing body of Chicago, including Senator Bowden, was working the room. Making deals. It appeared to be a cocktail party, but I knew what was going on beneath the surface. I had work to do myself.

"Paul, I've been looking for you." Councilman Bradford punched my arm lightly, causing the drink in his hand to slosh drops of liquid onto both of our shoes. "Ooopps, sorry about that." He rubbed his shoe on his pant leg. "So what did you decide?"

Bradford wasn't wasting any time. I could feel my blood pressure rising. "I've thought about what you asked, Councilman, and as I told you the first time, I won't do it." My voice rose.

"Hey, hey, now, don't get worked up about this." He took a swallow of his drink. "All you have to do is make a couple phone calls."

"Those phone calls you want me to make are illegal and you know it."

"Oh, I wouldn't say that." He chuckled, his face getting red.

"It's called insider information and it's against the law."

"Well then, Paul, I'm sorry." He dropped the polite smile from his face. "You know this will ruin any political ambitions you may have had." The councilman's eyes turned icy. "See you around."

"Say something." Dave's voice brought me back to my condo. "The last time you were this quiet you had your tonsils out."

Maybe Councilman Bradford wouldn't see me around. Maybe the change I'd been praying for wasn't a career in politics. Wasn't another step up the investment banking ladder. Maybe it was a job in Brewster. A job back home.

"Does your long silence mean you're thinking it over?" Dave was nervously snapping the band of his watch against his wrist. "Or is the idea so out of the question you can't think of a way to say no?"

I was definitely thinking it over.

～

And now, back in the house where I'd grown up, I still was.

I stuck my face into the shower spray then turned off the water, listening to the familiar *clunk-clunk* of Mom's aging pipes. It was funny how relaxed I felt hearing that old sound. My condo in Chicago was practically soundproof. I hardly knew anyone lived next to me. I toweled off, put on my robe, and padded down the hall to my old bedroom.

"Paul?" Mom called through the door a few minutes later. "It's eight-twenty."

My condo also didn't have a timekeeper. I'd forgotten Mom's habit of pointing out the passing minutes and wondered how she thought I got to work on time without her. I chuckled into the mirror as I knotted my tie. Slipping into my suit coat, I joined her in the kitchen, the smell of browning hamburger and onions greeting me. She was buttering two slices of toast. I assumed that was her idea of the "no breakfast" I'd requested.

"Ooo-la-la!" Turning from the counter she pressed her lips together in a sly smile. "Don't you look nice today. I was expecting to see you in your hunting clothes. Seems that's the only reason you come home anymore." She picked up a spatula and pushed at the hamburger.

Her voice held no accusation, but inwardly I winced. She was right. The only time I had been home over the past years was to hunt with Dave, squeezing in minutes here and there for quick conversations with Mom. She never complained about not having enough time with me. She took whatever I gave her as enough. Even Christmas this past year I'd begged off, using end-of-the-year financial deadlines as my excuse. Truth was, I had become so consumed in my work, work I thought only I could do, that I'd shut people out of my life. Her simple words, "seems that's the only reason you come home anymore," were convicting. Even if I didn't move back to Brewster, I was going to have to change that part of my life. I knew enough people in Chicago who had a façade about them, a falseness that said, *I'm paying attention to you because I might need you for business, no other reason.* I didn't want to become one of those people.

As I took a bite of toast I silently prayed, *Lord, take away any pretense and mold me into the man You want me to be.*

I folded Mom into my arms, spatula and all. "How about you and me for dinner tonight?" It was a start.

"Oh, Paul, I'm sorry." She stepped out of my embrace, pushing the hamburger quickly around the pan. "It's my turn to bring hotdish to the senior center tonight. It's our monthly meeting. You said not to make any special plans when you called, and I thought you'd be out hunting till after dark. But, goodness, I should have known hunting season doesn't start until next month." She shook her head and put a finger to her forehead in that "duh?" gesture teenagers often use.

The action looked comical and I laughed. It made Mom seem much younger than her early seventies, and I wondered where she'd picked up that mannerism. Obviously she had a side to her life I knew nothing about. A side I was going to have to get to know if I moved back. My evasive tactics had worked, apparently too well.

"How about if I leave a bit of the hotdish in the fridge?" She measured two cups of grated white and green vegetables into the pan. "I've got mushrooms in here just the way you like and you won't even notice the zucchini."

"Zucchini? Since when did zucchini become a hotdish ingredient?" I wasn't sure I liked the sound of this.

"I'm not going to waste good vegetables." Mom scooped a bowl of rice into the pan, sprinkling the mixture with a good dose of salt and pepper. "Ida Bauer, you remember Mrs. Bauer from the Dairy Freeze, don't you?" She didn't wait for my reply, talking as she pulled a can of mushroom soup from the cupboard. "Ida gave me two zucchinis from her garden yesterday." Mom clamped the hand-operated can opener onto the soup can. Grimacing, she looked up at me. "Would you open this for me? My hands are slippery from cooking." She glanced at the clock on the microwave. "It's eight forty-one."

I twisted the can open quickly and smiled at her. "Then I'd better run." Luckily in Brewster nothing was more than a few minutes away.

"Can you tell me what this big meeting is all about?" Mom spooned the soup from the can into the rice mixture and then stirred it all together with a wooden spoon.

"Dave wants to talk to me about some financial-type stuff." I was still being evasive, not wanting to let on I was even considering a move back to Brewster. Right now my thoughts on the prospect were fifty-fifty, and I didn't want Mom getting her hopes up about her only child moving home.

"Couldn't he do that over the phone?" My mother was never one to miss a point.

"Talk to you at lunch." I went out the door, a good way to avoid answering her. Knowing Mom, within a few more questions she would have known exactly why I was home for something besides hunting.

⌒

"So, now you've seen the *plant*, so to speak, what do you think?" With a hand motion, Dave steered me into the large corner office. He settled himself into a straight-backed chair, leaving the well-padded leather chair behind the cherry wood desk for me. His unsaid proposition was loud and clear.

It seemed odd to have Dave, my oldest friend, showing me through the bank where we'd opened savings accounts together when we were ten. I would have felt more comfortable riding our bikes through the drive-up and asking for a sucker than being escorted through the bank as its potential new manager.

"I like the *plant*, as you called it. The remodeling job turned out great." I was stalling for time. Had it been pure irony, or God's timing, that the very night Dave had appeared in Chicago to make his offer I'd been asked to pull strings to give a favorable investment deal to Senator Bowden?

My first instinct was to tell Dave, "I'll take it." But as attractive as the job sounded, it would be a major career change for me, and I knew it wouldn't be wise to accept it without more thought. And prayer.

"I'm going to level with you, Paul." Dave leaned forward, placing his forearms on my desk.

Well now, that thought told me something. *My* desk was it?

Dave cleared his throat. "Listen, I know we can't begin to offer you anything close to the salary you make in Chicago. I saw where you work, and hey, your office makes this place look rinky-dink. So let's do it this way. You tell me if you are at all interested in hearing more or if we should just wrap this up now and go do some preseason scouting." Dave stretched his neck. It didn't take a psychologist to know he was nervous. He stood suddenly. "I'm going to go grab us some coffee." He bolted from the room.

Alone in the office, I swiveled the chair to look out the one large window. An ancient car moved slowly down the street. I was pretty sure old Mr. Ost was behind the wheel. Everyone had called him old Mr. Ost when I was in high school, and he couldn't have gotten any younger. I marveled that he was still driving. A kid on a bike stopped at the corner, waiting for the slow-moving car to pass. Ah, that was Mr. Ost's secret. Everyone here watched out for him.

From the window I had a good view of Brewster's post office and the undeveloped lot between the bank and post office that was used only to pile snow from the city streets in the wintertime. This time of year it provided me a window on one of Brewster's hottest morning stops. As I watched, the kid on the bike screeched to a stop in front of the post office, hopped off, and ran inside, emerging moments later with an armful of mail. No home delivery here.

How easily the memory came back to me, my own summer days of picking up the mail for my folks. I'd felt so responsible, stopping to sort the mail at the inside post office counter, then riding through the alley to give my dad his mail at the hardware store before going home to give what remained to my mother. A kid in Chicago could hardly ride his bike around the block alone, much less all over town.

As I stared out the window a flock of sparrows commandeered the trees just outside the bank. I watched as one swooped to the ground, pecked quickly, then joined the other birds in the trees. It wasn't as if Chicago didn't have birds or trees, but I rarely saw any from my window at work. My condo, either, come to think of it.

"Here's your coffee." Dave walked in slowly, the two cups in his hands filled to the brim. "The gals in the coffee room said to empty the pot, so I did. Not such a good idea. I've burned two fingers already." He held a cup out to me.

I began to turn my chair, taking one last look out the window. There was a woman walking toward the bank building who looked exactly like Ruthie Hammond. My heart did a double take as my head swiveled between the window and the coffee cup Dave was pushing into my hand. It definitely was Ruthie. "Ouch!" The coffee spilled, burning my fingers.

Dave followed my gaze. "She's still doing that to you, huh?"

"You mean distracting me or burning me?" I wiped my hand on my slacks while Dave calmly sipped his coffee. His wry smile showed that he remembered every word I'd told him almost twenty years ago about the night I'd proposed to Ruthie Hammond.

Ruthie

The silver Bug I'd followed into town last night was parked in front of the bank. Any strange car in town probably belonged to a salesman. I stopped and peered inside. They'd definitely improved this version of the Bug over the old-model VW Paul had taught me to drive. The guy even had a daisy stuck in the vase on the dash. Cute. Very cute. Maybe someday I'd own a car like that.

Not on the salary you make. I pushed the thought aside as I walked around the car, not at all anxious for my meeting with Wayne Jorgenson. The loan officer had left two messages on the answering machine at the station. I knew exactly what he was going to tell me.

⌒

"Your account is seriously overdrawn, Ruth." As if punctuating his statement, Wayne clicked his pen. "We need to get this cleared up. Now if you think you might be getting some ad money in to cover things by the end of the day—"

Might as well get it over with. "That's not going to happen, Wayne. I got a late start selling today, and I'm not having much luck with the calls I have made. I tell you, people just aren't advertising anymore. They can't afford it. I don't know what else to do." I tried to keep the panic out of my voice. I didn't need Wayne to tell me that the station was in dire need of cash. I knew it all too well.

"Ruth, we can't have these continual overdrafts on the books." Even though he was five years younger than I was, he made me feel like a little kid. "You know the examiners frown on things like this." He stretched his hands in front of him, clicking his pen and waiting for me to fill the silence.

I had nothing to say. The money wasn't there, and it wouldn't be there by day's end. Probably not by week's end either. I couldn't manufacture the money, and trying to sell ads to struggling businesses was like trying to sell ice to Eskimos. They didn't need what I was peddling.

"I'll tell you what." Wayne sat forward. "How about if we write up a short-term loan? I know you're a little behind on your other loans, but I'm sure this is a temporary situation. In a few weeks, when the farmers around here start harvesting, the stores will be doing better and your ad sales should take off. We'll write in a balloon payment for the end of October. That should give you enough time to get things squared away."

I'd never been a financial genius. My forte was talking. I left the bookkeeping up to Jack and the bank. Lately, Jack had been sending me to the bank. He told me it would be good for me to learn another part of the business. The only thing I was learning was how to get deeper in debt. "Where do I sign?"

"It'll only take a few minutes to draw up the papers. Stay put."

I glanced over my shoulder as he left the office, noticing a young woman with her small son enter the bank. The boy was carrying a piggy bank that was obviously heavy.

"*Put your dime in here.*" I could hear my dad's words as plain as day. My mom had cut a small slit in the metal top of an old canning jar, letting me tape the sides of the lid with masking tape as if it were Fort Knox. "*Now every week when you get your allowance,*" a dollar, in dimes, that had seemed like a hundred, "*you put ten cents in here. That goes to the bank. Ten cents for church, and the rest is yours.*" A fortune.

I remembered adding more dimes, birthday dollars, and extra-chore money to that pint jar, trying to fill it quickly so I could open my first savings account at this very bank. Saving for my trip to New York. Paris. My very own purple hat. During frustrating teen years, I'd often imagined the day when I'd cash in my savings and fly away.

I'd long ago spent those dimes. Plus some. When I'd agreed with Jack to spend every penny of my savings to start the station, it had seemed in some way a ticket to a bigger world. Not anymore. How I wished I had listened to my dad's wise counsel, "*Always put ten percent in savings so you have something to fall back on in hard times. So you always have options.*" Besides losing my savings, I'd also lost my chance to dream. My options.

The only option I had now was to sign for another loan that would keep us barely afloat. I wasn't sure if Jack had me tending to the bank business because he really wanted me to learn this aspect of our joint venture or because he didn't want to deal with the bind we were in. I looked at the upside-down figures Wayne had left lying on the desk. Two thousand dollars with a minus sign in front of it. Ugh. My stomach did a flip-flop as I mentally added that amount to our outstanding loans. How we would ever pay them off, I didn't have a clue.

"Here we go." Wayne sauntered back into the office. "Now, Ruth, if you'll sign right here." He clicked his pen twice before holding it out to me.

I grabbed it, if for no other reason than to stop his annoying clicking habit. I wasn't anxious to sign my name to another loan and hesitated, running my eyes over the document, wondering what my dad would say if he could see these numbers. I gave my head a small shake. My dad had been dead for many years; no advice from him would be coming my way. I was on my own.

From the lobby I could hear the voice of my brother-in-law, Dave Johnson. It wasn't unusual for him to be in the bank. After all, his insurance office was right next door, and he was on the board of directors of the bank as well. But today his voice carried across the building. His pumped-up tone caused me to look over my shoulder. I strained to peer through the glass partition to see what could be so exciting. All I could see was the back of a man in a dark suit. Must be the salesman whose car I'd admired. I caught a snippet of the man's voice and for a second I could have sworn it was Paul Bennett.

"Sign right here, Ruth." Wayne tapped the document with his finger.

I directed my attention back to him, my ears practically growing, trying to catch another phrase from the man in the lobby. Trying to make sure it wasn't Paul. What would Paul Bennett be doing in Brewster, anyway? Especially in the middle of the week? And not even hunting season? I turned my head again, trying to catch one more glimpse. It couldn't be him. Could it? If it was, I had some hightailing to do. Ever since the senior prom fiasco, I'd made it a point to avoid Paul whenever he was in town. It was easier that way.

"Is it the amount that bothers you?"

Obviously, Wayne didn't understand when a woman had more important things on her mind. Things like old boyfriends. Things like regrets.

"I made the loan out for five thousand. I figured that would give you some breathing space. I can change it if—"

"No, no, it's fine." I put pen to paper, signing my name without thought. My body might have been in Wayne Jorgenson's office, but my mind was in the bank lobby. It couldn't be Paul out there. What business would he have here? I doubted he kept an account at the bank. Not someone making the mega-salary he apparently did. At least that's the way the local grapevine had it. His mother still lived in Brewster, and he did visit her occasionally, but always over a holiday or hunting season. Not the middle of August, for no reason at all. Surely, if he was planning to spend any time in Brewster, Vicky would have told me. She always kept me up to date on his visits, and I made sure our paths never crossed.

"That should do 'er." Wayne handed me a copy of the loan. He stood, clicking his infernal pen.

Reluctantly, I took my cue and stood too. Now that I was free to leave, I wasn't all that sure where to go. Certainly not into the bank lobby. What if it was Paul?

So what if it is?

My cheeky conscience had no idea what it was talking about. *Because I might shrivel up and die of embarrassment,* I answered myself.

Oh, get over it, Ruthie. I'm sure Paul has.

You're right. Absolutely right. The prom was almost twenty years ago. I'm a grown woman now.

"Could I use the back entrance?" I could feel myself growing flushed.

Chicken.

"I need to get back to the station, and it's so much closer."

About ten paces.

"Sure," Wayne answered, looking at me as if I'd suffered heat-stroke.

Well, I had…in a way.

⌒

"Vicky, you will never guess what happened to me in the bank today!"

I'd rushed out the back door of the bank, ran kitty-corner across the street, and hurried into the back entrance of the café. I'd timed it perfectly. Right between morning coffee time and lunch. Vicky was chopping onions, her mouth clamped shut, the only method she'd found that kept her from crying buckets.

Pulling up a stool I kept talking. "I went to the bank a few minutes ago to talk to Wayne, and while I was there I heard Dave out in the lobby talking to someone, and you will never guess who this guy reminded me of. Paul Bennett. Now what would Paul be doing in Brewster? I mean, it's not even hunting season or anything. Well, obviously it wasn't Paul, but I swear, Vick, this guy was a ringer for him. From the back, at least. I don't know why he was the first person who came to mind when I saw this guy. I mean, I never think of Paul anymore."

That's a lie. You never quit thinking about him.

"And besides, you'd know if Paul was in town, right?"

Vicky nodded, trying to say something through her sealed lips. I held up my hand, letting her know I understood why she couldn't talk. I spoke for her. "I mean, certainly he would have called Dave and they'd have plans or something. It would be so weird if I ran into him. I mean, we've hardly spoken in almost twenty years.

Well, we did at the funeral, you know, when Mom and Dad died. And, then when his dad died I saw him at the church. But there were all kinds of people around and...not that we'd have anything important to say to one another, but it would just be weird if...." I trailed off, realizing I was practically foaming at the mouth. I had no idea why seeing a guy who reminded me of Paul could do this to me. It wasn't as if we had left things unsettled or unsaid when we broke up. No, that wasn't the problem. We both knew exactly where things stood.

Exactly. Thanks to me.

The bell on the front door of the café sounded.

"You've got a customer and I've gotta get back to work." I hopped off my stool. "I still can't believe how much that guy looked like Paul."

Vicky held up a finger, indicating I should wait while she gave her pile of onions one last chop.

I realized I was sounding like a woman who had never gotten over her high school boyfriend, which wasn't the case at all. *Oh, really?* I pushed the thought aside. It seemed the only way I would stop talking about him was to leave. "No, really, I gotta go."

As I rushed out the door Vicky broke her silence. "Wait!"

"Nope, I'm outta here." I tossed the words over my back.

"Come for supper. Bring Jack."

I waved my hand to show her I'd heard and kept moving. I thought she added another sentence, but just then a diesel truck drove through the alley and her words bounced off my back.

Oh well, she could tell me tonight.

Paul

After my meeting with Dave, I walked across the street to *Victoria's Café.* I remembered how we'd teased Vicky when she'd named the café, telling her no one would call it by that name. She had insisted she wanted to give Main Street an upscale impression. But, as predicted, by the time the sign arrived everyone in town had dubbed the place *Vicky's.* Vicky was the only person who called the café *Victoria's.* Vicky and out-of-towners.

As I swung open the glass door, the bell hanging there echoed into the empty café. The smell of coffee filled the space. I poured myself a cup and slid into a booth.

"Paul!" Vicky pushed through the swinging door from the kitchen, wiping her hands on a towel. She held up one hand, palm out. "Onions." She wrinkled her nose, then broke into a wide grin. "Give me my hug." She held her arms wide.

I rose, scooping her into my arms. Vicky had always been slender, but I swore I could feel her ribs. "Don't you ever eat any of that cooking of yours?"

"Not often. I'm too busy. I tell you, it's getting harder and harder to find good help. Ever since that telemarketing office opened in the old implement building, most of the available workers went there. I can't afford to pay what they offer, not to mention benefits. So…" she pointed a finger at her chest, "I'm it today. I've got a high school girl covering the evening shift." She turned, pouring herself a cup of coffee. "Enough about me. Let's talk about you. Dave mentioned you'd be in town this week. What's up?" Vicky slid into the booth across from me. "Talk fast. My lunch crowd starts coming in twenty minutes."

The easy way Vicky slid in across from me, carrying on our conversation as if it hadn't been almost ten months since I'd seen her, Dave, and the kids, reminded me, once again, of what I'd been missing in Chicago. There were no pretensions here, no worries about invading someone's "personal space." The people were extended family. Sometimes they got on your nerves, but they cared about you no matter what. I felt a swell of contentment fill my chest as I sat across from Vicky. I didn't want to talk about life in Chicago; I wanted to hear what was happening in Brewster. The town that meant *home* to me.

I stirred some sugar into my coffee, relaxing in a way I hadn't in months. "Tell me about the kids. What grades will they be in this fall?" As hard as I tried, I could never seem to remember Angie's and Sam's exact ages.

Vicky took a long sip of coffee. "Angie's going to be in seventh grade—"

"Middle school already?" Where had time gone?

"No, big-city boy," Vicky swatted at me with her hand. "You're forgetting. In Brewster we don't call it middle school. It's just junior high. It's all one building."

How could I have forgotten? I'd spent nearly half my life in school here. Kindergarten through twelfth grade sharing one building. Brewster had built a new school and gym since I'd graduated, but, like the old school, it was all under one roof. The remembered smell of chalk almost overtook the smell of coffee as I lifted the cup to my mouth. *You've been away too long.* I filed that thought with the other differences I'd been noticing between Chicago and Brewster.

"What about Sam? I know he's not far behind Angie." I took a guess. "Fourth grade?"

"Close. He's going into fifth. You remember Sandy Quinn?"

I nodded. "Vaguely."

"I think she was a year behind you. She teaches Sam's class. She taught Angie too. Sandy's really good."

The bell on the door rang out and Vicky jumped to her feet as the first threesome of what would be the lunch crowd entered the café. "Oh, they're early today. Stick around. I'll try and stop back. No promises, though."

"Don't worry about me." I motioned to my cup. "I'll grab a refill and sit here for a minute. My mother is expecting me for lunch. I'll see you tonight. What time?"

Vicky answered my question by cocking her head. "Tonight?"

"Dave didn't clear his plan with you? He invited me for dinner tonight."

"Oh." Vicky coughed as if she'd swallowed wrong.

"If that's a problem, I'll stop by another time."

"No. No problem. We'll throw an extra burger on the grill. See you at six."

Jack

When we rounded the corner of the house leading to the back-yard deck, Ruthie let out a sound that sounded like a cross between a dog in pain and a pig squeal. She stopped dead in her tracks, turned around like she'd forgotten something, then did a one-eighty and froze.

"What's with you?"

I was sure she was going to send me back to our apartment to get some Jell-O concoction from the fridge, but she blinked her eyes at me, shook her head, and said, "Nothing."

I walked ahead of her. Women. Who knew? Probably some sort of PMS thing.

I would have recognized Paul Bennett anywhere. Almost twenty years and the guy still looked as though he could be quarterback of a football team, run an anchor leg of a relay, and hit a home run out of center field. And no doubt have the women fawning all over him too. I still didn't like the guy.

He shook my hand, then put an arm around my shoulder as if we'd been best buddies in high school. "Jack!" he said. "Jack Warner! You're looking good, guy. Still got that red hair, I see."

At least I had my hair. Paul's looked as if it were a bit thin at the forehead. There was an obvious scar near his hairline. Certainly the guy hadn't had some botched transplant job? From what I'd heard, he could afford the best. I angled for a better look.

"I hear you finally got that radio station you always talked about. Good for you."

Paul had actually talked to me in high school? That was a laugh. "Yup. Yup." I wasn't in the mood to make chitchat with him. I grabbed a beer from the cooler in the corner and sat backward on the picnic table bench. Ruthie had finally made it up the three steps of the deck. She looked distracted. I just knew she was going to send me back to the apartment for something.

"Paul." Ruthie stuck out her hand, stiff as cardboard.

"Ruthie." Paul leaned in for a hug, but Ruthie stopped him at the pass.

Good girl.

Those two had been stuck together like glue back in high school. It was nice to see Ruthie didn't have any lingering feelings for the guy. Why would she? She was living with me, after all.

"Auntie Ruth!" Sam tackled Ruthie around the waist. Angie waved so hard her hand looked like a piece of rubber. Aw, wasn't this sweet?

"Hey, guys. Glad you could make it." Dave appeared with a bag of charcoal.

"Oh, you're here." Vicky slid out the patio door with a humongous bowl of chips. "I suppose you remember Paul?"

Did I sense a note of sarcasm in Vicky's voice? If so, I was sure it was directed at me. Dave, Ruthie, and Paul had been a tight threesome in high school, Vicky joining them towards the end of senior year. Even though she'd only been a sophomore, she had to remember I'd never been part of their popular crowd. I hadn't been a part of any crowd, unless you called one music geek a crowd. Not that it mattered anymore. After all, I owned a radio station and was about to make an offer on another one. How many of them could say that?

I popped the top of my second beer, not missing the disapproving look Ruthie tossed my way. We'd been at Dave and Vicky's fifteen minutes already and between those two wound-up kids and the guy who was winding them up, Paul-Super-Stud-Bennett, I'd had it. And Dave hadn't even put charcoal in the grill yet. I took a draft and set my jaw. This could be a long night.

Vicky set the bowl of chips on the picnic table behind me. "I'll go grab the dip."

"You should have called. I could have brought some." Ruthie grabbed Vicky by the arm and practically yanked her through the door. "At least let me help."

Who'd ever be that anxious to get into a kitchen? Women.

I quickly finished off my second beer and reached for a third. If Ruthie did send me back to the apartment, I was going to take my good, sweet time. What did I want with this crowd, anyway? Let these guys live in the past. At least I had a future ahead of me.

I had a radio station.

I had Ruthie.

And Paul didn't.

Ruthie

"What is going on? Why didn't you tell me Paul would be here?" My voice was a harsh whisper.

"Ouch!" Vicky rubbed her arm. The white marks where my hand had been were turning red.

"Just what do you think you're doing?" I was right on Vicky's heels, following her into the kitchen. "Did it ever occur to you that I might not want to see Paul?" I'd heard of people hissing before; now I knew exactly how they sounded. It wasn't very attractive, but I couldn't seem to stop. "You could have at least warned me when I was in the café this afternoon."

"I didn't know then that Dave had invited him to dinner." Vicky calmly pulled a container of dip from the fridge and handed it to me. The red marks on her arm had already faded, thank goodness. "Besides, you didn't give me a chance to say anything anyway."

I took a deep breath. "How about a phone? Have you ever heard of a phone? You might at least have let me know he was in town." My voice was more level now, but I found myself holding the bowl of dip next to my ear as if it were a telephone. I placed the dip on the counter, rolling my eyes at myself. *Calm down.* I took another deep breath.

Vicky handed me a wooden tray. "I was really busy this afternoon and I didn't have time."

"Not even to make one phone call?" Not giving her a chance to answer, I went on, my reminder to calm down unheeded. "What am I going to say to him? I can't believe it. I mean, I've hardly talked to him in, what?" I did a quick calculation. "Eighteen years? And I'm wearing my grubbiest cutoffs and this ugly T-shirt. I don't think I even brushed my hair after I changed clothes." I sounded shrill. A vixen on a soap opera.

Or a grown woman who still feels ashamed about a hurt she caused years ago.

I had to get out of here. Settle down. I set the tray down on the counter, hard, practically missing the edge. The tray teetered and I nudged it with my hip. "I'm going to the bathroom." I marched down the hall. It was cool there compared to the kitchen. A haven of sorts.

Or a hideout? I yanked one of the vanity drawers open and pushed the thought away.

Don't hide.

I had to. It was easier to hide than face the embarrassment seeing Paul had brought back. I glanced into the mirror, then quickly looked away. It didn't take more than a glance to see the humiliation in my eyes. Had Paul seen it too?

I stood in front of the vanity, running my fingers through my messy hair, avoiding meeting my eyes in the mirror. It had been easy to hide when Paul was far away. Harder when I had to look straight into his intent blue gaze. I had to pull myself together. Had to go back out onto the deck and pretend my insides weren't a whirl of pure emotion. Shame. Regret. Attraction? I squished my eyes shut as hard as I could, then opened them wide. Might as well face reality. What was in the past was past, and there was nothing I could do about it now.

You could apologize.

Apologize? Now there was a thought. I stared into the mirror. What would that feel like? To apologize?

Freeing? For a second the knot in my heart loosened. The words, *"I'm sorry, Paul, so sorry,"* tumbled through my mind. My heart clenched again. Freeing? I didn't think so. Embarrassing would be more like it. Shameful. Humiliating. All of the above. No, apologizing wouldn't change anything.

I rummaged in the vanity drawer and pulled out a wide-toothed comb, tugging it through my hair as if it were some sort of punishment. Why in the world was I so unsettled seeing Paul? There was nothing between him and me. Nothing. Not anymore. For all intents and purposes, he was just an old high school classmate I hadn't seen in years. Oh, sure, we'd dated a bit.

Four years! Ouch! I yanked through a snarl in my hair. What was four years in the whole scheme of things?

He proposed. Did you forget?

No. I turned away from the mirror.

And you think he did?

I didn't even want to think about the answer to that question. I flipped my hair behind my ears. It was the best I could do without shampoo, cream rinse, volumizer, a blow drier, and my special brush. Paul could take it or leave it.

I thought you didn't care what Paul thought?

I don't.

Then what's all the fuss about?

Ignoring my conscience, I jabbed my chin in the air, turning my head slightly. There, that was better. I definitely looked better at an angle.

Still trying to hide?

This was stupid. I couldn't change the past. I was just going to have to live with it. It was a lot easier, though, when Paul wasn't sitting in the backyard. I flipped my head forward, rubbing my hands briskly through my hair, then tossed my head back. I dug in the drawer and found a tube of lipstick. Plum Breeze. *Plum.* My worst color. Why didn't that surprise me? I uncapped the tube and leaned into the mirror, my face looking unnaturally flushed. Oh good, red and plum, the perfect color combo.

I closed my eyes for a moment. Why had seeing Paul thrown me for such a loop? Was it because seeing him reminded me of the awful way things had ended? A night I had never had a chance to explain or apologize for? Or did seeing him remind me of all the plans I'd had back then? Plans that had never had a chance to happen. Plans I still hoped would come true.

I took a deep breath and turned the doorknob. Then stopped. What was I going to say to Paul? *Remember our senior prom?*

How about, "I'm sorry?" Or, "I still think about you?" Or… Great. Just great. I was sticking my foot in my mouth and it wasn't even open. *Come on, Ruthie.* I gave my head a shake. *Things could be worse. You make your living talking. Go out there and pretend it's just another boring day at work.*

~

I slid onto the bench beside Jack. "So, Paul, what brings you to town?"

See, it's not so hard.

A quick look passed between Paul and Dave. Did I say something wrong?

Paul held up a finger and pointed to his mouth.

Let him chew all he wanted. It was that much less conversation I'd have to dream up. I waited patiently, noticing the deep scar along his hairline. He hadn't had that in high school. I wondered what athletic feat he had to accomplish to get a battle scar like that? Or was it from the plane crash a couple years ago? My stomach clenched at the possibility.

Paul swallowed, exaggerating the motion, acknowledging his delay in answering my question. "Uh, Dave and I had some business to discuss and—"

"Yeah," Dave chimed in, "hunting business."

"…and I hadn't seen Mom in a while. It seemed like a good way to kill two birds, if you know what I mean."

"And how are things in…Chicago? Is that where you are now?" *Oh yeah, right, as if you don't know where Paul lives or how he is. You may not see him, but you make darn sure Vicky keeps you posted.*

"Good," Paul replied as if it wasn't really. "Life's hectic."

"We could use a little hectic in Brewster. Right?" I looked around. Had everyone fallen asleep? They had mouths too. Why weren't they using them? "And your mother? How's she doing? I haven't seen her out lately." Okay, this was the last question I had up my sleeve. Someone else was going to have to handle the conversation from here on out.

"Mom's okay. Not as steady on her feet as she used to be. Her arthritis seems to be getting worse. She overdoes it sometimes. It takes its toll." Paul reached for another chip. "Enough about me. Tell me what's been going on in your life."

Oh, so things could get worse. My mind went blank. I felt a cold trickle of sweat run down my back. *You know, Ruthie, if you had apologized years ago you wouldn't be feeling ashamed now. There's freedom in facing up to your wrongs.* So what was I supposed to do? Blurt out "I'm sorry" right here? No way. I clamped my teeth together, making sure not even an embarrassing whisper slipped through my lips.

Jack placed a hand over my knee, patting it possessively, saving me from saying anything. "We're doing great. Just great." He squeezed my leg, letting his clammy hand rest there. "I suppose you heard Ruthie's a partner with me in the station? We're just about ready to make a move on another station. Which reminds me, honey…"

I gave Jack a look as if he'd gone daft. He never called me honey.

"…we've got to talk to Wayne about getting another loan for that. Anyway, you watch—" Jack stopped and chuckled, his eyes hooded as he directed his words to Paul. "Well, I guess that'd be hard for you to do from Chicago. But I'm telling you, next year this time, people are going to be talking about us."

As if they weren't already.

I had a sudden urge to be anywhere but here. "I need a drink of water." I jumped off the bench and went into the house, closing the sliding door with a satisfying thud. Seeing Jack and Paul sitting on the deck together made me feel as though I were being squeezed between my past and my present. And I didn't like the looks of either. From my vantage point on the picnic table bench, I'd made a mess of everything.

I pulled open one cupboard door, then another. Where in the world had Vicky put her glasses? I'd grown up in this house; there wasn't a spot she could put them I didn't know about. I slammed the cupboard door, then opened it again. There. There they were. I blinked hard as I reached for a glass. I absolutely refused to cry over not finding a water glass right away. Then people in Brewster would really have a reason to talk.

It seemed people in Brewster had been talking about me my whole life. It had started with my breech birth and continued when, at age three, I'd tripped in the grocery store and needed two stitches in my tongue. In third grade I fell off the slide on the playground and got a concussion, and when I was eleven I tried unsuccessfully to back Dad's car out of the driveway. Sneaking into the city pool after hours in ninth grade added more grapes to the local grapevine. Even then I was counting the days until I could leave. But, first I had to live through the debacle at the senior prom. I think after that, even the people in Brewster were glad to see me go. After all, Paul was the town's all-American guy, and I was just Ruthie Hammond, the girl who'd hurt him.

I'd left Brewster after high school graduation, ready to wipe the dust of this rinky-dink town from my feet for good. I was headed for college. Bigger. Better. As soon as I had my degree I was going to take that trip to Europe. Find a job in New York City. See the Statue of Liberty with my own eyes. Whatever lay ahead, I was ready. But I hadn't been at college six months when the phone in my dorm room rang, changing everything.

"It's for you, Ruthie." My roommate let the receiver dangle from the wall and went back into our room.

I hurried to the phone, hoping it was the cute guy from English class. To this day I can remember how the phone receiver hung there, twisting first left, then right, as if it knew enough to try and stay out of my hand.

"Hello!" I could hear the anticipation in my voice.

"Ru-Ru-thie?" It was Vicky. Her next five words changed my life. "Mom and Dad are dead."

I remember sliding to the floor, the fabric of my shirt catching on the rough texture of the dorm wall. The room spun in slow motion, just as the phone receiver had done. Beyond that I don't recall much. Somehow I got home to Brewster. Someone must have packed the things from my dorm room and sent them after me. I don't remember. All I did know was that my life was over.

The next days were a blur. People stopping by our house with casseroles and curiosity.

"Do you think they even saw the truck?"

"If they had just gotten an earlier start home..."

"If it hadn't been dark..."

"Why did they go to Carlton, anyway?"

I didn't have answers for any of their questions. Especially not the most important one.

"What are you girls going to do now?"

These were the facts: There weren't any relatives living nearby. Vicky and I now had a Main Street business on our hands. Dad had been a pharmacist and owned the town drugstore. And Vicky had a year and a half of high school to complete.

The answers to the questions came slowly and painfully. No, they probably didn't see the truck coming their way, the policeman said. It was an old farm truck, missing a side mirror and a blinker. The farmer had started his left turn without looking. If he had, he would have seen the blue sedan beginning to pass. As it was, he turned right into them, the sedan no match for a truck filled with grain.

They'd gone to Carlton to celebrate their anniversary, Dad taking a rare afternoon off from work. The police assumed they'd done some shopping, drawing their conclusions from the mangled shopping bags in the back seat. We found out later, when the check cleared, that they'd had dinner at a seafood place, Mom's favorite. I liked to imagine they'd lingered over dessert, but that was pure speculation on my part. What else did I have to dream about?

Vicky and I had to sell the store. State law said a drugstore had to be owned by a registered pharmacist. The new owner offered me a job waiting on customers, which I gladly accepted. It was better than sitting in the house waiting for Vicky to get home from school. Family friends had volunteered to have Vicky stay with them. But Vicky needed me, and as humbling as it was to admit, I needed Vicky.

So, there we were, a sixteen-year-old and an eighteen-year-old, with over a hundred thousand dollars in the bank, one of us waiting for life to begin, the other one knowing life had just ended.

After that, people seemed to forgive me for hurting Paul. Either that, or they figured I got paid back...in spades.

We left the money in the bank and tried to get through each day the best we could. Vicky went to school and got a job in the café on weekends. I worked in the drugstore. Our parents' life insurance came in handy, but it would have been better to have them around. We both missed them. Terribly.

I told Vicky a million times she should go to college, but all she wanted was to marry Dave. She graduated from high school and worked in the café for two more years until Dave finished college. They got married that summer. Vicky used her half of the inheritance to buy the café when the owner decided to retire. I added my half to the dimes, quarters, and dollars I'd dreamed of spending somewhere far from Brewster. But by then the world seemed like a very scary place. I would have been free to leave Brewster again, but I was afraid—and confused. The last time I'd left my world had fallen apart. It was easier to make sure it stayed together if I stayed put for a while.

After a few years, I felt brave again. I moved to Carlton and got a job as a secretary in a radio station. That's where I ran into Jack. Within the year I was back in Brewster, most of my inheritance invested in station KBRS, my personal life invested in Jack. We hadn't moved in together until three years ago. It hadn't seemed like a bad idea at the time. Jack's lease was up, and we practically lived together at the station, anyway. Unfortunately, as the station slowly started going backward, so had our relationship. One sinking ship taking another one down with it. It was hard to tell which ship had developed the first leak, but one thing I'd learned, when a relationship is built on a business deal, that ship might as well not leave port.

I set the glass I'd been holding on the kitchen counter. I turned on the faucet, bent over the sink, and began splashing my face with icy water as if trying to wash away the mistakes of my past. No one but me would ever know I'd been standing here crying.

Paul

Last night after the barbeque I'd asked Dave if I could spend the morning at the bank. I wanted to talk with the staff and get a feel for the place. I thought spending some time where I might be working would give me a sense of what my decision should be. One minute I was convinced I would take the job in Brewster. The next I'd think about how hard I'd worked to gain my corner office in Chicago and doubts would set in. If I was honest with myself, I had to admit there wasn't much holding me in Chicago beyond the prestige of my job. Granted, my rise up the corporate ladder had gone faster than I'd ever dreamed, but the view from near the top wasn't as enticing as it had appeared from the bottom rungs.

It wasn't the responsibility that scared me; that I thrived on. It was the special requests my boss, Jim, had made lately. While his requests may not have been technically illegal, they didn't seem ethical, and that was the rub. And then there was Councilman Bradford pressuring me for inside information.

Was taking the job in Brewster my way of running from a challenging situation? Challenges had never intimidated me; instead, they motivated me. So, what was the problem? I didn't quite have the answer to that question yet.

I gathered the papers Dave had left for me to look over. Personnel policies along with retirement and benefit packages. The board offered a fair deal. Not nearly as much as my Chicago firm offered in terms of year-end bonuses, but overall, for a small town, it was good. And, Dave's offhand comment as I'd left last night about stock options sweetened the deal. I carried the papers into the bookkeeping department. Bookkeeping *area*, really. The banks I was familiar with in Chicago had whole floors dedicated to this function. Here it was three desks and two women, a short dividing wall and a glass panel separating them from two tellers out front. I'd been told two part-time people filled in on Mondays, Fridays, and Social Security check day, the busiest day of the month in Brewster's bank. The small size of the bank didn't seem to keep the staff from being enthusiastic about their work. If anything, it seemed to be the reason they enjoyed their jobs so much.

Peggy, the young teller I'd just met, turned from me and smiled broadly at the gray-haired woman who'd just come in. "Good morning, Mrs. Kuntz. Did you get your beans canned this week?"

"Yes, I did." Mrs. Kuntz replied. "Good thing too. Lorna called and said her and Milton are coming to visit me this weekend. I'll send some jars home with them. Goodness knows I can't eat all those beans. Did your son's team win his baseball game?"

"Yes, they did and no sliding this time. His pants were intact." Peggy chuckled along with Mrs. Kuntz. Obviously, they talked regularly. "What can I do for you today? Did you want to deposit your rent check?"

"Yes, that's what I came here for but…" Mrs. Kuntz rummaged in her purse, pulling out a check and a folded piece of paper. "I got this letter from the phone company yesterday, and I don't understand what they want." She pushed the letter across to Peggy.

Peggy glanced at the letter and then handed it back to Mrs. Kuntz. "You can throw that letter away. It's from one of those companies that tries to make you think you're their customer, and then they change your phone lines and charge you an arm and a leg."

Mrs. Kuntz nodded. "That's what I figured. I can't see to read all that fine print anymore. Here, you throw it away for me. And what about these?" She pulled three more envelopes from her purse.

"They just want money," Peggy commented, flipping through them quickly. "Do you want me to toss those for you too?"

Mrs. Kuntz nodded.

Peggy tossed the stack in the garbage can and began writing up Mrs. Kuntz's deposit, chatting all the while.

There was something about their simple exchange that struck me. It was as if they were old friends, a generation apart, one asking advice, the other gladly giving it. Even if it wasn't part of her job. Looking out for each other. I thought of the bank tellers I'd stood across from in Chicago. When I didn't use the ATM, that is. After a customer waited in a long line, the tellers were impersonal at best. I couldn't imagine what they'd do if an elderly lady asked them to sort through her mail.

As I walked toward the loan area I noticed my mother entering through the double front doors of the bank, the sun glancing in a shiny streak off the metal cane she carried.

When had she started using a cane?

I stopped to watch as she slowly made her way into the lobby. I hadn't noticed her even hesitating as she'd walked around the kitchen this morning. Was she hiding something from me? Come to think of it, she had stood with one hand on the kitchen counter or on the back of a chair whenever she'd moved. And, once she was sitting, she'd asked me to pour her a second cup of coffee, a detail that hadn't registered at the time. The image of her grimace as she handed the can opener to me yesterday suddenly had new meaning.

From my vantage point, my mother looked just like the women we'd called "old grandmas" during my high school years. Their curly gray hair, fading complexions, and loose-fitting dresses made the elderly women clones to our jaded young eyes. In my mind my mother had always been vibrant and active. I'd never seen her as aging, but today her years showed.

"Mrs. Bennett, good morning!" Peggy greeted my mother in the same familiar voice she'd used with Mrs. Kuntz. "Is your arthritis bothering you today?"

"Oh, yes, something awful." Mom's voice sounded weak. Just then she spotted me standing off to her left. I could see the effort it took her to appear as if nothing was wrong.

Peggy glanced my way, then back to my mother. "Do you know him? Oh!" she cried, putting together the puzzle, "*Mrs.* Bennett. *Mr.* Bennett. I bet this is your son. Am I right?"

"That you are, Peggy. That's my Paul. He's a good son. I'm sure I told you about him. He lives in Chicago."

"Yes, you did. I remember." Peggy looked almost as proud as my mother. "I moved here...what was it?" She looked to my mother for confirmation. "About a year ago now?" My mom nodded. "Your mother was my first customer the day I started working. She's mentioned you several times."

I stood there, doing my best to imitate a beet from Mrs. Kuntz's garden. How quickly one could feel like a little boy again.

"Paul, are you going to be home for lunch?"

Exactly like a little boy.

I clasped the papers I was holding and drew myself up, trying to transform myself from child to maybe bank president in the course of two seconds. The picture of my aging mother burned in my mind. "Better yet, Mom, why don't I take you out for lunch? I'll pick you up at noon and we'll eat at Vicky's."

"See, Peggy," Mom said, "I told you he was a good son."

Exactly like a little boy.

Wayne Jorgenson, the bank's lone loan officer, was busy with customers all morning, so I stopped in after lunch, leaving Mom to do some errands near the bank. She'd insisted she was perfectly capable of walking to the drugstore and the post office without my assistance, but she had agreed to let me give her a ride home in an hour.

Wayne was on the phone when I arrived, so I bided my time in the lobby looking over the workplace and watching customers come and go. I'd checked out the bank on the Internet before I'd left Chicago. The financial institution appeared to be sound from what I could see. I wanted to talk with Wayne and learn the lending policies of the bank and the outlook for the ag economy, an area I'd never concerned myself with before.

"He'll see you now." The secretary stood and held out her arm as if I were a visiting dignitary she was ushering around.

"Mr. Bennett." Wayne offered his right hand, clicking a pen with his left. "What can I do for you?"

No chitchat. No, "*How are you doing?*" No, "*Are you enjoying your visit?*" Even after I asked him to call me Paul, he got right down to business. I got my information and that was all.

Cordial. Aloof. Nervous. Those were three words that came to mind as I walked to the back office. I could hardly blame Wayne. Maybe he'd had his eye on the job I'd been offered. But there was something else, something I couldn't quite put my finger on that sent my antennae up.

Way up.

~

I had a half hour until I'd promised to meet Mom. My potential office was quiet. A good place to think. And pray.

Lord, show me Your will in this.

I closed my eyes and tried to recall all the things I loved about Chicago. The things I'd thrived on during my early years there were losing their luster. The fast pace. The downtown condo. The Cubs. Okay, maybe not the Cubs. I'd been a fan even before I moved there. Poor season or not, they were still my team. My brows furrowed. Surely there was more. Ah, yes, pizza. No one could argue with that. But Italian sausage and extra mozzarella weren't anything to base a decision on.

What about Corinne?

Yeah, what about Corinne? Though we'd dated a little over a year, it hadn't become steady until recently. I enjoyed her intelligence, her business acumen, and her sense of humor. But her subtle hints at something more serious had left me feeling more panicked than pleased. The pain of losing Mia still rocked me at times, making me back off from anything that hinted of possible heartache.

What about Corinne? I didn't have an answer to that question.

What about Ruthie?

My eyes flew open. Ruthie? What did she have to do with anything? I hadn't thought about Ruthie in years.

Years?

Okay, months.

What about last night?

Okay, since last night.

I could tell she'd been crying. I had no idea why. Ruthie had slipped through the sliding door, a glass of ice water in her hand. Her brown eyes sparkled in a way that threw me straight back to the night I'd tried to forget for almost twenty years. Her eyes had glistened in exactly the same way that night. The night of our senior prom...

"Okay, guys," the deejay whispered into the microphone, trying his best to add atmosphere to the end of our evening, "you seniors hold 'em close. This is the last dance." The strains of a popular romantic ballad filled the gym.

"Come here." I slowly walked backward onto the dance floor, beckoning Ruthie to follow. When we reached the center of the floor I wrapped my arms around her, the soft satin of her dress a cloud under my hand. "Mmmmm," I murmured, "you smell good."

Ruthie tilted her head, giving me what I called her Mona Lisa smile. Content. Slightly amused. Feelings behind that smile I'd find out about later. For now, knowing I was dancing the last dance of our senior prom with the girl I loved was all I needed.

All around I could see classmates and teachers, people I'd known almost all my life. It was strange to think that in a few weeks I'd never see many of them again. This gym and the people in it held some of the best memories of my life. Winning the district basketball championship, the goofy skits we'd done for pep rallies. Right here was where I'd danced with Ruthie for the first time, square dancing in fourth grade PE class. One thing I didn't have to worry about—Ruthie and I would always be together. I planned to make sure of that tonight. I took my hand from her waist and reached into the pocket of my tuxedo. Yup, it was still there. The white gold-and-diamond solitaire I'd saved for this whole past year. I'd had it on layaway in Carlton, sending as much of my paycheck from the hardware store as

I could spare each month, making sure I had the balance paid before tonight. I patted my pocket, then slipped my arm around Ruthie again, pulling her close.

Ruthie turned her cheek, laying it gently against my shirt. "Mmmm, this is nice."

It's as if You made us for each other, Lord. Thank You. I rubbed my cheek against the top of her head.

The last notes of the song filled the gym. Now. Now was the time. My heart thumped hard in my chest as I took a step back from Ruthie. As I reached in my pocket, the couples around us clapped softly, thanking the deejay for the music.

"Excuse me!" As football quarterback and basketball captain I was used to speaking in the gym. I had no trouble getting everyone's attention. "Uh, before we all leave tonight there's one more thing I'd like to do."

My classmates hooted, encouraging whatever my plan might be. Dave stood nearby, grinning from ear to ear. He knew exactly what I had planned.

"Paul?" Ruthie looked at me, puzzled, blushing furiously, looking around to see what everyone was laughing about.

By the time she'd turned back to me I had dropped to one knee and had the small blue velvet box open in my hand. The gym was so quiet you could have heard a pom-pom drop.

"Ruthie Hammond," I cleared my throat, finding myself suddenly nervous, "I'd like to ask if you would marry me?"

I heard Ruthie's quick intake of air right before the silence in the gym started sounding as though it were ocean waves crashing on an empty beach.

No one uttered a word. Not even Ruthie.

The coldness of the floor crept through the slacks of my tuxedo into my knee.

Superintendent Baumiller cleared his throat.

From somewhere to my left I heard a girl whisper, "Answer him."

Ruthie laughed a high-pitched, trembling giggle that made her sound much younger than eighteen. Her eyes darted from side to side as if she were trapped and looking for a way out. I'd been so sure of Ruthie's answer—until this second, when I looked into her eyes. In the short span it took for her eyes to fill with tears, for her to fill her lungs with the breath to murmur, "Paul, I can't…I just can't," I recalled snippets of conversations we'd had about getting married.

"*I want to travel,*" she'd said. "*I want to see the world. New York. London. Paris.*" She'd kissed me between the words as if she were a conductor punching a train ticket.

"*We will travel someday,*" I promised, reminding her we had to finish college first, that money would be tight, but after college we'd move back to Brewster, maybe start a family. There would be plenty of time to travel.

"*There's just so much I want to do.*" Her eyes sparkled as she dreamt of faraway places. I'd always assumed she'd dreamed of seeing those places with me.

Until now. Even the air in the gym seemed to be holding its breath, waiting for Ruthie to change her mind. Her eyes glistened as she shook her head and softly said, "I'm sorry, Paul."

I'd been hit hard on the football field. Even had the wind knocked out of me twice. Those blows felt like feathers compared to how her words struck me. My leg felt as though it were filled with lead as I tried to stand. The other kids turned their backs, trying to distance themselves from my humiliation. Not even a whisper cut through the silence pounding in my ears. Finally, I stood upright, the ring box lying open in my cupped hand. Ruthie blinked once, then opened her mouth as if to say something more. The snap of the ring box cut off anything she meant to say. I turned in slow motion, the distance to the gym door seeming longer than any relay race I'd ever run.

"Paul." Ruthie's hand brushed my back. "Don't…" I kept walking. "It's just that…" Her words came in a rush. "If I marry you I'll be stuck in this town the rest of my life. I'd rather die."

Die? *Die?* What was so bad about dying? At that moment, death seemed like a great option. I kept walking.

"Paul, wait. You don't understand."

I turned to face her. Except for the deejay at the far end of the gym, the room had emptied, the purple and silver streamers suddenly looking more garish than romantic.

"I understand perfectly." My voice surprised me. It sounded calm. Perfectly modulated. As if I were the leading man in a romantic farce. If that were the case I might as well play the part. This act would be over soon.

I reached in my pocket and pulled out the car keys. "Here," I said, tossing them to her. "I'll walk."

"Paul, don't. Don't do this. Let's talk about...I didn't mean..." The tears that had brimmed in her eyes now ran freely. They slid down her cheeks and onto the light blue satin of her dress, staining it dark, a storm cloud in a perfect sky.

I turned to the door, tossing words over my shoulder, my grand exit line, "Have a great life, Ruthie Hammond."

It was a good thing that was my last line, because right after I said it a lump formed in my throat so large even gulping great breaths of night air wouldn't budge it.

✑

"Mr. Bennett?" The secretary's voice startled me into the present. I shook my head, the hunter green-and-beige tones of the bank carpet suddenly replacing the memory I'd been reliving. "I hope I'm not disturbing you, but the *Brewster Banner* just arrived and I thought you might like to look it over while you're here."

"Thanks," I said, reaching for the thin weekly paper, my mind reeling from the vivid memory.

Absently, I paged through the paper. I recognized three of the people in the four-generation photo on page three and noticed that the Freshman Student of the Month was a dead ringer for his dad at the same age. I turned the page, my mind more focused now. My eyes scanned the columns, assessing which businesses in Brewster had enough money to run weekly ads. The grocery store, the bank, Vicky's café, the livestock barn. Dave's insurance agency, the drugstore Ruthie's dad used to own, and the local chiropractor. My eye was drawn to a muddy-colored photo on the bottom corner of page five. My heart did a small flip as I recognized Ruthie and Jack. I noticed the call letters of the radio station and the tag line, "*Your voice in the country.*" I wasn't sure if it was the picture of Ruthie or the picture of Ruthie and Jack together that gave me pause. After my recall of our prom night you'd think I'd be glad to see her with someone else, but I had to admit, against all odds and my better judgment, there was something about Ruthie that still captivated me. Although I'd never managed to forget prom night, I'd long ago forgiven Ruthie. Not without struggle, however.

During my first three years at college I avoided women altogether, which was good for my grade point average but lousy for my social life. I thought about Ruthie a lot, especially on late-night treks from the library back to my dorm room. There were very few people hanging around outside the library after midnight, and something about the empty sidewalks and the way the moonlight filtered through the trees always made me think of long walks I'd taken, hand in hand with Ruthie, around the two-mile perimeter of Brewster. Over and over, I found myself longing for the good times we'd shared. The way we could tell each other anything and be understood. The way Ruthie would look at me out of the corner of her eye in class, then turn her head and look directly into my eyes, a grin plastered across her face. More than once a teacher had said, "Miss Hammond, maybe you could share with the class what it is you find so fascinating on that side of the room." Ruthie wasn't one bit embarrassed to point her index finger at me and say, "Him." The teachers quit asking. I couldn't count the number of times I relived our first, gentle kiss. Then, when I'd think I couldn't stand remembering any more, I'd remember prom night.

How many times had I lain in bed, talking to the ceiling, appealing to Ruthie to change her answer? She never did. There was no answer from the dingy beige ceiling.

Eventually, instead of talking to Ruthie I started talking to God. I'd grown up in a Christian home, been raised to trust God, and I'd thought I did. But it was then, during those late night hours when I felt as though I were the only person in the universe, that I found a faith of my own. God led me to an understanding I couldn't find on lonely campus sidewalks or on my dorm room ceiling. It didn't happen overnight, but in time He led me to forgiveness.

Over the years I gained a perspective I hadn't had when I was a high school senior. Ruthie had always had an indefinable spark, a love of life, a sense of living life to the fullest. A spirit that had drawn me to her in first grade.

In the intervening years I came to see that Ruthie hadn't turned down my proposal because she didn't love me. I knew she did, otherwise I wouldn't have asked her in the first place. Ruthie had a need to discover what life had to offer before she could commit to anyone. She needed to try out her wings. Leave no stone unturned. Experience all the clichés people made fun of but that had truth at their core. Ruthie had dreams to fulfill, and if she didn't at least try to live her dream, she would feel life had let her down. Ruthie would have been miserable, and so would the person who had kept her from pursuing her dream. Which would have been me.

I'd come to see that Ruthie had been the wise one that night, saying no, when yes was the easy answer. The answer just about anyone else would have given in that situation, even if they'd have to change it later. As painful as that night had been, I'd come to respect Ruthie for instinctively knowing both of us needed more time to find out what life had to offer. If it hadn't been for Ruthie, I might never have spread my own wings. Never have found a deep faith. Never have graduated from college. Never had a career in investment banking. Never met Mia. Never had Jenny. I'd already lived a life beyond anything I could have imagined in high school and, in a sense, I had Ruthie to thank for it. I only hoped she could say as much.

The intercom buzzer on the phone interrupted my thoughts.

"Judy, line two." The disembodied voice immediately added, "Oops, wrong button. Sorry."

I shook my head, trying to clear my mind. Enough of dwelling in the past. I had a future to decide. I closed the *Brewster Banner*, my mind debating the pros and cons of the decision before me.

Lord, what am I supposed to do? Help me to know what Your will is in this decision I need to make. Show me clearly what You would have me do.

I glanced at my watch. I still had fifteen minutes until I needed to meet my mother. Fifteen minutes to try to come closer to an answer. Swiveling the chair, I gazed out the window. I'd always done my best thinking outdoors. Hiking through a field in the fall was when I'd had some of my best ideas. It didn't matter if the hunt ended with me filling my limit or not. I considered the day a success just to be outside in God's glorious creation. If nothing else, gazing outside would help clear my mind.

The birds in the hedge were busy. I watched as a robin pecked at the ground, then took off in flight, startled by something. My eyes followed the bird as it swirled above the hedge, then swooped toward the post office.

I could see a woman slowly making her way across the street, going toward the post office at a much slower pace than the robin. The robin flew out of sight, and my eyes took up the slower track of the woman. It was calming to follow her deliberate gait. Right foot, then left, lift her cane and start again. Cane?

Once again, when I realized the slow-moving woman was my mother, I was struck by how much she'd aged in the past months. When I viewed her at a distance, her frailty was more apparent than when she was close, where her words and expressive face distracted me from the deterioration of her mobility.

In the time it took Mom to cross the street, several cars had driven by, two swinging to a stop in front of the postal building, their occupants in and out before Mom paused at the curb. I held my breath as I saw her hesitate, carefully lifting her cane onto the curb before raising her right foot. Just as I was ready to release my breath, her foot seemed to catch on the edge of the sidewalk. In a fruitless gesture I reached out as if to balance her, but before I could push back my chair she was laying flat on the pavement.

By the time I'd sprinted the space between the back door of the bank and the post office, Mom was standing. Two Brewster business-people had Mom by each arm. One was holding her cane, the other was brushing her off. A few other people stood by, ready to help. Ruthie elbowed her way through the small crowd, taking her place by Mom's side as if she had no better place to be. The businessman handed Ruthie the cane and stepped back. A couple other folks sent curious glances our way as they walked out the post office door. I'd forgotten what a popular spot the post office was this time of day.

"Are you sure you're okay?" Ruthie's voice was calm. "Nothing hurts?"

"Only my pride." Mom's eyes twinkled, but I noticed the trembling of her hand as she patted at her hair.

"Mom, what happened?" My breath was coming in short bursts. I hadn't sprinted in years.

"I fell down," Mom explained matter-of-factly, "as little children and arthritic old ladies are prone to do. I'm perfectly fine. No need to worry." She turned to me, slipping her arm through mine, ignoring the smudge of dust on each knee of her pant legs. "I'm ready for that ride home now."

Seeing that she was all right, the two other businesspeople went into the post office. Ruthie handed the cane to my mother. "I've always thought that curb was higher than the rest of the curbs in town. I'm going to have to remember to be more careful around here too."

"Thank you for helping me, Ruth." Mom leaned heavily on my arm, a much sturdier support, apparently, than her cane. As we began to walk Mom's foot caught again, and Ruthie grabbed Mom's other arm to steady her, knocking the cane onto the ground.

"Better that thing than me," Mom said, trying to make light of the situation.

A line from an old Jeff Foxworthy comedy routine flashed into my mind, "*Here's your sign.*" Jeff's kind of signs pointed out when people had been blind to the obvious. I'd been praying for God to show me what to do. Having my mother lean so heavily on my arm was almost as clear as if I'd been handed a sign. I couldn't help but laugh at God's sense of humor.

Regaining her composure, Mom turned the both of us toward the bank where my car was parked, but not before I caught the wide-eyed, *your-mother-needs-help* glare Ruthie flashed behind Mom's back.

Funny how, after all these years, I could still read Ruthie loud and clear.

God too. It didn't take a rocket scientist to decipher this sign. Holding my mother's arm firmly, I took a deep breath of Brewster's sun-drenched summer air, the crystal-clear air I'd be breathing year round.

The decision made, I felt more like running than stepping along slowly beside my mom. But then life in Brewster was much slower paced than life in Chicago. I'd better get used to it. I sighed deeply, contentment filling every pore of my body.

I was coming home.

Ruthie

"Look at it this way, Cal," I said, crossing out the dollar figure I'd just written and lowering it by ten percent, "you're getting one week of ads for free." I looked casually toward the front of the store, giving Cal a chance to think. The *New Fall Merchandise Now In* sign hung at an odd angle. Fall had been here a good month already, but knowing Cal, that sign would hang there until Christmas.

Cal scratched his head, then took off his thick glasses and cleaned them slowly. I snuck a glance at my watch. At this rate I'd never work in the other two ad stops I'd planned to make before lunch. The cool, musty air of the old wooden building closed in on me. *Hurry up. I have work to do.* At least now that school had started I had hopes of finding ad sponsors for the high school games KBRS broadcast. *If I ever get out of here, that is.*

Immediately my conscience pricked me. Cal had known me since I'd been born, had even wrapped his thick arms around me one time after my parents had died and I'd burst out crying in the middle of the hardware store while trying to replace an iron. What did I know about irons back then? What did I know about much of anything life had in store? It hadn't mattered to Cal that he'd been filling a paint order for someone. He'd hurried away from the paint mixer and pulled me into his beefy chest, wrapping me into a hug that eventually dried my tears. I sighed. I owed Cal some time.

"Don't know what to tell you, Ruth. I'd sure like to help you out, but people ain't buying hardware like they used to." Cal blew on his glasses and started cleaning them again. "Three quarters of the folks in Brewster are getting Social Security. They don't need new shovels and rakes. A piece of sandpaper and a roll of masking tape now and then are all they're good for."

79

"We'll advertise sandpaper and masking tape then." *Come on-n, Cal, please.* He had no way of knowing that the longer I sat here the less time I had to call on my other accounts. Accounts whose business I needed just as badly as his.

"But I'm the only one in town who sells that stuff."

"Sure you are, but when they come in to buy their tape they'll see all the other things you have for sale and pick up other items too." I looked over Cal's shoulder at the sparsely stocked shelves. "Besides, you don't want them driving to Carlton to buy the same things you have right here." I didn't sound very convincing.

"They drive to Carlton anyway." Cal held his glasses up to the light then began rubbing at them again. "Sandpaper and masking tape," his voice was low, as if even he couldn't believe it had come to this. "It's hard to make a living off of that. I remember back when I was working for Mr. Bennett..."

Could the man talk any slower? I pasted a smile on my face. I heard this same story every time I stopped to renew his ad contract. At least he did renew it. That was more than I could say for two of the businesses I'd stopped at yesterday.

"...yup, those were the good old days, I say." Cal nodded slowly, finally putting his glasses back on his face.

"They sure were," I agreed, holding my pen out in a way Cal couldn't help but subconsciously get my message. *Sign here.*

The radio on Cal's desk was tuned to our station. I could hear Jack giving the weather report, possible frost this week. According to Jack, fall was coming early this year. At least he'd shown up for work this morning. I wouldn't have bet money on it. He'd tiptoed into our bedroom sometime after two o'clock last night. I'd pretended to be asleep. I had discovered long ago listening to Jack's excuses only caused me to lie awake longer.

I drummed my fingers silently against my knee as Cal signed his name. Unfortunately, he wrote as slowly as he spoke, each letter stroked in a deliberate manner. C-a-l-v-i-n. Methodically, he dotted the "i." All I had left was to listen to his story about the penmanship award he'd received in fourth grade and then I'd be out of here.

"There you go." Cal pushed the contract my way, holding the pen until he finished telling the penmanship story.

"You still have award-winning handwriting," I told him as I did every month, trying hard to unclench my teeth as I spoke. I held out my hand, hoping he'd get the hint.

"Thank you." Cal beamed as though he were a fourth grader again. "I'd better get back to work and I suppose you've got things to get to too." He placed the pen in my palm.

Finally.

I stood. "Thank you once again, Cal. See you next month."

He walked me to the door, held it open, and smiled the same wonderful smile I'd known all my life. "Take care, Ruth."

"Thanks, Cal," I replied, and then without thinking I reached out to give him a quick hug, suddenly grateful not only for his advertising, but also for the way he'd always supported me by simply caring. "You take care, too," I added, meaning it from the bottom of my heart.

I stepped out the door, the warmth of Cal's embrace still on my shoulders and looked both ways down the sidewalk before deciding which way to go. To the surprise of almost everyone in Brewster—and especially to me—Paul had been offered and accepted Bob Marsden's former position at the bank. He had completed his move back to town only a few days ago and ever since I'd been on edge. I moved around town as though I were a private detective, ever on the watch for the elusive Paul. I wanted to see him, and yet I didn't. I had nothing to say to him, yet felt there were volumes of words I should speak. Ever since the night of Vicky's barbeque a few weeks earlier, I'd felt all the things I'd left unsaid the night of senior prom hanging in the air. As if my unspoken words had hovered there all these years, waiting for me to give them voice. Those words would have to hang there a while longer. I had no intention of running into Paul anytime soon. I turned left, toward Vicky's café. She was on my list of clients to see today, and a cup of coffee would be a good way to celebrate Cal buying an ad package. I yanked open the door to Vicky's.

"Paul!" My heart started hammering in my chest as Paul side-stepped to avoid a collision.

"I see you're addicted to the coffee here too," he said, unruffled as could be.

I consciously turned up the corners of my mouth. "Um-hmmm," I hummed, very intelligent-like.

Paul stood, cool as a bank president, while a bead of sweat broke out on my upper lip. I squirmed inside my skin, words of apology clogging my throat. I knew I'd never speak them here, but that I wanted to say them at all surprised me.

My eyes darted away from his crinkled blue gaze into the bottle green eyes of a tall, raven-haired woman standing at his side. My hands started sweating too. If luck were with me, maybe I would simply explode and be done with it. It didn't happen, so instead I stared. It wasn't often women in kiwi green business suits and what looked to be navy Manolo Blahnik heels stood in the entryway of Vicky's café. Stood in Brewster, for that matter. I was positive her jet black hair was dyed, but instead of looking cheap, it added to her air of cool sophistication.

"Ruthie," Paul's voice cut through my assessment. For a brief moment we both gazed at the woman, his expression a mixture of pleasure and pride, mine flat-out curiosity. "I'd like you to meet a friend of mine from Chicago."

Friend?

"This is Corinne. Corinne, this is Ruthie, Vicky's sister and a classmate of mine."

"It seems as though half the people I've met have been class-mates of yours." She laughed, her voice crystal clear and perfectly modulated. I would have hired her in a second as a radio talk-show host, but somehow I didn't think that was her idea of a promotion. As she transferred her navy clutch purse to her left hand, I noticed she wasn't wearing a ring. I hadn't read all those Nancy Drew books in the Brewster library for nothing. She stretched out her hand. "Pleased to meet you, Ruth."

I swiped my sweaty palm against my side, hoping to appear half as collected as this Corinne person. My brown cotton sweater and wrinkled beige skirt didn't seem nearly as stylish as when I'd looked in the mirror this morning. I shifted in my tight brown Payless pumps. "Nice to meet you too." I sounded phony, a cut-rate version of someone named Corinne.

"This is a charming little town you live in," Corinne said as Paul stepped around me, leading their way out.

She had the *little* part right.

I marched past the table of regulars I usually sat with, giving Vicky a meet-you-in-back tilt of my head. I pushed through the swinging doors into the café kitchen, the smell of morning breakfast filled the air. Bacon and sausage patties. Beef stew simmered on the stove. The lunch special, I guessed. Impatiently, I waited.

"Vicky," I called, poking my head into the full café, "your stew is boiling."

"Turn it down, please, I'm busy." With the coffeepot in her right hand she filled Pastor Ammon's cup with decaf, then proceeded around the table topping off other cups, some with decaf, some with regular, chatting all the while.

Couldn't she see this was important? "I think it might be burning."

The second the swinging door closed behind Vicky I blurted, "Who was that?"

Vicky turned the burner down and stirred the stew. "This isn't burning."

I shrugged my shoulders, grimacing sheepishly. "Who is she?"

"Ruthie, I have a business to run." Vicky turned from the stove. "In case you haven't noticed, I have a full house out there, which doesn't happen all that often anymore. If you want to hang around, grab a coffeepot and go to it, otherwise, I've got cups to fill." She paused, her hand on the door. "I think she was someone Paul was seeing in Chicago, and for your information she seemed very nice."

A totally unexpected stab of jealousy cut through me. Voices from the busy café floated through the door as Vicky left the kitchen, then it was quiet except for slow bubbles breaking on the surface of the stew. I had no claim on Paul. No reason to feel jealous and yet…I did. Except for holidays, I hadn't been to church in years. I'd pretty much given up that sort of thing when my parents were killed. But I still had a sense of right and wrong, and I knew this feeling was wrong. To put it in church terms, I was covetous.

I coveted everything about her. I wanted to *be* her. I wanted her fancy name. *Corinne*. I wanted her stylish suit and designer shoes. Even her dyed black hair would be better than my plain brown. I could try to fit the junk in my purse into her chic navy bag, and whatever sort of job she had in Chicago, I wanted that too. But, most of all, I wanted Paul to look at me the way he'd looked at her.

Jack

Something was eating Ruthie, but danged if I knew what it was. She came storming into the station doing a perfect imitation of a shrew from Shakespeare. Not that I knew much about Shakespeare, but once, for speech team, Mrs. Webb had asked me to do a dramatic interpretation on Shakespeare, which I refused. All those judges would have had to do was take one look at me, a tall, skinny, pale-faced redhead and any dramatic Shakespeare reading I attempted would turn into a comedy routine. No, I knew my limitations even then.

Just like I knew them now. Crabby, drawer-slamming women were never my area of expertise. I knew enough to keep my distance and I did.

Like last night. I had sneaking into our apartment down to a science. The worst part was popping the lock, but that part I couldn't help. Ruthie always locked the door before she went to bed. Not that Brewster had a high crime rate. Must be a woman thing. I'd slowly opened the door and taken a giant step over the squeaky spot directly in front of the doorjamb. After that it was just a matter of slipping out of my shoes, undressing in the hall, then quietly dropping my clothes on the chair inside the bedroom door while I grabbed the gym trunks I'd left there from the night before. I slipped into bed without Ruthie even suspecting I'd been to the casino seventy miles away and back.

I didn't think it would exactly be a lie to say I'd had a business meeting. I ended up playing blackjack next to a guy who seemed pretty impressed when he found out I owned a radio station. He said we should talk sometime. He was looking to make some investments and radio might be the way to go. I told him about the scoop I had on a station in Carlton that was for sale. If I could get him to bankroll this little project, it would take a lot of the pressure off from the bank here in Brewster. And having two stations would look that much better when I tried to buy a third. Maybe this guy would be my one-way ticket to the big markets. Maybe we could be partners. Of course I'd have to run it by Ruthie, but three o'clock in the morning probably wasn't a good time to do that.

It didn't look as if this morning was a good time either. Yep, I knew when to stay out of her way. Unfortunately, she didn't know enough to stay out of mine when she was having a hissy fit.

"Jack," she stood opposite the microphone, arms folded tightly across her chest as if she were trying to hold herself together from the sides, "we need to talk."

If there was ever a four-letter word a man should fear, it's the word *talk* coming from a woman. I'd learned that *talk* meant Ruthie would talk and I'd sit there and wonder how soon I could make my getaway.

"I can't talk now. This song is almost over." I swiveled the chair around to the stack of tapes lining the back wall, pulling three out at random, pretending to search for more. Thinking quickly, I added, "I promised to play a six-pack and I've got five more to go, then the noon weather report is up, and I was counting on you to get it off the wire service for me."

She stood still, not making a move to get the weather report. I jerked my head toward the office, hoping she'd get the hint and maybe get off her high horse on the way. The last notes of a steel guitar faded away and my radio voice kicked in. "That was an old one from the Judds. Now let's listen to daughter Wynonna. This is KBRS, your voice in the country." I punched the play button. "The weather report?" I reminded, just in case she hadn't heard me the first time. "Could you get it for me?"

"I think you should move."

I'd never seen Ruthie in quite this state of mind before. Who knew what she was thinking? I really didn't want to find out. I stood, swinging my arm toward the chair seat, leaning forward, a gallant knight. "It's all yours. I'll get the weather report myself. The rest of the music is right here." I pushed four tapes towards her. "Feel free to pick something else."

"Not that." Ruthie pushed the stack of tapes back at me, sending them sprawling. "I think you should move out of our apartment."

Did she now? "And where do you think I should move to?"

"I don't care. I just don't think we should live together anymore. This isn't working for me."

"Isn't working for you, is that it? Have you forgotten we own this radio station together? That you wouldn't even have this business if it weren't for me?"

"We don't have to live together in order to be in business together." Unlike other times we'd argued, her voice was dead calm. "The song is ending," she added in that same detached tone.

I stabbed at the play button on the second machine, the tune of the Judds' song I'd played previously going out over the air. "I like this song so much I'm going to play it again," I shouted into the mike as if I were having the time of my life playing the part of a hotshot disc jockey.

Ruthie turned on her heel and walked out of the broadcast room.

Move out of our apartment? I couldn't afford an apartment on my own. Besides, we'd probably be moving to Carlton as soon as this deal went through. If I could just get a chance to tell Ruthie about my plan, I knew she'd change her mind. Wouldn't she?

I ran after her. "Ruthie, let's talk."

Ruthie

The words were out of my mouth before I'd realized I'd said them out loud. *I think you should move.* They surprised me as much as they seemed to surprise Jack, but the moment I said them I knew they were words I'd wanted to say for a long time. I couldn't believe the sense of relief I felt, as though the last piece of a huge jigsaw puzzle had been slipped into place, or *out,* in this case.

For the first time since I'd known him, Jack ran after me. "Ruthie, let's talk," he pleaded. The thing he didn't understand was there was nothing left to talk about.

Jack hadn't fooled me for a minute last night. Sneaking into bed at three-sixteen, smelling of smoke, stale air, and beer. The bars in Brewster closed at one, so I knew he had to have gone to the casino to be tiptoeing in so late. That's all we needed—him to be gambling away the little bit of money we had coming in.

I had turned my back to him, pulling the covers up to my chin, pretending I was sound asleep. In fact I hadn't slept a wink. How had I made such a mess of my life?

Instead of sleeping I'd spent the wee hours of the morning wrestling memories. Memories I'd been trying to avoid since Paul had moved back to Brewster.

Seeing Paul with Corinne had been like running into a wall. I couldn't keep the thoughts at bay any longer; they were right in front of me. I couldn't help but imagine what it would have been like if it were me standing there in the café next to Paul. Having him take *my* elbow. Having him put his hand on the small of *my* back, ushering me out of Vicky's as if I were fragile as crystal.

I'd tossed and turned as I tried to unravel the mystery of how my life had taken such a wrong turn. My plans had been to get a degree in broadcast communications, an internship at a big-city station, and then a job at a major network. Radio or television, I didn't care; I just knew it would be my gift of gab, my words, that would bring my release from Brewster.

Instead, there I was in our crummy apartment, at our struggling radio station, at Wayne Jorgenson's desk at the bank, trying to use my words to bail us out of trouble. Not what I'd had in mind at all.

It seemed as though moving in with Jack had been the start of the end. Until then I'd held on to the dream of moving on. At first, Jack and I had been simply business partners, focused on one thing…getting our start in radio. Building one small station into a solid foundation from which to add more. We found out reality didn't mesh with our dream. Almost all of the businesses in Brewster seemed to be struggling to make ends meet. Advertising on the radio was about the last item in their budget. Still, it seemed, everyone loved the idea of having a local radio station; they just didn't like the idea of having to pay for it. "Stop by next month," they'd say when we'd ask for their business. If we were lucky we'd hear, "I suppose I can take the small ad package for one month." And so we were taking out loans to cover our costs, convinced, like every other business-person in town, success was a flip of the calendar away. *Wait till harvest. Wait till spring. Next year will be better.* Somehow we'd limped along like that for years. How had that happened?

In the meantime Jack and I dived into the community in high gear. Showing up with our remote mike, broadcasting from the county fair, setting up a table in Magner's Grocery store during Pumpkin Days, broadcasting live from Pumpkin Fest, using every trick in our slim book to promote our station and the town. We'd made an effort to get to know people. Not that it took too much of an effort, considering this was home base for both of us, but people needed to view us as businesspeople, not high school kids. We tried our best to let them know we had high hopes. Little did they know our hopes rode on the first ticket we could get out of town.

Jack and I had been thrown together night and day as we worked to make a go of KBRS. When we weren't on the air or selling ads we were putting our heads together concocting new ways to make the station prosper.

A few local guys had asked me out back then, but I quickly realized hitching my dreams to a dairy farmer didn't fit one bit with the grand career I had planned. Pretty soon they quit asking, and my world shrunk to the station and Jack.

Looking back from the vantage point of my rumpled bed, it was hard to understand how the years could pass by so unmarked. As if one melded into the next in a seamless weave, binding Jack and me into an intricate web. A web I hadn't seen being woven. And here I was, trapped.

Why had I stayed?

Now *that* was a question.

I'd gotten out of bed and stepped to the window, leaving Jack the whole bed to himself. The streetlight on the corner illuminated the empty street out front. Not a car or a person in sight. Certainly not the fast-paced life I'd dreamed of for more years than I could count.

What had kept me here?

Convenience? Complacency? Fear? Had I really thought staying in Brewster, staying with Jack, would get me where I'd dreamed? Hitching myself to this little town and Jack hadn't gotten me any further than if I'd driven down the road and joined up with one of those dairy farmers I'd scoffed at. I'd spent so much time with Jack that for a while I did think I loved him. At least that's what I thought love might feel like if I couldn't recapture what I'd had with Paul. I'd been so young then. What did I know about love?

Three years ago I'd told Vicky I was moving out of the tiny, one-bedroom house I'd rented for years.

"What?" she responded. "Where will you live?"

"With Jack," was my smug reply, anxious, finally, to move anywhere. Even if it was still in Brewster, it was a move. At the time it had felt like a kind of freedom to say those words. Only now did I see it was bondage of its own kind.

"You're not getting married, are you?" Vicky knew, very well, the relationship Jack and I had was based on a dream and nothing more.

"No," I answered. Then, feeling a need to fill her appraising silence, I added, "I love him." What else would you feel for someone who shared your dream?

Vicky's reply still rang in my ears. "If you're not committed enough to get married, you're not committed enough to live together."

"This is my life, Vicky—not yours." I blew righteousness into the air. Sometimes Vicky could sound more like a mother than a little sister. *Or a conscience.* I moved the next day.

In the stark light of night I could see with clarity that what I'd thought was love was, at its essence, a longing to *be* loved. A longing to be loved by someone, and that someone wasn't Jack. Why had it taken me so long to understand that?

I wasn't quite sure what the future held, but I knew I didn't want my future to be like my past, same old–same old. If I didn't make changes now, my life would never change. I would ask Jack to move out—and if he wouldn't move, I would.

I'd marched into the kitchen and pulled a notepad from the drawer. Grabbing a pen, I'd sat at the counter and wrote:

Dear (big-city station manager):
Have you ever wondered where the next exciting
new voice for your station will come from? I have the
answer you've been looking for...

At least I'd hoped that was the answer.

Paul

"That's h-o-r-s on you, buddy. One more and I'll skunk you."
Dave tossed the basketball my way. I was off my game tonight, even
though I knew Dave had been taking it easy on me since "o." We'd
been shooting hoops in Dave's driveway a couple nights a week lately.
Sam and Angie usually joined us, but tonight they'd dropped out
early. Vicky had called Angie in to help with supper and insisted Sam
come inside and practice his saxophone. Through the closed windows I could hear him squeaking through the scale. I was glad I was
outside. Dribbling the ball slowly, I walked to the far end of the
driveway.

"Going for a three-pointer? You haven't even made the gimmes
tonight." Dave deserved to taunt me because I usually creamed him
at this game. "Why don't you admit defeat and put yourself out of
your misery?"

I stood in place dribbling, my back to the basket, my mind somewhere besides the driveway.

"Hey, buddy, it's your turn," Dave reminded.

Crouching low, I pivoted, then sprung into the air, pushing the
ball into a perfect arc that ended up nothing but net. "'H' on you," I
said tossing Dave the ball.

Dave didn't even try to match my shot and tossed the ball right
back to me. I knew he'd never had an outside game, and if I was going
to come from behind I was going to have to take advantage of his
weak spots.

I dribbled to the side of the makeshift court, eight feet straight
to the left of the rim. I could make this shot with my eyes shut. A

second before the ball left my fingers Dave asked, "So what's the deal with Corinne?"

My ball ricocheted off the rim and into Dave's hands. Not quite fair, but then maybe he was taking advantage of *my* weak spots. "She broke it off."

Dave tossed the ball from where he stood. Swish.

I matched his shot. He missed the next. I caught the ball on the fly, curved my arm behind my back, and sent it up. Miraculously it went in. Dave tried to match my move and missed.

"'O' on me," he called sending the ball back to me.

Oh. My thoughts exactly when Corinne had said she was coming to Brewster to talk. Oh? Oh.

I dribbled the ball in place. "She said she couldn't see a long-distance relationship working." I drove in for an easy layup, talking as the ball rolled off my fingertips into the basket. "She's looking to settle down and…well, I couldn't tell her I was ready for that yet."

Dave retrieved the ball and bounced it a few times, looking at me with an expression I couldn't read, then went in for the layup. The ball balanced on the rim for a second, then rolled out. "R," he announced, as if I didn't know.

"Said she loved Brewster." I put in a shot from four feet out, with my left hand. "But her job's in Chicago."

"Makes sense." Dave's left-handed shot missed the rim altogether. "S." We were tied.

"Dad," Sam called, "Mom says to come and eat."

"Tell Mom it's a tie game. She'll understand."

"No way," Sam said. "She's already got the salad on the table. If you're not coming I'm staying to watch."

"That's right, Sam," I said, "you stay right here and watch me put your dad out of his misery." I dribbled to my favorite spot at the far corner of the driveway and lobbed the ball into a high arcing curve that again was nothing but net.

"E!" Sam crowed. He jabbed his fist in the air. "Yay, Paul!"

Dave didn't even attempt the shot, ruffling Sam's hair instead. "Just wait till next time, buddy."

"Yeah, Dad." Sam bounced the ball from hand to hand. "Next time Paul and I will take on you and Angie. And we'll win. Won't we, Uncle Paul?"

"For sure," I answered, inwardly smiling at the easy way Sam called me uncle. Technically we weren't related, but Dave was the closest thing to a brother I was ever going to have, and it was easy for me to claim the title. I grabbed the sweatshirt I'd tossed on the grass early in the game and pulled the car keys from my pocket. "Now you guys get in there and eat or Vicky will come out here and cream all of us." I turned to go.

"Eat with us, Uncle Paul," Sam said. "Mom made tons of noodles and a whole pan full of sauce. If you don't we'll be eating spaghetti all week. Besides, Angie already set a place for you."

I glanced Dave's way. Over the years I'd eaten at their table so often it almost felt like mine. "If you don't mind. Mom's at the senior center for dinner tonight, so I'm on my own anyway."

"Come on in," Dave motioned, opening the kitchen door wide just as Ruthie slid into the extra spot set at the table. Her eyes met mine for a frozen second, then she quickly glanced away, her hand brushing invisible strands of hair away from her face.

If I hadn't seen only five plates on the table with my own eyes I would have sworn Vicky really did plan on having me stay for supper. As if she were a magician, an extra plate appeared in her hand as she stood over the spaghetti pot on the stove saying, "Who's first?"

"I am!" Sam elbowed his way past Dave and me as though we were a wimpy defense line on a crummy football team.

Vicky heaped noodles on Sam's plate, added a ladle of steaming meat sauce to the top, and stabbed a fork in the middle as if she'd planned to serve the meal that way all along. "Who's next?" She had a smile pasted on her face and was giving Dave a wide-eyed stare even I could see meant, "*I didn't plan on this.*"

Dave took his cue. "Okay, Angie, you're next. Grab your plate and get in line." He was waving his arm, a cut-rate maitre d' who wasn't expecting any tips. "Ruthie, Paul, grab your plates. Its buffet-style tonight."

For lack of any other ideas, I picked up a plate and stood at the end of our short line. Even with the distance of a plate between my chest and Ruthie's back and the smell of tomato sauce in the air, I could still detect her familiar perfume. I inhaled slowly. Now, that brought back memories. Good ones. By the time I got to the head of the line, Angie and Sam were already vying for attention from Ruthie, who didn't seem to be in any hurry to eat. Or to meet my gaze.

"Did you ever eat worms?" Sam dangled a noodle from his fork and slurped it into his mouth. A fifth grader's idea of good table manners.

"Did you ever hate boys?" Angie's way of putting her brother in his place.

Ruthie took a sip of milk, stared hard at Vicky, and said, "Not until this week."

Vicky heaped spaghetti noodles on my plate, added a ladle full of sauce, then pleasantly added, "Did Dave tell you Ruthie has moved in with us for a while?"

No. He didn't.

Ruthie

Did you ever hate boys? Not until this week. Whatever had possessed me to say that in front of Paul? Even though I was alone in Vicky's basement, I could feel my face flush. I hoped Paul knew I'd been talking about Jack, trying to be clever to cover my failure... again. What if Paul had thought I'd meant him? I closed my eyes, searching for some sense to my emotions behind my eyelids.

Apologizing to Paul couldn't possibly be any more difficult than sitting beside him had been tonight. I'd spent more energy pretending to ignore him than an apology would ever take.

After I'd moved out of our apartment, I'd been so determined to move on. Yet here I was paralyzed by my past. My past with Paul. My past with Jack.

It had taken a week for Jack to realize I'd meant it when I told him I didn't think we should live together anymore, and even then I don't think he thought I was serious. In the end, he refused to budge and I didn't have the emotional energy to argue. I suppose I could have packed up his stuff and set it outside the door, but in a small town like Brewster, the fact we wouldn't be living together anymore was talk enough. I was the one who ended up moving, and in some strange way I felt victorious.

I couldn't afford an apartment on my own, so I was back in Vicky and Dave's basement, the same place I'd camped when Jack and I had first started the station. It felt as though I were going backward and forward at the same time. My clothes shared the closet with an outgrown snowsuit of Sam's, Vicky's wedding dress, and two feet of old clothes I didn't bother to look at. The top shelf held my folded sweaters, a beat-up Candyland game, and assorted stuffed animals. I thought I spotted my old Barbie doll amidst the collection, but I was in no mood to reminisce. I had enough to think about in my present day life without venturing back to simpler years.

Jack and I had worked out an arrangement so that our paths barely crossed. I took the morning shift on-air. He took the afternoon. We'd hired an eager high school boy, Mike Anderson, who was more than happy to play country tunes from after school until sunset, the time the station went off the air for the day, unless we had a high school sporting event to announce. We took turns with those. Jack did the books. I sold ads. For a couple days, anyway, it seemed to be working.

I'd come back from the station early today, telling Mike to tell Jack I needed some time to unpack. Jack didn't need to know what I'd really needed was time to sort through my life.

There was nowhere else to sit in my new room, so reverting to high school days, I'd sat cross-legged on the bed and made a list of things to think about:

> ~Radio station?
> ~Own apartment?
> ~Paul?

No! I'd drawn a dark line through his name. I was going to concentrate on getting the station out of debt, sell my share, and finally, *finally*, leave this town that had done nothing but hold me back from the life I was meant to have.

I leaned back on the pillows, folding my arms under my head, imagining the life I knew was my destiny. It was easier than facing the life I was living. Soon I'd be a wisecracking disc jockey for a major radio station in Chicago.

Oh, it's Chicago, is it?

What's wrong with Chicago?

Isn't that where Paul moved from? Where Corinne, your latest role model, lives?

Oh, for stupid. She's not my role model, and what's Paul got to do with anything?

Maybe you're trying to show Paul you can still have the life you've always dreamed of. That he'll find out soon enough there's nothing for him here in Brewster. That you were right all along…the only life worth living is somewhere besides here.

There're lots of people who are perfectly happy in Brewster. I just don't happen to be one of them.

Have you ever given it a chance? A real chance?

Good grief, I've lived here practically my whole entire life and I'm miserable. If that's not enough of a chance, I don't know what is.

I shook my head. Arguing with myself was getting me nowhere. I had a life to plan. I closed my eyes and continued my fantasy. My face would be plastered on billboards throughout town, the call letters of the station a mere afterthought under my name. People would recognize me as I walked down the sidewalks of Chicago in my designer shoes. I'd be invited to prestigious events. Be presented awards for my entertaining banter. Handsome, eligible bachelors would ask me out to dinner at exclusive restaurants—

"Come and eat." Angie had tapped at the door before poking her head around the doorjamb. "Mom said to tell you the spaghetti's ready. We've gotta eat early tonight because Dad has a meeting and Sam has to study for his spelling test."

Nothing like being brought back to reality by spaghetti. Not quite the exclusive dining I'd been dreaming about, but for now it would suffice. Having someone else do the cooking did wonders for my appetite. I was starving. I swung my legs over the side of the bed and followed Angie's bouncing ponytail up the stairs. I would have plenty of time to worry about my life during the long evening ahead.

As I slid into my chair, Sam burst into the kitchen followed by Dave and Paul. For just a moment my eyes locked with Paul's. As quickly I slid them away, wondering if, in that brief moment, he saw my unspoken apology. My regret? Or was it simply my shame? I didn't feel very hungry anymore.

"Sam," Vicky reminded, "the ball belongs outside."

Sam bounced the ball once on the kitchen floor, pivoted, then swayed as if he were in a one-on-one battle with Paul guarding him.

Paul shifted from foot to foot, then wrapped his arms around Sam. Sam laughed, "Foul! Foul!" Paul ruffled Sam's hair, palmed the ball, and rolled it out the door.

My heart did a queer flip-flop seeing Paul like that, in his jeans and T-shirt, his hair a mess from playing ball. I had a quick memory of the many times I'd stood on the sidelines in my cheerleader's uniform watching Paul run up the score for the Brewster Badgers, knowing I'd be getting a ride home from him after the game. Those had been good times.

What do you mean, good times? I thought you hated everything about this place.

Maybe not everything. I sipped my milk, remembering the shambles my life had become. That I did hate. Suddenly I wasn't hungry at all.

Dave took his usual seat at the head of the table as Paul slid in on the opposite end at a ninety-degree angle from me. Good. I wouldn't have to look at him, except for what my peripheral vision picked up. It would be easier to get through this meal if I didn't have to look at him.

Sam and Angie teased each other until Vicky filled her plate and joined us at the table. "Paul," she asked, "would you say grace?"

"Glad to."

Automatically, as was their family habit, Dave, Vicky, Sam, and Angie reached to join hands. Angie slid her fingers into mine at the exact instant Paul's warm hand wrapped around my other hand.

So, you don't have to look at him, you just have to hold his hand. Great, just great. I squeezed my eyes shut, trying to ignore the feel of Paul's grasp.

He paused a moment, head bowed, grip firm. The warmth of his hand seeped into mine. It felt strangely comforting.

"Father," he began, his voice unwavering, "I thank You for the people around this table. Dave, Vicky, Angie, Sam, and Ruth. They are like family to me."

Paul was thanking God for *me?* My eyes shot open.

Like family?

How could he think about me like that after what I'd done to him at our senior prom? I felt an odd mix of shame and wonder and peered at him through the corner of my eye. Who was this man?

I didn't hear another word except for "Amen."

It was funny how, even hours later, as I crawled into bed I could feel the warmth of Paul's hand, solid and comforting. I closed my eyes to go to sleep, his words around me like a warm blanket, "*Father, thank You for Ruth.*"

My conscience screamed. *You just got rid of one guy. Quit mooning over another one.*

I'm not *mooning*, I just thought what he said was…interesting.

Listen, you don't need a man, you need a plan. And you have one, remember? Turn the station around and leave Brewster.

Right. The warm feeling evaporated. I turned onto my side and pulled the covers under my chin. The stack of bills waiting at the station floated across my vision like mutant sheep. A perfect prescription for a rotten night's sleep.

Paul

My first month at the bank was like the combination of a family reunion and graduate school. The *Brewster Banner* had run a front-page article titled, "Bennett's Back," with two photos, one showing me running in for a touchdown in the last football game of my senior year, the other the standard businessman pose of me behind my desk at the bank. The minute the paper hit the street a steady stream of people marched into my office, hand extended, saying, "It's good to have you back, Bennett."

On the other hand, Wayne Jorgenson, my one loan officer at the bank, was testing me. Questioning me about loans and policies I had no way of answering in my first days on the job. Making sure I knew that *he* knew more about this bank than I did. His behavior didn't bode well for a good working relationship. But I kept trying.

"Wayne, could I see you in my office?" The doors to the bank wouldn't open for another fifteen minutes, which gave us time to have an uninterrupted conversation before customers would want to see either of us.

"In a minute." Head down, Wayne clicked his pen over a stack of papers on his desk. I had the feeling he wasn't busy but stalling. After a few moments he slowly pushed back his chair and followed me into my office. "I have someone coming in at nine," he said before sitting down. His way of letting me know I'd better make it fast.

"I wanted to get up to speed on a couple loans you've been handling." I picked up the file on top of my desk. "Let's start with this one." I read the tab. "KBRS." Ruthie's radio station. "I noticed you gave them another loan a few weeks ago. It seems to me they're already extended beyond the collateral we have. Is there something I'm not aware of?"

Wayne leaned onto one arm of the chair, crossing his legs, taking up time. "Uh, no, nothing special." He clicked his pen. "They've been having some cash flow problems, so that loan was just to tide them over until harvest. You know," he added, then amended, "well, maybe you don't know coming from Chicago, and all." He sniffed. "After harvest people around here usually start spending more. Once the crops are in." Click, click. "Nothing to worry about. Things will pick up."

I glanced down the comment sheet inside the file folder. "It looks to me as though this has been an ongoing situation. There are several notations over the past two years that look like what were supposed to be short-term loans to solve a cash flow problem have sat on the books accruing interest with no pay down at all."

"Ummm. Hmmm." Wayne shifted onto the other arm. "I'm sure Ruth brought in a payment last month."

I brought the KBRS loan portfolio up on my computer screen. "Not according to our records."

"Maybe it was the month before." Click, click.

"No. According to this, the last payment was four months ago. Have you called them in to talk about it?"

"Just talked to Ruth a few weeks ago."

"It looks like that talk resulted in another short-term loan. Did she say what their long-term plan was? When we can expect payment?"

Wayne tugged up the sleeve of his shirt, exposing his watch. "I'm sorry, but we'll have to talk about this another time. I've got someone coming in at nine, and I have to get some papers ready for him to sign. Don't worry, the station's doing fine. If they were in trouble, Jack would be in to talk to me." He patted the edge of my desk with his fingertips. "Good talking to you. Any other questions, just ask."

To say I had an uneasy feeling about this loan was to put it mildly. I was in an awkward position. If I called Jack and Ruthie in to talk about the loan, Wayne would think I was pulling rank on him. If I let the situation go on any longer, it might be too late for KBRS to pull themselves out of trouble. All this added on to the fact that

Ruthie didn't seem to want to have a thing to do with me. The few times I'd bumped into her at Vicky and Dave's she'd answered my questions as if she were at the dentist and had her mouth full of cotton. Yes. No. Ummmm. Then she'd make an excuse to leave the room. Jack seemed to have about the same amount of time for me. For now it didn't seem as if I had much choice but to let Wayne handle the loan. But I would monitor it closely.

Another problem faced me outside of the bank. I had been planning on moving into a place of my own as soon as I had a chance to get settled into my new job. I had made it clear that my stay with Mom would be temporary. I didn't think either of us liked the idea of a grown man living with his mother. But after the other morning, I wasn't sure what to do.

"Paul?" Mom's voice came from her bedroom. I was surprised I heard it over the whine of my shaver. "Paul, could you come here?"

She was sitting in her bed. One leg over the side, as if she intended to get up, the other straight in front of her, as if she wasn't sure. "I seem to have a kink in my hip this morning. I can't get this leg to cooperate. Could you help me scoot it over?" She slapped at her knee as I easily swiveled her body to the edge of the bed. "Naughty leg."

"There, is that okay?"

"Perfect. Now where is my cane?" She looked at the night table. "I try to leave it close in case I need to get up in the night. Oh, there it is." She pointed to her dresser near the foot of the bed. "Could you hand it to me? I don't dare stand on this silly hip without it."

With effort she rose from the bed, suppressing a groan of pain as much as she could. "You'd better pray you inherit my good looks and not my arthritis. Now go get ready for work. I'll be fine after I stand here a bit."

"I have some time." I wanted to linger a minute to make sure she was okay. "What do you have planned today?"

"I was going to go to the church to decorate the altar for Mission Sunday. We always like to get people thinking about it a few weeks ahead of time. But I may have to put that off until tomorrow if this kink doesn't work itself out. Don't worry about me. I'll keep busy. Now go."

The thought of leaving her alone in the house had me worried, but the thought of her venturing through town didn't seem any better. It was obvious that she was becoming more and more dependent on her cane just to get around the house. And she often needed me to do things that would have been no trouble for her to do on her own before. While she had never asked me to stay with her—in fact, she often asked if I'd had a chance to look for a place— it was clear she was quickly becoming dependent on my presence. I wondered what she would have done if I hadn't moved back to Brewster. I wondered what I would do now that I had.

As I walked back to the bathroom to finish shaving, a conversation I'd had with Corinne when I'd driven her to the airport in Carlton to catch her plane back to Chicago tumbled through my mind.

"Are you sure this is what you want? Living here?" She nodded her head backward in the direction of Brewster, which was quickly receding on the horizon.

"Yeah, Corinne, I think it is." I glanced in the rearview mirror. Brewster's two small water towers were the only thing making up the town's skyline. Ever since I'd put my furniture in storage in Chicago and moved the rest of my things to Brewster, I'd felt at peace about my decision. I gazed out the window at the round hay bales lying in the fields on either side of the highway. This was God's country, no doubt in my mind.

"I'm going to be frank with you, Paul." Corinne slid the tips of her fingers into the pockets of the jeans she'd worn for the drive.

"That's what I like about you, Corinne. You're always up-front." I knew whatever she had to say would be well thought out and to the point, but tactful. Those qualities were what had drawn me to her in the first place when she'd approached our firm about signing on with her ad agency. When I'd bumped into her in the foyer of church one Sunday, we started meeting for coffee. I'd since come to value her opinion in many areas of my life. "Tell me what you think I need to know."

"I understand how you might feel you need to be closer to your mother, but you know," her voice was gentle, "she's not going to be here forever, and then what?"

A quick vision of Mom's house emptied of all the furniture came to mind. I'd never imagined that before. Strange image. "To tell you the truth, I hadn't thought quite that far ahead."

"After what happened to Mia and your baby, I can see why you'd think you might want to leave Chicago. In fact, I'm surprised that if you were going to leave you didn't do it sooner." She turned toward me, shifting as much as her seatbelt would allow. "Lots of people do that, you know. Try to run from a hurt."

I rubbed the scar on my forehead. "I thought about that and it's not what I'm doing. I've been praying for a change for some time, and I feel this is what God has led me to."

"You're something, Paul." She laughed softly. "Most guys in your position would maybe think of marriage as the change God was directing them to, not moving a thousand miles away. You didn't do this to get away from me, did you?"

I paused before answering. Her words were convicting. "I'll be honest with you. I'm not entirely sure."

Corinne's proposal had certainly upped the ante on our relationship. I'd been content with our arrangement to see each other exclusively. We both had demanding jobs, our leisure time was limited, and we had an understanding that worked fine for both of us…or so I'd thought. Until the night Corinne had suggested we consider marriage. Suddenly the three years I'd had with Mia wrapped around me like a tight cocoon, or maybe it was me wrapping myself around those years. Either way, I realized I wasn't ready to let go of them yet.

"I'll wait," Corinne had said when I explained.

But that had been when I still lived in Chicago. Her trip to Brewster had been to tell me that if I couldn't move ahead in our relationship, she needed to move on. I understood, but I felt the emptiness of knowing she was no longer in my life, even while she was sitting next to me.

I reached across the car seat and grabbed her hand. "I am going to miss you, you know."

She squeezed my hand. "I know." She was silent a moment, then went on, "Don't take this wrong, but I don't see you in Brewster long term. I hope you don't have some idealized version in mind of the place you grew up. It's a great little town, but that's the point, Paul, it's little."

As if to help make her point I pushed down the blinker and pulled out to pass a slow-moving tractor.

"You have a great future ahead of you. Much bigger than what Brewster can offer, and I don't mean anything bad about Brewster when I say that. But there's only so much that can happen in a town that size." She released my hand. "I'm predicting there won't be enough challenge for you there and you'll come back to Chicago. When you do, I hope you'll call."

We rode the rest of the way in thoughtful silence.

～

I stared at the KBRS file lying on my desk, my mind replaying Corinne's words, *I'm predicting there won't be enough challenge for you.* Clearing up this loan would be a challenge, but after that?

"Mr. Bennett," my secretary's voice broke into my thoughts, "your mother is on line two."

I opened the KBRS file as I picked up the phone. "Paul," Mom sounded breathless, "could you manage to come home for a second? I'm in a bit of a pickle."

～

I arrived home to find my mother clinging to the kitchen counter, macaroni and a broken casserole dish surrounding her bare feet.

"I didn't dare move," she said when I ran in.

Not enough challenge? I thought as I shifted my VW into gear to head back to the bank. Between Wayne Jorgenson, KBRS's delinquent loan, and my mother, right now my life seemed nothing but a challenge.

Ruthie

I had a mission. I was single-handedly going to get KBRS back in shape. When that was done I planned to ask Jack to buy out my share of the station or find another buyer and then I'd be out of here. I'd already received two "not hiring right now" letters from the inquiries I'd sent out, but that didn't bother me. I'd sent out close to a dozen, and it was going to take a little time to turn the station around, anyway.

Once I had a light shining at the end of my tunnel it was easy to focus. All I had to do was sell more ads, take the money to the bank, and watch the balance on our loans decrease. If I had it figured right, it might take a little under a year of hard work to get my half of our short-term loans paid down. When that happened, my share of the station might actually be worth something. Not much, but that wasn't the point. The point was that then I'd be free.

"Hey, babe," Jack called to me as I walked past the broadcast booth. His greeting didn't even irritate me. I wasn't going to have to hear it all that much longer. "I need to talk to you about something kind of important."

"Not now." I was on my way out of the station. There were ads to sell, and in my frame of mind there was nothing more important than that. I raced past Jack and out the door.

Jack and I had managed to work together these past weeks without talking. If we needed to communicate, we left a note on each other's desk. As long as he was on-air when he was supposed to be and paid the bills when they were due, I didn't see that we had anything to talk about. Right now selling advertising was more important than talking.

"But, look at it this way, Jim." I flipped a page in my notebook and underlined the numbers. "If you purchase this package, you'll get ten more ads per week for not much more than what you were paying with your old package."

Jim Magner nodded his head. "I can see that, Ruthie, and it'd be a deal if I thought it helped. But I'm beginning to wonder if anyone pays attention to those ads. KBRS isn't the only place I advertise, you know. I send out my weekly flyer with the grocery specials in it. Coupons to cut. That sort of thing. Advertising gets expensive. Especially if you don't know if it brings in customers."

I could feel a cold bead of perspiration roll down my spine. Mr. Magner couldn't pull his advertising; he was one of our larger accounts.

"I can understand your concern, Jim, but I can assure you the folks of Brewster listen to KBRS. I've made arrangements with the local car mechanics. Whenever they have a car in for servicing, they tune the radio to KBRS. It's the first thing people hear when they get in their car. Once they listen they realize how much local information we give them and they keep on listening."

Jim Magner laughed. "No one ever accused you of not being a saleswoman, Ruth." He paused for a moment, and then offered a surrendering sigh. "Okay, sign me up for another month."

I breathed a silent sigh of relief and wrote up the contract. If only all my calls were this cooperative. I'd already been turned down by the two gas stations in town, as well as the dentist. And Cal, from the hardware store, told me he was going to skip this month altogether. My plan wasn't working out quite like I had planned. At least I could count on my brother-in-law.

"Hey, Ruthie." Dave smiled and pushed himself away from his desk. "How's it going?"

"Going is about all I can say for it." I hadn't meant to sound discouraged, but my voice echoed my feelings.

"What's up?"

I dropped myself into a chair, tossing my notebook and files onto his desk. "Nothing. That's the problem. There's nothing going on. This town is drying up and the station is going right along with it."

The smile fell from Dave's face. "Things are tough, aren't they? I hear it all day long too. I try to tell people they need to upgrade their insurance coverage, but they can't afford it. It makes a person wonder what's going to happen to these small towns. Have you been over to talk to Paul?"

My heart did a funny flip-flop at the mention of Paul's name. "Why would I talk to Paul? I finally moved out from living with Jack and there's no way I'm going to—" Suddenly it dawned on me. Dave wasn't trying to match me up with Paul; he was asking if I'd talked over my business situation with him. I could feel my face turning an ugly shade of red.

"Me thinks the lady doth protest too much." Dave had a sly grin on his face. He knew exactly what I'd been thinking.

There was nothing to do but change the subject. "Shakespeare, you're not." I opened my notebook. "So, are you going to increase your ad contract and help this poor damsel out of her distress?"

Dave sobered again. "I'd love to help you out, Ruthie, but between the advertising I do in the *Brewster Banner* for the insurance agency and what Vicky does for the café, we're pretty much maxed out in that department."

"It doesn't hurt to ask." I tried to keep the desperation out of my voice. "You are going to renew what you have been doing, right?"

"That I can do. Sign me up." Dave sat straight, stretching his back as if he, too, had had a long day. "Seriously, Ruthie, I think you should go talk to Paul," he paused, then went on quickly, "about your loans. You know I'm on the bank board and I know the station has been having some problems. It will only get worse if you don't get a handle on it."

"That's Jack's department."

"It may be Jack's department, but your name is on those loans too. You need to know exactly where you stand so you know what you're up against." Dave was silent for a moment, then added, "Ruthie, the prom was over eighteen years ago. Go talk to Paul."

Now I wasn't embarrassed, I was mad. Sometimes Dave acted more like a parent than a brother-in-law. "If I need advice I'll talk to Wayne. He's the one who set up our loan in the first place."

Dave leaned forward, his elbows on the desk. "I'm only telling you this because you're family, Ruth." He lowered his voice to almost a whisper. "Did you ever stop to wonder why we offered the job to Paul instead of Wayne?" Dave leaned back, his voice at normal level. "It helps to get a second opinion sometimes. I'm only telling you this because I'm concerned."

"You don't need to be. I've got everything figured out." I picked up my files and walked to the door.

"I sure hope so."

I swung my purse over my shoulder and tried to keep the resentment from my voice as I walked out. "Thanks for the advertising."

I didn't sound nearly as thankful as I really was.

⤳

I stormed down the street, reliving our conversation. Who did Dave think he was, anyway? Trying to tell me I didn't know what was happening to my business!

"Hello, Root." Mrs. Bauer called my name from across the street. Her pronounced German accent made me cringe. You'd think she would have figured out by now that this was *America*. "Dit you have a nice wisit with your brudder-in-law?"

Another thing I didn't like about this little town. No privacy. "*None of your business!*" I wanted to scream. Instead I pretended I didn't hear. Next thing she'd be in the café saying I was stuck up.

Why shouldn't she say you're stuck up? You're acting that way.

A lump of frustration pressed its way into my throat. All I'd ever wanted was to live somewhere else. Somewhere big and exciting, not Brewster where everyone acted as though my business was theirs.

She's just an old woman, Ruthie. She's known you your whole life. Even if her questions bug you, she means well.

I couldn't even have a pity party without my conscience joining in. "Hello, Mrs. Bauer," I called, hoping the wave of my fingers distracted from the catch in my voice. I hurried off in the opposite direction. If I was going to do any crying, it wasn't going to be on Main Street.

Jack

If Paul Bennett thought he had more to tell me than Wayne Jorgenson I wanted to hear it. I hadn't dropped into the bank to talk about our loans; that was Ruthie's department. I'd dropped in to talk to Wayne because I thought he'd want to know my latest plans. Apparently, now that Paul was in the picture, Wayne didn't have the pull he did before. Once he heard me out he told me, "You'd better go talk to Mr. Bennett."

Mr. Bennett, was it now? The guy obviously had Wayne cowering, but he didn't intimidate me. When you knew a guy from high school days, it took some of the starch out of his stature.

"Hey, Paul." I strode into his office with my hand out, ready to shake. The way I saw it, we were equals. He had his business to run, I had mine. "Nice digs you got here."

"Thanks. I like it too."

Well, who wouldn't? Cherry desk. Mahogany bookshelves. Upholstered chairs. It wouldn't take a guy long to get used to that. Not quite the metal desks and vinyl chairs we had at the station. So the guy had a better office than me. I wouldn't hold it against him.

Paul gave my hand a firm shake. "What brings you here?"

"Have a little news about the station. I stopped in to touch base with Wayne, and he thought you might be interested in hearing it too." I helped myself to one of the fancy chairs. Nice.

"What's up? I noticed you've been having a bit of a cash flow problem. Is there anything I can help you with?" Paul sat back in his chair just like the big guys in the movies do when they want to lord it over the little guys. I half expected him to prop his feet on the desk. Quickly he sat back up. *You're right*, I thought, *I command more respect than that.*

"This darn chair," he commented, leaning over to adjust the mechanism. "I practically fall over backward every time I sit down. Sorry about that. One of these days I'll either get it figured out or break my neck." He grinned, but I knew better than to fall for that "*we're buddies, aren't we?*" routine. "Do you know anything about how these things operate?"

"Sorry, no can do." I wasn't about to turn into Paul Bennett's handyman.

Paul adjusted himself in the chair. "There, I think I'll stay upright for the duration. What did you want to talk about?"

"There's nothing I want to discuss. Wayne thought you might want to know that I'm leaving the station."

"Leaving?" Paul sounded as though he didn't know the meaning of the word.

"Yeah, leaving."

"Leaving, as in taking a vacation?"

If I didn't have his full attention before, I had it now. "No, leaving as in *leaving*. As in, bye, gone, greener pastures leaving."

"And what plans did you have for your interest in KBRS?" Paul turned and typed quickly on the keyboard at his side. I saw the KBRS loan screen pop up.

"Well, I really didn't have any plans for it. I know the station hasn't been doing all that great, so instead of asking Ruthie to buy me out I thought I'd let her have my half." My speech had sounded a lot better when I'd rehearsed it in the lobby while I'd been waiting. "I got a job offer from a big station in Minneapolis and I took it."

"Have you talked to Ruthie about this?"

"Well, no. I tried but she was on her way out, and I didn't have a chance to tell her. Not yet, anyway."

"And do you think she'll be agreeable to your plan?"

"Oh, you know Ruthie." I stopped, remembering *I* was the one who'd been with Ruthie these past years. "Oh, right, maybe you don't know her so well anymore. She's not that concerned about financial stuff. I'm thinking she'll think it's great to own the station all by herself."

"You are aware the station has considerable debt."

"Oh, sure. But without me there drawing a salary I'm thinking Ruthie can use that money to pay it down." Couldn't the guy see I was doing Ruthie a favor?

"You do know your name is signed on the station's loans along with Ruth's?"

"Well, yeah, but I thought if I gave Ruthie my half of everything it would even out. You know, the collateral and stuff. She'd get all that." My reasoning didn't seem to be making much of an impression on Paul. All of a sudden my Ralph Lauren sweater seemed a little too tight. I ran my finger around the neckline. Why should it bother me what Paul Bennett thought of my plans?

"Jack." Paul leaned forward, both elbows on his cherry desktop. "Signing your name to those loans meant you are responsible to make payments on them until the balance is paid off. As long as you are part owner of KBRS you are required to pay off that debt. If you walk away from the station and Ruthie can't make the payments on her own, we will be forced to get the money from you in order to meet your obligation. It doesn't matter if you still work there or not. You do realize that, don't you?"

"Don't worry, I'm sure it will be fine with Ruthie. At this point I think she'll be glad to have me out of there and have the station all to herself. Maybe you haven't heard, but we're not together anymore. My idea, of course. She's a great gal, but working together and living together twenty-four-seven, well, it got to be too much togetherness, if you know what I mean. Maybe you'd like another shot at her."

Paul's eyebrows raised in surprise. Okay, so maybe that was the wrong thing to say to a bank president. I just meant I knew they had a history and, like they say, sometimes history repeats itself. "Hey," I held one hand up, palm out. "I didn't mean anything by it. You're free to see whoever you like. Just thought you'd be interested to know we're through."

Paul cleared his throat. "I'm thinking you need to talk this over with Ruthie, uh, Ruth. She may have some thoughts on getting left with your half of KBRS."

Well, of course she would. "Will do, my man, will do." I got up from his fancy chair and gazed around his plush office. "Like I said earlier, you got nice digs here, but the fact remains they're in Brewster, North Dakota." I couldn't help but chuckle. "See you around, pal."

I wasn't worried one bit because I knew something Paul didn't. I knew Ruthie, and I *knew* she'd never let the station go under. With or without me.

Ruthie

"You're *what?*" I was finishing up the last song of three-in-a-row. I'd agreed to sit in for Jack while he ran some errands before lunch. A few moments ago he'd waltzed back in the station and into the broadcast booth.

"Calm down, babe." Jack patted my arm. He may have meant to be comforting, but after what he'd told me, his gesture seemed condescending, to say the least. "There's nothing to get worked up about. I was offered a broadcasting job in Minneapolis and I decided to take it. I thought you'd be glad to get me out of here." He lowered his voice and said, in a poor imitation of John Wayne, "This station ain't big enough for the two of us."

"Very funny." I wanted to tug at my hair, but that would let Jack know I was worried. I had to be rational about this. There was no way I was going to let Jack walk away from KBRS. If anyone was supposed to be leaving, it was supposed to be me. "What makes you think you can just up and leave? We've got loans up the whazoo, have you thought of that?"

"I've already talked to Wayne. He didn't think they would be a problem. Paul, too, if that makes you feel any better." Jack nodded at the microphone.

"I know, I know." I rolled my eyes, then spoke into the mike. "Here's another one, back-to-back." How I managed not to sound like a crazy woman I couldn't imagine. I turned to Jack. "Could you have picked a worse time to tell me this?"

"I tried to talk to you earlier, but you bee-lined it out the door."

"You could have told me it was something important."

"I did, but by then I was talking to your back."

I closed my eyes and gave my head a shake. Maybe I'd wake up and discover this was all a dream. A bad dream. I opened my eyes. No such luck. Jack was still standing over me in the broadcast booth. "I can't run this station alone. No way. It's hard enough with just the two of us. Being on-air. Selling ads. Doing the bills. Paperwork. I can't do it alone, Jack. I won't. You have an obligation to me. To this station."

"Babe, believe me, I'm doing this for you."

"Oh, puh-lease. You're doing this for Jack. When the going gets tough, you go."

"No really, Ruth, I've thought this out. You'll be better off without me drawing a salary. You can use part of what I get paid to pay down our loans, and part to hire another high school kid. You know how they love to sit behind that mike and play disc jockey. While they're working you can sell ads and do whatever needs doing."

"Apparently you've forgotten that high school kids have to go to high school." My voice rose. "They can't work here while they're in *school*."

"I checked into it. Mike Anderson has study hall first period and can sign up for co-op work class for second. He'd be glad to work here and that'd give you most of the morning to sell ads."

"You've got this all figured out, don't you?" I swallowed hard, opening my eyes wide. I would not cry. I would not. A stony silence filled the air as I repeated to myself, *don't cry, don't cry.* Even though some days it felt as though I ran the station by myself, Jack just couldn't leave. There was no way I could do this alone. A feeling of panic began a slow burn in my chest.

Once again he nodded toward the console. His timing was uncanny. I squeezed my eyes shut as tight as they would go. I felt a migraine coming on. I spoke into the mike, the most unenthusiastic deejay around, "It's another triple play, folks." I punched the play button. "And what did you plan to do about your half of what we owe on the station?"

Just then the phone rang in the outer office. Jack picked up the extension we had in the broadcast booth, the one with the ringer turned off for when we worked alone.

"K-B-R-S." He sounded smooth, as usual.

I could hear the young girl's voice from where I sat. "You already played that song. Like, right before."

I was reaching for the stop-play button when I heard Jack answer, "That was our two-in-a-row contest and you're the winner. You win a free soft drink at Vicky's Café. Stop by the station and pick up your coupon. And, keep listening." He hung up grinning. "Pretty quick thinking, huh? I'd better go make a coupon."

That quickly he seemed to have forgotten our conversation. The fact that he owed a lot of money whether he was leaving or not. I wasn't about to let him get by with it.

"What'd you do? Win the lottery? Where do you think you're going to come up with the money to buy out your half of the station? The half *I* put down for you from *my* inheritance. Not to mention giving away prizes we can't afford." I sounded shrill but I didn't care.

"You know, babe, you're right. This isn't the best time to talk about this. I'd better go draw up a coupon so that little girl thinks she really won my contest." He stood and reached for his billfold. "Or maybe I'll just put a buck in an envelope. I think that's what a pop costs these days."

"You could apply it to our loan."

"Good grief, Ruthie, it's just a dollar." He opened his billfold. Empty. I could have told him that. "Guess I'll go make a coupon."

I swiveled my chair so my back was to him, pretending I was searching for songs to play next. I rubbed my temples with my index fingers. I felt physically sick. I was supposed to be the one with a new job in a new town. I was supposed to be the one leaving. This couldn't be happening to me.

Brewster had always felt confining. As though the town itself was keeping me from something. Now this broadcast booth was starting to feel like solitary confinement. I wanted to run. I wanted out. Instead I spoke into the mike, "It's a wonderful day at KBRS, your voice in the country. You gotta wanna live here."

Right.

Paul

"Ruth Hammond here to see you. From KBRS." My secretary had made it a habit to provide a mental connection for me about the customers who came to see me. It helped as I often scrambled to associate names and faces with people I'd known years ago. She obviously didn't know about the history I had with Ruthie. Which was just fine.

"Ruthie." I stood as she marched into my office, closing the door firmly behind her. I reached across my desk for a handshake. The way I always greeted customers.

Ruthie waved away my hand. "I'm in no mood for niceties, Paul." Her eyes were narrowed, her gaze piercing, as if she were searching for a target. I had a feeling Jack had told her his news. She threw herself into a chair and tossed a ring binder on my desk. "I've got a huge problem," she spoke slowly, as if trying to keep a simmering rage in check, "and from what I hear, you're part of it."

"I am?" Slowly, I eased myself into a sitting position.

"Yes, you are." She pressed the palms of her hands flat on my desktop. Leaning forward she spoke forcefully, anger apparent, words bubbling from her mouth in full boil. "Just what do you mean by telling Jack he can take off and leave me with the station? In case you don't know, we're in debt up to our ears. Past our ears. I can't imagine you would let him waltz out of Brewster without any obligation to repay his half of our loans. When we started the station we agreed it would be a fifty-fifty deal." She didn't stop for a breath so I took one for her. "Of course, I was the one who had the money for the down payment. The money from my parents' life insurance. But Jack promised me he'd pay me back. He hasn't paid me one dime and if you—"

"Hold on a minute." I raised my hands in protest. "I didn't—"

"Yes. You. Did." She jabbed an index finger at me with each of her words. "Jack told me he's talked this hairbrained idea over with Wayne and with you and you said it was perfectly all right if he left for this job in Minneapolis, which, personally, I think he has fabricated out of thin air." She splayed her fingers in the air, as if releasing invisible magic dust along with her anger. Obviously Jack had told her only his version of this story. I knew the whole story and would have shared it, but right now Ruthie needed to release her feelings more than I needed to defend myself. I let her talk. "I can't run the station alone. And I won't. I can't believe you would tell him he could take off on me. Do you want the station to fail? Is that what you want? Do you want me to fail? Is that what everybody wants?" Her voice cracked.

I'd long ago learned silence is often the best response to questions like hers. Usually the person isn't asking for an answer; they are simply releasing pent up frustration. And if I remembered right, Ruthie's anger was a foil for fear. I folded my hands on my desktop and waited, watching a mix of emotions crowd her face. "It's just that life seems so *hard*." Ruthie blinked back tears. "It wasn't supposed to be like this. You got to leave. You got to have a wonderful dream-job life." She whisked a tear from under one eye. "What did I get? I got stuck here. I had dreams too, you know." She looked straight at me, eyes brimming.

"I remember." My voice was soft. I did remember.

Ruthie burst into full-blown sobbing. "I'm sorry. I wasn't going to do this. I'm so sorry."

I didn't know if she was apologizing for getting mad, for crying, or for what had gone wrong between us so many years ago. It didn't matter. She was hurting. It's funny how certain actions are imprinted into a person. I didn't hesitate for a second. I didn't wonder if what I was doing was professional. I didn't think, *I'm the bank president and Ruthie is my customer.* I did what I'd always done when she had cried; I walked to her chair, pulled her up into my arms, and held her. Simply held her.

She cried for a long time, sniffing and swiping at her face but never stepping out of my embrace. Her soft perfume worked its way again through my memory. It smelled like powder and rain. I liked it. A lot. It brought those heady days of our relationship right back. I closed my eyes and took a deep breath, remembering. Ruthie, too, took a deep, shuddering breath, then tilted her head to look up at me. "Is this how you treat all of your customers?"

"No, it isn't," I replied. Her brown eyes sparkled with tears and with just a hint of amusement at their corners. Without thinking, I leaned forward, tilting my head toward her quivering lips. Her eyes closed. Mine did too.

Then I came to my senses.

With an awkward quickness I pressed my forehead against hers, as if that's what I'd intended all along. I dropped my arms from around her and adjusted my suit jacket, the impact of what I'd nearly done slamming me square in the face. Almost kissing a customer. I should fire myself. "I'm sorry, Ruthie. I don't know why you do that to me." It was obvious what my intention had been.

"Why *I* do that to *you*?" Ruthie stepped back, running a hand through her hair. "If I had my wits about me I'd say *you* were the one who almost kissed *me*."

Well, there, she'd just said it. So much for pretending it hadn't happened. "That's not the way I meant it. You're right, I did. But I shouldn't have." I straightened my tie, feeling like I was back in high school, trying to apologize for breaking a rule I didn't know existed. "Could we try to pretend that didn't happen just now and get back to business?"

Ruthie pulled a tissue from her purse and blew her nose. "If you promise to forget my sobbing, I'll try to forget the rest. Deal?"

"Deal."

I took my place behind my desk, where I should have kept myself in the first place. Ruthie resumed her position in the chair across from me.

"Now where were we?" I moved a paper clip with my thumb, trying to regain my composure. I was used to dealing with farmers smelling of grain and diesel fuel, not discussing problem loans with soft perfume lingering in my memory. It was distracting. I took a deep breath to clear my head. "Ruthie, you need to know that I did *not* tell Jack it was okay for him to leave the station and leave you with the loans."

She rolled her eyes skyward then looked at me, a wry smile turning up one corner of her mouth. "You know, that doesn't surprise me. If I'd have thought about it for even a millisecond, I could have figured out Jack's story didn't come from you. So, let's try this again. Here's the deal." Ruthie put a palm on each knee and leaned forward intently. "He told me he's taking a radio job in Minneapolis, but he's got his name signed to those loans just like I do. The way I see it, he can't leave unless he pays off his half." She leaned back into the chair, crossing her arms defiantly. "Right?"

"You're half right." I sighed. There were parts of this job I didn't like, and this was one of them.

"What do you mean, half right?" She braced her hands on the arms of the chair looking as though she would spring from her seat. "We went into this fifty-fifty. Jack said—"

"Ruthie, I'm going to explain this to you but you have to promise to remain calm. Okay?"

She nodded, sinking back into the chair.

"You're right in that Jack does have his name signed to those loan papers. Most people would think that means he owes exactly half of what you have borrowed."

Ruthie nodded. "That's what I thought."

"You're not going to like this, Ruthie, but that's where you're wrong. When two people sign a loan it means either one of them can be held responsible for repayment. Either one of them. Not each one in equal portions." She pressed her lips into a grim line and stared off into a corner of my office. "When things work in a partnership such as you and Jack have, the income from the business pays your salaries, expenses, and loan payments. But if Jack chooses to leave, he is not legally responsible for a penny unless you quit making payments on the loans. Then both of you become responsible for the debt."

"Let me get this straight." Ruthie tilted her head from side to side, rubbing her neck. She spoke slowly. "Jack is free to walk away from the station and leave me with every cent we owe?"

I nodded. "As long as you keep making payments, your creditors—the bank in this case—well, it's business as usual." I held up a cautionary finger. "However, if you get behind on your payments, then the bank has a legal obligation to try and collect what you owe."

"From whom?"

"From either one of you. Both of you."

"And if you can't get the money?" Ruthie rubbed her temple.

"We would be forced to foreclose on your loans."

"Meaning what, exactly?"

"Meaning we would take whatever collateral you have pledged, any assets, and apply them to your outstanding balance." I could see realization dawning as Ruthie's face paled.

"And if our assets wouldn't cover our debts, then what?" Her voice was strained.

"You'd be looking at a bankruptcy situation."

Ruthie gave a quick nod. "I wouldn't have the station." She held up her index finger and touched it. "I wouldn't have a job." She touched her middle finger. "I wouldn't have anything to show for all my time here." She talked to herself, counting off each loss on her fingers. "And I'd have no credit rating, either. Talk about being up a creek without a paddle." She gave me a wry smile. "So basically you're saying the only option I have is to keep making my payments."

"If you don't want to declare bankruptcy, yes." I rubbed at the scar on my forehead. This wasn't easy for me either. "I'm sure you already know your loan payments are behind schedule."

"Which means…?" Ruthie leaned an elbow on my desk and laid her cheek in her hand. She looked defeated. As though nothing more I could tell her would matter.

"Which means interest is accruing, and every month you don't pay, the balance gets bigger rather than smaller."

"I see." Her voice was flat. "Is there any way out of this?"

I looked at the loan balance on the computer screen and paged through the KBRS file. "It'll be tough." Ruthie had enough to absorb; I didn't think it would help to itemize just how bad the station's situation was. The collateral limit had long been exceeded and their financial statement was several years out-of-date. There would be time to tell Ruthie the details later. Right now coping with Jack's announcement was news enough. Inside I was seething. Wayne Jorgenson should have never lent KBRS that much money. I was going to have a talk with the board about the situation. The guy did his customers no favors by lending them more money than they could repay. And who knew how many other files looked like this?

Ruthie pressed hard at the bridge of her nose with her fingertips. "I guess I should have paid more attention." She said the words more to herself than to me. "Could you get me a printout of our past payments? And what we owe now? I suppose it's best if I know all the bad news."

I pressed the intercom button. "Peggy? Could you please get me a payment history on the KBRS loan account? Thanks." I turned to Ruth. "It's probably going to take a while. If you want, you can stop by on Monday and pick it up. Or I could drop it off at the station if it's done before I leave."

"Are you going hunting with Dave tomorrow?"

Her question caught me off guard. "What?"

"If you're going hunting with Dave in the morning, you could drop it off at the house when you swing by."

I'd almost forgotten about the hunting plans Dave and I had for Saturday morning. "Yeah, that would work."

Slowly she gathered her notebook and purse. "I usually say *thanks* when I leave the bank, but today that doesn't seem appropriate." She gave me a half smile.

"I can't tell you not to worry; the station is in pretty deep. But I can tell you I'm going to be thinking about your situation too. The bank has a lot of money invested, and it's in both our interests to see if we can work this out. We're here to help. Remember that."

"Thanks." Ruthie chuckled. "See, I told you I always say *thanks*." She paused by the door, her eyes squinting as if she was amused by something more.

"What?" It still surprised me how clearly I could read her face.

"Remember when I came in here and started crying? And you came over and—"

I didn't need to be reminded of my unprofessional behavior. "I thought we agreed to forget—" I interrupted.

Ruthie interrupted right back. "That's what I call full-service banking." Her eyes twinkled. "Sorry, I couldn't resist."

"Go on," I laughed, pushing my hand through the air as though shoving her out the door. "I'll drop those papers off tomorrow."

She turned to go, then stopped in the open doorway, turning back, not quite looking at me. "Oh, and what you told me to forget?"

She didn't say, but I certainly remembered. The almost kiss.

"Well, I didn't. It would have been nice."

And before I could think I found myself answering, "It would have."

Ruthie

It would have been nice? *It would have been nice?* Whatever possessed me to say those words? Whatever possessed me to have a complete breakdown in Paul's office? Whatever possessed me to walk into his arms? To look into his eyes? To stand on my tiptoes just enough so that he had no option but to lean my way? Arrgghh! My face felt like a forest fire as I walked out of the bank entrance.

There was no way I was going back to the station in my frame of mind. The only place I could think to go was to the café. Maybe Vicky would have a minute to sit and dissect what had just happened.

The café was nearly empty when I slipped into the far-corner booth, but almost immediately a steady stream of businessmen and farmers began filling the tables and other booths. I looked at my watch. I should have remembered three o'clock was coffee time in this town. Vicky moved swiftly from table to table, filling cups. I knew I had no choice but to sit and wait.

I leaned my head back against the vinyl booth, hardly noticing the clinking cups and conversation going on around me as I relived my meeting with Paul. I wondered what he was thinking? I took a sip of the ice water Vicky had slipped on my table, remembering the feel of his arms around me as he'd held me in his office. Warm and comforting. As if he had been trying to absorb some of my burden. In all the time I'd been with Jack I'd never felt that sort of support from him. Why hadn't I noticed?

I took another sip of the water, remembering the look in Paul's eyes as he'd looked into mine, offering a kind of solace. That was when he'd leaned down to—

I shook my head, clearing the embarrassing thought from my mind. *Focus, Ruthie. An almost kiss is the least of your worries. First things first. The station. What are you going to do about the station?*

What was I going to do? Paul had more or less told me the station was in big trouble. It wasn't as if I didn't already know that, but I hadn't thought it was going to be solely *my* responsibility to get it solvent either. The more I thought about it the angrier I got at Jack.

At times I'd imagined selling the station, leaving the station, but never, ever, running it by myself. I didn't think I *could* run it alone. Which would mean I might lose it.

I picked up a spoon from the table and flipped it round and round with my thumb and forefinger. It reminded me of my thoughts, going round and round with no direction. What was I going to do? Sure, not having Jack around would mean a little more money each month, but was it anywhere near enough? I pulled a pen from my purse, grabbed a napkin from the holder against the wall, and started jotting numbers. When I listed my measly income next to the figure I guessed I owed the bank—*we* owed the bank—it looked pretty pathetic. There was no way Jack was going to get off the hook on this. Or was there? A heavy weight settled on my chest. According to Paul, it didn't sound as though I had a lot to say about it. As long as my name was signed I was responsible for the whole amount. Jack or no Jack. Tears welled in my eyes, and I used the napkin I'd been writing on to dab them away.

"Root? Are you okay?" Mrs. Bauer stood by my booth.

For a moment I'd forgotten where I was. I'd slipped into the café, not trusting myself to go back to the station and see Jack. Who knew what I'd say or *do* to him? It certainly wouldn't include tears and the prelude to a kiss. I gave my head a shake and looked up at Mrs. Bauer. "I'm fine, Mrs. Bauer, just a little headache." At least I wasn't lying.

Mrs. Bauer dug in her gigantic beige purse, pulled out a wadded-up tissue, and unfolded it. "Here." She placed a yellowed aspirin tablet on the table. "This vill help. I keep those handy for my arthritis. It's a proplem some days."

If I hadn't grown up listening to her brogue, I would have needed an interpreter.

Just because you're mad at Jack, doesn't mean you have to take it out on Mrs. Bauer. I sighed, picked up the grainy aspirin, and tossed it down with a sip of water. At least she was concerned. I could be grateful for that.

She softly patted my shoulder. "Maybe you shoult go talk to Harolt over at the drugstore. I remember vhen your father owned that store, vhy sometimes he saved me the price of an office call at the clinic. I vould chust tell him vhat vas wrong vit me, and he coult show me something right on the shelves that vould help clear up whatever it vas I had. Your dad vas a goot man for this town. Your mom too. Such a tragedy." She shook her head. "Ven my husbant died—"

I didn't feel like listening to her old stories, but I knew from experience there was no stopping her. "Would you like to sit down for a minute?" I sounded surprisingly friendly considering the state my life was in. *It's easy to sound friendly when it's a distraction from your problems.* I twisted the small pendant hanging from my necklace. I'd be facing those problems soon enough; listening to Mrs. Bauer for a few minutes wouldn't change anything, and it wouldn't hurt to sit here until my emotions settled. Maybe then I could go back to the station and try to reason with Jack.

She slid into the booth across from me. "I'll chust sit here until Martha comes. Ve meet here for coffee every day at tree."

I suppressed a smile, imagining Martha Just and Mrs. Bauer in a tree having coffee. She checked her watch, then carefully placed her huge purse into the inside corner of the booth. You never knew when a purse-snatcher might dash through this crime-free town.

"As I vas saying, ven my Fred died, your mother—"

"Coffee, ladies?" Vicky stood by our booth, a pot in each hand.

I widened my eyes and just barely shook my head, giving her the high sign that coffee would only prolong this impromptu session of girl talk.

"That woult be splendid!" Mrs. Bauer turned the mug on the table right side up and slid it toward Vicky. "You'll have a cup, too, von't you, Root? My treat." She slid another mug Vicky's way. "Caffeine is goot for headaches, did you know that? Your dad vas the one who tolt me that."

Vicky didn't even try to hide the Cheshire-cat grin she had on her face. She'd listened to Mrs. Bauer enough times to know exactly what I was going to hear. "You girls have a nice visit."

"I vas telling you about your mother." Mrs. Bauer certainly didn't have any problems with her memory. She picked up right where she'd left off. "After Fred died your mother came to wisit me twice a mont for a whole year." She sipped at her coffee, two loud slurps followed by lip smacking. "Your mother vould bring me, oh, banana breat or a small dish of casserole. Vell, dis would have been back ven you were chust starting to walk. She'd bring you right along. Chust because she hat a little one didn't stop your mother. No, you'd be standing on my doorstep too. At first there vere some days I didn't even vant to answer the door, but your mother chust kept coming. I told her one time she was as bad as an old alley cat, showing up on my doorstep. Your mother laughed and told me alley cats *come* for food, they don't bring it." Mrs. Bauer covered her mouth with a wrinkled hand and chuckled, looking a bit like a young girl with the gesture.

Vicky stopped by and refilled our cups, ignoring my hand as I reached to cover my cup. "Martha must be busy today," she commented, turning to fill the cups of the four men at the table behind her. I didn't miss the wink she gave me. What was that supposed to mean?

"I learnt a lesson from your mother." Mrs. Bauer blew on her coffee and sipped loudly. "Sometimes you chust have to do."

Sometimes you just have to do? What in the world was that supposed to mean? I recalled a phrase my dad used to say, words I hadn't thought of in years. "*You'll never find out unless you ask.*" True. I supposed I owed Mrs. Bauer that much for offering to buy me coffee. I took a sip, then asked, "What does that mean, sometimes you just have to do?"

"Oh," she laughed, "you young kids don't know those old expressions. It means you chust go on. Even ven you don't feel like it."

Like now.

"You chust get up and answer the door. You chust do the next thing you're supposed to do even ven you don't feel like it, and pretty soon you haff a life again. Not exactly the same life as before. But it can be goot too."

Unexpectedly, my eyes filled with tears. I wished I were that little girl again. The little girl who had a mother's hand to hold. Who had her whole life ahead of her instead of the mess my life had become. I blinked, causing a tear to spill down my cheek.

"Rootie, vat is wrong?" Mrs. Bauer wrapped her warm, papery hands around mine. "Iss it your hettache?"

I shook my head, even though it was starting to pound. That's all I needed—another emotional breakdown in front of Mrs. Bauer and in Vicky's café to boot. I'd be front-page material for the *Brewster Banner.*

"Other tings, then?" Mrs. Bauer massaged my hands.

I nodded. Tears continued down my face.

"Do you vant to tell me about them or should I chust pray?"

Tell Mrs. Bauer about my problems? About Jack leaving me in debt? Leaving me stuck in this stupid town for who knew how long, when all I'd ever wanted was a chance to leave? No, I couldn't tell my problems to Mrs. Bauer. "Pray," I wheezed, my voice squeaking out between tears.

Pray? Oh, Ruthie, you are getting desperate. Asking Mrs. Bauer to pray for you? As if that's going to do any good.

Well, it's better than pouring out my guts to her. And, besides, it couldn't hurt. Could it?

"I vill pray for you, Root. I do anyvay. I'll chust pray more." She gave my hands a big squeeze, then released them. "You should come to church with Wicky and her family. God might have answers you don't know about."

I smiled politely. A sermon wasn't going to help my problems.

"Vell, my gootness!" Mrs. Bauer looked at her Timex. "Martha must be busy today. I have a chiggen I vant to get started for subber."

I smiled to myself. Listening to Mrs. Bauer was a trip to a foreign country for free.

"I'd better get a moof on." She dug in her purse and laid a dime on the table. "This iss for your sister. I don't know vhat this town would do without our café. Good to wisit vit you, Root." She reached over and squeezed my hand.

"You too, Mrs. Bauer." I squeezed back. The faint warmth of her handclasp seemed to spread through my body, and I realized it had been good.

Vicky swung by my table on the way to the cash register. "In case you're wondering about Martha, she only stops in on Tuesdays and Thursdays. Mrs. Bauer comes in every day and *wisits* with whomever she can find. Lucky you, it's Friday."

"Thanks for telling me, *Wicky*." I rolled my eyes, but inside I was imagining my mother on Mrs. Bauer's doorstep twice a month for a whole year, me standing beside her, my hand in hers, waiting for Mrs. Bauer to answer her door. I didn't remember that time of my life, but I was suddenly grateful that Mrs. Bauer did. That she had shared her memory with me. Given me a piece of my mother, and a piece of myself, I hadn't known existed.

If you were living in New York, you would have never heard that story from Mrs. Bauer today.

For a fleeting second the image of me standing hand in hand with my mother vanished, replaced by the nothingness that had been there before. I wrapped my hands around my coffee cup. I liked the warmth of the cup and the memory better. I let the image wash over me again. What had I been feeling those days, standing next to my mother?

Love? Hope? Those were the emotions I imagined that little girl had been feeling. The little girl Mrs. Bauer had helped me recapture. I watched as Mrs. Bauer made her way to the cash register, stopping for a few words at every table.

Sometimes you chust have to do.

This time I knew exactly what Mrs. Bauer meant. I had a life to live and a *goot* one too. I added a quarter to the dime she had left on the table and slid out of the booth. No matter what Jack did I wasn't going to lose KBRS. I was going to get the station straightened out, sell it, and then I would be free to get on with the life I was meant to have, away from Brewster. I would just *do*, for now.

Dan Jordan, Brewster's self-appointed real estate guru and the owner of the station building, stopped me with a hand on my arm as I walked by his table. "I've been wanting to talk to you." His voice was low. I could see the other men at the table stirring their coffee, pretending they weren't curious as Dan followed me to the café door. "The lease on your building is up soon. I heard Jack was leaving, and I was wondering what your plans are."

Was there a sign on Main Street? How had the news gotten around so fast that Jack was leaving? Living in this town I should have known my problems wouldn't be mine for long.

"Plans?" I responded as if I had no idea what he was talking about. "Why would I have any plans?"

"Well, uh," Dan rubbed the side of his nose with a forefinger, "I figured you, uh, might be thinking of making some changes, and I want to know if there's anything I can do to help." He cleared his throat. "Your dad did some things to help me get my business going, and ever since the accident I've always felt I should look out for you girls. Kinda like he did for me, you know." His voice petered out in light of my withering stare.

"No, Dan," I replied as if I had a million dollars and not a care in the world. "It's business as usual." Inside I saw that little girl clinging to her mother's hand.

He wants to help. Let him.

No, I was too afraid to do that. I felt my heart curl up tight into itself. I'd managed perfectly fine all these years. I didn't need Dan's help. I didn't need Mrs. Bauer's prayers. I would find my way out of this problem all by myself...as I'd done my whole life. In my mind I let go of my mother's hand. I pasted a smile on my face. "Thanks for your concern, but everything's fine."

I pushed at the café door and almost fell on my face as Kenny Pearson pulled open the door at the same time. "Women falling at my feet," he quipped, catching my arm before I went completely down, "just what I like." I forced a smile as he held the door for me to leave, remembering he'd told me he couldn't afford to advertise his gas station on the radio anymore. Then how could he afford to be coming to the café to have coffee? His wife was a year younger than I and pregnant with their third child. If things were that bad maybe he should bring his coffee to work in a thermos.

I thought you were going to focus on your problems. You're getting as bad as they are, Ruthie, nosing into everyone else's business.

I am not! I'm just concerned.

Maybe they are too.

I shook the thought away. I certainly had more to worry about than Kenny Pearson drinking a cup of coffee. I stormed down the street toward the station as the image of hands reaching toward me continued to fill my mind. I wasn't sure if they were hands reaching out to help or simply to keep me where I'd always been. Either way, I didn't need their help. I could manage just fine on my own.

Paul

"I tell you, Dave, I think I'm going to have to fire him." The corn stubble crunching under our hunting boots gave my words a staccato-like punctuation. High above I could hear a flock of ducks quacking their way across the sky. Hopefully, they were heading to the same pond we were. I'd picked up Dave well before dawn, leaving the KBRS loan papers on the kitchen counter. The thought of the outstanding balance on that loan account made me angry. "I don't like coming into this job and having the staff think I'm a hatchet man, but Wayne is doing the bank more harm than good."

Dave shifted his gun, careful to keep the barrel pointed down. "What, exactly is the—" he paused, taking in a gulp of air, "problem?"

"The problem is that he can't say no. I'm sure Wayne wants to be a good guy and help people out, but he's doing them no favors by letting these businesses get so far in debt. Not to mention what it's doing to the bank's bottom line." I pointed to Dave's right. The pond I'd scouted early yesterday morning was about a half mile south.

He veered that direction, taking off his camouflage cap and wiping his brow. "Tell me what," he puffed heavily, "you plan to tell the board."

I motioned for Dave to stop, raising my binoculars to scan the horizon. Dawn was about to break. If we didn't get to our spot soon, it would be too late to plan on duck for supper. "Let's get a move on." I strode out a good step and a half ahead of Dave. "It's not just the KBRS loan, although how Wayne ever let that get so far out of line I'll never understand. But there are several other loans that are way beyond what's acceptable. I don't know what the guy was thinking."

"I think I might." Dave stumbled on a clump of dirt but kept moving. "When the bank holding company bought the bank over in

Carlton, I think the whole board got caught up in the excitement of the new venture." Dave paused to catch his breath, unbuttoning the top two buttons of his camouflage jacket, muttering, "I gotta start working out more. Playing 'horse' in the driveway isn't cutting it." He took four quick steps to catch up with me, continuing the conversation. "When the board appointed Bob Marsden as CEO, we decided to base him out of there." Dave stopped in his tracks. "Hey, slow down. How far is this place, anyway?"

I turned back, Dave was a good three paces behind me. "Not that much farther. Come on." I could see the first rays of sunlight breaking on the hillside. If we weren't in place soon, we weren't going to have a chance.

"If you want me to explain this to you, you're going to have to walk slower. I'm bushed." Dave kneeled to retie his boot. A stalling tactic if I ever saw one. "Where was I? Oh, yeah. Wayne isn't the kind of guy who operates well on his own. He's been used to a lot more supervision than he's been getting since the transition." Dave stood, stomping his feet as though he were trying on a new pair of boots. "There," he said, "that feels better." Finally he started walking. "The board is going to have to take the blame for some of the problem, but you know how it goes, someone has to pay the price. And it sounds like it's going to have to be Wayne."

"I'm afraid so. I don't have the time to micromanage his work." I patted at the air, motioning Dave into a crouch. We crawled into the scrub brush near the edge of the pond, positioning ourselves on our stomachs and elbows, guns at the ready. A flock of ducks was circling high overhead. I hoped the water and brush around the pothole looked more attractive to the ducks than the hard cold ground felt to me. But it didn't matter how uncomfortable I was. Any problems I thought I had seemed much smaller out here in God's outdoors. I watched as the ducks circled lower, positioning themselves into landing mode. Everything fell away as I marveled at the beauty of the flock against the rising sun.

Just then a barrage of shots rang out from the west, about a mile north of our spot. The flock we were waiting for kept flying. "Shoot," Dave said.

"No," I replied, "I think that would be 'shot.' As in there goes ours."

"I suppose this means you're going to make me walk some more?" Dave's breath finally seemed to have caught up to his words.

"Let's wait. Maybe we'll get lucky and some of the ducks those other guys missed will settle over here." I didn't want to let Dave know the walk hadn't been a piece of cake for me either. It was hard to admit, but staying in shape wasn't as easy as it had been in high school. Having a full-time job plus a mother I was hesitant to leave by herself for long put a real crimp in any workout plans I might have. We lay in silence, the only sounds a light breeze rustling the grasses around us and the occasional chirp of a meadowlark. I hoped that bird was thinking of heading south soon. The way today felt winter wouldn't be far behind.

"Boy, some coffee would taste good right now." Dave pulled off his glove and blew on his fingers. "Vicky filled a thermos before she left for the café. I've got it back in the pickup. What do you think?" Dave pulled a small pack of tissues from his pocket, removed one, and blew his nose.

"I think you're turning into a wimp. Tissues? Coffee?" I laughed. "I suppose you've got two mugs to drink it with too."

Dave grinned. "Can I help it Vicky is so organized?"

"Let's go. Maybe we'll scare up a pheasant on the way back." I stood, tucking my gun under my arm, barrel down.

We trudged though the field, making our way slowly through the high grass rather than the shortcut through the stubble field. The wind picked up and bit into my cheeks. Hot coffee did sound good. And drinking out of mugs would be much better than sharing the thermos top with Dave. He was lucky to have Vicky.

A stab of loneliness coursed through me as I recalled the way Mia used to bring a mug of hot chocolate into my home office on cold Chicago nights. "Extra marshmallows for a mellow guy," she'd always say, her words reminding me to forget about work and enjoy what I was working for. I missed her and the life we'd had together, but I knew I could never have Mia back. Dr. Lucy had helped with that during a time when I thought all that lay ahead of me was aloneness.

After the plane crash, my pastor had suggested I meet with Dr. Lucy, whose specialty was grief counseling. What he didn't tell me was that Lucy was her first name and she wasn't any older than I. At first I wondered whether someone that young could help me, but it turned out she had experienced her own share of loss. A brother who had died of leukemia, both parents gone after short bouts of cancer, and two close friends killed in an auto accident, one of them her fiancé. Lucy had a unique talent for drawing out my grief, helping me to feel the pain and yet using those feelings to draw me closer to God at a time when it would have been easy to turn away.

It also would have been easy to turn to Lucy. *Dr.* Lucy, as I reminded myself often enough. To say she was attractive was putting it mildly, and in spite of her job she had a spark to her personality I found extremely appealing. She was compassionate and accepted all my feelings, both my love for Mia and my anger at her for being gone. My sadness. My loneliness.

In Lucy's office I felt a return to normal life was possible. It was easy to imagine that Lucy was the key to getting back. I was shocked at how drawn to her I'd felt after just a few sessions. She seemed to pick up on my feelings, and before I could say anything I'd feel foolish about later, she pointed out it was common for a client to feel attracted to their therapist as they began to heal. She pointed me to a verse from Proverbs she liked to use with her clients who were grieving the loss of a spouse: *Above all else, guard your affections. For they influence everything else in your life.* Dr. Lucy reminded me the love I'd had with Mia was special, and that I should guard my love until I knew I was ready to share it again. It would do no honor to Mia, or to me, to search for affection simply to replace what I'd lost. To replace the irreplaceable. "God is working in this," she counseled, "be patient."

When she told me she was closing her Chicago practice and moving to live near her only sister in Memphis, I had a moment's panic wondering how I would cope without her listening ear. Lucy reminded me how far I'd come since those dark early days, and I left her office if not completely healed, at least a lot closer to it. Her parting gift was a CD of praise and worship music. "Some of my favorites," she'd said right before she'd squeezed my arm and added, "be well."

Her words gave me confidence that I would be well. I had grieved for a part of my life I knew was gone, and while I couldn't replace Mia, I could, I *would*, find love again. Being back in Brewster, seeing Dave and Vicky and their easy way together, made me think maybe I was ready now to share my heart. Maybe I should have given Corinne more of a chance. Maybe I should look around and see who God might have in mind for—

Ka-pow! The blast of Dave's gun practically scared the socks off me, not to mention sending my memories far afield. I watched as a pheasant fell from the sky a good distance from where we stood. Dave grinned. "Not a bad shot, huh?"

"I thought you wanted coffee," I reminded him. "Do you see how far away that bird is?"

"It's never a long walk when there's a pheasant on the other end." Dave set out to retrieve the bird, calling over his shoulder, "I'd rather eat pheasant than duck any day."

I caught up with him in time to hear him panting, "I gotta get a dog. This retrieving is for the birds." He chuckled as he bent to pick up the bird. "Hey, did you get that? For the *birds?* I gotta remember to tell Sam that. He'll get a kick out of it."

Dave's offhand remark reminded me of the scene I'd be returning to. Not a loving wife and two children but my mother struggling to make her way around the house, acting as though each step was not a struggle when it was plain to see it was. As much as I cared for her, my thoughts during my walk made me realize I wanted more in my life to look forward to than returning to my childhood home with Mom waiting inside the door.

"Promise you'll come over for supper?" Dave stood on the running board of his pickup, which was parked in front of his house. He was proudly holding his pheasant by the feet. "Vicky refuses to cook anything wild, and Angie won't touch the stuff. I'll cook this baby in a mushroom sauce that'll make those gourmet Chicago chefs want to take up hunting."

"I'll be over," I promised, my mouth already watering as I stuffed my hunting gear into my VW. For some illogical reason I always drove to Dave's house for hunting, then we'd take his pickup. His habit of oversleeping in high school might have started the tradition. "Game of 'horse' first?"

"Nah, I think I'll pass." Dave stepped onto the sidewalk. "I've had enough exercise for one day."

True to his word, Dave had cooked a meal folks in large cities would pay big money to eat. Saturday night was my mom's bridge night, and Ida Bauer had offered to pick her up at seven. No worries in that department. Vicky's weekend cook had called in sick, so she had taken Angie along to the café to help cover the dinner hour. It was just going to be "the guys" around the table. Dave stood at the counter sharpening a filet knife on a steel rod as I walked in. "Hope you're hungry," he said, examining the knife with a squinted eye. He gave the knife a couple high-pitched swipes, then pointed to the table with the keen edge, a general summoning his troops. "Let's eat." He set the knife down.

"I get the drumstick," Sam called before the pheasant was even on the table.

"Hold your horses, buddy." Dave balanced the meat platter in one hand, a bowl of rice in his other. "Grab the corn, Paul, and then I think we're ready."

"Hey, guys." Ruthie walked in the door as we finished saying grace. "What's cookin'?" She stopped short when her eyes caught mine; clearly she hadn't expected to see me. "You eat here almost as often as I do," she blurted.

"Ha!" Sam bellowed, his mouth full. "That's funny. He does not. He never eats breakfast here and you do all the time."

"Sa-am," Dave cautioned. "That's not polite."

"Well, she does." Sam nabbed the other drumstick, even though he'd barely started on the one already on his plate. "You gotta taste this, Auntie Ruth. Dad cooked tonight."

"Oh, he did, did he?" She sounded skeptical. "What's on the menu?"

"Chicken," Dave and Sam announced in unison. Dave sliced himself a thigh.

"In mushroom sauce," I added, picking up on the glint in Dave's and Sam's eyes.

"Honest," Dave said, nudging the platter her direction, "it's good, even if I do say so myself."

Ruthie grabbed a plate and fork and then slid into the chair farthest away from me, her eyes glued to the food. I wasn't sure if she was that hungry or just trying to avoid my gaze. The memory of our meeting yesterday seemed to hang in the air, somewhere between her chair and mine.

"Mmmm," Ruthie mumbled, halfway through the large piece of breast meat she'd taken, "this is good." She swallowed, then added, "You should give this recipe to Vicky. I bet it would go over like hotcakes at the café."

"Like hotcakes?" Sam roared. "Try, like *pheasant*."

"Samuel Johnson." Ruthie's fork clattered on her plate. "Are you telling me this isn't chicken?" She pretended to have trouble swallowing. "If it's not, you have dish duty tonight."

"Hey, Dad said it too." Sam looked desperately to Dave for help.

Dave stabbed another piece of meat onto his plate. "Sorry, son. You were the one who let the cat out of the bag. Or should I say *pheasant?*"

"That's lame, Dad." But Sam laughed anyway.

I didn't miss the quick wink Ruthie sent Dave's way as she tucked the last bite of pheasant meat into her mouth. "Time for dishes," she said to Sam. "You wash. I'll dry and put away."

〜

"I'm full." Dave patted his stomach then flipped through some channels on the family room television, settling on the History Channel. The same World War II documentary seemed to be showing from the last time I'd sat here. Ruthie's and Sam's voices drifted from the kitchen, wrapping around the narrator's voice in a comfortable way that made the evening feel as if I were home.

"So," Dave said, tapping the sound up a notch on the remote control, his eyes darting toward the kitchen, "we never did finish our conversation this morning. I was going to ask about the KBRS loan. What's happening?"

It took a minute for my mind to shift into work mode. I shrugged my shoulders. "That's a tough call. Now with Jack leaving—"

"Then it's true," he interrupted. "I heard that at coffee yesterday." He nudged the volume up some more. "Ruthie was so quiet around here last night I didn't dare ask. Kinda hoped it was a rumor." He leaned forward in his chair, his voice low. "Can he do that? Just up and leave her with all that debt?"

I nodded, my lips in a grim line. "I'm afraid so."

"Oh, man." Dave scrubbed at his cheek. "Is she going to be able to make it?"

I shrugged one shoulder. "I don't know." An image of the way Ruthie had looked when I'd impulsively tried to comfort her in my office yesterday appeared. The word "nice" came to mind. I doubted that's what Dave was waiting to hear. "It'll be tough," I replied.

"It just seems to go from bad to worse for her lately."

"I know," I said, well aware of the challenges facing Ruthie. My mind had worked overtime last night trying to concoct a plan to help her out. I'd finally resorted to prayer. Maybe God could think of something for her my earthly mind couldn't fathom.

"Is there anything I can do?"

Before I could even shake my head a bloodcurdling scream came from the kitchen. "Yeee-oooowwwww!!"

I jumped to my feet, not sure if the high-pitched yell was coming from Ruthie or Sam.

"Owiee! Owiee! Owiee! Mo-mmmm! Daaaaaa-ddy."

Definitely Sam.

In the seconds it took me to reach the kitchen doorway the water in the sink had turned a sudsy pink. As if she were some sort of Florence Nightingale in an apron, Ruthie was wrapping a damp dish towel tightly around Sam's palm.

"Call 9-1-1! Call 9-1-1!" Sam had changed his owiee mantra into emergency mode.

"Take a deep breath, Sam." Ruthie's voice was calm. "You're going to be fine. You need to sit down and let us take a look."

"No-oooo," he moaned, backing himself into a kitchen chair, his knees all but buckling.

"Listen to Ruthie, Sam." Dave was eyeing the blood seeping through the towel. He didn't sound much better than his son. "Take a deep breath," he added, taking one himself. "What happened?" He plopped into a chair.

"It was the filet knife," Ruthie said, pressing on the makeshift bandage. "I told Sam to leave it for me, but—"

"I was being really careful," Sam interrupted, his voice strained. "Oooo, that hurts." He winced as Ruthie slowly unwound the towel.

"We need to see if you need stitches." Carefully she undid the layers, sending me a pleading glance.

I picked up my cue. "Hey, buddy, that better not be your shooting hand. We've gotta take your dad and Angie on in a game of 'horse' one of these days. We're still the champs, remember?"

Sam nodded, a brave little smile creasing his face. "It's my left hand," he added, wiggling the fingers of his right as if checking to make sure they still worked.

Ruthie tilted her head towards Sam's exposed palm, her eyes seeking my opinion.

I nodded once.

"Stitches for you, mister," Ruthie said.

"You sure?" Dave asked, his eyes looking everywhere but at Sam's wound.

"I'm sure," I replied.

Dave pushed his chair back. "I can't look but I can drive." He fished in his pocket for the pickup keys as Ruthie rewound the towel. "Let's get you to the emergency room. Might as well get our money's worth out of that insurance I'm always pushing." Dave put his hand on Sam's shoulder as they walked out of the house. I wasn't sure if it was a sign of support for Sam or literal support for Dave.

"What are you doing?" Ruthie's question cut into my thoughts.

What was I doing? I hadn't moved since I'd run into the kitchen. "Praying, I guess." I hadn't realized my lips were moving in silent petition.

She eyed me, amused. "For Sam or Dave?"

I couldn't help but grin back at her. "I think they both need some help."

She blinked slowly, in silent agreement, then her eyes opened and locked on mine. We stood facing each other in the suddenly empty kitchen. The soft sound of dish soap bubbles breaking seemed to fill the air. The last time we'd been alone together I'd almost kissed her. The time before that she'd followed me out of the Brewster High School gym trying to explain why she couldn't marry me.

After a few seconds, Ruthie was the first to break the increasingly awkward silence. "This place looks like an army trooped through here." She pushed Sam's chair into the table, sliding the tablecloth around as if it needed rearranging. She straightened the chair where Dave had sat. Grabbing a paper towel, she stooped to wipe a single drop of blood that had fallen on the floor.

Not knowing what else to do, I started straightening the other chairs around the table. "You were pretty impressive." I nodded my head at Sam's empty chair. "Where'd you learn that stuff?"

Ruthie looked at the chair and shrugged. "I'm addicted to *ER*."

"I've got to start watching more TV," I commented.

Ruthie laughed. "No, the real reason I knew what to do was from the remote broadcast the station did at Pumpkin Fest last year. The hospital staff was demonstrating emergency techniques all day, and our booth was right beside theirs. Who knew?"

"God works in mysterious ways," I chuckled.

"If a booth at Pumpkin Fest was His way of preparing me for tonight, then He sure does." Her eyes met mine again with something in them I couldn't read.

My laughter died as Ruthie turned back to the sink. This was one time I wished I could know what she was thinking. Did she really think God had prepared her for tonight? I didn't know how she felt about those sorts of things, but I wanted to. Now didn't seem the time to ask. I glanced around the kitchen, and except for the pinkish dishwater in the sink, the room looked entirely normal. It didn't appear as if anything traumatic had just happened, or even that two adults were awkwardly trying to reestablish a friendship.

"Is there anything I can do to help?" I asked.

"No," she replied, turning to face me and then leaning casually against the counter. She looked awfully cute standing there in an apron that didn't match her clothes. "I'm just going to get rid of this creepy dishwater, and then things should be back to normal."

Funny, I wasn't feeling one bit normal. I pulled my VW keys from my pocket. "Maybe I'll head over to the hospital and see how Sam's doing. Want to ride along?" The invitation spilled effortlessly from my lips. I realized I wanted her company, even if the drive to the hospital would take less than ten minutes.

She shook her head. "I'd better stick around in case Vicky and Angie come home. They won't know what happened. But thanks," she added.

"No problem." I tossed my keys from hand to hand. "Guess I'll take off then."

"Okay," she said, her eyes not leaving mine. "Drive carefully."

"I will," I responded, not moving, not wanting to leave. "You're sure you don't need any help?"

"Absolutely not." Ruthie pushed herself away from the counter and plunged her hand into the pink suds. "Ouch!" She yanked her hand back. One small red prick of blood seeped from her index finger. She stuck it in her mouth, speaking around her finger. "That was dumb."

I shoved my keys back into my pocket, stepped to the sink, and carefully pulled the plug. As the water drained I pulled the filet knife from the cool water and laid it on the counter. "We're going to have to declare this thing a lethal weapon. You okay?"

Ruthie nodded. "I think so."

"Let me have a look."

"I'd better not need stitches too," she said, gingerly removing her finger from her mouth. "Unlike Dave, I don't have insurance. I'd have to get you a needle and thread."

"Let's pray we don't have to resort to that." I took her hand in mine, turning it to get a look at the cut.

"You seem to do a lot of that. Praying, I mean."

"Yeah, I do," I replied, smoothing my thumb over her finger. "It helps me sort things out. Settles my soul. I like to think it helps others too." Here was my chance. I looked at her. "What about you?"

She shifted her feet, but left her hand in mine. "Not much. I'm kind of used to doing things on my own. And now with Jack leaving..." She lifted her eyes to mine.

I finished her sentence, "...you're really alone."

She nodded.

"Sounds like you could use a friend." I wasn't sure if she knew I meant God or if she thought I was offering. Either way, for now, however she understood it, it might be enough.

I felt her hand relax into mine. "I could," she murmured.

Whatever awkwardness had been between us fell away, like ice falling from tree branches after an early winter storm. I ran my thumb over the small white slit that outlined her cut. "I think you're going to be fine."

"Thank you, Dr. Bennett." Ruthie gave my hand a squeeze then turned her hand to slide it from mine. But when our fingers met, instead of sliding away my fingers entwined with hers as if they had a mind of their own. Her hand felt warm and soft, the complete opposite of the knife blade glinting on the counter. Her hand felt like something I might want to hang on to for a long time. Our eyes held for a moment, long enough for me to recognize a spark of connection between us. Then Ruthie glanced away.

"You'd better get to the hospital." Ruthie wiggled her fingers, loosening my grip. "If I keep you here any longer, Sam will be healed by the time you get there."

"My prayers don't usually work quite that miraculously. But you never know." Our hands slowly slid apart. I reached in my pocket for my keys. "Guess I'll get over there then."

"Tell Sam I'm putting the knife in the drawer…way in the back."

"I will." I walked to the door, my eyes landing on the KBRS loan file I'd set on the counter early this morning when I'd picked up Dave for hunting. I laid my hand on the file. "I'm praying for this too."

Ruthie looked surprised, then gave a small laugh. "That could be a full-time job in itself."

"God's got all the time in the world," I said, my hand on the doorknob.

"Yes," Ruthie said, "I suppose He does. Unfortunately, I don't think I do."

I turned to face her, looking her square in the eye. "Then I'll have to pray harder."

Ruthie

How could he do that? Offer his prayers for me with such confidence? As if he fully expected an answer? Soon. And for me? After what I'd done to him and had never once said, "I'm sorry." How could he do that?

I stood by the window, watching Paul's silver Bug move down the street. For a second I wondered what it would be like to be sitting next to him, but then I remembered how I'd felt when he'd looked into my eyes a few minutes ago. There was a time when he'd known all my dreams. Could tell them simply by looking into my eyes as he'd just done. Only now he knew exactly what had come of those big dreams. Nothing. Absolutely nothing. I felt my face flame. I'd mortified Paul in front of half the town in order to pursue those dreams and here I stood, still in Brewster, still wishing I were anywhere but here.

As he drove out of sight, my eyes fell to my hands, fingers entwined much like Paul had held my hand moments ago. It wasn't hard to remember just how his touch had felt. Nice. Very nice.

What was I thinking? I pulled my fingers apart and retied my apron, anxious to do something to get my mind off the past. Off the emotions stirring inside me. Even I couldn't identify what those emotions were, but they felt unsettling, nonetheless. Carefully I squirted a dollop of dish soap onto the knife blade, rinsing it clean. I dried it and laid it far back in a drawer. There. It wouldn't hurt anyone else, at least not tonight. I rummaged in Vicky's other drawers looking for plastic wrap for the rice, the one dish still left on the counter. Where did she keep it? Oh yeah, in the drawer by the back door. I leaned that way, my hand landing on the countertop, on the file folder lying there. K-B-R-S.

I recalled how Paul had placed his hand there a few minutes ago, offering his prayers. At the time I'd been comforted. Now, alone in the kitchen, I wondered what Paul must have thought when he saw that folder lying there. It had to have been obvious that I hadn't touched it since he'd dropped it off this morning. In truth, I hadn't seen it. Had forgotten about it. Paul must have thought I was some sort of Pollyanna to let the file lie there all day, not even bothering to pick it up and look at it. I looked at it now. I flipped through the pages rapidly, not wanting to know the figures but needing to know them all the same.

Oh gosh! My eyes widened when I saw the total of all the KBRS loans. That could hardly be, could it? Suddenly the warm feeling I'd had while Paul had been here evaporated. I looked over the documentation. The two big loans I'd been well aware of, but how had we accumulated so many smaller loans? Of course, when you added them up they didn't seem small at all. I sank into a kitchen chair. How had I let Jack get me into this mess?

Jack? Didn't you have some say in this too?

Well, yeah, but Jack was the one who did most of the business with the bank. I was out there working like crazy trying to sell ads.

Go ahead, Ruthie, blame Jack. It's always someone else's fault, right? Remember, you thought Paul was the one who would keep you in Brewster if you married him. Now you're saying it's Jack's fault. Maybe it's not Jack. Maybe it's you. No one is keeping you in Brewster but you.

What about all of those loans?

Oh, okay, now blame the loans for keeping you here. What's wrong? Are you afraid of the truth?

Maybe.

You had such big plans for your life. What would happen if you tried to make them come true?

I might fail.

So what if you fell flat on your face? It's not much different than where you are right now. If you left Brewster at least you'd fail where no one was there to laugh at you. No one would be around to judge you. And, what if you didn't fail? What if your dreams finally came true?

Yeah, what if? With the loan total figures seared in my mind, I closed the file and picked up the box of plastic wrap. I tore off a portion with a jerk, watching helplessly as it curled in on itself as if melting in a flame. I couldn't even tear off a piece of plastic wrap without botching the job. What made me think I could fulfill my dreams?

Oh sure, talk yourself out of it before you have to do something about it. You've done that your whole life.

The truth hurt. I yanked off another piece of plastic, making sure it didn't fall back on itself this time. I had let Jack hold me back for way too long. I'd let my excuses hold me back even longer. No more. I stretched the clear rectangle over the edge of the bowl. There. Job done. If only I could seal away my problems so easily. I pushed the bowl into the fridge. Away. Just like I was going to be. I was going to find a way out of this town once and for all.

And how would that happen with loans up the wazoo?

"Be quiet!" I yelled at my chiding conscience. "Maybe I'll ask Paul to pray for that too."

Prayer, now there was a thought that finally shut my conscience up. First Mrs. Bauer and now Paul. You'd think a person with so many people praying for her wouldn't have a care in the world.

I turned out the kitchen light and headed down the basement stairs toward my corner room. It was cold downstairs, much like my heart. Maybe God wasn't listening to their prayers. Maybe God had given up on me long ago, about the same time I gave up on Him.

Jack

If only the folks in Brewster could see me now. KMIN was big time. This station made KBRS look like something little kids built out of milk cartons.

I followed the operations manager, Doug Sommers, down the narrow hall. Broadcast booths and recording studios lined the way. Most were empty.

"You're lucky to get this slot, Jack." Doug opened a sliding door into the room where, I guessed, I'd be doing my show. "The employment rate in the radio industry has fallen quite a bit over the last few years, and it's all because of these babies." He patted the top of one of two computers that sat on the wide countertop lining two walls of the room. "I've been in this business twenty years and I've never seen anything like it."

I'd never seen anything like it either. Two computers. A huge reel-to-reel tape deck. A telephone with several lines blinking. Boom mike. Weather screen. Not quite the weather report Ruthie and I used to get by looking out the window. NASA could launch missiles from this setup. The only thing missing was the music. I glanced around hoping to see the familiar stacks of tapes along the wall like we'd had in Brewster. All that covered the walls was equipment, cartoons, and notices tacked up for staff to read. I was almost afraid to ask, but I needed to know. "And the tunes are where?"

Doug's eyebrows creased the center of his forehead for a moment as he reached under the countertop and patted more computer equipment. "They're right in here." It looked like any other computer hard drive. He chuckled. "We like to think of this as the biggest jukebox you've ever seen." His gaze wandered over my shoulder. "Oh, here's our star."

I'd been so busy staring at the unfamiliar equipment that I'd missed seeing the gorgeous babe who had sauntered in behind me. No doubt checking me out. Instinctively I straightened the hem of my Polo sweater. I wanted her to know she was looking at a class act.

"Sunny, this is Jack Warner." Doug sounded wary. "He's taking over the evening slot. Sunny's our morning drive-time deejay." Ah, radio prime time. No wonder he'd called her their star. "You probably saw her face plastered on a few billboards when you drove in."

Actually, I had. She looked even better up close. I stuck out my hand, which she greeted with a cool look. Oh, playing hard to get. I could handle that.

"Are you going to be in here long?" Sunny spoke to Doug, her voice perfectly modulated. No wonder radio was her game. "I need to lay down some voice tracks for the breaks."

"No problem." Doug ushered me out, sliding the door closed behind us. He lowered his voice. "Don't let her get to you. She's protective of her time slot, is all. Everyone around here is always worried the next guy is going to take over their spot." He slid open another door, waving me in. "Then again, from what I heard of your air-check tape, maybe Sunny should worry."

I didn't tell Doug, but he didn't need to worry about Sunny and me getting along. Nope, give Sunny a little time and I knew she'd like me just fine.

"Here's where you'll be doing your show." The room was filled with even more equipment than the one he'd just shown me.

"Heh, heh." Even I could hear the nervousness in my voice. I cleared my throat. "For some reason I thought that last room was where—"

Thankfully, he cut me off. "No, that's our PB. We use that for pre-recording only."

PB? I knew he didn't mean peanut butter. I cleared my throat again, running my finger around the neckline of my sweater. I hadn't realized how tight it was. I might have to return it. "PB?" I asked, trying to joke my way into information. "Where's the 'J'?"

"Production bank," Doug said, casting me a puzzled look. "You are familiar with this system, right?" Doug scanned the computer screen, punched at a rectangle on the screen and watched as a list of songs to be played in the next hour popped up. "We overprogram," he said, pointing to the last few songs on the screen.

Overprogram? What was that supposed to mean?

"They'll never get on." He tapped at a different colored box and the main screen returned, showing the next six songs and commercials to be aired. "It's got the ten break, twenty, forty, and fifty all laid in there for you."

I didn't have a clue what he was talking about. Ruthie and I just stacked our old tapes in the order we planned to play them, reading commercials in between. If we didn't feel like listening to a song, we didn't play it. I had no idea what the heck a ten break was. Not to mention a twenty, forty, and fifty. "What happens if a song reminds you of your old girlfriend?" I asked, trying to buy time. Trying to understand how the system worked. Maybe I shouldn't have fudged my experience in the interview.

Doug gave me a sidelong glance. "You could turn the sound down," he said. "But usually the deejays lay down their tracks a day or so ahead of time. All you need to listen to are the last few snips before you lay in a commercial."

Snips? Lay in a commercial? Hoo, boy. I felt a cold bead of sweat form on my upper lip. "Uh. Umm. The station I came from was in the process of converting to a similar system. I may need some coaching to get up to speed."

"Sure, no problem. You can stay and talk to Marv on his shift tonight. He'll be in around midnight setting up his show for the next couple days; then he's going to take a couple days off."

"You mean he'll be on the air and not even be here?" Incredible. I thought of all the things I could have done in Brewster if I would have had access to this kind of equipment. Well, actually, I couldn't think of much I could have done in Brewster, but here? I could be listening to myself on the radio while I played poker with the guys.

"That about does it." Doug held out his hand. "Glad to have you on board, Jack. We've got big plans for you. See you Monday night at seven."

Seven to midnight was a lot better than the night shift. Of course, I'd had my eye on morning drive time, but that would mean I'd have to get up at the crack of dawn, so maybe evening drive time would be better, three to seven. Put in a good afternoon of work with a whole evening ahead to enjoy. Maybe with Sunny. The more I thought about it, that *was* the shift I was eyeing. It wouldn't hurt me any to put in time on the evening shift for a while. Coming from a Podunk station like KBRS, I had a bit of a learning curve to catch up on. Perfectly understandable. A few weeks of catch-up and Doug would see I was ready for that evening drive-time slot.

I inched the sliding door behind Marv open a crack. I'd bided my time, listening to a half hour of Marv's show from my car in the parking lot. Only after he'd announced, "Here's five in a row," did I make my entrance. No sense catching the guy on air. "Hey, I hear it's Marv the Man." I stuck out my hand.

"I've gotta make a bathroom run. Wait here." He pointed to a dark spot on the carpet just outside the door, then ambled down the hall in no hurry at all.

I stood outside the doorway, trying to scrape away the spot with my foot. *Glad to meet you too.*

"Who are you?" Marv barely glanced my way as he slid onto his high-backed stool. He swiped at a rectangle on the computer screen, nodding at whatever information popped up.

"I'm your competition." I stuck out my hand, which he slapped with cold, clammy fingertips, reminding me of trained seals I'd seen on TV.

"Not much competition in this time slot." He held up a finger for silence. "You're listening to K-M-I-N." His voice was animated, completely unlike his welcome, if you could call it that. "Keep listening to

K-Minnesota for the latest in alternative rock." He swiveled his chair towards me. "What're you here for?"

Might as well start over. Hopefully on a better foot. "I'm Jack. Jack Warner." I pointed a thumb at my Ralph Lauren sweater even though he didn't look like the designer type. "I've been assigned the evening shift but I need to get up to speed on the production system here. Doug said you'd be the guy to see."

"Where'd you come from?" He turned back to the console.

"Someplace smaller than this." He didn't need to know more than that. Rural North Dakota didn't have much of a ring to it.

"Umph." He grunted. "Hang on a minute, I've got to lay down another liner."

"Liner?" I sounded like a hick.

Marv spoke into the mike, "This is K-M-I-N. K-*Mine*, from *yours* truly." He flicked a switch near the mike. "That's a liner." He looked me up and down in a way that made me think he wasn't checking out my designer shoes. "So, what do you know?"

I almost said, "Nothing. I know nothing." At least that's the way it felt after a day of new equipment and lingo that sounded like a foreign language. But then the answer filtered through the day that had felt so strange. The answer I'd had since junior high. My voice filled with confidence. "Music," I answered, my voice strong. "I know music."

A slow smile spread across Marv's face as he looked me square in the eye. "We're gonna get along fine," he said. "Just fine. Got a place to stay?"

"Still looking," I replied, multiplying the $39.95 I'd been paying at the Super Six Motel against the prices I'd been quoted on the downtown high-rise I had my eye on.

"Not anymore, you're not. I've got an extra room." Marv swiveled back to the mike. "This is Marv the Man at the mike, comin' at you from Minneapolis, at K-M-I-N."

"Liner?" I asked, realizing he wasn't on-air, he was taping.

"Liner," he replied, rewinding it for playback.

"You'll lay it in between snips later, I suppose?"

"You got it." He flicked a switch and his recorded voice played into the room, "*This is Marv the Man at the mike, comin' at you from...*"

～

There was much to learn that night. So much to take in, I didn't have a second to think of what I'd left behind in Brewster.

Not about Ruthie.

Or the bills.

Ruthie

Bills. I flipped through the pile. Royalty fees. Rent. Mike's part-time hours. I'd dropped my health insurance months ago. I slammed my hand on the desk, the force of my frustration sending the stack fluttering to the floor.

Great, another mess to clean up.

The three weeks Jack had been gone seemed like three months. Tears hung at the back of my throat most days, along with an ever-present fear. What was I going to do? Ever since the night Sam needed stitches, a new easiness had sprung up between Paul and me. An easiness that almost made me forget how much money I owed the bank. But when I thought of the figures, it was hard to separate what I owed from the man who was supposed to collect it. Whatever was going to happen to the station wasn't going to happen tonight. I pushed the bills into a pile and stuffed them into my carry bag. Right on top of the loan history file Paul had left me two weeks ago. I still hadn't had time to really look at it.

Haven't had time or haven't made time?

Of course I hadn't had time. Trying to cover Jack's time on-air as well as my own didn't leave many moments to try and figure out a solution to the financial problems I was facing. "*On my own!*" I mentally screamed to Jack. Mike Anderson, the high school kid who worked part-time, had a natural knack for radio, but the two morning hours he filled in for me weren't enough. I spent what little time I had away from the station racing around town trying to sell ads. I was determined to keep the station solvent. Pay off my debt. I wasn't about to let KBRS go under just because Jack had given up.

In all my dreams of leaving Brewster, it had always been on my own terms. Leaving to go somewhere exciting—not leaving with failure dogging my heels. When I finally left, it would be with my head up, my debt clear.

I locked the station door, vowing to look at the papers soon, but with Pumpkin Fest tomorrow there wouldn't be any time until next week.

As I stepped outside, the cool October night air bit into my cheeks. If only my thoughts felt as clear and crisp. It had been a bad day and an even worse three weeks. My brain was mush from trying to organize the remote broadcast I'd be doing all day from Pumpkin Fest. Sponsors had been hard to find since most of Brewster's businesses were setting up booths and paying extra to hire help for the day. They didn't have money for radio advertising. I took a deep breath. I'd have to chalk this one up as public service, something the FCC monitored. If I didn't get any credit from the people of Brewster, at least I'd get it from the government. Go figure.

The streets of Brewster were empty; the only sign of life was a dim light in the window of Vicky's café. The café closed after the dinner hour, and Vicky should have been at home already. I suspected she had forgotten to turn off a light, but I thought I'd better check to make sure that's all it was. Instead, when I walked around back and peeked in the window, I found Vicky and Angie bustling around the café kitchen getting pies ready for Pumpkin Fest tomorrow night. I should have known. I opened the back door, oven-warmed air surrounding me like a soft sweater.

"Thank You," Vicky said when she spotted me, her eyes roving skyward, her arms covered in flour up to her elbows. "Every year I swear I'll never do this again." Vicky was busy rolling out a ball of pie dough. The café kitchen counter was filled with pie tins waiting to be lined with Vicky's well-known flaky crust. "I know Pumpkin Fest is Brewster's claim to fame, but gosh, it's a lot of work."

"Mo-om," Angie countered, "I won the pumpkin carving contest last year. It's fun!" Angie was busy cracking eggs into the large mixing bowl on the counter.

I was already exhausted, but I knew Vicky needed help. I set my bag in a corner, hung my coat on a hook, swallowed the tears that had threatened to fall all day, and rolled up my sleeves.

For longer than I could remember Brewster had been celebrating Pumpkin Fest on whatever October Friday fell closest to Halloween. As a kid I'd loved the day for the same reason Angie did. It was fun. Pumpkin carving. Booths manned by local merchants, who handed out candy and prizes to people who came from miles around to celebrate. All day and into the evening old-time music filled the old high school gym where the festival was held. Brewster had built a new school and gym in the years since I'd graduated, but Pumpkin Fest had remained a fixture in the old building.

As a high school student I'd rolled my eyes at the festival, forced to sit through an afternoon celebration while playing old-fashioned music on my saxophone with the school band. I was much too sophisticated to even pretend I enjoyed the music. Much too mature to join in the pumpkin-carving contest. Too cool to collect a sack full of candy from the booths lining the gym floor. The only reason I liked Pumpkin Fest was because it got me out of an afternoon of school.

Later, after I'd returned to Brewster to run the radio station, the day was nothing but work. Setting up a remote broadcast from the old gym was annually plagued with problems. Old folks, or kids, tripping over cords we needed to run the broadcast, no matter how much duct tape we used to secure them to the floor. Trouble with the equipment. People to interview who turned mute when faced with a mike. Then, at sunset, when the station went off the air, I'd pitch in to help Vicky serve her famous pumpkin pie and coffee to hungry Pumpkin Fest celebrators. Sure it was fun if you were ten, or seventy, but to me it was nothing but a headache. And with Jack gone, this year was going to be a nightmare. Dread was the word that came to mind.

"Ruthie, grab a knife," Vicky instructed, "and poke those pumpkins in the oven. See if they're done." A puff of flour flew through the air as Vicky pointed to the knife rack.

I opened the oven door, the smell of baking pumpkins filling the kitchen. "I thought we talked about this last year," I said, poking through the tough skin to the tender core of the vegetable. "I thought you were going to start using canned pumpkin."

Vicky wrinkled her nose. "It goes against everything I believe about pumpkin pie. Make that pie-*ssss*." She flopped another doughy crust into a waiting tin. "Angie, you can start the mixer now, but be careful with that spatula. I don't want rubber flecks in the filling. Not good for business." She raised her eyebrows at me, smiling. "I guess that would be one way to get out of this job."

"Whoops," Angie said. "Mom, I need a paper towel." Filmy egg residue ran down the side of the mixing bowl.

Vicky tossed a roll to Angie. "Wipe it up and start *slow*. How're the pumpkins?"

"I think they're done," I said. The pumpkins had collapsed into themselves.

"Could you grab the potholders and put the pans on top of the stove to cool? Be careful. There'll be a bunch of boiling liquid in the bottom of the pans."

A splash of liquid hit the top of my hand as I jostled one pan out of the oven. "Ouch!" The quick pain turned the tears I'd felt earlier into instant anger. A surge of bitter thoughts flashed through me. It didn't seem to matter how hard I worked, the station was going backward. Fast. Fear mingled with anger as pent-up emotions from the past weeks bubbled to the surface and angry words poured from my mouth, bouncing against Vicky and Angie as though they were targets. "I don't know why you're knocking yourself out for this stupid festival, anyway. Why am I bending over backward to do a remote from the gym? No one in this town cares about it. Why should you participate in it? Why should I?" I slammed the pan on the stovetop, more hot liquid splashing over the sides and just missing my hand. Angie stared at me as if she didn't know me. "Half the businesses in town no longer participate."

The soft clicking of Vicky's rolling pin was the only sound in the kitchen. Finally Vicky answered softly, "Maybe it's because half of those businesses are no longer in business."

Even Angie's wide-eyed stare still couldn't stop me. "Well, then maybe this town should quit having Pumpkin Fest." I pushed the first pan of cooked pumpkins to the back of the stove, making room for more. "Whoever heard of celebrating *pumpkins,* anyway? It's a lot of work and it's dumb."

Vicky glanced at Angie, who had turned the mixer on as if to cover up my words. Her head was down and her shoulders were slumped. Vicky turned her gaze to me. "It's not just about pumpkins." She had that fake-cheerful sound in her voice adults use when trying to shield their kids from bad news. Or a crabby aunt. She added a few drops of water to the mound of flour and shortening in front of her. It seemed as if she could make piecrusts in her sleep. "Mrs. Bauer would tell you it's about celebrating the fall harvest and community spirit."

"Then Mrs. Bauer should be doing this." My voice held a bitter tone even I didn't like.

"She did when she was younger," Vicky said softly. "It's our turn now."

"What if I don't want a turn? What if all I want is out of this town?" I faced Vicky, my hands on my hips as if ready to do battle.

"Mom, is that enough?" Angie turned off the mixer, sounding near tears. She scraped at the sides of the large bowl with a spatula, not looking up.

Vicky peered into the bowl. "Just a little bit more. You need to make sure you can't tell the white part of the eggs from the yolks. It should look solid gold when it's mixed completely." She gave her daughter a nudge with her elbow, careful not to get flour on Angie's sweater. "Why don't you take a little break and go call Steph? When you come back grab a couple Cokes out of the cooler for us. You're helping me so much you deserve a break." Angie pressed her lips together in a grim semblance of a smile. Thanks to me, I knew.

"Diet, please," I called as Angie went into the main part of the café to make her call and get our drinks. An uneasy silence hung in the air. Inside I boiled. I knew my anger was misdirected. If I were yelling at anyone it should be Jack, not Vicky, and certainly not Angie.

You could tell Me.

The unfamiliar voice twanged my conscience, sending a stab of quick remorse through my chest. Vicky didn't deserve what I'd said, but then I didn't deserve to be stuck at the station alone either.

Tell Me.

I wasn't about to start a conversation with myself in the middle of the café kitchen. The least I could do would be to simply be quiet. Push my anger back where it should have stayed. Buried inside.

Vicky was still, her eyes closed, almost as if she were praying. Or counting to ten. The hands I'd placed so defiantly on my hips fell to my sides. I waited for the tongue-lashing I knew I had coming.

"I have learned wherever I am to be content." Vicky picked up her rolling pin and began pressing on the pie dough with slow, steady strokes.

I snorted. "What's that supposed to mean?"

"Oh, sorry, I wasn't saying that to you." Vicky continued to calmly roll the dough into a thin circle. "I didn't even know I said it out loud. It's just something I say to myself when things seem out of my control. That's what the apostle Paul said when—"

I cut her off. "Oh, so now you're quoting the Bible to me. Why don't you just come right out and tell me I acted like a jerk in front of Angie? Go on, I can take it. This week has been rotten enough already." My vow to be quiet sure hadn't lasted long.

"Ruthie." Vicky put down her rolling pin and leaned forward, her hands on the edge of the marble rectangle she used to make piecrusts. "You act like living in Brewster is the source of all your problems. Like it's some sort of prison. The apostle Paul said those words after he really *had* been in prison. There are no prison bars holding you here. The only thing holding you captive is your stubborn attitude. Maybe if you changed your attitude your life would change." She picked up her rolling pin and began working. "And, as long as you brought it up, I don't appreciate you saying those things about Brewster in front of Angie. Some of us love this town, you know."

Tears hung at the back of my throat. What did Vicky know about my life? "That's easy for you to sa-ay." My voice cracked. "You've got a husband and two kids and a business you love." I blinked rapidly. I wasn't about to let Vicky see me cry. "I don't have anything I ever wanted. I've been stuck here my whole life!"

Vicky folded the flattened dough in half and transferred it to an empty tin then turned and looked me in the eye. "Don't you think I've ever wished for something different?"

"You? You've got everything you ever dreamed of. All I've ever wanted is to live in a big city and have an exciting life." I turned back to the oven. There was one more pan filled with misshapen pumpkins to remove and tears to blink away.

"Ruth, this may surprise you, but you don't have the corner on the market of dreams. There are things I'd like to do, go to college, travel. But right now I know we can't afford it…the time or the money. But I don't spend my time thinking about how miserable my life is because I can't fly off somewhere. I try and focus on the things that are good in my life right now. And you were right. Those things are Dave and the kids and this café. I think if you looked around, you might find something good here too."

"In Brewster? Give me a break." I pulled the pan of baked pumpkins toward me. "I can see where it might be okay for you, but I don't see myself spending my life here. As soon as I get this station stuff straightened out I'm gone. Ouch!" Liquid from the pan soaked into the potholder, scalding my fingertips. Instinctively I jerked my hand back. The roasting pan tipped precariously, resting half on the oven rack, half off, a stream of hot liquid running from the pan onto the oven door, then to the floor. "Help!" With one hand I attempted to hang on to the pumpkin-filled pan, fumbling to regain a grip on the potholder with my other hand. There. I managed to nudge the pan enough so that it flattened itself back onto the oven rack.

Another flash of anger filled me. So much work just to try and entertain the folks in Brewster. Who cared, anyway? I sure didn't. I was going to be gone by next year at this time for sure.

"That was a close call." Vicky was on one knee wiping the hot liquid from the floor. "Careful you don't step on that clump of pumpkin that fell." She pushed it away from my feet. The tips of my shoes were wet. Luckily, they were an old pair I was past caring about, like just about everything I owned.

I yanked the last pan from the oven, setting it firmly on the stovetop. Enough liquid had spilled that I didn't need to worry about any splashing on me. "Next year," I said firmly, "I want you to say no when they ask you to do this because I will not be here to help you. I plan to be far away from here."

"I'll miss you." Vicky's soft remark drifted up from where she was kneeling at my feet, wiping up the water I'd spilled.

A sudden, lonesome feeling filled me. The tears that had hovered all day filled my eyes. "Well, I'll miss you too," I said, sounding just the opposite. I grabbed a paper towel and dabbed at my eyes before Vicky looked up, then at my shoes. "But," I added, "I will not miss this town."

Vicky tossed the soggy paper towels into the wastebasket. "I'll mop the floor when we're done." She said the words more to herself than me. Squirting soap on her hands, she washed them, her back to me. She sighed heavily. "I know you think this whole Pumpkin Fest thing is corny. But, I don't know—" She grabbed a towel and dried her hands. "I kind of look forward to it. I get to see all these people I don't often get a chance to talk to. Most from Brewster, but a lot from towns around here too." Vicky picked up a large spoon and started scraping the soft flesh from the inside of a pumpkin. "There are so many interesting people, and they've all got a story to tell..."

Angie burst through the swinging door, three sodas in her small hands. "Auntie Ruth, grab yours. Quick!" I took two of the cans from her hand, glad she hadn't heard my last outburst. "Who's got a story to tell?" Apparently, she'd forgiven my earlier words as well.

"I was just telling Ruthie that I like listening to the stories people tell me while they're having pie and coffee at Pumpkin Fest." Vicky handed Angie a large spoon and motioned for her to start scooping.

Angie dug in, then tapped her spoon hard on the edge of the bowl; a large chunk of pumpkin fell off. "Like when Dad proposed to you at Pumpkin Fest?"

"Ha!" I laughed. "He did not. Where did you ever hear that?"

"Mom told me." Angie dipped out another spoonful of pumpkin. "I think it's romantic."

"Ha!" I laughed, again. "Pumpkin Fest? That old gym? Romantic?" Vicky shot me a warning glance. I stopped talking, not wanting to take away from the story Angie thought she knew. I'd already done enough damage with my mouth for one night.

"It's tru-ue!" Angie's voice rose in excitement. "Tell her, Mom."

"Oh, good grief." Vicky threw one empty pumpkin shell into the garbage and started on another one. "You've heard that story a million times. I'm not going to tell it again. We've got too much work to do. Here." Vicky handed me a recipe card stained from years of use. "Start measuring those spices into that bowl."

"Dad had already graduated from high school," Angie took a sip of her pop. "Right, Mom? He came home from college just for Pumpkin Fest."

Vicky rolled her eyes at Angie, but smiled. "Yes, he had." Obviously the story was going to get told no matter what Vicky said.

"And Mom was working at the café. She did that after Grandpa and Grandma Hammond died." Angie gave a little hiccup. "Well, I s'pose you know that."

I nodded. "Just a second." I held up a finger indicating she should wait. "Are you sure this calls for three *tablespoons* of cinnamon?"

"Remember," Vicky reminded, "this is for Pumpkin Fest, not just one pie."

"Okay." I started measuring. "Go on." I found I was anxious to hear this story I'd thought I knew.

"Mom was a senior in high school," Angie continued.

"I'd already graduated, but I was still much too young to get married," Vicky interjected.

"But Mom, you wanted to let Auntie Ruth go back to college and—"

"Angie, I was very much in love with your dad, but nineteen is too young to get married." Vicky rearranged the tins lined with unbaked piecrusts. "Let's get these pumpkins done or these pies will never get baked by tomorrow."

Angie's statement made me lose count of the number of tablespoons of spice I'd been measuring. Vicky hadn't gotten married barely out of high school because of *me*, had she? She'd dated Dave steadily for four years by then, and they seemed to be as much in love as I thought two people could be. It had never occurred to me Vicky might have gotten married so she wouldn't be a burden to me. Could that be true? Was there more to this story than I'd thought? I rolled my hand at Angie. "Continue."

"Mom was barely out of high school, and she'd spent the whole night right here in this kitchen making pies. Well, maybe not the *whole* night, but most of it. And then she worked in the café most of the day 'cause it's always busy on Pumpkin Fest day. Right, Mom?"

Vicky nodded along with the story, as if she was reciting it herself. "It's still that way."

"But after supper—" Angie paused, pushing hard on her spoon and coming up with a large chunk of pumpkin. She transferred it to the bowl and continued, "Mom went over to the gym to help serve pie. They closed the café for the night even back then."

"See?" Vicky said, "They've always had a hard time finding enough help. Besides, everyone should be at Pumpkin Fest, anyway."

Angie nodded emphatically, obviously agreeing. "There were hundreds of people there and they were running out of pie, and Dad came up behind Mom—he'd ducked under the tables where they were serving—see, they kind of made a square with the tables." Angie formed her arms into an imaginary counter. "Like a pretend café and—"

"Ruthie knows that, Angie." Vicky was chuckling. "We still do it like that."

"Oh, yeah, I forgot. Well, my dad asked if she wanted him to help." Angie's eyes sparkled as if this were her favorite fairy tale, and in a way, I imagined it was. "And they served all the pieces of pie and all the coffee. It was all gone." Angie chopped her hand across the air making sure we knew she meant *all* gone. "The other ladies who were helping stacked the empty pie tins and took them back to the café, and my dad and mom said they'd stay and wipe off the tables. So they did and then Mom said, 'Gosh, I spent all that time baking those pies and I never even got to eat a piece.' And, like he was a magician, my dad reached in a box that was under the table and pulled out one whole pie that he had hidden! Then remember, Mom?" Angie sounded almost as though she'd been there. "You hit him with the wet dishrag and said, 'You could get arrested for doing that.' And then you grabbed two plastic forks and said, 'Let's eat it!'" Angie's clear giggle filled the kitchen.

I couldn't help but smile, imagining Dave and Vicky eating their purloined pie.

"They ate the *whole* pie!" Angie dropped her jaw in a *can-you-believe-it* way.

"We did," Vicky said. "And then—"

"No, Mom, let me tell it!" Angie didn't wait a breath to let Vicky get a word in. "And then Dad ate the last bite of pie, licked his fork, and said, "Vicky Hammond, I love you. Will you marry me?" She grinned from ear to ear.

"How come you never told me this story?" I asked Vicky.

She shrugged her shoulders. "You always thought Pumpkin Fest was so dumb, I guess I thought you'd laugh or something."

"But you were excited to be getting married, weren't you?" The thought that Vicky had said yes because of me had my mind twisting. I only dared say so much in front of Angie. "I mean Pumpkin Fest proposal, or not." Vicky and Dave had always seemed like the perfect couple. Perfect for each other. Perfectly content.

I have learned wherever I am to be content.

Vicky's words echoed in my mind. Had she clung to those words even as a teen? When our parents died and all she had was me? Me. Ruthie. The person who had never made it a secret that all she wanted was to leave town. Vicky hadn't really even had me to depend on, had she?

No, but she always had Me.

Chills ran down my spine. That voice again. The thought hadn't come from my mind, that I knew. I dumped another tablespoon of cinnamon into the bowl, trying to chase away this odd feeling.

"See, didn't I tell you it was romantic?" Angie was dreamy-eyed, staring at a spot somewhere over my head, somewhere far away from this messy kitchen.

As if her words had pulled away a curtain, I suddenly remembered a time when I, too, thought that old gym was the most romantic place on earth. I recalled the many prom grand marches I'd watched. First as a young girl standing by my mother's side, then as a junior high student standing with my girlfriends and peering between the crepe paper streamers. We'd loved that old gym. It had been our second home. The place where we attended pep rallies before ball games, where we had gym class and ferocious volleyball matches.

And then there were the proms. The proms I had attended, not simply watched. Dressed in a gown I had only imagined for years. Walking down that crepe paper aisle holding tightly to Paul's arm while the younger kids watched me. Angie was right—it had been exciting and romantic.

Until the last song of your senior prom. Remember?

Oh, I remembered all too well. Ever since that night the old gym had lost any luster it had ever had. I got busy, quickly dumping the rest of the spices into the bowl.

"Now what?" I asked Vicky, anxious to get away from Angie's starry-eyed view of life.

"Mix the spices in with the eggs. I'll get this pumpkin mashed." Vicky threw the last pumpkin shell away.

I spooned the spices into the bowl while Angie carefully turned on the mixer. Out of the corner of my eye I observed my niece's innocent face. Of course she was starry-eyed. She didn't know about things like broken hearts. Feelings of shame and embarrassment. Bills she couldn't pay and dreams that never came true.

I have learned wherever I am to be content. Vicky's earlier words filled my mind. I turned the mixer speed to high. Anything to drown out those words.

Old Bible words may have done something for Vicky, but obviously she didn't know anything about my problems or dreams. Being content in my situation would be impossible.

But even with the mixer on high and Angie's crystal-clear voice rereading the recipe ingredients out loud, even those sounds couldn't quiet the still, small voice that kept repeating…*Content. Content. Wherever I am…*

Paul

I heard Pumpkin Fest before I saw it. The sounds of several accordions and a drum stretched into the parking lot of the gym, working through the windows and past the sound of the heater in my VW. The gravel parking lot was nearly full, as were the several blocks surrounding the gym, but I managed to drive into a space left by a large pickup that had just pulled out near the entrance. Lucky.

I was anxious to get inside. It had been years since I'd attended Pumpkin Fest. The last time was the year Dave had proposed to Vicky. He'd made me ride home from college with him "for moral support and to split the gas. Engagement rings are expensive, you know." I knew.

I pulled open the heavy double doors of the gym and the muffled music I'd been hearing became a clear welcome. I'd wanted to get here earlier, but with all the people in town, the bank had been busy all day. I found it hard to believe they still celebrated Pumpkin Fest on a weekday, but from the looks of it most everyone here was retired. Gray hair was definitely the color of choice. I had a feeling that no matter what day the local merchants decided to celebrate, people would find their way here. I could also understand why they kept it to a one-day festival. There just weren't that many businesses in town to man the booths for more than one day.

A firm hand grasped my shoulder. "Paul. Good to see you here." I turned; Bob Marsden's hand was now shaking mine. Though he was my boss, he acted more like my friend. I liked that. "Can't miss Pumpkin Fest, even though I'm in Carlton most days. It's a good chance to visit with some of the customers I don't see too often anymore." His eyes scanned the crowd near the door. "I'm sure they'll like seeing you here too." Bob took a step back, tapping the shoulder of the woman next to him, who was surveying the crowd. "Have you met my wife, Olivia?"

She turned, her dark hair swinging with her. She'd been just enough older than me in school that I didn't have many memories of her. Other than the fact she'd been beautiful back then. She still was.

"Paul Bennett," she said, as though I were an old friend. She held out her hand, her clasp warm and firm. "Bob's spoken very highly of you. It's good to have you back in Brewster." She smiled. "Some of us stayed here and held down the fort while you checked out the world."

"You did a great job," I replied. "Brewster is a good town to come back to." She nodded. "I hear you wrote a book," I said.

There was a dimming in her eyes, a quick flash of pain, then her smile was back in place. "Yes, I did."

"Congratulations."

She ducked her head modestly. "It's not published yet. I'm still trying."

"Well," Bob said, putting his hand in the small of Olivia's back, "I guess we'd better join the fray."

"Good to finally meet you again, Paul."

"You too, Olivia."

As Bob eased her forward, she lifted her hand in a quick wave. "Call me Libby," she said as they melted into the crowd. I sidestepped as a knee-high toddler almost collided with my leg. Now that it was almost dinnertime, families were starting to arrive.

"Looks like your little sister is winning the race," I teased the young boy following the toddler.

"I know," he said, exaggerating his motion so it appeared he was running in place, smiling as he joined in on my joke.

I remembered Chicago, a place where kids didn't talk to strangers. I was glad I was here. My eyes skimmed the large space, not stopping until they landed on the KBRS sign. I hadn't realized what I was looking for until I found it. Ruthie. There she was. My stomach did an odd flop. Was it because of our past, or because she looked so cute in a pair of nice-fitting blue jeans and a crisp white shirt?

Holding a microphone to Ida Bauer's mouth, Ruthie was animated. Under the music I could hear the local radio broadcast, "...and you think this is the sixty-sixth Pumpkin Fest you've attended?" Ruthie sounded as if this were the most interesting thing she'd ever heard.

"Vell, yes. At least dat's vhat I tink." Mrs. Bauer licked her lips as if being interviewed gave her a dry mouth. "I chust know I am tankful to Gott dat I coult be here each year. And for you young people," she patted Ruthie's arm, "who do such a goot chob in carrying this tradition forwart." If Ida weren't careful she'd be running for mayor next.

"Thank you, Mrs. Bauer." Ruthie nodded a smile at Ida, turning back to the KBRS booth, continuing to talk. "That's it for our live coverage of Pumpkin Fest. The sun is setting, which means we've got to get off the air, but there's lots of celebrating left in Brewster tonight." She quickly ran through the schedule of events for the evening, including a plug for Vicky's homemade pumpkin pie. "That'll do it for me, Ruthie Hammond, live from Pumpkin Fest in Brewster, North Dakota. If you're not already here, you're in the wrong place." She made it sound like the most exciting place a person could want to be tonight. And from the sounds of the crowd, it was.

I wondered if Ruthie really was excited to be here. I'd seen her last night when Dave, Sam, and I had stopped by the café after helping to get things set up in the gym. She'd looked tired and I'd imagined she was. Even with the financial problems she was facing, Ruthie still jumped in to help Vicky make a go of it. I had to admire her for that.

"Uncle Paul!" Sam tackled me around my waist. "Come here." He grabbed my hand. "I want to show you my teacher." He dragged me through the crowd to Vicky's pie booth.

There was a line at least ten deep waiting for a piece of pie. My mom was in a chair, manning the coffee spigot, filling Styrofoam cups as fast as the pot would give up the coffee. Once they were filled, however, she seemed to be having trouble setting them on the table. I hoped she wasn't holding up Vicky's booming business. My mother had volunteered to help Vicky for years, refusing any pay Vicky offered but unable to refuse the free café meals Vicky simply wouldn't bill her for. In years past Mom had manned the pie-serving area, but that was much too hectic for her diminished walking ability. I was pleased to see that Vicky had found a safe spot for her.

"Teacher!" Sam abruptly stopped in the middle of the pie line. "This is my Uncle Paul. Not really my uncle, but he's kind of..." His explanation of our relationship was too much for his introductory skills.

I stuck out my hand. "Paul Bennett."

"Miss Quinn," she replied, shaking my hand. Then she laughed. "Sorry, *Sandy* Quinn. It's sort of an occupational hazard, introducing myself as *Miss*."

"Miss Quinn's not married." Sam just had to get that in, the little conniver.

I knew enough to ignore Sam's remark. "I think I remember you. Weren't you in Vicky's class in high school?" She was a far cry from the gangly girl I recalled. She'd grown up. Very nicely, I couldn't help but notice.

"One year behind." Sandy tucked a strand of blonde hair behind her ear. "I heard you were back in town. Have you had culture shock yet?" Her eyes swept the crowded gym that was divided into booths that were thronged with people, mostly farmers wearing farm equipment ads on their duck-billed caps.

"Culture shock? Nah." I shook my head, looking around at many familiar faces. "It's home. What about you? You've been in Brewster since...?"

Sam stood there grinning.

Sandy swept her hair behind her ear again, even though it wasn't out of place. "I taught in Carlton for several years, then my mom died and my dad went into a severe depression. He couldn't cope on his own, so I moved back to help. He's been recovered for years, but—" She shrugged her shoulders. "You know how it goes. Here I am." The line moved and we all went forward. "It's okay, though; I like it here. It's home." She brushed at her hair again, tilting her head to smile up at me. "Well, I guess you know that. About the home thing."

"Pie?" Angie called over the table to get Sandy's attention.

Sandy moved to the table. "Have time for pie?" she asked, a light color rising in her cheeks. At my nod she answered Angie, "Two pieces. Coffee too."

"I'm gonna go to the fishing booth, okay?" Sam ran off, a huge grin covering his face. His matchmaking plan had obviously succeeded.

I waited while Angie dished out our pie and my mother filled two cups of coffee. Neither Angie nor my mother were doing a very good job of keeping their thoughts off their faces. "Have fun," Mom said, as if Sandy and I were off on a first date…in junior high. I could see Angie behind the serving area whispering to her friend, Steph. They looked our way and giggled. I offered to pay but Sandy insisted it had been her invitation. While she dug in her purse I could see Ruthie at the far end of the gym, kneeling on the floor and pulling up duct tape and cords. She'd rolled back the sleeves of her white shirt and was winding the cords around her elbow. I had a strong urge to go help. The thick cords looked heavy and Ruthie was alone. I'd found myself thinking about her a lot lately. I knew the burden she carried, trying to manage the station without Jack. I saw her often canvassing the businesses along Main Street trying to sell ads for the station. Trying to pay back the large loans that had accumulated at the bank. I felt a stab of anger at Wayne Jorgenson. If he hadn't let that account get so far out of line, Ruthie wouldn't be facing the predicament she was. But it was no use wasting my thoughts on Wayne tonight. He'd been warned. He knew exactly what he'd done and that it had better not happen again. Just then Ruthie looked my way. Our eyes met and she gave a quick wave, wiggling her fingertips, almost dropping the coil of cord on her shoulder. I raised my hand, ready to wave back.

"Here we go." Sandy thrust a wobbly paper plate into my raised hand.

I glanced over my shoulder. Ruthie had turned away and was putting the heavy cords and microphone into a case. I had to respect her. It couldn't be easy doing a live broadcast all day by yourself. I knew she had stayed at the café until almost one in the morning helping Vicky. Then she'd been on the air at seven-thirty this morning. I knew. I'd been listening.

"Should we sit over here?" Sandy motioned with her pie plate to the bleachers that lined the gym. A section had been pulled out near Vicky's pie stand for just that purpose. We made our way past the lower level, which seemed to be reserved for those too unsteady to climb any higher. Somewhere near the top Sandy paused. "How's this?"

"Perfect," I said, realizing as I sat that from this vantage point I had a perfect view of the KBRS booth. As Sandy talked I found my eyes wandering over the crowd, always finding their way back to Ruthie.

"After Mom died," Sandy said, sipping her coffee, "Dad got worse and worse. At first we thought he was just lonely, but pretty soon he wasn't even getting out of bed in the morning."

Ruthie was standing on her tiptoes, trying to remove the staples from the KBRS sign that lined the back of the booth. I wished I could reach up there for her. It would be no problem for me at all.

"My sister and I talked it over and decided I should be the one to move back and help him." Her eyes roamed the gym, stopping the same place mine had. "Looks like Ruthie could use some help," Sandy remarked. We watched as Ruthie tugged at a corner of the sign. "Oh, she got it. As I was telling you, my sister has four kids and couldn't just pick up and leave, so it was up to me, being divorced and all. It was easier for me…"

As she talked I found myself praying, "Lord, ease her burden. Give her the strength she needs to go on." I realized as Sandy got up to refill her coffee that I was listening to Sandy but praying for Ruthie.

Ruthie

Why did I feel such a quick stab of jealousy seeing Sandy Quinn and Paul together? I yanked hard at the KBRS sign, but the staples held as though they were made of superglue. I certainly had no dibs on Paul, and Sandy had been nothing but nice to me in all the years I'd known her. "Come onnn…," I muttered as if the sign could hear me. I stood on my tiptoes trying to loosen the upper corner. Even from my awkward position I couldn't keep my eyes from straying to the top of the bleachers where they sat, deep in conversation. Sandy's head was bent toward Paul as if whatever he was saying was the most fascinating thing she'd ever heard. There. The sign came down. I rolled it up carefully. I wasn't planning on being back at Pumpkin Fest next year, but maybe someone would buy the station and they'd need it.

Pretending I was surveying the crowd I looked again at Paul and Sandy. She was gesturing in the air with her hand. Paul was nodding. I suspected they had a lot in common. Sandy had returned to Brewster after spending time away, even if it was just in Carlton. And, like Paul, she had an aging parent who needed a support system. Of course they had a lot to talk about. With a *crack* that echoed through the gym, I stood the sign on end against the back of the booth and started yanking at the skirting around the table.

Why are you so interested in the fact that Paul is talking to Sandy?

I'm not that interested. It's just that he is…he *was* a very important person in my life at one time and I care about him.

Are you sure that's all?

I remembered last night when Vicky, Angie, and I had been rushing around the café kitchen trying to get the pies ready. Vicky had pulled the last pies from the oven, fragrant spices filling the air. As if on cue Dave poked his head around the kitchen door. "Need any tasters?"

"No!" The three of us yelled in unison.

Sam and Paul followed Dave into the kitchen. "You mean there's nothing we can taste?" Dave pouted. Vicky held out a mushy chunk of pumpkin that had somehow escaped the mixing bowl. Dave popped it into his mouth. "Phooey!" He spit it out. "That stuff's not very good without the pie-stuff in it."

Paul stood in the doorway, his hands in the back pockets of his jeans. "We were over at the gym helping get some of the booths set up." Paul looked at me as he spoke, as if he needed to explain to me why he was there. "It seems smaller than it used to back in high school."

"That's because Pumpkin Fest is smaller, buddy." Dave stuck a crumb of piecrust that had fallen on the counter into his mouth. "Brewster doesn't have near the businesses today it did back then."

"No," Paul explained, "I meant the gym. It seems smaller."

I busily wiped the counter, brushing away imaginary crumbs. I wondered if Paul was remembering how his proposal to me had echoed in the silent gym. And how my foolish rejection, "I can't Paul…I just can't," had bounced around, seemingly forever. The gym had felt like a huge, cold cavern that night. No wonder it seemed smaller to him now, filled with the trappings of a city celebration.

"It's probably because you're used to all those big buildings in Chicago." Count on Vicky to offer a logical explanation. She brushed her hands together, looking at Dave. "We'd better get these kids home. They've got school tomorrow, and then I'm counting on their help after school at the pie booth. I'm about done here. Can you take them home? I'll be along in a bit."

"Sure thing." Dave slid one pie into a corner of the counter. "This one's ours," he said, smiling at Vicky.

Angie gave me a knowing look, whispering, "They save a pie just for them. But they let Sam and me have some too."

I nodded, as pleased as Angie that her parents continued their romantic tradition.

"Okay, everybody, let's go." Dave clapped his hands.

"Go on, Ruthie," Vicky said. "You've got to be on the air early, and all I have left is to cover these pies and run a mop over the floor. I'll be right behind you."

Sam and Angie hopped into the cab of Dave's pickup as Dave slid behind the wheel. There wasn't much room left for two adults. "I'll walk," Paul suggested.

"No way." Dave waved him in as though he were driving a bus, not an old pickup with one bench seat. "It's cold out. Get in."

Sam and Angie squished together while I squeezed in beside them. No stretch of the imagination would call Paul heavy, but I knew five inches of seat space wasn't enough. "I'll wait and go with Vicky," I said, moving toward the open door.

"Oh, come on," Dave called, "we can do it. It's only a couple blocks to Paul's house. Everybody suck it in." Angie and Sam inhaled like old asthmatics. Obviously they'd played this game before.

Gamely, Paul slid in. Somehow in the arranging I ended up with one leg on the seat and the other draped over Paul's knee. The kids let out their breath in a loud huff as Paul closed the door. "Here we go." Dave shifted into gear and we bounced down the alley behind the café, our version of the Brewster Hillbillies. One big happy family.

The cab of the pickup had been ice cold but our five kitchen-warmed bodies quickly fogged the windows. Dave rubbed away a small spot, enough so he could see to drive.

"This is cozy," Angie said.

She was right. It was.

When Dave pulled to a stop in front of Paul's house, Paul pulled at the door latch. The door flew open and he tumbled sideways. I grabbed at his arm, keeping him steady enough so he could get a foot out to balance himself. The kids giggled. "Thanks for the ride," he said looking at Dave. Then he looked at me, one side of his mouth turning up. He didn't need to say a word to send happiness coursing through me. Ever since the night I'd cut my finger, there'd been an easiness between us that was hard to explain but felt right.

The sides of my mouth curved up all on their own.

"See you tomorrow." Paul smiled back.

"Yeah, buddy, see you tomorrow." Dave shifted into drive.

"Bye, Uncle Paul," Sam called. "See ya."

We drove off, and I closed my eyes. I knew I was the only one who'd noticed that Paul had been looking directly into *my* eyes when he'd said, "See you tomorrow."

For the first time in years I'd been looking forward to Pumpkin Fest.

⤳

Sam came barreling to a stop in front of the KBRS booth. "Did you see that Uncle Paul and Miss Quinn are eating pie together?"

"I did," I answered, my voice feeling as fake as my smile.

"I introduced 'em," Sam said, pulling his whole conniving body up tall. "She's not married and he's not married, so—"

"I'm not either," I interrupted, wondering why I was having this conversation with a fifth grader.

"Yeah, but, you're already my aunt."

Perfect logic for a kid. I sighed.

"Gotta go. Mom said she needs help." Sam dashed off, making a sharp curve by the candy dish sitting on the table of the drugstore booth.

I knew I should hurry and get my equipment put away. I'd promised Vicky I'd help serve pie as soon as I signed off the air. I wished now that I'd asked my high school helper, Mike, to come pick up the equipment and take it back to the station. I knew he'd be showing up at Pumpkin Fest soon; it seemed everyone in town was already here. But Mike had already missed most of the fun, and I hated to ask him to miss any more. Well, I'd just have to run this stuff out to my car by myself. I hoisted the cables onto my shoulder, tucked the KBRS sign under my arm, and headed outside into the cool night air.

There was something peaceful about being outside the celebration. Hearing the muffled sounds of music and voices drifting toward the three-quarter moon that hung high over town. Gravel from the parking lot crunched under my feet. I took a deep breath, crisp air replacing the body-warmed air I'd been breathing all day. It wasn't always this nice for Pumpkin Fest. I recalled one year when I'd lugged equipment out here in a snowstorm. But tonight bright stars were suspended above my head. The same stars Paul and I used to admire when he'd drive me home after winter basketball games.

The same stars you wouldn't be able to see if you lived in a big city. The jarring thought bit through my momentary sense of calm.

Quit it, I told myself. There's nothing wrong with enjoying this night.

I have learned wherever I am to be content. Vicky's words of last night replaced my bitter thought from a moment before. She was right; her words did make me feel calm.

Not her *words. Apostle Paul's.*

Well, it didn't matter whose words they were, for a fleeting moment they had restored my sense of well-being in this night... until I thought of Sandy Quinn and Paul sitting so cozy atop the bleachers inside.

When he'd said, "See you tomorrow," it had seemed as though it were some sort of promise. Now I realized he'd meant it, as Sam would put it, "See ya." As in, "See ya around." Not, see *you*. As in, *personally.*

I opened my car door and threw the cables in, tossing the poster onto the back dash where it bounced against the glass and fell onto the floor. Who cared? I slammed the door and marched back to the gym, a woman with a mission. Clear out and move on. I yanked open the door.

"Need help?" Paul stood just inside holding the next two boxes I'd planned to carry out. His two simple words were a pin, popping my balloon of jealousy and self-pity.

"Oh hi!" I said, sounding as though this were the first time I'd laid eyes on him all night. A sudden, warm relief flowed through my body. I didn't have to do this all by myself. "Help would be good." My voice faltered and I cleared my throat. "That cold air did a number on my vocal cords," I said, but I knew better.

In one more trip we had all the equipment in my car. I pushed the lock button, even though Brewster had a crime rate of next to none. However, you never knew when some kid might think he needed a microphone, and goodness knows, I didn't have money to replace anything. The muffled sounds of celebration wrapped around us.

"Thanks," I said, turning to Paul. "A lot." I pushed my hands into the back pockets of my jeans, not wanting to move from my spot. "I'd better get back in there and help Vicky."

"Yeah," Paul answered. "I said I'd help too." He didn't move. He just stood there, staring into my eyes. "You did a good job broadcasting today."

"You listened?"

He nodded, not taking his eyes off me. "I had the radio on in my office. You made me want to run right over." He smiled.

I smiled back.

Three people walked through the parking lot toward the gym, their soft conversation mingled into the night. "Well, uh—" I scuffed my foot across the gravel. "I imagine Vicky needs me."

"Would you like to have some pie with me later?" Paul's words came quickly. "After things slow down? I never did get a taste last night." He chuckled softly.

I thought of the piece he'd just eaten with Sandy. "Sure," I answered. "If there's any left."

"I'll hide some," he said, looking very serious.

Slowly, side by side, in comfortable silence we walked back to the gym. I highly doubted Paul knew the story of Dave hiding a whole pie the night he'd proposed to Vicky. After all, I hadn't known about it until Angie's revelation last night.

I think it's romantic, Angie had said.

Funny, suddenly I did too.

Jack

Sheesh, I didn't know what Doug was making such a big fuss about. So I'd said a couple words on-air I shouldn't have. You'd think it was a federal crime or something. Howard Stern did it all the time.

"Actually, Jack, it *is* against federal regulations." Doug Sommers picked up his pen. "There are seven words we're not allowed to say on the air. I thought you knew that." I did know it. Marv had told me. But he didn't tell me the exact words. So I'd guessed wrong. "Shock-jocks do it all the time," I protested. "How do they get by with it?" I couldn't believe he'd called me into his office for something this petty.

"We could get socked with a heavy fine. Those stations are in much larger markets and, frankly, they make so much money they don't care. We do." He jotted something on a piece of paper. A note in my file? I hoped not. Doug dropped his pen on the desk. "You're good, Jack. Don't blow it for this station or yourself." He sat still, his gaze firm on mine. Okay, I got the message. "There's something else I wanted to talk to you about—"

"Doug—" The cute little receptionist I'd talked to this morning peeked around the door. What was her name? Oh, well.

"Hey, babe." I winked.

Her eyes rolled up. "Doug, Mr. Lambert is on line two." She handed him a note, walking by me on her way out without even a nod.

Doug held up a finger. "This will only take a minute." He punched the button for line two. "Harry, how're you doing?"

As he talked I gazed around his office. The walls were lined with records. The big old kind my folks used to play. Silver. Gold. Platinum. Awards Doug had won from record companies over the years for helping a song, or an album, rise to the top. In between, on whatever wall space was left, were photos of Doug with radio personalities and rock stars who had passed through Minneapolis. His office looked like a rock star's rec room. Not that I'd ever been in one, but I'd seen photos. Yup, I was going to have an office like this someday.

Doug hung up the phone and picked up his pen. "Jack, I wanted to let you know a couple things…" I didn't like the tone of his voice or the tapping of his pen. I shifted in my chair, grasping the arms as if they were a life preserver. "We just got the new book in and our numbers are down."

At least this time I knew what he was talking about. The book. The Arbitron ratings. Radio's bible. Every station lived or died by "the book." From the tone of Doug's voice it sounded as though KMIN was dying. He opened the booklet lying on his desk. It looked more like a slim magazine than a force that could get a disc jockey fired. I swallowed hard. Doug tapped his pen down the page. "I'm not blaming you for these numbers, Jack. You haven't been here long enough for us to gauge the results of your time slot from this."

I let go of the chair arms. Okay, I wasn't going to have to flip burgers after all.

He went on, "But I've got to tell you our numbers are down across the board. They have been for almost a year now. People just aren't listening to the kind of music this station broadcasts. From the looks of things," he tapped the pages again, "they're looking for music with more substance. Not the heavy-metal stuff we play. Station management is looking to switch formats." He closed the book. "Just thought I'd let you know."

Was that it? New format I could live with, no job I couldn't. I almost laughed out loud. "I've got years of experience with country." Thought I'd better put in whatever plug for myself I could. "I love country," I lied.

"Glad to hear you're flexible, Jack." Doug stood. "I'll keep you posted."

I relaxed. At least I wasn't going to have to slink back to Brewster and try to get back on Ruthie's good side.

"My name's Jack and I'm back!" The crowd cheered as I slipped behind the mike after my break. "Is everybody having fun?" Hoots and whistles filled the Backstreet Bar. "Are you ready to par-tee?" Everyone screamed. This gig was going to be a breeze. Of course, most New Year's parties were. "Here's a song to help you get trashed." I punched a button and cranked up the volume, congratulating myself for having a job that was such a blast.

"Buy you a drink?" A gorgeous blonde pushed an amber-colored shot into my hand. Not my first of the night.

I tilted my head, draining it in a swallow. "Sure," I said, after it was gone.

She laughed. "Okay, I get it." She crooked her finger at the bartender, pointing to my empty glass. A server hurried over with another shot, and the blonde slipped her a ten. "Watch out for us," she said, her voice high-pitched and scratchy. Like bad feedback from a mike. "So," she said, leaning a bare arm across the CD deck on the table, "how do you get a job like this?"

"Good looks," I said, giving her a wink. I knew her type. Fascinated by a disc jockey who could rev up a crowd. Wanting in on the fame and the fun. With a voice like that, this gal didn't have a chance. Why dash her hopes? If it was fun she wanted, I could show her some. "Meet me on my next break," I said. Over her shoulder was a skinhead-type kid waiting to talk to me. He didn't look old enough to be here, but that wasn't my job. "What's up, man?"

The kid shrugged one shoulder. "Wanted to talk to you about music, man."

Musicman. I hadn't thought of my old nickname in ages. I looked at this kid. Except for baggy pants that barely hung on his hips, I could see some of my younger self in him. Head bobbing in time with the music. Eyes squinted as his ears tried to pick out backbeats. That had been me a whole lot of years ago when nothing had mattered but the music. What had happened?

The real world, that's what happened. I'd gotten into this job for the music. I stayed in it for the music. But the trouble was that disc jockeys barely listened to the music they played anymore. Everything at KMIN was on computer. A touch on the computer screen and the next song was set to play. In fact, the deejays didn't even pick the music. That, too, was done by random selection by computer software. It seemed all I had to do was sit in front of a computer screen and monitor what had already been done. Sure, there were voice tracks for commercials to lay down and weather updates to record. But none of that involved music.

Even deejaying in the Backstreet Bar was not about music…it was about money. Forty bucks an hour. In cash. Not reported. All mine. The gig made a nice little supplement for my casino runs.

At KMIN I was making double what I'd earned at KBRS, but I didn't have a dime more at the end of the month. Half of the dump I shared with Marv was more than my rent in Brewster, not to mention gas for the commute. And the mall was a great place to stop on my way to work. A guy had to look hip for gigs like this. Then there were beers after work. It was important to get my name out there, let people know what station I was on. Drum up listeners. Still, it seemed I should have something left to show for my hard work.

Well, at least gigs like this helped supplement the old cash flow. And part of the package was chatting up customers who wanted to talk to the deejay. Although I'd rather be talking to the blonde than this skinhead. "What's new?"

"Have ya heard the new CD by Hitch?" The kid's eyes glowed. "Man, that third track is somethin'. You should hear the licks comin' from the bass."

Hitch? It sounded more like a farm part from Brewster than the name of a group. Half these groups were gone before they started. There was no way a guy could keep up. Especially when the station gave us a preselected list of what to play. Not much chance of catching the latest that way. This kid would be amazed at what I could tell him about the music business. I wasn't so sure I wanted to disillusion him at the start of a whole new year. I'd have to bluff. "That so?"

"Their drummer used to play with The Blue Penz."

Never heard of them either, but I had to give the kid credit—it was obvious he loved music.

Like you used to. Remember?

Yeah, I remembered. But a guy had to make a living. The kid continued to talk as I reloaded the CD system for the last hour of this gig. It would be the hour after midnight. One hour to usher in the New Year. I wanted to pump 'em up with music, then, just before closing, bring the crowd down enough so they wouldn't beg for more. Give me enough time to get to the casino. Maybe tonight I'd hit it big. Then it would be a happy new year.

"What're your favorite groups?" The kid had moved closer to hear my answer.

Favorite groups? I couldn't remember the last time I'd listened to something a machine hadn't picked. Favorite groups? My favorite groups were the people sitting around the blackjack tables. I squirmed in my seat. This was embarrassing. Musicman didn't know music.

"Ten...nine...eight..." The crowd began counting down the seconds. I looked over the kid's head and motioned to the bartender with two fingers. Make it a double. I needed a drink. Or two.

"I got a girl to kiss," the kid said. "Happy New Year." He backed off. "Check out Hitch if you get a chance."

"Will do." I'd never see the kid again, anyway. The crowd screamed. "HAPPY NEW YEAR!" I yelled into the mike over the sounds of sappy "Auld Lang Syne."

"Hitch," the kid mouthed, pointing his index fingers at me as he moved away. He then took one finger and pointed it at the ceiling.

Whatever that was supposed to mean.

I could see his upraised index finger weaving through the crowd. I looked up just in case I wasn't getting something. Nothing there but ceiling tile.

Whatever.

With one hand the bartender sat two drinks on the edge of my table. Then added a third. "From her," he said, nodding at the scratchy-voiced blonde. "You sure you can handle this?"

I wasn't sure if he meant the blonde or the booze. But it didn't matter because the answer was the same either way. "No problem, man. No problem."

Paul

"Happy New Year!" The staff at the bank called out their good-byes. We'd closed the lobby doors an hour early to give everyone a chance to finish up the bookkeeping tasks associated with the end of the year and then get home to their celebrations. They were in a good mood. Looking forward to whatever the night held.

"Happy New Year," I called back, wondering if it would be. I punched the "off" button on my computer. I knew I'd be back tomorrow to do year-end work. In the banking business December thirty-first meant end-of-the-year reports. It was hard to believe the year was ending. It seemed I'd barely moved back and already hunting season had passed. Thanksgiving and Christmas too.

Happy New Year. Maybe if I said it enough it would happen. I'd never been one to celebrate wildly, but I always enjoyed doing something special to mark a new year. However, in the two years since Mia had been gone, I'd spent New Year's Eve alone. Even Corinne couldn't drag me out of my condo last year. She'd attended a get-together without me. Funny, though. I was finding myself looking forward to the "friends only" party Vicky and Dave were giving at the café. I knew Ruthie would be there.

It didn't make any sense, this growing attraction I had for Ruth. Neither professionally, nor personally. Professionally I knew it wasn't good to mix friendship and business. In fact, there were rules that prevented a bank officer from giving loans to family members or preferential treatment to friends. While our business dealings had been strictly business, excepting that near-kiss fiasco, somehow I felt I had more on the line with Ruthie than a pure business transaction. At least I was hoping I did.

Ever since Pumpkin Fest I'd found myself admiring her for carrying on alone. Running the station by herself as if she'd done it that way all along. She always sounded upbeat on the air, and I noticed on the loan reports she was making weekly payments on her loans. The amount wasn't much considering the debt, but I couldn't help but notice how hard she was trying.

I tapped the remaining papers on my desk into a neat pile. Even though I knew the stack contained several days' worth of work, it gave the appearance of starting the new year with a clean slate. I looked out the window. The wind had picked up. Snow was swirling, curling itself under my VW. I'd better get going. I shrugged into my heavy topcoat.

Personally, I knew Ruthie and I had a long history together that had ended badly. Very badly. I knew our breakup had spurred me on to a life I'd never dreamed of, and a faith I hadn't tested before. But every time I saw her I could sense her unease about our past. I was positive many folks in Brewster recalled the circumstances too. One thing about a small town, your past never really was—past, that is. But I'd learned all too well that *all* things could be forgiven. Not forgotten, but forgiven. If only I could help Ruthie understand. I'd been praying for a chance to do just that.

The bank door clicked shut behind me. I pushed on it, checking to make sure it was locked, then high-stepped through the snow to my car.

No, this attraction I had to Ruthie didn't make any sense at all. But that didn't seem to matter to my heart.

Happy New Year.

I hoped it would be.

Ruthie

"Happy New Year, Angie." I hugged my niece. I noticed she was wearing the sparkly bracelet I'd given her for Christmas. The one I'd found on a sale rack in Target. I'd tried to make up in creativity what I didn't have in money. "Happy New Year, Sam." He gave me a high five, then allowed me to pull him into an embrace. It wasn't midnight yet, but it still felt good to pass out hugs. This simple New Year's party was a far cry from the bar scene Jack had insisted on over the past years. It felt good not to reek of smoke and stale beer.

The front door of the café swung open, sending a swirl of snow into the entryway of the café. Ben Pearson held the door against the howling wind as his wife, Cindy, and their daughter, Steph, ran into the café. Ben eased himself inside. "Looks like a blizzard out there." Ben stamped his feet. He was a slim duplicate of his twin brother, Kenny.

"Hold this." Cindy thrust a crockpot into my hands. "Just a minute." She reached into the deep pockets of her parka and pulled out a tangled cord. "Here's an extension cord to plug it in." She slipped out of her heavy coat and tossed it on the growing stack of coats in the booth nearest the door of the café. "I hope we make it home tonight. It's getting bad out there." Her cheeks were bright red from the short distance she'd had to walk outside from their pickup, and she rubbed at them with her hands. "Okay, I can take that now."

"That's all right, I'll get it." I carried the crockpot filled with miniature meatballs to the food table. I was glad to have something do to. Jack and I had never made much of an effort to make friends in Brewster because we were always thinking that *next* year we'd be moving on. I knew these people, but not well enough to feel like a part of their group.

Vicky had closed the café at nine, inviting a small group of their friends, and kids, to join us after kitchen cleanup. Two tables near the back of the café were covered with potluck hors d'oeuvres. I'd brought my specialty. Cream cheese flattened into a circle, covered with cocktail sauce, and topped with a small can of drained shrimp. No sense overtaxing my cooking abilities. The tables from the center of the café had been pulled to the sides, leaving the middle open for a rousing game of charades. Guys against girls.

"Okay, Sam, here's our chance to catch up." Paul clapped his hands twice. "It's all up to you, buddy." Sam drew a slip of paper from the soup bowl filled with choices. "I've never heard of this," he groaned. Vicky glanced over his shoulder then whispered into his ear.

"No fair," Ben called, joining the game.

"It's okay," Dave said. "She's helping our side."

"Oh, yeah," Ben amended. "Go-ooo, Vicky."

Sam tilted his chin toward the ceiling, eyes closed, thinking. He nodded to his mom, who started timing. Sam cupped his hands around his mouth.

"Song," Paul said.

Sam nodded and held up three fingers.

"Three words." Paul was leaning forward on the edge of his chair, concentrating.

Sam held up one finger.

"First word."

Sam nodded and pointed to his waist.

"Belt," Paul called.

Sam shook his head.

"Waist? No. Uh—"

Sam tapped at his belt.

"Leather?"

Sam shook his head and held up two fingers.

"Second word?"

Sam nodded and pointed to his eyes.

"Eye!" Paul yelled.

Sam nodded, motioning with his hands as though he were pulling taffy.

"Longer?" Paul asked. "Come on, guys, help me out here. Eyes?"

Sam shook his head. Continuing his pulling motion.

"Eyes?" Ben offered the word again halfheartedly.

"I already said that. Come on, we're getting creamed." Paul put his hands on his knees. He spoke rapidly. "Okay, we know the second word is something to do with eyes." Sam nodded vigorously. "Go on to the third word."

Sam pointed at Vicky.

"Mom?" Paul shouted. "Woman?"

Sam ran over and pointed at Angie, then Steph.

"Girls?"

Sam nodded as though his head would come off, chopping at the air, then holding up one finger.

"Girl," Paul called.

"Yes!" Sam shouted. "Ooopps." He clamped his hand over his mouth. "Sorry."

"Eye. Girl. Eye. Girl." Paul repeated the words.

Sam held up one finger.

"First word." Paul was sitting up straight now.

Again Sam pointed to his belt. His eyes widened. He ran over and pointed at Dave's shoes, then at the top of the table.

"Brown?" Ben asked.

Paul jumped in the air. "'Brown Eyed Girl'!"

Sam jumped, too, thrusting his fist into the air. "Yes!"

Paul's blue eyes flew to my brown eyes. "Brown Eyed Girl." Our song. Or what had been our song. He sat down, his eyes glued to mine. Even after all these years, it was plain to see he remembered as well as I did.

Cindy Pearson hummed a few bars. "I love that old song," she said.

So had I. It was old even back when Paul had claimed the song as ours. Every time it came on the radio, he would turn up the volume and sing as though he were Van Morrison and I was someone who would never break his heart. The way he was looking at me now, it seemed he still thought of me that way.

It was the same way he'd looked at me at Pumpkin Fest. Right before Vicky poured herself a cup of coffee and flopped down on the bleachers beside us. My heart had plummeted. I hadn't realized how much I'd been looking forward to sharing time with Paul. I'd brushed off the disappointment. It was probably best that Vicky joined us. No sense in getting too friendly with him or anyone else, for that matter. I planned to be out of Brewster before long, anyway.

The two months since Pumpkin Fest had flown by. I was now two months closer to leaving Brewster and feeling much better due to the flurry of extra advertising leading up to Christmas. While it certainly wasn't enough to pay down my loans, the extra income did help keep me caught up with current bills. Speaking of which, the BMI statement would be on my desk soon. The license fee all stations had to pay for the right to play music. We'd borrowed the money to pay it last year. I doubted that would happen this year.

What would happen this year? As hard as I was working, the station wasn't even holding its own. It was one thing to leave Brewster because of an opportunity. It was a whole other thing to leave because of failure. I vowed that would not be the case in this new year. I was going to make the station succeed. I had to.

"Whose turn is it?" I looked at Vicky. Charades was one way to keep my mind off my troubles.

"It's Steph's." Vicky held out the bowl. "Pick one."

Steph looked in the bowl. "There's only one left."

"Then I guess that would be yours."

Steph looked at her slip and groaned, pacing past the café coffeepots while she thought. A couple of the guys walked over to the food table. Steph looked at her slip again. "I can't think of anything."

"Tell you what," Vicky said, "let's take a break. We're so far ahead the guys can't possibly win."

Dave and Paul booed.

"What was yours?" Sam asked Steph. She showed him the slip. *"The Encyclopedia?"* He sounded amazed. At least I wouldn't have had to worry about that conjuring up any old memories. "Good idea about the break, Mom." He headed to the food table along with Steph and Angie. I fell in line.

"Okay, listen up everybody." Vicky raised her voice. "While you're getting your food I want you to be thinking about the next game. It's almost midnight, and I want everyone to think about what was the best thing that happened this past year and what you're looking forward to next year."

Being gone. I didn't have to think about that at all. And the best thing about this year? That it would be my last year in Brewster, of course. I knew I couldn't say either of those things here. At least I had time to think while I filled my plate. I scooped up two of Cindy's meatballs.

You know, Ruthie, you've spent half your life wishing you were somewhere else. Have you ever thought what your life might be like if you tried to appreciate where you are?

I cut a wedge of the shrimp spread I'd made.

What? I should repeat after Vicky, "I have learned wherever I am to be content"? Forget that. I'll never be content in Brewster, and saying a few Bible-sounding words won't change that fact.

I added three crackers to my plate, thinking back to the night of Pumpkin Fest when, just for a moment, I had felt content. The cool air, the clear sky, people who had known me since I'd been born filling the gym behind me. *Wherever I am...*

You were in Brewster that night and you felt content.

Ha! One night. Or rather one moment of one night. That hardly counts for anything.

Maybe if you stopped and thought about it, you might find Brewster has a lot to offer.

Stopped? Thought? No. I couldn't stop and I wouldn't think. I'd learned there were some events in life that if you couldn't get over them, you just pretended you had. I plopped two cocktail wieners on my plate and a hunk of mystery cheese. If I had ever had a future in Brewster, I wouldn't feel as discontented as I did. No, this would be the year I made the changes I should have made years ago.

"Okay, everybody, gather round." Vicky sat cross-legged on the floor, her plate of food in front of her. She popped a chip into her mouth. "I'll start. The best thing about this past year would have to be my family. Dave. The kids."

Almost in unison Angie and Sam groaned.

Vicky swatted a hand their direction but kept talking. "I can't imagine what my life would be like without them and, well…" Her voice faltered and she took a deep breath. "Anyway, the best thing about the coming year is that we have a whole new year to be together."

Dave acted as though he couldn't find a comfortable spot to sit on the floor. Shifting around, moving his plate, blinking rapidly.

What would it be like to have someone love you like that?

"I'm next!" Sam raised his hand as if waiting for a teacher to call on him. When he realized he had no competition, he lowered his arm. "The best thing was playing basketball in the driveway with my dad and Uncle Paul. Angie too. Paul and me are way ahead."

"Are not," Angie said.

"Are too," countered Sam. "Right, Paul?"

Paul shrugged, a half smile climbing his face. "What can I say? When you've got a great partner…" He pointed a finger at Sam. Sam pointed back, like some sort of guy hug, without touching, of course.

"Paul, you go next," Vicky directed.

"This is easy for me." Paul looked around the circle. "The best part of this past year was moving back to Brewster. I know some of you get tired of small-town life, but believe me, you've got the best life in the world right here."

Oh, please. Do tell.

As if he'd heard me, Paul answered, "Good people. A safe place to live. No commute to get to work." Some of the guys chuckled. "Hunting a mile out of town. A grocery store five blocks from anywhere in town." Now the women laughed. "You don't know what some people would pay to have this stuff. The only trouble is, money can't buy it." He stretched his legs out in front of him, leaning back on his hands. "The only way you can have it is to live here. And now

I do." The room was quiet as Paul's obvious love of Brewster filtered around.

Well, now, what do you have to say to that?

Obviously the guy hadn't been back long enough to remember how it really was. It'd get to him eventually. Then he'd be wishing he were back in Chicago.

"And what about the coming year?" Vicky asked.

Paul continued leaning back, as if he had cornered the market on contentment. Again his eyes swept the circle, ending with me. "I'm looking forward to getting to know most of you a lot better."

He'd said, "most of you," but the way he was staring, it felt like he meant only me. I flipped my hair off my neck. Gosh, it was warm in here.

The game continued around the circle. I wracked my brain, trying to come up with something acceptable to say. It was hard to think with Paul's eyes meeting mine every time I looked his way.

"Ruthie, what about you?" Vicky asked.

I took a deep breath, buying time. "Well, I guess—"

"Ten...nine...eight..." Angie had started the countdown to midnight. My favorite niece.

People straggled to their feet, looking at the clock, counting the seconds out loud. "Three...two...one. Happy New Year!" Dave and Vicky fell into each other's arms. Angie gave Sam an awkward hug then turned to embrace Steph. It was hard to miss the way Ben Pearson had practically thrown Cindy over backward and was kissing her loudly. The others laughed then started trading polite hugs with their friends. I picked up some of the plates from the floor and set them on the food table. Brushed crumbs from around the cracker basket. Hid a limp piece of celery under a lettuce leaf. Even when I'd been with Jack, I'd always hated this part of New Year's. It felt awkward and forced, hugging half-strangers in a smoke-filled bar. Kissing Jack happy-new-year when I knew darn well the new year wouldn't be any happier than the past one if we spent it in Brewster.

I glanced at my watch. I doubted I could leave gracefully at twelve-o-one. The way I figured it, I had another twenty minutes before I could truthfully say I had to get home. I had to be on-air tomorrow when the sun came up. For something to do, I stirred Cindy's meatballs.

"Can I help?" Paul stood at my elbow, looking as out of place as I felt.

"Nope," I said, relieved for the company. "I've got dibs on this job."

Paul chuckled, then pick up a carrot. "Does anyone really like New Year's parties?"

"Only if you're ten and get to stay up past your bedtime." I moved the cheese tray an inch to the left, then moved it back again.

Paul reached in front of me to grab a piece of cheese but instead of standing back up, he turned his head my way and whispered, "Wanna ditch this party?" He had a gleam in his eye. "Go drive around in a snowstorm?"

Immediately I thought of the other stormy nights Paul and I had driven around Brewster. Plowing his old VW through snowbanks. Laughing when we'd get hung up on a high spot. Flagging down Dave, or whoever else happened to be driving around, to help push us out.

I understood why Paul would want to brave a snowstorm again. There was a sense of adventure about bucking snowbanks that even mild-mannered adults needed sometimes. What I didn't understand was why he suddenly wanted to leave this group of friends he'd just said made his year complete. But the way he was staring at me, his eyes all crinkled at the corners, well, there was no way in the world I was going to say no. "Only if I can drive," I said softly, a conspiratorial grin sliding onto my face. "My coat's in the kitchen." Just in case anybody was listening I added loudly, "I'm going to carry some of these dirty dishes to the sink." I still didn't understand how Paul could treat me as though I'd never hurt him, as though there might still be something special between us. All of a sudden I wanted to find out.

"I'll pick you up around back." He walked away from me as if we'd never talked. The perfect spy. Paul walked to Vicky and gave her a hug as I gathered up dishes. "Thanks for the party," he said.

"You're not leaving," Vicky protested. "We've got more games to play."

"Sorry," he said, faking a huge yawn. "It's been a long day."

I made my getaway into the kitchen while Paul played decoy for Vicky's watchful eye.

With the headlights off, Paul pulled up to the back door of the café. As if we were accomplishing a Chinese fire drill, he ran around to the passenger side while I jumped behind the wheel. A gust of snow followed us into the car.

"Let's go," he whispered.

"Okay," I whispered back, pushing in the clutch and shifting into reverse. Driving Paul's new VW was like riding a bike; I hadn't forgotten what he'd taught me all those years ago. I'd just lost my touch. We jerked down the alley, two riders in an ornery bull. I depressed the clutch again, trying to find a better gear, then realized we were already at the street. I stepped on the gas but without a gear to grab, the car roared uselessly. I shifted into first and we popped into the street, a bull released from his chute. A thick blanket of snow had covered the ice-packed layer below. The car did a three-sixty then came to a stop.

"Whoa," Paul said, then grinned. "Think you can do that again?"

"Sure," I replied. "That was pure skill. Couldn't you tell? I drive for NASCAR in my free time." The side street was deserted, thick snow falling onto a heavy blanket already covering the ground. I shifted into first, releasing the clutch carefully. "One good thing about Brewster is not having to worry about traffic."

Did you notice, you just thought of something good about this town?

Increasing our speed, I shifted into second. "Where would you like to go?"

"Drive around town. Let's see who's still out tonight." He tuned the radio to an oldies station out of Carlton. I'd noticed it had been set to KBRS. Interesting.

"Hang on," I warned, pushing the gas pedal hard. A large snow-drift blocked the road. The car faltered, then bucked its way through. I downshifted.

"Good job." Paul tapped my hand on the stick shift, making me wish I had taken off my gloves. "Looks like the Magners are at Dan and Jan's." Sure enough, the Magners' Crown Victoria was parked on the street in front of Dan Jordan's. "Drive past my mom's house. She was having some of her bridge club over. I want to see if they're still there."

There were three cars in front of Paul's house. "I hope they don't have to have a slumber party," I commented as we bucked through another snowdrift.

"They drive big cars. I think they'll be fine. I worry more about them walking out to their cars in this storm. It's icy under the snow." Paul turned the heater down a notch. "I may have to look at getting a different vehicle. This VW is low to the ground and light too. I suppose a four-wheel-drive would make more sense in North Dakota. But I don't know," he tapped at the dash, "I've got a 'thing' for VWs. If you know what I mean."

I knew exactly what he meant. Ever since he'd taught me to drive that tan, beat-up '65 Beetle of his when we were freshmen, I'd had a 'thing' for VWs too. That old car held a lot of memories. "Remember the time we were going to drive out to the lake? It was in the spring." I remembered how rain had poured down on the car as Paul and I splashed our way over the gravel road leading to Brush Lake four miles out of Brewster. Three miles out of town we'd gotten stuck, practically up to the floorboards. "What were we thinking?"

"Obviously we weren't." Paul laughed. "I tried to push us out and ended up looking like mud-man."

"Then we walked to that farm. I can't remember whose it was, but he got his tractor to pull us out."

"And before I got home that night, my folks had already heard about it."

"Mine too."

Our eyes met at the shared memory. A connection between us time had not erased. I looked back to the road, remembering a time when Brewster had been filled with adventure. When had it changed? When had I changed?

I swung the car onto the highway that ran through town. How many times had we driven up and down Main Street, as we called it? Hundreds? More like thousands. It was the place to see and be seen. If anything were going to happen, it would happen here. Back then it seemed this street had been paved with possibilities. Not simply a highway out of town. What had happened?

"Turn here." Paul pointed to my left. "Someone talked to me about putting up a building in this area in the spring. Might as well look at the spot."

I made a sharp turn onto the side street leading to Brewster's small warehouse district. Two blocks of steel-sided buildings housed a small manufacturing plant, a car repair shop, and several storage buildings. It was plain to see we were the first vehicle to drive this street since it started snowing. Snow flew off the bumper as I down-shifted, trying to gain in traction what I couldn't do with speed.

"Step on it," Paul urged.

"I am," I said, shifting into second and stomping on the acceler-ator. We lurched through the thick snow, managing to plow our way to the middle of the second block. The car came to a slow halt, then died. We sat staring out the car window at a sheet of white, the street-light on the corner barely visible.

"Good idea, huh?" Paul said.

"Fabulous," I replied, restarting the car. Already the cold from outside seeped into the interior. The car hummed to life, crept for-ward a whole inch, and stopped. I looked down at the loafers I was wearing. I hadn't planned on climbing snowdrifts tonight, just run-ning from the café into a warm car and then into Vicky's house.

"I'll push," Paul said zipping his parka to his neck. His footgear didn't look a whole lot better than mine. At least he had thick socks on. "Here goes." He dived out of the car into the swirling snow. I shifted into first, rolling down the window a crack so I could hear

Paul's directions. "Hit it!" he called. I stomped on the accelerator. The car rocked forward, then back into place. "Again!" The car rocked unproductively for several moments, wheels spinning. Finally Paul jumped back in the car. "We're stuck," he declared.

"Brilliant deduction, Sherlock." The cold air that accompanied him into the car seeped through my wool coat, causing a shiver to run down my back. I pulled the collar of my coat up. "Now what?"

Paul turned the heater on high and settled into the seat. "We sit tight and wait for the bars to close. I'm sure some other fools will think driving around in a snowstorm is as good of an idea as I did." Eyebrows raised, he looked at me out of the corner of his eyes, a wry smile creeping onto his face. "Good thing I filled up the gas tank before I went to the party, huh?"

"Good thing they improved the heaters in these Bugs. Remember your old one? That heater seemed like it was run by a hamster on a wheel." How many nights had we driven around scraping frost from the inside of Paul's car windows? At the time it had seemed like fun. Tonight I was thankful for the new and improved version. I settled in for the duration. Paul turned up the volume on the radio. Van Morrison was singing. It wasn't "Brown Eyed Girl," but the familiar sound of his voice automatically turned my head toward Paul's. Our eyes locked. It was déjà vu with almost twenty years in between. When the last notes of the song faded away, he turned down the volume.

"I didn't forget," he said.

"Neither did I." My voice was a whisper. I hadn't forgotten any of it. The good or the bad. Especially the bad.

"I'm so sorry," I suddenly blurted, apologizing in three simple words for almost twenty years of guilt. For cruel words spoken in immaturity. For regret I couldn't undo. Big warm tears fell from my eyes.

"I know," he said gently, taking my hand and pulling the glove from my fingers before wrapping his cold hand around mine. I could sense he knew exactly what I was saying. "You're forgiven."

His words made me cry all the harder. The shame of what I'd done felt as cold as the blizzard raging outside. "I don't know how—"

I gasped for breath, "—you can forgive me for that. It was so mean and so—so wrong."

Paul let go of my hand and put his arm around my shoulder, pulling me close to him in an awkward embrace between the bucket seats. I scooted over, resting my wet face against his soft parka.

Tears continued to flow. "I've felt…terrible…for almost twenty years." My voice sounded like a scratchy record with a jumping needle.

"Oh, Ruthie." Paul hugged me to his chest, his voice full. "Do you think you're the only person who has ever done something foolish? Ever hurt someone? I forgave you so long ago you probably wouldn't believe it."

"You…did?" I spoke into his coat, my voice muffled.

"Um-hmm, I did," he said. I felt as though a great weight was being lifted from my chest. "Do you have time to listen to a story?" He stroked my hair.

I nodded into his parka. "Unless the city snowplow makes rounds at one in the morning." My tears continued to flow, but my breathing had calmed.

His hand settled on my shoulder and he began to talk. "I want to tell you about something foolish I did." He breathed deeply, as though preparing himself for a long journey. When he spoke his voice was soft. "There's a Bible verse I found two years ago, after Mia and Jenny died, that helped me—helped me forgive myself." That was the first time I'd ever heard Paul say their names. Mia and Jenny. I'd imagined any wife of his to be stuck up and cold. Someone who wouldn't like me. Someone I wouldn't like. But the tender way he'd said their names made me realize Paul could never love someone like that. My throat filled with more tears as he went on. "The verse goes something like, 'Please, Lord, don't hold against me the sin I've so foolishly committed.' You see, Ruthie, people have been doing foolish things since the beginning of time…including me."

He paused, his breathing uneven. When he spoke again his voice was thick. "I'm sure you heard that Mia and Jenny were killed in a plane crash." I nodded, my head rubbing against his parka. "You knew

I was in the plane, too, didn't you?" So that scar on his forehead *was* from the accident. "What most people don't know is that I was the pilot of the plane."

"You?" My heart started hammering.

Except for the swirling wind, silence filled the car. Now it was his turn to nod, his chin lightly brushing against my hair. "Yeah, me," he said as if two words held the weight of the world.

"What happened?"

"A foolish mistake," he said. "My foolish mistake." His hand rubbed against my coat as though he were trying to sooth himself with the repetitive motion. "I'd rented a plane to fly us to a lake cabin in Minnesota for a week of vacation. Jenny was just a few months old and we had her in a car seat in the back of the plane. Mia sat back there with her. We were leaving to go home. It was the end of July and as hot as blazes. I remember seeing heat waves coming off the runway. I just didn't think…" His voice trailed off, then he picked up again. "We loaded the plane. Suitcases, baby stuff, my golf clubs, some souvenirs we'd bought. I should have known…but, I don't know, I didn't even think about all the weight we were carrying and how hot it was." His voice turned matter-of-fact. "It's harder for planes to take off in hot weather." He stopped as though memorizing something he should have known. "I did the run-up and everything was fine. Mia and Jenny strapped in their seats, cabin door secure, the plane ready to roll. We started down the runway and the plane seemed a little slow, but I knew it was warm and that's not unusual. What I'd forgotten to take into account was that the runway was carved out of National Forest property. A short strip, cut into thick evergreen trees."

I could almost see what Paul was going to say. I closed my eyes, as if that would change the outcome.

"The plane started lifting, just fast enough so that by the time I realized we wouldn't clear the trees it was too late to do anything. The landing gear clipped some branches, we lost air speed, and than we flipped over into the forest." Paul stopped, letting the image his words had created sift around us. After a while he spoke again. "I keep thinking I could have done something if I hadn't been knocked out. I had a broken pelvis and a bad gash on my head." The scar. "Otherwise I was fine. But Mia and Jen—ny." His voice cracked. "When I came to, they were both—dead."

We were quiet as the wind howled a lament for the lost.

Paul took a deep breath, held it, then exhaled forcefully. "See what I mean by foolish mistakes? You don't have the corner on the market, by any means."

What could I say in the face of tragedy like that?

"I'm sorry," I said, and this time my words were for his grief. My childish behavior of twenty years ago suddenly seemed just that. Childish. Hurtful, to be sure, but not something to weigh me down for half a lifetime. How had Paul ever managed to put his life back together? To forgive himself? "How did you go on?" I asked.

He sighed. "It wasn't easy, and it didn't happen overnight." He shifted his position, and I realized my side had developed a serious kink. I sat up, wincing at a muscle spasm. He took my hand in his again as if needing someone to help bear his pain. I was glad I was right there.

Content wherever…?

He pressed hard at his forehead with his other hand. "I was an emotional mess for a while. But that was okay; I needed to cry. Needed to grieve. Lucy—" he paused, "*Dr.* Lucy was a Christian counselor who helped me understand that grieving can heal." Paul sighed and looked into my eyes. "You know, Ruthie, even during that hard time I thought of you. Thanked God for what you had done for me."

"Me?" My eyebrows folded together in puzzlement.

"Yes, you." He placed his thumbs between my brows and rubbed at the crease, gently smoothing my brow. Soothing me. "If it hadn't been for what happened between us all those years ago, I don't know if my faith would have been strong enough to carry me through. I went from your arms into God's."

An image formed in my mind. My empty arms held out to Paul, calling him back. God's arms reaching out, wrapping around him, holding him close. Just the image was comforting. What must it feel like to have those arms around you?

Content.

Paul ran his thumb along the side of my hand. "Way back in first grade you started teaching me what it meant to love someone. By the time we got to high school all I wanted was to marry you and live in Brewster. Run my dad's business. Raise some kids. Hunt with Dave. I couldn't imagine anything in life could be better than what I already had. But you had other plans…"

I closed my eyes, not wanting to see whatever pain might be in his.

"…and so did God. He had a bigger dream for me than I could dream for myself." Paul looked out the side window into the blowing snow. "I've thought about this a lot. I think God wanted to show me more of the world. Maybe it was so I would never feel I'd missed out on anything. That what I have here in Brewster is the best God could plan for me…in a roundabout way." He turned his head to me, a soft smile on his face.

"I went to Chicago and had a job most people in Brewster couldn't imagine. Heck," he laughed, "I can't even explain it to people all that well. There was money. A lot of money. Prestige. Meeting all kinds of important people. The stuff you read about in novels. If it hadn't been for what I'd learned from loving you, I might have been swayed by all that." He held up his hand, as though to stop me from speaking, even though I was speechless. "Don't get me wrong, Ruthie. I wasn't a saint in all this. I was hurt and I was mad at you. Really mad. But deep down I knew what it felt like to love, and I wanted that again." His eyes softened as he gazed toward the soft light of the dashboard. "As it was, most of my life in Chicago seemed superficial. Money couldn't buy what I wanted. Meeting important people was exciting for the three minutes they spoke to me, but once they found out I wasn't buying what they were selling—self-importance—they moved on to the next guy. I carried Brewster around in my mind as if it were some sort of mental-haven. The one place where I knew life was real. Where I could go to find home. Then I met Mia." He stopped. "Are you sure you want to hear this?"

"I do," I said, wondering about the woman who had finally captured his heart.

"She was a bond trader." Paul lowered the zipper on his parka and pulled open the collar, his voice lighter now. "I met her at a business seminar."

Already I had a picture of her in my mind. Sleek. Sophisticated. Nothing small town about her.

"She was from a small town in South Dakota, so we had that small-town connection in common right away."

There went that idea.

"Within a year we were married."

Leave it to a guy to leave out the details.

He paused and looked out at the snowdrifted street. "We had some good times, and it would be easy to idolize her, but we had our problems too. Especially right after Jenny came. Both of us had waited a long time to get married, and we agreed we wanted a baby right away. Mia said she wanted to quit work and stay home with the baby, and I wanted that too. But when the time came, she changed her mind. She wanted an income of her own. And she liked the power that came with her job. All of a sudden she didn't want to give it up.

"Here I'd been thinking we should move to the suburbs so our kids would have a yard to play in, and she was gearing up to recharge her career." Paul shook his head. "We had some pretty big fights. I'd spent twelve years doing nothing but climbing the corporate ladder, waiting for the day I'd have a wife and kids, and then Mia decides she wants to keep climbing. That was one of the reasons we went to the cabin in Minnesota. We were going to talk about what to do—on neutral ground, away from the city. Mia was bored out of her mind at the lake. Said she'd spent half her life waiting to get to a big city and she wouldn't move. Period."

If I hadn't just heard about Paul's dreams, I might have been on Mia's side. As it was, I felt sorry for him. All those years of longing and it wasn't what he'd dreamed at all.

"We were leaving the lake a day early. We'd had a big fight about the whole thing that morning and decided to pack up and leave. Jenny was cranky…" Paul stopped and sighed heavily. "It'd be easy to blame the accident on our fight. Jenny. Whatever. But I don't want to make excuses. I was the pilot and I used bad judgment. And believe me, I've searched my soul to find forgiveness for that. We hadn't even made up." He hung his head, shaking it back and forth as if he still couldn't believe what had happened. "Do you know what it's like to live with the fact that the last words you said to someone you loved were mean words?"

With my memory of our prom night as clear as if it were yesterday, I reached up and put my hand on his cheek, turning his face to mine. "I know *exactly* how that feels."

Tears brimmed his eyes. "You do, don't you."

"Um-hmm," I murmured, blinking back fresh tears of my own.

Paul swiped at his eyes with the back of his hand. "After Mia died I had an opportunity to run for public office, but the people who wanted to back me wanted my help in a shady business deal first. I'd seen what lust for power and money had done to Mia. To our marriage. I was offered big money to participate, but at that point I knew money couldn't bring Mia or Jenny back. Money couldn't buy what I wanted, and all I wanted was peace. In my mind. In my heart. And, like before, my need threw me right back into God's arms. Where I was supposed to be all along.

"I can see now God used Mia's death to bring me back to Brewster. Don't get me wrong; He didn't cause her to die. That was my faulty judgment. But I truly believe God uses *all* things for His good purpose. Her death opened the door for me to return to the place I've wanted to be ever since I left." Paul leaned his head against the car seat as if he were exhausted. He squeezed my hand. "I haven't talked about that day in over a year." He drew a shaky breath. "Thanks for listening."

All I'd had to do was sit there. His three grateful words brought on a new flood of tears. I burst out sobbing as if I hadn't cried in years, rather than in minutes. I sniffed, fumbling for a tissue without letting go of Paul's hand. It felt good to be crying. Cleansing in some way. Paul slid his hand from mine and put his arm over my shoulders, pulling me again into his down-filled parka. His tender gesture unleashed another round of tears, and I sobbed out years of pent up emotions. For myself and for Paul, if that was possible. His arms felt like a protective shield around me.

Wherever I am, I'm content.

The comforting words crept around my tears, settling around my heart in a way I hadn't felt before. How could I possibly be content sobbing in a snowstorm? I didn't know, but I was.

When my tears finally stopped, I sat up. A large spot on Paul's navy coat was almost black. "I hope your coat doesn't freeze," I said, blowing my nose.

He patted the dash. "Like you said, 'good thing they improved these heaters.' Feel better?"

I nodded. "I do. Thanks. How about you?"

He reached over and smoothed the side of my hair that had been against his jacket. "It felt good to talk it out. A lot of that stuff I'd thought, but I hadn't said it out loud."

I blew my nose, again. "What a way to ring in the New Year. Sorry I got us stuck."

Paul turned the radio up so we could hear it again. "I prefer being stuck in a snowbank over party games anytime."

I smiled, tucking my tissues into my pocket. "I don't know if that's saying a whole lot. The lesser of two evils?"

He laughed, took my hand, and threaded his fingers through mine. "You never did get to answer Vicky's question. What were you going to say?"

"Say?" Vicky's New Year's party seemed ages ago.

"About the best of this year, the best of next," he reminded.

I'd thought I was off the hook. Apparently not. "Honestly?"

"Um-hmm." He rubbed his thumb over my hand.

"Honestly, I was thinking by next year at this time I'll be gone from Brewster."

"Leaving?" He looked at me sharply, then his face softened. "You still have that dream, don't you?"

I nodded, suddenly not so sure I did. Had I clasped onto that dream as a teenager wanting a bigger world and simply never let go? Believed with every fiber in my being that somewhere else, anywhere else, would bring me happiness?

Wherever I am, I am content.

Was that possible? Wherever? Even in Brewster?

Paul

Back when I was in college, if someone had asked, "What would be your idea of a really great New Year's party?" I can guarantee my answer wouldn't have been, "Sitting in a snowbank with Ruthie Hammond." But ask me that question a week after that night, and that's exactly what my answer would be.

Even as I shuffled through the stack of loan files on my desk, I could feel a smile cover my face as I thought of the two of us huddled together in my Bug. I had just decided North Dakota blizzards had a definite appeal when the headlights of a pickup had bounced down the snow-covered street. Mike Anderson, Ruthie's part-time high school help, jumped out of the truck and knocked on our window. We scrambled to sit up straight as if it were our parents coming to check on us in church, rather than us huddled together trying to keep warm in a blizzard.

As Ruthie rolled down the window Mike squinted into the car. "Need any help?" A huge grin covered his face when he realized it was his boss he'd come to rescue. With a guy.

"What are you doing out at this hour of the night?" Ruthie asked, sounding more like a parent than an employer. Sounding almost disappointed we'd been found. "And in a blizzard," she added as if Mike should just hop into his truck and head on home. I got out of the car, ready to enlist his help before Ruthie chased him away.

"Good thing I came along," Mike said, ignoring Ruthie's comments and stepping back to survey the deep snowbank. "You shouldn't be driving this kind of car in this deep snow." He swung a thumb over his shoulder at his pickup. "You need four-wheel drive to buck these snowbanks."

Two more husky young men jumped from the pickup cab. I could see Emily Marsden, Bob Marsden's daughter, peering out the side window of the truck. I wondered what she was doing out so late? Her dad was CEO of the bank holding company. My boss. I wondered if she'd report this to her dad. It would be fodder for ribbing at the next board meeting, for sure. But then again, I guessed she was out past her curfew. She'd probably have more to explain than my situation. The two burly guys stood there, swatting at their arms to stay warm. I wondered how the four of them had fit into the cab of the pickup? But then I recalled the night before Pumpkin Fest when five of us had gladly crammed into Dave's pickup cab. They were more than likely enjoying their drive around Brewster as much as I had that night.

"Lend a hand, guys?" I high-stepped to the back of the Bug, thinking I should have known better than to walk around North Dakota in January without boots. Snow sifted under my pant legs, soaking into my socks. The wind whipped around my head. I pulled the hood of my parka up. The wind blew it right off.

The two football-player types joined me and on Mike's count of "One. Two. Threeee!" Ruthie gunned the engine and the three of us pushed. Within a second the car had flown forward almost as if it hadn't ever been stuck at all.

"Thanks, guys." I pulled off my glove and shook their hands. I noticed they weren't wearing gloves, boots, or headgear. Invincible. Just as I'd been at their age before I'd learned the world wasn't in my control. I sent up a quick prayer for their safety in the blizzard and thanks for their help.

"We'll follow you home," Mike announced, sounding much older than he looked. "Just to make sure you don't get stuck again."

And making sure I wasn't going to get a chance to give Ruthie a goodnight kiss.

⁓

I was still waiting for that chance a week later, my thoughts drifting to Ruthie whenever I had a free moment. Remembering the smell of her hair as she cried on my shoulder. The wistful sound of her voice as she told me about wanting to see the world beyond Brewster. Why did my chest tighten whenever I thought of her being gone?

I closed the loan file on Kenny Pearson's gas station, vowing to keep my mind on business. Reviewing loan files was tedious work, a task I usually delegated to my staff. However, I was looking for particular information, information on Wayne Jorgenson's loan practices I didn't feel free to ask my secretary to find. Even though he'd mangled the KBRS loan, I was willing to grant him one big mistake. And a big mistake it was. Unless Ruthie came by a miracle, I highly doubted the station would make it through the year. If that happened, Wayne would have the failure on his conscience for a long time. I knew all too well no one was perfect. His misjudgment in this one case might be forgivable. However, if his freehanded loan practices extended to other customers, the bank couldn't afford to keep him. We'd received notice the state bank examiners would be coming to the bank next week, an annual visit that let the board know the state of the union, so to speak. I was determined not to be caught flat-footed when the examiners questioned me about the loans on our watch list.

I opened the next file. Jason Wynn, a small grain farmer a couple miles out of Brewster. He was the third generation on the homestead farm. Like most farmers in the area, he was trying to make ends meet any way he could. He'd added some cattle to his operation, and his wife worked at Magner's grocery store.

I pulled Jason's financial statement from the file, looking at the values that had been placed on his machinery. Being away from Brewster for so many years had left me at a disadvantage when it came to farm loans. I wasn't familiar with the equipment that was being used. What was a five-year-old seeder worth? A seven-year-old combine?

I buzzed my secretary. "Nancy, would you please bring me the files of Curt Sailer and Roy Wahl? Thanks." Two farmers I knew were solid. Two clients who had been customers of Bob Marsden, not

Wayne. While I waited I dialed the number of Brewster's implement dealer, checking on the going rate for used farm equipment.

"Here they are." Nancy laid two thick files on my desk.

A couple minutes later I could see not only were the assets inflated on Jason's financial statement, but Wayne had also neglected to bring the loan up for its mid-December annual review. A sure sign he was trying to hide poor loan performance.

Quickly I looked through two more of Wayne's clients' files. One file looked fine. In the other it was apparent the income projections for the small consignment shop run out of a young mother's home were completely unattainable. I could feel anger rising in my chest. What had he been thinking? It was his job to help her recognize what a reasonable income might be for a small shop. If he didn't know, there were area bankers he could call and ask, state programs he could tap into for advice. He was doing this young woman no favor by lending her money she'd never be able to repay.

I pulled a yellow legal pad close to the file and started making notes. I might have to fire Wayne before the examiners came, if for no other reason than to prove we could see he was incompetent and had taken action. Angrily I jotted numbers, punching the calculator harder than necessary. It was one thing to see a business fail because of a bad economy or a crop not worth harvesting because of hail damage, but it was another thing to know a business was going under because of a negligent loan officer. If we didn't get rid of Wayne soon, the bank could be liable for bad business practices.

When the page was full, I tossed the pen down. I sat back in my chair, pressing at the bridge of my nose with two fingers. When I'd moved back to Brewster, I'd expected challenges. I'd long ago learned there was a learning curve with every new job. I hadn't, however, expected those challenges to come from an inept employee. I thought of Jason, trying hard to keep his family farm. That young mother trying to stay home with her kids and still bring in a little money. Ruthie's radio station. Once again I felt anger bubbling in my chest. I took a deep breath, making sure the air filled my lungs.

Lord, settle me down. Help me think clearly. I exhaled slowly. *How could Wayne do this, Lord? Give me wisdom to deal with these customers who are going to need guidance. Help me deal with Wayne in a respectful way. Show me…*

What kind of training did he have?

The question filtered through my prayer, no thought from my own angry mind. W*hat kind of training did he have?*

Was it possible Wayne didn't know better? That he didn't know how to read a financial statement? Figure out income projections? Had he blustered his way through his job, trying his best while simply not knowing?

Help me deal with Wayne in a respectful way. I'd meant my prayer as a way to fire Wayne fairly. God seemed to be answering in a completely different manner. It wasn't the first time God had used prayer to change my heart toward someone. I'd found myself petitioning God on Jack's behalf more than once since he'd left.

Slowly I closed the files. My anger was gone, replaced by questions. I picked up the phone. "Dave, could you stop in and see me on your way home from work? I need to talk to you about Wayne."

⌒

"Whew!" Dave stomped his feet as he walked into my office, snow falling from his shoes. "It's a blizzard out there." He paused, a sly grin covering his face. Too casually he brushed half-melted snow from his hair. "Almost like New Year's Eve." Obviously, he'd heard all about Ruthie and me getting stuck.

"Very funny," I said, motioning him to have a seat. Actually, it was kind of funny thinking of him knowing about me sitting in a snowbank for two hours with Ruthie and not saying a word for a whole week. I'd bet he about burst waiting for this opportunity. I hid my amusement. I wasn't about to give him any bait for his fishing trip. "So," I said, ignoring the *I-know-all-about-it* look in his eye, "tell me about Wayne."

Dave wiggled his eyebrows at me but without a word settled into the chair across from my desk. It was nearing supper time, and the bank staff had left for the day. In between customers I'd spent the afternoon wondering if I'd judged Wayne before knowing the full story. I realized I knew nothing about him other than his bad lending practices. The more I thought about it, I understood that very few loan officers would deliberately get a client into trouble. Instead of feeling angry at Wayne, I suddenly felt compassion for the man. Maybe he didn't know.

"Go ahead and fire him," Dave said. "If you say he needs to go, I'll back you up to the board."

I shook my head. "No, it's not that simple. I want to know more about the guy. Where'd he work before here? What kind of background does he have?" I picked up my pen and twisted it through my fingers. "He's made some bad decisions, but before I decide anything, I'd like to know more about him."

Dave pulled on his ear. "Let me think. From what I know, he used to live over in Flander. Remember that old farm we used to hunt near in high school? The one we always threatened to bring a couple gallons of paint and just throw it on the house?"

I nodded. We'd also talked about shooting out the windows before we'd discovered anybody lived there. A crime I was glad we hadn't been dumb enough to commit.

"That's where Wayne lived. His dad left the family when Wayne was a kid. I heard his mom lost the farm and then moved over here when Wayne was maybe in eighth grade. I think his mom raised him and his brother pretty much by herself. She still works at the retirement home." Dave loosened his tie and unbuttoned the top button of his shirt, settling more comfortably into his chair. "I think he went to a two-year college in Carlton on some sort of track scholarship. I'm not sure what his major was. He came back and worked at the implement dealer for a few years, selling equipment. He ended up as parts manager before he got hired here. I wasn't on the board then, so…"

"Who hired him?"

"Do you remember John Erickstad?"

"I know the name." I racked my brain for more information. "Refresh my memory."

"He was the bank president before Bob Marsden." Dave crossed an ankle over his knee, as if settling in for the long haul. He put his hands behind his neck. "John ended up resigning, and that's when Bob got in as president and they asked me to join the board. There was a real shake-up around here from what I understand."

"I think I'm remembering some of this. Wasn't there something unusual about his resignation?"

Dave leaned forward, laying his arms on my desk. "Yeah, like I said, this was before I got on the board, so some of what I know is what I've been able to pick up from listening closely. The other board members don't like to talk about it too much, but rumor had it John was putting false loans on the books and pocketing the money. The examiners caught it. They tried to keep it quiet by letting John resign rather than firing him. You can about imagine what folks in this town would say if they found out something like that was going on at the bank. From the sounds of it, things were a real mess around here. Shortly before John got caught, he'd hired Wayne straight from the implement dealer. Sort of a favor, I guess. Wayne's mom was a cousin of John's, or something. Then the examiners figured out what was going on, John left, and Bob was asked to step in and straighten everything out." Dave sat back and tugged at his chin, pausing while his words settled. "You know, sitting here and telling you this stuff, it sounds like Wayne was hired and then got left on his own. I'll bet the guy was swimming as fast as he could just to keep his head above water. Things around here were so tense I'm guessing he put his face in the water and tried not to make waves."

I was thinking the same thing. Unexpectedly the image of a shabbily dressed young boy standing in a front yard that was mostly dirt came to mind. A boy who'd called to Dave and me as we'd hiked past his farm near Flander with our guns, "There's a pheasant nest over there." He'd pointed to a field overgrown with weeds. A young Wayne, willing to help two high school kids fill their limit when it was his stomach that more than likely needed filling. A boy who'd been on his own most of his life. A young man who hadn't had many breaks, who probably thought he'd struck the big time when he was offered a job at the bank.

Now he was married and had two kids of his own, and I had been thinking of firing him.

Dave scrubbed at his eye as though it were itching. "Gosh, all of a sudden I feel kind of sorry for the guy."

"Me too," I said, marveling at how quickly God could change my perspective. I tore the pages of notes I'd made from the legal pad, tucking them into a new file folder. Just like that, they'd turned from evidence into teaching tools. "I think I'll hold off bringing this up to the board. Let me talk to Wayne first, okay?"

Dave nodded, his thoughts far away. "Hey, do you remember that time we were hunting out by his place and this kid told us there was a—"

"Yeah, I do," I said, not needing Dave to finish the thought.

"I bet that was him."

We were quiet. I imagined we were both thinking just how far Wayne had come from that dirt-poor farm to his job as loan officer at the bank.

I tapped the corners of the files on my desk into line. I had work to do with Wayne, but unlike less than an hour ago, now I was looking forward to the task ahead. I'd come back to Brewster hoping I would make a difference in people's lives by helping them achieve their dreams. I had thought that would come in the form of lending money and giving financial advice, managing the investments of the bank. I had never dreamed I would be given the task of mentoring a young loan officer. God certainly worked in mysterious ways. I felt a sense of anticipation when I thought of the days to come.

It's not exactly as if you needed motivation lately. Ruthie seems to be motivation enough.

Where had that thought come from? Flustered, I glanced at Dave, hoping he hadn't somehow read my mind. Ever since New Year's I'd found myself thinking about Ruthie more and more. It had felt good to talk to her that night, as though I could tell her anything and she'd understand. I found myself manufacturing excuses to stop by Dave and Vicky's, hoping Ruthie would happen to be there. I wanted to ask her out. I hung around like a schoolboy with a bad crush. But every time I tried to put together the words, something held me back. Part of my hesitation had to do with the tenuous status of the KBRS loan. Eventually, it was going to fall on my shoulders to tell Ruthie the fate of her business, and I knew mixing in a personal relationship would not make the task any easier. I hadn't quite put my finger on the other part of my hesitancy. Was it simply junior-highish cold feet? Or was it something more?

"So what's up with you and Ruthie?"

I'd been so caught up in my thoughts I'd almost forgotten Dave was still in my office. The fact that he *had* practically read my mind unsettled me more. Was I that transparent?

"What do you mean, what's up?" I asked, lifting the stack of files and bouncing them into order, collecting my thoughts.

Trying a defensive maneuver?

"What makes you think anything is *up?*" I sidestepped around the desk.

More maneuvering?

"I'm going to put these files in the vault."

Ah, retreat.

Dave followed me down the short hall, a counteroffensive if ever I saw one. "A guy would have to be blind not to notice that you and Ruthie left the New Year's party at *exactly the same time*," he said, sounding as though he had a degree in spying. "And when you come over to our house, you hardly ever want to talk about hunting or the game. You just scan the room until Ruthie walks in, then you start talking to her as though the rest of us aren't even there." He stopped at the edge of the vault, waiting while I laid the files in the fireproof cabinet so Nancy could refile them in the morning. As I began locking the vault he continued, "Angie thinks whatever is going on is pretty romantic. Sam is wondering why you talk so much to Ruthie and not his teacher. I'm wondering if you know what you're getting into."

"What do you mean?" I asked for lack of a defense, reaching up to set the alarm. Was this God's way of telling me to back off? My own alarm, of sorts?

"Don't get me wrong, buddy," Dave went on, "I love my sister-in-law like a—well, like a sister. She's great, especially with Angie and Sam, and I don't know what Vicky would do without Ruthie to vent to when I get on her nerves." Dave rubbed his neck, leaning back into his hand. "Heck, there was even a time when I thought if you and I couldn't be brothers, we'd be brothers-in-law. But a lot of time has passed since then and Ruthie has changed. So have you. But, hey," he added, stepping out of the way of the heavy vault door as I swung it closed, "if you and Ruthie still have something between you, I won't stand in your way. I always thought you were a great couple."

"We're not a couple," I replied, being reminded of the Brewster rumor mill. I wondered how many other people already had that in mind? They didn't need to know the idea had crossed my mind more than once. "We got stuck in a snowbank. That's all." Dave shook his head and smiled as I spun the combination dial on the vault door, my thoughts spinning as randomly. Was Ruthie the person God had in mind for me, or were the years we'd shared growing up leading me down a safe, convenient path? Was I relying on my memory of Ruthie years ago and not looking clearly at how we'd changed in the years between?

Suddenly, as if a silent alarm had gone off, I knew exactly what my hesitation in asking Ruthie out had been. It had to do with her faith. I wasn't sure she had any anymore. After my experience with Mia, I'd promised myself, and God, that I wouldn't get involved with someone who didn't have a strong faith. And I wasn't at all sure where Ruthie stood in hers.

For as long as I could remember, Ruthie's family had gone to the same church as mine. We'd even sat in the same pews each Sunday, her family four rows from the front, our family two rows back from them. I'd spent many a Sunday morning watching stained-glass-tinted sunlight bounce across Ruthie's dark brown hair. Since I'd returned to Brewster, I'd noticed that Dave, Vicky, and the kids still sat in that same pew, my mother in hers. I hadn't seen Ruthie in church except for the Christmas Eve service, although she could have decided to attend another church. While uncommon in our small town, switching churches wasn't unheard of. But somehow I doubted that.

Until I knew more about Ruthie's faith journey, I wasn't sure what to do about the emotions I had every time I saw her—or thought about her, for that matter. Should I pursue a relationship with her? Should I back off before my feelings threatened my better judgment and the promise I'd made to God?

Lord, I prayed as Dave followed me back to my office, *reveal Your will in this area of my life. If a relationship with Ruthie isn't Your will, then take away these strong feelings I have for her. If it is, then show me clearly that Ruthie is seeking to grow in her faith and that You have something more intended for—*

"Want to run over to the café and grab some supper with me?" As if on cue Dave's stomach growled. "Vicky's high school gal has early play practice tonight, so she's short on help. We're having dinner at the café."

"No thanks," I replied against the soft thump of excitement in my heart, thinking I might bump into Ruthie if I went along. "I'd better get home and check on Mom. Her new medication seems to be helping, but I still feel I should keep an eye on her." I turned off my office lights. Soft illumination from the streetlights outside flickered through the swirling snow, dimly lighting our way to the outside door.

"Catch you later then." Dave shuffled kitty-corner across the icy street to the warm lights of the café.

A cold blast of wind slammed the bank door closed behind me. I wanted nothing more than to follow him, knowing Ruthie would more than likely be sitting there with Angie and Sam, her hundred-watt smile brightening this cold winter night. Instead I turned and walked in the opposite direction to my car, an icy blast of wind hitting my face like a slap.

It wasn't simply a need to check on my mother that had led me to turn down Dave's invitation. Mom had been doing very well on her new medicine and really didn't need my chaperone services. In fact, I'd been toying with the idea of looking for a place of my own if she continued to improve.

The real reason I'd turned down Dave's offer to join him for supper was that I didn't merely want to follow Dave to where I knew Ruthie would be. I wanted to give God a chance to reveal the plan He had for me.

And for Ruthie.

If He had one, that is.

I put my head down and rounded the corner of the bank, turning into the biting snow. The faster I could get to my car, the better. It was seriously cold.

Whomp! Whatever it was practically knocked my feet out from under me.

"Paul!" Ruthie's voice was warm with surprise.

"Ruthie!" I grabbed at her coat sleeve, trying to stay upright.

"Sorry," she laughed, her voice crystal clear in the midst of the twisting wind. "I was cutting through your parking lot from the station. I'm eating at the café tonight. Want to come along?"

"Sure," I said, the excuse of my mother not even crossing my mind.

As if I were a star soldier in the army, I did an abrupt about-face, as though I'd been meaning to go to the café all along. Ruthie threaded her arm through mine, and I found myself wishing my coat weren't quite so heavy.

"We'll either both stay on our feet or both fall over," she said, as we slowly made our way over the snow-slicked street. The warmth from her body seeped through her coat and into mine. I didn't care how long it took us to get to the café; it didn't seem all that cold anymore.

I wasn't sure if this was God's timing or pure coincidence, but I sure wanted to find out.

Ruthie

The café was packed. Dave was stepping between tables pouring coffee from pots in both hands. Angie sat with Paul and me as though she were a miniature chaperone. One who was in charge of conversation. A chaperone who talked with her mouth full.

"Did you guys have Snow Week when you were my age?" Three French fries in her mouth weren't going to stop her from talking. "Yesterday was Team Colors day and tomorrow is Dress Up day. I'm not sure if I should wear my Christmas dress or if that's too dressy." She swallowed her fries and then took a huge bite of her cheeseburger. "I'm going to call Steph when I get home and see what she's wearing."

"You guys doing okay?" Dave stood by our booth, not bothering to hide the wily grin plastered across his face. I knew exactly what he was smiling about. Ever since New Year's he'd teased me about getting Paul's Volkswagen stuck on purpose, and my protests did nothing to change his tune. The fact that Paul and I were sitting together, on the same side of the booth no less, just gave him more fuel for his little bonfire. The fact that the only empty seat in the café had been on the opposite side of the booth from Angie didn't stop his scheming.

He'd stood—so nonchalantly it was obvious what he was doing—on Angie's side of the booth, removing any chance of me sitting by her, when he'd said, "Sit here." I'd had no choice but to slide in, Paul right beside me.

"Angie, you'd better finish up and get in the kitchen and help your mom with dishes." Dave winked, as though we had put him up to making Angie disappear.

Angie washed down her mouthful of food with a swig of root beer. "I think Sam got sick on purpose," she said, shoving the last of the burger into her mouth. She swished two French fries through a puddle of ketchup, chewing in exaggerated slow motion, stalling kitchen duty.

"He was home all day with an earache." Dave tapped once on the table with a coffeepot. "Now hurry up and go help your mom. Besides," Dave now winked at Angie, "these two might want to be alone."

Angie stopped chewing, her mouth open. Wide.

"Eww, Angie," I said, observing the half-eaten French fry in her mouth.

She snapped her mouth shut and widened her eyes. Obviously she hadn't thought of the possibility her dad had just suggested. I could have kicked him. His motives were as clear as plastic wrap.

"Really?" Angie said, grabbing her plate and scooting out of the booth. "That's so cool." She pushed her back against the swinging door, twirling her way into the kitchen. "Guess what, Mom? Ruthie and Paul..." Thank goodness the door silenced the rest of her sentence.

Paul swung around to the other side of the booth. "Do you suppose this will be in the *Brewster Banner* on Wednesday?"

"Headlines, for sure," I replied, shrugging out of my heavy coat. Vicky could save a bundle on her heating bill if she could tap my embarrassed warmth. "*Bank President Eats Hamburger with Café Owner's Sister*, watch next week's paper for more information." Now why'd I have to go and add that last part? About next week? My already overheated face flushed more. I didn't want Paul to think I'd meant we we're going to start meeting for dinner every week. I focused on the menu, even though I knew it by heart. Would I ever learn when to keep my mouth shut?

From nearby tables I could see people glancing our way. Some tried to mask their curiosity, others flat-out stared. Good grief, you'd think they'd never seen two single people have dinner together before. I knew the Brewster grapevine would be in high gear tonight.

"I missed this," Paul said, his eyes looking right back at the people who were staring at us. A look of amusement filled his face as he turned his gaze to me. "In Chicago, if anyone looked at you at all, you'd get a blank stare, at best. Here," he cocked his head sideways, toward our audience, "you can see what they're thinking. It's funny." He turned his eyes to his menu. "I like it."

"Like it?" I said, incredulous anyone could like being under the microscope of Brewster's old gossips. "What's to like about it?" Just then the café door swung open and three people walked in, a man, a woman, and a young boy, about eight. All heads turned. "Wonder who they are?" I asked, not recognizing the strangers. At least everyone wasn't looking at us anymore.

"See?" Paul replied. "That's what I mean. No one around here stays a stranger. My guess is that someone in here knows them. I'll bet they're visiting relatives in town and they stopped by for supper before heading home. Or maybe they're just passing through on their way across the state. Either way, I'll bet someone in here will know before long."

"You're as bad as everyone else. Making up stories about three people you've never seen before."

Before I could say another word, Paul jumped from the booth and walked over to the family who were standing near the door, looking for a place to sit in the packed café. He stuck out his hand. "Welcome to Brewster. If you're looking for something to eat, you've come to the right place. It's kind of packed in here tonight, but we've got a couple empty spots in our booth if you'd like to join us. Oh, by the way, I'm Paul Bennett." Paul ruffled the top of the young boy's stocking cap. "We'll find an extra chair so my buddy can sit on the end. How's that sound?"

The young boy's eyes darted to his dad's. When he saw him nod, he nodded, too. Paul grabbed an empty chair from behind the cash register and carefully lifted it over the heads of Mr. and Mrs. Meier and Cal Link, from the hardware store.

That move was Cal's invitation to join in. "You look familiar," he said to the woman in Paul's small parade. "You from around here?"

Oh, good grief, this was beyond embarrassing. Three people, who were probably looking for a quick meal while passing through town, were getting the third degree from Cal. I gave the woman a sympathetic smile. If she were lucky they'd get to eat before the vultures in town picked them apart.

"Well, actually," the woman was smiling at Cal, "I used to spend a couple weeks here every summer with my grandparents, Erna and Emil Stading."

I knew the Stadings. Emil had passed away several years ago. Erna had been in the hospital, but had died a couple days ago. They were probably here for the funeral.

"You don't say," Cal answered, turning his chair our way. "I knew them both real well. They were good customers of mine."

Mrs. Meier chimed in, "Erna was in my homemakers' club. Such a nice woman." She clucked her tongue. "I was so sad to hear she died. You must be her granddaughter, Jill. Or are you Hannah?"

"Jill," the woman answered. "How'd you know?"

Mrs. Meier chuckled. "Your grandma talked about you two girls all the time. Let's see, are you the one living in Rapid City?"

"You've got a good memory," Jill said as she slid into the booth where Paul had been sitting. Her husband followed her. "This is Craig," she said as he stuck out his hand. "And, our son's name is Justin." The young boy flapped his hand in a quick "hi."

"This is Ruthie." Paul slipped in beside me, his close presence and the addition of three new people making this suddenly feel like a cozy family dinner instead of the talk-of-the-town it had been a few minutes ago.

Paul handed them our menus as Dave added three more water glasses to the table, greeting Jill, Craig, and Justin as if they were regulars.

Jill spoke. "We were just commenting on what a friendly town this is. We stopped at the gas station when we pulled in to town and Ken, is it, the man who works there?" I nodded. She meant Kenny, but Ken was close enough. "Ken came out to fill our tank and wash our windows."

"We haven't had service like that in years," Craig added.

"He knew my great-grandma," Justin chimed in, nodding his head as though he was very glad Kenny had known his grandma.

"I knew her too," I replied, wanting his approval somehow.

"Gosh, Mom," Justin was wide-eyed. "Great-grandma must have been famous. Everyone here knew her."

"I suppose it seems that way," Jill said, lightly rubbing the back of Justin's hand. "In a small town people look out for each other." She looked at Paul and me. "That's why we never insisted Grandma move to Rapid City; she had such a good support system right here." She paused, her eyes filling with tears. "Thank you. Thanks for living in this town and watching out for my grandmother."

I opened my mouth to protest. What had I done, other than say hello? Hold the heavy door at the post office so she could come in on occasion? Reach a can of coffee off the high grocery store shelf? Isn't that just what people did? "I didn't—" Paul's soft touch on my arm stopped my words.

"You don't know what that means to us," Jill went on. "We couldn't get up here very often. Work, and all. We called every week, but Grandma was always so busy with her friends and things, sometimes it was almost impossible to get ahold of her. She had such an active life right up to the end. She could have never driven herself to church, or other places, if she'd lived in Rapid City. It's too busy. But here, here, she lived a blessed life. We're so thankful."

"Mom, look!" Justin pointed at the menu. "They've got chocolate malts with *real* ice cream!"

"Lucky you!" Jill laughed out loud. "It doesn't take much to please him," she explained. "All the places around us make malts with soft serve. But Justin's favorite kind is made with hard, hand-scooped ice cream." Justin nodded enthusiastically. "You're lucky to live in a place with good, old-fashioned…" Jill paused, searching for the word, "…stuff!"

She had the old-fashioned part right, but lucky? I didn't think so.

"I recently moved from Chicago," Paul added. His fingers brushed mine as he reached for his water glass, sending a warm tingle up my arm. I watched him as he spoke, his face a mirror of content-ment. What would that feel like?

"Then you know exactly what I'm talking about," Jill said.

"I sure do." Paul took a sip of water. "I think the same thing everyday."

And I think just the opposite.

Maybe if you changed your thoughts, your attitude would change.

Oh sure, what I thought would suddenly transform the town of Brewster? Transform me? Save the station? Hardly.

Whatever is true and noble, whatever is pure and admirable—if anything is praiseworthy…think about such things.

Out of nowhere words from my confirmation verse from many years ago popped into my head. I knew I didn't remember the verse exactly, but I remembered being mad when our pastor had assigned it to me. I'd wanted a verse with more drama. One that said some-thing about *going out into the world.* I didn't want the *preach the gospel* part, just the part that said *go.*

Think on these things…

I could hardly help thinking on those things during the friendly chatter that filled the hour. Snatches of the verse rattled through my brain as Mr. and Mrs. Meier and Cal threw in their three cents. Mrs. Meier told about the time Jill's grandma had mistaken three tea-spoons of baking soda in her muffin recipe for three tablespoons. "Our mouths puckered up just as if a group of handsome farmers had walked into our homemakers' meeting," she said, causing us all to burst into loud laughter. Paul grabbed my hand and squeezed it, pure joy in his grasp.

Content. Content wherever I am. Those now-familiar words barreled through whatever negative thoughts I had left. I was actu-ally enjoying visiting with these people I'd never met, hearing stories about Erna Stading, a woman I thought I'd known forever but now realized I'd never really known at all. And I'd never even given it a thought how Kenny Pearson ran out to fill my gas tank each time I pulled in. Sure, when I needed to fill up in Carlton, I had no trouble figuring it out by myself. But it was nice to have someone else do it and throw in some friendly chatter too. When I thought about it, Kenny was kind of like a shining knight coming to help a damsel in distress. *Noble*, that would be Kenny.

Whatever is pure and noble…think on these things.

What else in Brewster hadn't I been seeing? Hadn't even thought about?

"Thank you so much." Craig reached over the table to shake my hand as he slid out of the booth. He turned to Paul, who was standing. "Great meeting you. I'm guessing I'll be in the bank in the next few days to settle some of Grandma's affairs. We'll talk more then."

Jill reached across the table and grabbed my hand. "I never thought coming back for Grandma's funeral would include any fun, but this was! You and your husband have made this such a great evening."

"He's not my—" I opened my mouth to protest, but Jill talked over my words. Thank goodness the café had emptied and no one else had heard her remark. Headlines, for sure.

"Like I said before, Grandma was so lucky to live in a town with great people like you." Jill slid out of the booth while I stayed glued to my spot, digesting her assumption. "You're so lucky to live here. It almost makes me want to move."

Move. Now there was a word I could identify with.

Are you sure? Or are you clinging to an old dream?

"That was great, wasn't it?" Paul, with a sigh of satisfaction, held out his hand to help me from the booth.

Noble? Ruthie, think about this…

I found myself agreeing, "It was fun."

And for once, not one negative thought came to change my mind.

"Auntie Ruth!" Angie came rushing from the kitchen as Paul stood paying the bill he'd declared "my treat." "I wanted to tell you to come listen to the awesome song our girls choir is singing at—"

"Sure," I interrupted, my buoyant mood making any request doable. "When is it?"

"We're singing at church not this Sunday, but next."

Oh. Church. I'd thought she meant her school choir. "Sure," I repeated, not near as enthusiastically. "I'll have to see if Mike can cover for me that morning at the station." I was hoping he'd have plans. It wasn't that I *minded* church; it just didn't do anything for me. The rare times I went, I spent the hour planning what I'd do when it was over. But for Angie, I could sacrifice an hour.

But not for God?

"I'm looking forward to it," I lied.

⌇

Oh, great. Communion. My eyes spotted the silver stack of communion cups and the cloth-covered bread cubes on the altar first thing. The only thing communion meant to me was an extra-long service. Great. The one Sunday I decided to come to church and it had to be this one.

Angie was already sitting in the choir alcove at the side of the church. She caught my eye and waved. I mustered up a smile as I slid into the pew beside Vicky. Sunday was a big day at the café. Coffee after church for many, lunch there for twice as many. Even though the café was open on Sundays until two, Vicky always made a point of taking an hour on Sunday to be in church. I admired her dedication, even if I didn't understand it.

"Good morning!" Pastor Ammon's amplified voice rang through the sanctuary. "I'm glad to see so many of you here on this blustery winter day. Welcome to all who are visiting."

Was he looking at me? He'd been the pastor of this church for at least ten years. Surely he knew I was a member.

How would he know when you only show up a few times a year? I shifted position. These pews hadn't gotten any softer since the Christmas service. And the service hadn't gotten any shorter. Responsive reading, followed by a hymn, a unison prayer, then Scripture reading.

"Would the children please come forward for the children's message?" Pastor Ammon's announcement started a stampede toward the front of the church. I couldn't remember ever being that excited about anything to do with church, especially when I was that young. My folks had often told the story about when I was a first grader I used to call the sermon, "the long talk." My thoughts hadn't changed a whole lot since then.

"Does anyone know what this is?" Pastor Ammon fished something out of a small jar and held it high.

"I can't see it!" yelled Billy Pearson, Kenny's five-year-old son.

My thoughts exactly. If you're going to demonstrate a point, at least make it one we can all see. Good grief.

"Look harder," was Pastor Ammon's only comment, holding his hand closer to the circle of children.

The kids squinted their eyes. I found myself squinting too. I still couldn't see it.

"A speck?" said a timid little voice. I craned my neck. Erica Frank.

"It's as small as a speck," said the pastor, "that's for sure."

Erica beamed.

"Try harder," he urged.

The kids, collectively, moved their heads toward his hand as if by doing so they could fathom what it was.

"A seed?" Mike Jangula, probably a second grader now, asked.

"That's right!" Pastor Ammon sounded very excited. "Did you listen to the Scripture reading? Can you guess what kind of seed?"

Ooo-boy, I was wracking my brain. I should have been listening better. I caught myself. It wasn't me on the spot. I darted a glance at Vicky to see if she'd noticed my imagined dilemma. She looked as though she already knew the answer.

Several kids yelled together, "Mustard seed!"

"Good listeners," Pastor Ammon praised. "Do you see how very tiny this is?"

"Yes!" shouted the kids.

"Do you remember what Jesus said about this mustard seed?"

Several kids rolled their eyes back into their heads, obviously trying to rewind their VCR brains. Silence.

The pastor filled in. "Jesus said that if we have faith, even if it's only the size of this mustard seed, we can do all sorts of impossible things." He paused. "Can you think of some things that might seem impossible?"

"Flying to the ceiling." "Growing eleven feet tall." The answers came fast and imaginative. "Getting a baby brother," called Erica, an only child. The congregation chuckled. "Getting a horse." "Having a million dollars."

Being content?

I folded my arms across my chest. This was a children's sermon. What was I doing filling in answers? When was Angie going to sing, anyway?

Pastor Ammon concluded. "Remember, when things seem impossible, if you have even this...much...faith," he dotted the air with the practically invisible seed, "you can do anything."

Impossible, I thought.

That's the point.

Angie's song wasn't quite as awesome as she'd led me to believe. The air-filled voices of seven junior high girls wouldn't be ready to head for Nashville any time soon. I nodded along, anyway. The melody was catchy, despite the air.

I daydreamed through the sermon, thoughts of the station tumbling through my mind. Ad sales had never been good in the winter, and this year was proving that record true. Mike Anderson had informed me he was going out for track and wouldn't be able to work as much come March. And Paul had called, asking me to set up a special meeting about the status of the KBRS loan. His voice had held none of the ease of our dinner two weeks ago. I didn't know what he planned to tell me, but I knew it couldn't be good. I couldn't manufacture money out of businesses that were barely holding their own. I just hoped the bank would let me hold on. What was I going to do if they didn't?

"...and so, the night He was betrayed," Pastor Ammon's gentle words filtered through my thoughts, "the Lord took the bread, broke it, and said, 'Eat. Do this in remembrance of Me.' And, likewise, He took the cup, poured it out and said…"

Speaking of what was I going to do, what was I going to do now? I opened my bulletin. How much of this did I have left to sit through? I should have sat in the back and left after Angie's song.

"…do this in remembrance of Me."

Those words always made me uncomfortable. I felt unworthy somehow. Judged, in a way.

You're the only one doing the judging. Maybe you're supposed to be uncomfortable. That might be the whole point. If you don't like what you see, change it.

And how would I do that?

Listen.

Listen to what?

Just listen.

Since I wasn't getting any other answers, and the service wasn't over, I had no choice but to sit in my uncomfortable pew and listen.

"This table is open to all," Pastor Ammon said. "All who profess faith in Jesus Christ. We are all unworthy."

He thinks that too?

"All in need of grace."

Unexpectedly, tears filled my eyes. How could he know?

He doesn't. God does.

"I invite you now, to come. Come to the table."

This was the part I never liked. Should I go? Maybe I should just sit here. Everyone might talk about me if I did go up. "Look at Ruthie Hammond up there taking communion after living with Jack all those years." Yeah, okay, I'd stay here. This service would be over soon and I'd be out of here.

"Come. For all is ready." Pastor Ammon paused, then reached into the little spice jar sitting on the edge of the communion table. He picked out one of the nearly invisible seeds and held it high. "Remember, if you have faith the size of this mustard seed, it is enough to do the impossible. Come."

Something propelled me out of my seat. Whether it was Vicky giving me a nudge or something else entirely, I didn't know, but I found myself walking to the altar.

Maybe I was unworthy. Maybe I shouldn't go up there. But if Pastor Ammon said all you needed was faith the size of a mustard seed...well, I supposed I had at least that little.

Or that much.

Jack

"Here's a new one by Koby Teith!" A swear word followed my blunder. Okay, regroup. Try it a third time. Doug Sommers stepped into the recording booth as I spoke into the mike. "Listen up, folks, it's Toby Teith!" Arrgghh! I slapped at the mike, swearing again.

"Go home, Jack." Doug's tone was flat. "You're drunk."

A ready protest fell from my lips. "No, I'm not. I'm just having a dad bay. Bad day," I quickly amended.

"You're lucky you're not on live or I would have fired you a long time ago." Doug stepped over and turned off the backup tape machine. "I'll have Marv cover for you this time. Go sober up."

"I'm not drunk," I said, a little too loudly.

Doug stared at me, not saying anything.

"Okay, so I stopped and had a couple beers before I came in. Since when is that a crime?"

"It's not a crime as long as you can do your job." Doug looked at the floor, then at me. "What is a crime is the talent you're wasting, Jack." He shook his head, kind of like my dad used to do when I'd disappointed him as a kid. "I've saved your skin with management more times than I can count. You're good, Jack. Really good. But you're going to throw it all away if you keep this up. Now go home and come back tomorrow. Sober."

Words of denial were on my tongue; I bit them off. No use killing the messenger. I flipped off the machines and slid off the stool. The room spun and I caught the counter with my hand before I tipped over. So, okay, maybe I'd had more than a couple. I shrugged into my leather jacket, pulling the car keys from my pocket. Luckily, I passed no one on my way out of the building. I started my car, the latest from KMIN blaring from my new speakers. I punched at the station button; they might have gone country, but that didn't mean I had to. I backed out of my parking space. My apartment was west. The casino was north. If I had the whole day off, who said I had to go home?

⌒

I loved those sounds. Dropping coins. The low, persistent call of bells signaling another winner. Soon that would be me. But none of that quarter stuff. I threaded my way through the exciting sounds and flashing lights to the blackjack tables. It was quieter there. A place a guy could concentrate. A place where I could rely on skill, not pure luck.

"Hey, Jack, my man!"

The dealer greeted me by name. I liked that. "Greg," I said, pushing a twenty across the table.

"Starting small tonight?" he questioned sliding one chip my way.

"Yeah," I replied. "Not sure if I'm in the mood." He didn't need to know a twenty was all I had left. I watched him deal a hand before I laid my chip on the felt. He dealt me an ace of hearts. The thumping in my chest grew harder. If only I had another twenty I'd double down. Double my winnings. As it was, all I could do was tap the table with my finger. Hit me. Greg backhanded me a three. Shoot! A measly three? That meant I had fourteen or four. He had a face card showing. I didn't like this one bit. I wanted to spend the night here, not drive home on my quarter tank of gas. I tapped the table again. A six. If he wasn't hiding an ace, I'd at minimum get to sit here for another hand. I wiggled my fingers over my cards and watched as he completed dealing to the table.

"Want your usual, Jack?" Heather, one of the cocktail waitresses, sidled up to me.

"Yeah," I replied, distracted. My whole night depended on what Greg had dealt himself. He slid his face card to the side and turned over a ten. Push. At least I was good for another hand.

"Shuffle!" Greg called out, gathering the cards. A pit boss walked nearby and watched as Greg expertly mixed the decks.

"Here you go, Johnny and soda." Heather placed my drink at the edge of the table. "How're you doing?" Maybe she was interested, but I didn't have either the time to lead her on or a buck for a tip.

"Fine," I mumbled, barely glancing over my shoulder. She got the hint.

Greg handed me the plastic marker to cut the cards. Impatiently I shoved the marker into the middle of the decks. Let's get going. He settled the cards into the shoe and dealt to the table. A ten of spades. My fingers drummed on the table as he expertly fanned the cards across the felt. Ah, he'd dealt himself a four. Ha! It was all I could do to keep from grabbing my wallet to look for another twenty. This was a setup for a win. I didn't have to look, though; I knew my wallet was empty. I tapped my index finger once. Hit me. A second ten. I wiggled my fingers over my cards. I was sitting good. Greg turned his card. He had an eight. That made twelve. I liked this a lot. He dealt to himself one more time. A queen. Busted! I sipped at my drink as Greg passed a second chip my way. It wasn't good manners to gloat. I let the chip ride.

Two hours later three stacks of chips rode the table between my elbows. Heather removed my third empty glass and replaced it with another amber-colored drink.

"Here." I tossed her a chip. Twenty bucks. All I'd had earlier in the night. Now I could afford to give it away.

"Thanks, Jack." She grinned. She knew sticking around me would pay off. "Good luck."

I nodded, turning back to the table.

"I'm off for tonight." Greg fanned the cards face down across the table, a red rainbow of color. "Thanks for playing with me."

What the heck, I tossed him a chip too. He'd been good to me. Greg tapped the chip on the table, giving me a firm nod. I was a good player and he knew it. An unfamiliar female dealer took his place. Betty. Not very pretty, but I didn't care how she looked as long as she dealt me the cards. She waved her hands over the table, showing off her manicure. She had the card symbols—a heart, a diamond, a spade, and a club—imbedded in each of her maroon fingernails.

Apparently Betty loved her cards. She was getting better looking already.

I tossed her a chip to ensure good numbers. "Ready, Betty," I said with a wink. She gave me a weary smile and handed the cutting duties to an old woman at the end of the table. I laid two chips inside the circle. Within seconds Betty had dealt me two eights. I split the cards, moving my two chips onto one eight, adding two more chips to the other. My palms were sweating. All I needed were two big cards and I'd win eighty bucks. Ha! A miracle, two tens. I got 'em. Now all I had to do was wait for Betty to bust her own hand. Sure enough, she went over twenty-one. She swept up the cards as she distributed the chips. I let them all ride. A hundred and sixty bucks. If I won this hand I'd cash out. I didn't know how much I had sitting in chips in front of me, but it had to be plenty. One of the cardinal rules of gambling was to not count your winnings at the table. Even Kenny Rogers knew that.

Shoot. Two cards that added up to fifteen. I hated middle numbers. What to do? Betty had a nine showing. There weren't many face cards on the table. Maybe there was a string of small numbers in there. Maybe Betty would be forced to deal herself out of the game. My heart thumped an anxious rhythm. I let my cards ride. Betty turned her second card over, another nine. Eighteen. She won. She swept my hundred and sixty bucks of chips into her tray. Lucky Betty.

I couldn't quit now. I'd play until I won that hundred and sixty back. Then I'd quit, cash in my chips, fill my car with gas, go home, and get some sleep before work. I tossed two more chips onto the table. Betty whisked them away almost as quickly. I knew I could win it all back; I just had to wait for the cards to change. Somewhere along the line Heather had replaced my drink. I'd been too caught up in the cards to notice.

One lousy chip. That's all I had left. Betty had gone, replaced by Harold. While he shuffled the decks, I looked around the casino. It had practically emptied. The night crew was vacuuming, polishing slot machines.

"You in, buddy?" Harold had already dealt a card to the only other guy at the table.

"Yeah." I slid my lone chip into the circle as he dealt my cards. What did I have to lose?

Your last dime, I thought as Harold took my chip and any chance I had of winning.

"I'm out," I said, finally pushing myself away from the table. My legs felt cramped and I kicked them forward, one foot at a time, trying to bring some life into them. How long had I sat there, anyway? It had felt like barely more than an hour or two. I looked at my watch. Whoa! Where had the night gone? I had to be at work in an hour! I hurried out to my car, hoping my few gallons of gas would get me back to the station. Hoping no one would notice I hadn't changed clothes. I'd ask Doug for an advance on my paycheck, again.

I pulled out of the parking lot, my foot pressed hard on the accelerator. I was going to have to watch myself at work today. Doug would be eyeing me closely after yesterday. I glanced into the rearview mirror. I needed a shave. I scrubbed at my face. Ah, heck, male models sported that morning-stubble look all the time. If anyone said anything, I'd say I was updating my look. Yeah, that would fly. I winked at myself in the mirror.

The sound of a siren caught my attention. Must be a fire somewhere. I edged over to the side of the road and while I waited for the truck to pass I closed my eyes. A sharp knock on the window jerked me out of my instant sleep.

"Can I see your driver's license, sir?" A patrolman stood by my car window. Where had he come from? I reached into my back pocket and handed him the license. He looked it over. "I'd like you to get out of the car."

"Is there a problem?"

"Your car was moving in a suspicious manner." He handed me a tube and told me to blow into it. His next words changed my world.

"You're under arrest for driving under the influence. Get in the patrol car."

⤳

"Doug, I need a little help." My one phone call went to the only guy I knew who I thought would help me out. I needed bail money. And a driver.

"Sure, Jack, no problem." Doug didn't sound happy, but he did say he'd help. That was all I needed.

"Where can I take you?" he asked after I'd been released and we were in his car.

"I'll have to get my car later." The officer had made that clear. I looked at my watch. "I suppose it's too late to make my shift." I gave him a grim smile. "Why don't I go to the station, anyway? I can catch up on some other work; maybe fill in for Marv's shift later being he's covering for me. I really appreciate this, you know."

Doug put the car in gear and drove slowly away from the police station. He spoke softly, "Then you're not appreciating the right thing." He shook his head. "What you should have been appreciating is the talent God gave you. Instead you wasted it. I'm sorry, Jack. The truth is, you pushed your luck. You're fired. Now where can I take you?"

Fired? I couldn't be fired. I had rent to pay. Credit card payments that were already overdue. I also kind of liked to eat. I couldn't be fired! "Doug," I pleaded, "give me one more chance. I promise I won't—"

"Sorry, Jack," Doug interrupted, "you've already had more chances than a guy should expect. You want me to take you home?"

I nodded. The dirty apartment I shared with Marv was no place anyone would call home, but it was all I had for now. Until Marv learned I couldn't pay the rent. A cold bead of sweat formed on my upper lip. What was I going to do? I had no money. I didn't have a job, and I wouldn't have a place to live if Marv kicked me out.

"Here you are, Jack." Doug stopped in front of my apartment complex, shifting the car into park. He stuck out his hand. "You're a talented guy, but talent isn't worth anything if you can't use it for some good purpose. I hope you find out what that purpose is." He slipped a business card into my hand. "Call me when you get things straightened out. I'll see what I can do."

I got out of the car, staring first at the grimy apartment complex, then at the card in my hand. I'd expected to see Doug's business card. Instead I found myself looking at a card that read:

When you don't know where else to turn, turn to God.
Christian Counseling Center of Minneapolis

Oh yeah, right. Like I was going to get religion and everything would be peachy keen. I laughed, stuffing the card deep into my coat pocket. No use getting picked up for littering too.

Turn to God. That was a good one. I kicked a crushed beer can out of my way as I walked up to the apartment, slipping a bit on the icy, unshoveled sidewalk. Ouch! A muscle yanked in my back. All I needed was a doctor bill.

Rubbing my back, I walked into my apartment, the musty smell of old wood and hopeless lives filling my nostrils. I bypassed throwing my coat on the layers of clothing piled on a chair near the door. I'd keep it on since the apartment was freezing. Marv's method of economizing. I sank onto the lumpy brown couch and surveyed the room. A television with aluminum foil assisting the antenna, a coffee table that was more stained rings than wood, and furniture the Salvation Army wouldn't want. And none of it was even mine. My eyes scanned the room again. This was what I had to show for my life? No money. No job. A shared apartment in a bad part of town. I slapped at the couch, a cloud of lint drifting into the dirty sunlight filtering through the window.

Maybe a beer would help. I jammed my cold hands into my coat pockets as I walked to the kitchen. That beer wasn't going to warm them up any. Pulling my right hand from my pocket, I reached for the fridge. The business card Doug had given me fluttered to the floor. I covered it with my foot. I'd trash it later. I opened the fridge and leaned in for a beer, but my hand, with a mind of its own, reached down to recover the small white card.

Turn to God.

Empty-handed, I closed the fridge door and stared at the card. No money. No job. I didn't know if it was God I needed, but what I had been doing certainly hadn't been working. A surge of nausea crept over me. The memory of last night's accumulated drinks, smoke, and the antiseptic smell of the police station combined to make me sick at myself.

One phone call. I'd make one call to this number. Maybe no one would answer. If someone did, they wouldn't know who was calling. I wouldn't give them my name. I'd just call and see what they had to say.

Paul

"Bob. Paul." Bill Murphy, the head bank examiner, shuffled through a stack of papers on the table, nodding at Bob and me in turn. Bob Marsden was spending the morning at the Brewster bank to sit in on the exit interview of the exam team that had been at the bank all week. "We've completed our exam," Bill said, "and overall we'll be giving the bank a good rating. However…"

I knew what was coming. The examiners had spoken at length with me earlier in the week about several loans they planned to classify as substandard.

"If you'll turn to page six of the exam report." Bill handed Bob and me a neatly printed sheaf of papers and waited until we found the right page. "You'll see we have several loans listed there. Paul," Bill turned to me, "you're aware of the fact that we found insufficient collateral on many of these loans, the Wynn farm loan perhaps the most glaring example." I nodded. "We were also missing up-to-date financial statements on many of the loans. Documentation has been lax, to put it mildly." Inwardly, I winced. This wasn't the way I did business. I liked my "i"s dotted and my "t"s crossed. I knew most of these loans had been Wayne's, but I was his supervisor and felt that the ultimate responsibility fell on my shoulders.

I'd had several long conversations with Wayne over the past two weeks. My hunch had been right. John Erickstad had hired him shortly before John's misappropriation of funds came to light. Everyone in the bank had been worried about possibly being laid off. Wayne simply tried to lay low and do his job. A job he'd had no training for. Bob Marsden had his hands full trying to straighten out the mess in addition to getting the recent acquisition of the bank office in Carlton up to speed.

I'd worried Wayne would take offense, get defensive, when I questioned his lending practices...

"Wayne," I'd stood in his office doorway that morning, trying hard to sound compassionate instead of boss-like. "I'd like to talk to you in my office after the lobby closes today."

"What about?" He clicked his pen rapidly, his eyes not meeting mine.

"I'd like to go over our loan policy with you and talk about some training programs I'm considering sending you to."

"Oh. Oh!" He sounded like a kid who'd been ready for a fight, only to find out the other guy wasn't swinging.

Later that afternoon I prayed hard, then called Wayne into my office. All it took was one sentence. "Wayne, tell me what I can do to help you do your job better."

The young man who'd walked into my office with his shoulders squared, prepared to defend himself, suddenly sagged. "My job better?" he'd said, his voice rising as though inflected with junior high hormones. He regrouped. "I thought you were going to ask me about the loans I've made. The—"

I held up my hand, stopping his flow of words. "I already know about the loans you've made. I want to know what we can do to help you do your job better."

It was almost as if someone turned on a light in his face. He sat up straight and said, "You could send me to banking school."

So, he knew.

He went on, his voice soft. "John hired me straight from the implement dealership. I didn't have any training in banking at all, except for one economics class I took at Carlton Junior College, and that didn't help much. John had told me he was going to send me to banking school, but once all the—" he paused, clearing his throat, "trouble started, well, John wasn't here anymore and Bob was so busy I didn't know if I dared ask to go. I was afraid Bob would find out how much I didn't know." Wayne dipped his head, looking down at his folded hands. "I really wanted this job." He lifted his chin and looked me in the eye. "I still do."

"Well then," I said, leaning towards him, "let's get to work."

That same afternoon I'd given him a brief primer on reading financial statements and doing cash-flow projections. The young man was a quick learner, asking question after question. Before Wayne left for the day, I'd called and enrolled him in the next banking school session.

He shook my hand with a force equal to a jackhammer. "Thank you," he said, a wide grin covering his face, words falling from his mouth, releasing burdens. "You don't know how much I appreciate this. I feel as though a load of bricks just fell off my shoulders. My wife has been praying for something like this for a long time."

So have I, I reminded myself, even though I'd thought the answer to that prayer would be firing Wayne, not mentoring him. *So have I.*

As eager as Wayne was to learn, that still didn't clear up his earlier mistakes, as the bank examiner was reminding me.

"We gave special scrutiny to the KBRS loan." Bill Murphy shook his head as he tapped at the numbers. "It's in bad shape, as I know you're aware." He looked at me again. We'd discussed this too. "Frankly, we don't see any hope of recovery."

Neither did I.

I just didn't know how I was going to tell Ruthie.

Ruthie

Two strange cars had been parked outside the bank all week. I could glimpse the cars from the KBRS window when I sat at my desk to do paperwork. They parked at the far end of the small bank parking lot, same spots each day. I'd never timed it right to catch whoever owned the vehicles getting in or out. As I punched Mike's hours into the calculator, I wondered if Paul had hired two new staff members. The bank didn't seem understaffed, but who was I to decide that?

Exactly, Ruth. Who are you to be snooping into the bank's business? You're doing the same thing you claim to hate about folks in Brewster.

Oh, good grief, I wasn't snooping; it was plain old curiosity. I hit the total button and opened my eyes wide at the figure. Mike couldn't have worked *that* many hours, could he? Quickly, even though I knew exactly what the balance showed, I opened the checkbook. I could pay Mike, but I wouldn't be doing much else.

"Hi, Ruthie!" I about jumped out of my chair as Dave rounded the doorframe. Mike was on-air right now, and I'd assumed I was the only other person in the building.

"What are you trying to do? Give me a heart attack?" I quickly closed the checkbook cover. I didn't need anyone else knowing how broke the station was.

"Nah," Dave said, sliding into a chair, "I'm heading over to the bank. The examiners have been here all week, and they want a short meeting with the full board before they take off."

So that's who the strange cars belonged to.

You're getting as bad as Mrs. Bauer.

I am not, my brain said to itself, muscles clenched like teeth, *it's common curiosity.*

"Where have you been keeping yourself?" Dave asked, pulling off his gloves. "I've hardly seen you all week."

I shrugged. "Been busy, I guess. Paperwork." Dave didn't need to know there wasn't much work to do after KBRS went off the air at sunset each night. I wished I had paperwork to do. What I had been doing was spending most of my time right here, at my desk, trying to squeeze pennies from an empty piggy bank, staring at my checkbook balance, going through old advertising files, trying to see if there was any possible source of revenue I'd missed.

There wasn't.

I'd even called around trying to find out the value of the station and the equipment. Maybe selling was an option.

It wasn't. I'd found out every station out there had switched to computerized equipment. The only thing the KBRS equipment would be good for was a museum. Or a bonfire.

I ran my fingers through my hair, trying to make myself look busy, not harried. My eyes caught on the amount of money I owed Mike this month. I'd barely made that much in the last two weeks in advertising income. Maybe I should confide in Dave. Maybe he would have some idea what I could do. It would be so good to share this burden with someone.

You can share it with Me.

The thought that wasn't mine caused me to pause. Share my problems with God? What could God do? Put money in my checking account? Right.

If you have faith like a mustard seed...

Since when had my brain turned into Saint Ruth? Ever since that Sunday when I'd gone to listen to Angie sing, my mind kept finding all sorts of opportunities to remind me of words I'd heard that morning in church.

Maybe it's not your mind, maybe it's Me.

This was getting annoying.

Talk to Me.

If I were going to talk to anyone, it wouldn't be myself. I took a deep breath. I could trust Dave with my problem. "Dave—"

"I'm worried about Vicky," he interrupted.

"Vicky?" I asked, caught off guard. Vicky had the most perfect life I knew. What could he possibly be worried about? "Is there something wrong?" My heart was hammering, a powerful thumping that felt ominous.

"She works too hard," Dave said, leaning forward, his elbows on his knees.

Was that all? Join the club. Self-pity and resentment coursed through me as I thought about these past months. Suddenly I realized most of what I'd been doing lately had been sitting and worrying while Vicky ran the café from before sunup until after the supper hour.

"She can't find enough help for the café so she tries to do it all herself. She's running herself ragged. Angie goes in after school sometimes, but she's only in junior high; she's got schoolwork to do. And, besides, she's too young to handle a job like that."

"Can Vicky afford to hire more help?"

Dave blew an ironic puff of air through his nose. "Money isn't the problem."

I wished I could say that.

"The café is making good money. The problem is that ever since that telemarketing place opened on the edge of town, most of her help has gone there. The work is easier. The hours are better. You don't have to be on your feet all day. They offer better benefits."

"Maybe I should go work there." I tried to make it sound like a joke, but it didn't seem all that funny, considering I hadn't had health insurance in more than a year.

"I don't know what to do." Dave sat back in his chair. "I'm afraid she's going to work herself to death. Have you noticed? She's nothing but skin-and-bones. I've talked to her about selling the café, but a business in a small town doesn't have that much to offer a potential buyer."

I didn't let on how true I knew his statement was.

"And, besides," he went on, "that café has been Vicky's dream since before we were married. She loves her work. I don't know what she'd do without it. She calls it her ministry." Dave laughed. "Can you believe listening to some of those old farmers telling their stories over coffee everyday is a ministry? Vicky thinks it is. She tells me how much she loves cooking for people. Mr. Ost, for instance. Vicky claims he wouldn't get a hot meal ever if it weren't for eating at the café. And visiting too. Did you know Ida Bauer goes there every day for coffee?"

Yes, as a matter of fact, I did. I simply shook my head, pretending I didn't know. Obviously, Dave needed to talk.

"I used to think Ida came to the café so she wouldn't miss out on any gossip, but Vicky says she comes in for company, not coffee or gossip. She's lonely. She'll talk to anyone who happens to make eye contact with her."

Or even people who don't. I recalled the day Jack had told me he was leaving the station. How Mrs. Bauer had slipped into my booth, offering compassion and prayer.

Maybe that's her ministry.

Before I had a chance to answer that thought, Dave continued, "I suppose it would get lonely sitting all alone in her house all day. Every day." He scratched the side of his mouth. "I just wish Vicky didn't have to work so hard. What I wish," he tapped his palms on his thighs, eyes twinkling, "is that she had an *assistant* minister! That's what she needs. Well," he pressed his hands on his legs and stood up, "I'd better be getting over to the bank." He looked at his watch. "Whoa! I've got to run."

So much for confiding in Dave.

Confide in Me.

After he left I looked, again, at the small balance in my checkbook, the number of hours Mike had worked, and the two paltry advertising checks lying on my desk. Beside them lay the income tax forms I needed to start filling out.

What income? I drummed the desktop with my fingers. I wondered what federal prison looked like? What was I going to do?

Confide in Me. If you have faith the size of a mustard seed...

Arrggghh! I was sick of this. It was like living with a minister in my brain. I shoved my chair away from my desk and sat back, stubbornly folding my arms tightly across my chest. *Okay, God!* I screamed in my head, as much out of frustration as to get the unsettling thoughts out of my mind. *Here it is. I'm broke. I'm alone. I'm scared. I don't know what I'm going to do. So there. What are You going to do about it?*

As if in answer to my challenge, the phone rang. I snatched it off the hook before it could complete a full ring. If God were calling, I wanted to hear what He had to say.

"K-B-R-S," I blurted into the receiver, a challenge in those four letters.

"Ruthie?"

I pulled the receiver from my ear and glared at it. If this was God, He sounded a lot like Paul.

Were you really expecting Me in person?

Oh, for pete's sake! I really hadn't been expecting anything. I'd get put in a nut house if anyone could read my mind.

"Ruthie," Paul said, as if he didn't have a clue he was interrupting a conversation with myself, "I'd like to set up an appointment to talk to you tomorrow. Anytime is fine. Let me know what works for you."

He sounded so formal. So...so, un-Paul like.

Well, when you're expecting God—

I wasn't expecting anything!

"Would tomorrow at two work for you?" Paul asked, sounding very much like a bank president. He'd mentioned that we were going to have to talk about the station's situation sometime soon. I thought he'd catch me someday when I stopped in the bank. I hadn't anticipated him setting up an appointment. Once again my heart started pounding an ominous beat. Tomorrow at two? After Mike came in? Sure. Fine.

I didn't feel fine at all.

Paul

"Ruthie, you're going to have to sell the station." No, that was too direct. I cleared my throat, practicing the words I would have to say in a few minutes. "Ruth, I'm sure you've known for a long time that the station isn't doing well." I wiped my palms on the legs of my slacks. Nerves were usually never a problem for me, but all day I'd had a hard time concentrating, knowing the bad news I was going to have to deliver to Ruthie.

The examiners had been clear. We needed to get the KBRS loan off the books and the bank board had concurred. It was up to me to carry out the job.

Earlier in the day I'd talked with Wayne at length about what had happened with the radio station loan. He fully understood his part in the failure of the station. As I'd pointed out just where and when the station loans had gotten out of hand, he was so full of remorse all he could do was repeat, "I'm sorry. I didn't realize. I'm sorry." He didn't have the background yet, or the fortitude, to explain to Ruthie why the bank was taking this action.

Nancy leaned into the doorway. "Ruth Hammond is here to see you."

"Send her in." I breathed deeply and said a quick prayer. I was going to need all the help I could get. I wiped my right hand on my pant leg again as Ruth entered my office. "Ruthie!" I walked around my desk to greet her, my hand extended as though we were about to make a big deal, rather than end one. I needn't have worried about my sweaty palms. Hers were clammier than mine.

"Pa-ul," she said, her voice faltering. She pushed her lips into a grim smile. It was obvious she knew that whatever the reason for this appointment, it wasn't good.

I closed the door. This meeting was going to be tough enough. I didn't need any interruptions from the staff or from folks who thought nothing of walking into my office to say hello, no matter whom I happened to have sitting across my desk.

"How are you?" I slid into my chair, opposite of Ruthie, my mind a complete blank beyond the inane question I'd just uttered.

"Good," she replied, looking down at her hands, not sounding good at all.

I opened the KBRS file, looking at the pages as if I didn't have the complete thing memorized. *Oh, Lord, give me the words…*

Instead He gave them to Ruthie.

"I'm not exactly sure why you wanted to meet with me today." The words tumbled from her mouth in a quick stream. "But I need to tell you that I know the station is doing badly. Well, worse than that." She paused, clenching her fist, then spreading her fingers wide as if throwing one word into the air, "Awful." She went on. "No one wants to buy advertising. There aren't enough businesses, even in the surrounding towns, to make a radio station work. I've tried, Paul, I really have." She sighed, closing her eyes briefly. I could almost hear her telling herself, *I won't cry. I won't cry.* She opened her eyes, blinking quickly a couple times, and then she stared at my desktop as if it were a movie screen showing a picture that held no hope. Finally, she moved her eyes to mine. With no expression in her voice at all she said, "I give up."

I'd expected tears. I'd thought she might get mad. Those emotions I knew how to handle. What I hadn't expected was the sound of defeat. When I'd asked God for help with this burden, I hadn't meant for Him to give it all to Ruthie. But here I sat, hearing her flat voice, seeing the absence of emotion in her eyes, helpless to do anything but dismantle her dream.

Ruthie

The first time I said the words, I didn't feel anything at all. I would have thought those three words would come out of my mouth in one huge sob, or maybe in a gut-wrenching scream, certainly not in the flat, emotionless tone they did. I looked straight at Paul and said, "*I give up,*" as if I were speaking a language I didn't understand. I honestly felt nothing. Like a condemned criminal waiting for her sentence, there was no fight left in me, nowhere to run. I said the words again, "I give up." Surprisingly, the second time I spoke, the words felt something similar to freedom. No longer would I have to worry if I could coax Cal at the hardware store into signing a contract for another month, listening to his penmanship story one more time. I wouldn't have to read the specials at Magner's grocery store out loud three times every day, and I wouldn't have to worry if I'd have enough money to pay Mike for his part-time work. Maybe closing the doors of the station was a blessing in disguise.

Since when have you started counting blessings? Since when is being penniless and without a job a blessing?

I remembered the years Jack and I had spent investing our lives in KBRS, dreaming of something bigger. I thought about the past months when I'd worked at the station from early morning until late at night, trying to make up in time what I couldn't in dollars…and for what? It had all come to this. *Absolutely nothing.* If this was a blessing, it was going to take some time before I could count it.

"Tell me what to do," I said, looking Paul straight in the eye. Now that I'd admitted defeat, all I wanted was to draw up a battle plan, fight the fight, and then retreat. Where? I didn't have a clue. All I knew was that I wanted this mess to be *over.*

I wasn't the first person to ever lose a business, and I wouldn't be the last, but right now that's exactly what it felt like.

Paul

Ruthie knew the only option was to close KBRS. I was surprised to learn she'd been checking out scenarios for some time. She knew there was no market for the outdated broadcasting equipment beyond having a rummage sale for the inventory of cassette tapes, a couple calculators, and the telephones. Ruthie thought she might give the reel-to-reel tape player to Mike as a sort of consolation prize for sticking with her until the end. She had a building lease to clear up and not much else.

Except to plan what her future held.

I broached the subject cautiously. It was never easy to close a business, but I knew how hard Ruthie had worked to make the radio station succeed, even after Jack had left her with all its problems. She'd poured her heart and soul into the business and was now left with nothing.

"Ruthie," I said, trying hard not to sound as though her future was as bleak as it appeared, "have you given any thought as to what you're going to do?"

For one moment she gave me that deer-in-the-headlights look, as if she'd never thought beyond locking the station door, then she straightened and said, "Yes, I have thought about it and…" She stopped, her voice faltering. She half-coughed, choking on the words to come, "And, I don't have a clue."

It was only then her face crumpled, her back slumped, and her hands came up to cover her face and muffle her crying.

This was the part of my job I felt untrained to do. Give me facts. Give me figures. I knew what to do with those. Give me raw emotion, and inadequacy was my only response.

I walked around the desk and stood next to her, gently rubbing my hand across her shoulders. *Lord, give her hope. Give her a future planned by You.* She crossed her arms on my desktop and sank her head deep into their fold, sobs shaking her entire body. Hope seemed the furthest thing from this room.

I found myself patting her back, murmuring, "There. There." Sounding more like an old grandma than a banker who knew what he was doing. "We'll work this out," I said, my voice more confident than I felt. Ruthie gave a shuddering gasp, a new wave of emotion flooding the room. *Why are You doing this to her, Lord? Why? I've never seen someone so broken. Where are You in this? Where?*

Suddenly Ruthie leaned over, her hand fumbling in her purse. She pulled out an already crumpled tissue and wiped her face. I grabbed some tissues from the box my secretary had placed on my desk the day I started work, saying, "You'll need these." I'd thought she meant I'd need them for a winter cold. Apparently, tears went along with banking more than I knew. I handed some to Ruth, grateful to have something to offer besides empty words.

"It must be your cologne," she said, her throat still heavy with tears as I went back to my chair. I must have looked puzzled because she went on, smiling through her wet eyelashes. "Practically every time I'm with you I end up crying." She dabbed at her eyes, a small hiccup of emotion pulsing her body.

I remembered the day Jack announced he was leaving Ruthie with the station and its debts…she'd cried in this exact spot. I recalled New Year's night when Ruthie had sobbed against my coat in the stalled car…a mix of emotions that needed voice. And now, again in my office, tears for the end of a dream. Was it our shared past that made her feel vulnerable around me? Made me feel so compassionate toward her? Maybe her tears were not the burden they seemed. Maybe they were a gift of some kind. Was this God's way of drawing us closer? If it was, He had a confusing way of doing it.

I rearranged the papers on my desk, waiting while she blew her nose. She pulled a compact out of her purse, flipped it open, and looked into the small mirror. "Beyond redemption," she declared, rolling her mascara-smudged eyes and snapping the compact shut. She scrubbed below her eyelashes with the tissue.

"No one is ever beyond redemption," I said softly, my tone telling her it wasn't makeup I was referring to.

She rolled her eyes again, raising her eyebrows as if to say, "*Apparently you don't know me*." She lowered her head, continuing to dab at her tear-smeared eyes.

But I did know her. I knew all about her. I knew her finances. I knew her self-doubt. I knew how she'd been left almost alone when her parents died and how she'd become the next thing to a mother to her sister, giving up any dreams she'd had so Vicky could achieve hers. I knew about Ruthie's past with Jack, and I knew her anguish about the future. The only thing I didn't know was where her heart was with God.

I know.

I paused, the silent words giving needed assurance. I didn't need to know as long as God did.

"Ruthie," I said, waiting to hear what God would have me say. "I'll help you work through this."

She nodded, a wry chuckle escaping her lips. "Thanks," she said, "but do you know what I need right now more than a banker?"

I waited, fairly certain of her answer. She was going to give me the amount of money she owed the bank. A dollar figure that appeared astronomical to someone with no income. An amount of money that even if it had been ethical for me to offer to lend her, I didn't have available.

Ruthie stuffed the wad of tissues into her purse, looked me in the eye and said, "It's what you said a while ago, at Vicky and Dave's that one night. I need a friend."

A friend? She wasn't asking for someone to bail her out of trouble. She wasn't requesting special favors. A friend. All she wanted was a friend.

I am her Friend.

Of course God was her friend. I just wasn't sure Ruthie was ready to hear that right now. I had a feeling she meant another kind of friend. One she could see. I opened my mouth, ready to tell her she had lots of friends. Vicky, for one. But just as quickly I remembered how busy Vicky was, managing the café, tending to her house, and keeping track of the kids. Dave had commented only yesterday that he hardly had a chance to see Vicky lately, much less talk to her. I was positive Ruthie knew that too.

I am her Friend. Show her.

Show her? Not tell her? Show her.

"Will I do?" I found myself asking, not sure that a friend in banker's clothing was what Ruthie had in mind.

For a moment her eyes widened, as if I wasn't the answer she'd had in mind to her question. But just as quickly one corner of her mouth turned up and she said, "I don't see anyone else in line."

Little did she know, God was right behind me.

Ruthie

You'd think closing a business would be easy. Lock the door and throw away the key, or at least give it back to the landlord. I found out the process wasn't nearly as easy as I'd thought. For one thing, I had a few advertising contracts that ran until the end of the month. I didn't have cash to refund any ads that didn't air, so I felt obligated to keep the station running until the contracts had been filled. I also had files to clean out, a few pieces of office equipment to sell, and paperwork to settle with the bank.

I knew some financial advisors would tell me to declare bankruptcy, file the papers, clear my record. But there was something deep inside me that didn't make bankruptcy an option. I talked over the other possibilities with Paul a couple weeks after I'd let the initial shock that I was going to close the station settle in my brain.

"Is the bank going to foreclose on me?" That was my number one worry. If the bank pressed the issue, I would have no option but to follow suit.

"I don't think so," Paul responded. "For one thing, you don't have enough collateral to make it feasible to collect the loan, so for us to go after your assets would be futile; and secondly, if you, in good faith, continue to make payments, well…the bank likes to do what it can to work with our customers." He scrolled the cursor down the computer screen, looking over my numerous loans. "But, frankly, Ruthie, I don't see how you can continue to make these payments. Do you have any idea what you'll do once the station closes?"

I shook my head. I hadn't allowed myself to think beyond the day at hand. If I did I was afraid some sort of paralysis would set in, leaving me incapable of even showing up at the station and unlocking the door. I was going through the motions of my life and that took all the energy I had.

"Have you heard anything from Jack?" Paul asked. "If you can't make the payments, we could go after him for the money."

"Jack?" I laughed, the first bit of macabre humor I'd found in this whole situation. "He didn't have a dime when he left, and I can't imagine he has a penny more now."

Paul nodded. A person didn't have to know Jack for long to know he was all talk and no action. "It's going to be a stretch for you to pay this off." Paul's eyes darted toward the computer screen that was filled with loan numbers and balances.

Even though I couldn't see the numbers clearly from where I sat, I knew there were years' worth of payments blinking on that screen. "My idea," I explained, feeling my face flush, "is to pay whatever I can each month out of whatever kind of paycheck I'm getting." Boy, that sounded lame. I couldn't believe those words had come out of my mouth. I felt like I was begging in some way. Pleading that the bank would let me make my meager payments and not force me into bankruptcy. "I know it won't be much, but I at least want to try to pay off the money I owe. Will the bank let me do that?" My voice was high and unsure, much like that of a child asking permission to do something when she already knew the answer was no.

"Your intentions are admirable, Ruthie." Paul looked directly at me, making my feeble plea seem not quite so small. "We have customers who are more than happy to give the bank back our collateral, cars that have been trashed with three years worth of payments left, that sort of thing. They walk away from their obligation with hardly a qualm. It's refreshing to talk to someone who's honestly trying to do what's right." Paul smiled. "Really, it is."

I smiled back, a shape my mouth hadn't been in much these days. It felt good. It also felt good to know Paul appreciated what I wanted to do.

The problem was, how was I going to do it?

A month later I held the door as Mike walked out carrying the large reel-to-reel tape player that had been the first item Jack and I had purchased for KBRS. It was a bit like watching a thief steal a dream. The trouble was I couldn't run after Mike and yell, "Stop! Come back!" Somewhere along the line, this dream had turned into a nightmare and I couldn't wake up. I walked back into the station. It looked as if a flock of vultures had dropped in for easy pickings. Bits of paper littered the floor. Dust balls appeared in corners I'd swept clean the night before.

True to his word, Paul had become the friend I'd wished for in his office a month earlier. He'd stopped by the station almost every day, asking if there was something he could help me do. He'd looked over licensing agreements for me, helped me drag Jack's heavy desk across the carpet so I could vacuum under it, and then helped move it back. He'd also helped me tag most of the office items with fire-sale prices. As he dumped the cassette tapes into a large cardboard box and I labeled it *fifty cents each or three for a dollar,* I teased Paul, "If this is what they mean by full-service banking, I'm all for it." He threw back his head and laughed, then ruffled my hair with his hand, letting it linger softly on my head, longer than necessary. I reached to my head, taking his hand in mine.

I'd been so focused on closing the station, trying to avoid thinking about what was next, I hadn't noticed the easy closeness that had developed between us. Until now. Suddenly it didn't seem so easy.

Paul looked at me, a glad softness in his eyes.

Kiss me, I thought, unexpectedly wanting more than the friend I'd asked him to be.

Instead he squeezed my hand and released it saying, "What do you want me to do now?"

Hold me. I pushed away the unsettling thought. Even if my future was uncertain, I wasn't about to hitch my hopes on a man. I'd done that once before and look where it had taken me…or hadn't taken me. I was in the middle of a mess, literally and physically, and this time I was getting out of it for good.

"Could you put this box of tapes on the counter near the door? I think people will notice them better than if I leave them on the floor. Then I think that's about it." There, that would get Paul away from me. Away, where I couldn't smell his crisp aftershave. Couldn't feel the warmth of his hand in mine. Away, where I couldn't see him and think *you are so handsome.* I'd been the one to say I wanted a friend, but if that were the case, why did I have these feelings every time he was near?

I could hear Paul place the box on the counter in the outer room. He loudly dusted his hands together, then patted them on his jeans. He poked his head around the corner. "If you don't have anything else for me to do, I'm going to run. There's a Wildlife Club meeting tonight that I think I'll try to catch."

"Oh, I'm sorry!" I could feel my face turn red. He'd caught me red-handed with my thoughts. "I didn't know you had a meeting tonight. You didn't have to—"

Paul stepped into the room and put his hands on my shoulders, stopping my frantic apologizing. "I wanted to be here."

Again, I felt a longing toward him. The reason I'd maneuvered him out of the room in the first place. "Well, thanks," I said, not noticing anything but the steadying warmth of his hands on my shoulders and the way his lips seemed to be suddenly moving toward me. I froze. Every fiber in my being cried out for him to kiss me, while another part of me yelled, "*Don't!*" afraid a kiss might ruin the friendship we had.

His hands slid up my neck, cupping the back of my head, holding me as though I were a fragile vase. Then, just as I was going to tilt my head into his hands and raise my lips to his, he pressed my head forward, touching his forehead to mine. "You're welcome," he said.

So many thoughts had raced through my mind in the past minute I couldn't, for the life of me, think what Paul was talking about. I nodded dumbly, hoping he knew exactly what this conversation was about.

"Good luck with the sale tomorrow," he added, dropping his soft hands from my head, reminding me that I'd thanked him for helping.

"Thanks," I said, my head feeling strangely loose without his firm hold.

⌒

All but a few of the older tapes had sold. Folks from Brewster had trickled in and out all day. Most had come out of pure curiosity, some to buy the remnants of a broken dream. The two files cabinets had sold immediately. Dave bought them both. I hoped he really needed them and wasn't just trying to bail me out. Jack's desk had gone to a local business, and Ben Pearson had purchased mine for his daughter, Steph. He was reaching for his billfold when he stopped, his hand moving from his back pocket to the desktop. He picked up the small Statue of Liberty figurine I'd left standing there, the sole sentinel left of my dream, her tarnished torch shining on nothing.

"Hey," Ben asked, "is this for sale too? One of the kids might like it."

I took the small statue in my hand, rolling it around much like my thoughts were spinning. My Aunt Lillian's long-ago words echoed in my mind, "I wonder where in the world we'll find Ruth someday?" *Find Ruth?* I remembered again how I'd thought she meant I would be lost. Well, she was right, I was. Lost, right here in Brewster. Only this time there was no mother, no father, who would rescue me.

"For sale?" I repeated dumbly, as if there were a going price for dreams. "No." I shook my head. "It's not for sale. Just take it." Why not? Everything else was gone.

So there they went, my dreams in Ben Pearson's pocket, cradled by cotton instead of my heart. Since I was feeling so generous I'd thrown in the desk chair for an extra twenty dollars, providing he'd let me use the set for another day or so. I still had a couple drawers to empty.

I sat behind my desk, automatically glancing toward the spot on the wall where the large clock had hung. A faded pale circle was all that remained. How many times had I looked at that clock over the past years, gauging the hours, the minutes, the seconds until air time? Now I gazed at my wrist, wondering at the time, then wondering why

I needed to know. I had nowhere to be, nowhere to go. I had all the time in the world to do exactly as I pleased. If only I knew what that was.

Automatically my eyes searched the empty spot on the wall again, so used to monitoring the time even a bare wall couldn't stop me. As if a movie were playing on the wall I recalled the last time I'd needed that clock…the final broadcast from KBRS.

I'd let Mike Anderson have the honors, letting him play disc jockey one last time. I'd put in my share of time behind that mike, I didn't feel the need to countdown the minutes as if it were some sort of death row watch. But it felt like it all the same.

I'd watched the clock slowly tick by the minutes, stepping into the broadcast room in time to take over the microphone from Mike, reading the final words I'd written out just in case my mind went blank. "This is Ruthie Hammond from KBRS saying goodnight and goodbye." I read the words I'd scribbled, a sudden lump forming deep in my chest. "This is your voice in the country." *The voice that would be silent after tonight.* Tears burned my eyes. "It's been a pleasure serving you." *It really had been.* "Thank you for listening." I turned from the mike, glad I hadn't written anything more.

Mike Anderson poked his head around my shoulder, practically swallowing the microphone, "Th-th-th-that's all, folks!" Brewster's own Porky Pig. I couldn't help but smile through my tears as he turned off the mike, then said, "I planned that for awhile." An impish grin covered his face.

I wasn't smiling anymore.

I pressed my eyes shut, trying to stop time. Turn it back to when the future held hope. I opened my eyes. Nothing had changed. Empty walls and a littered floor were all that remained of this failed dream.

What was I going to do? The question had popped into my mind at least once every five minutes over the past month. I'd managed to keep from thinking about it by keeping busy. Being on the air as much as possible, handing the broadcasting duties to Mike only when he breathed down my neck saying, "I wanna play some music." I cleaned files. Organized tapes that didn't need rearranging. Scrubbed the bathroom floor, then did it again. All the while pushing the question, "What am I going to do?" further back in my mind. After today, pushing the thought away wasn't going to be an option.

I reached for my desk drawer. I didn't have to think about my future for a few more hours, at least not until I cleaned out the last two drawers of my desk. I tugged at the drawer handle, the overloaded drawer first sticking then rolling loosely off its track, thumping onto the floor. I dumped the contents into a pile in the middle of the dirty carpet. It was surprising how quickly important papers turned into junk when the reason for their importance was no longer in existence. Within minutes most of the paper filled the only other object in the room, a large black garbage bag. Quickly, I went through the papers in the second drawer, finding nothing of importance worth keeping. It was humbling to see the flimsy paper I'd put so much stock in, paper that had at one time, only weeks ago, made me feel important, lie meaningless in the trash. I upended the drawer and was just about to return it to the empty slot in the desk when I noticed a small slip of paper stuck in the corner. I grabbed it, ready to toss it on top of the garbage when I caught a glimpse of the heading: United States Postal Service, Box Rent Paid. Of all the things I'd thought to do over the past month to close KBRS, the one thing I hadn't thought of was closing the postal box. I'd even stopped picking up the mail in the past week, knowing there were no advertising checks I was expecting. And, having closed all my accounts around town, I wasn't, for once, expecting any bills either.

Pocketing the box rent slip as a reminder I shoved the drawer into place. I tied the top of the trash bag and slid it to the door. I'd take it out when Ben came to pick up the desk and chair. I closed the KBRS door behind me, probably the second to last time I'd lock it. What was I going to do after tomorrow?

Well, I didn't have to think about it now. I pushed the ring of keys into my pocket and headed to the café. I'd ask Vicky if I could use their postal box number until I made other plans. When I'd told Vicky I would be closing the station, she'd empathized with me. She knew the work and money I'd put into the station over the years, knew it had turned into my dream as much as Jack's.

"What will you do?" she'd asked after I'd explained what it would take to close KBRS.

"I don't know," I replied, shrugging my shoulders in a way that covered my worry. Inside I felt a rise of panic. I had nowhere to go. No college degree to market. I was in the exact same spot I'd been almost twenty years ago after our parents had died. Living in Brewster. No job. No hopes for the future. Well, maybe not the exact same spot. Now I had no inheritance to fall back on. Just enormous debt. "Something will turn up," I said, sounding as though I had corporate headhunters calling me daily.

"You could help me here," Vicky said. Even though we'd been at the house at the time, I knew she'd meant the café.

"You never know," I'd said, while at the same time I'd thought, *never in a million years.* If I was ever going to get out of Brewster, now was the time. Either now, or I'd have to hire someone to drive my coffin out of town when I was eighty. Working at the café was not an option. But this afternoon as I crossed the street to Vicky's café I still didn't have a clue what was.

As usual, Vicky was busy pouring coffee, dashing in and out of the kitchen as she single-handedly tried to fry up a hamburger and serve pie and coffee to the late afternoon crowd.

"Could you?" she said as I walked in the door. She held up both coffeepots. "All you have to do is pour." She set the pots on the hot pad and dashed back to the kitchen.

I hung my coat on the coat rack and grabbed the pots, making my way around the tables, topping off half-empty cups.

"I see you got promoted!" Mr. Baumiller, my old high school superintendent, hadn't gotten any funnier since he retired.

I chuckled politely. *Very funny.* I was tempted to overpour his cup on purpose. Quickly I turned to the next table, cutting off his chance for more brilliant remarks.

"You going to be working here now?" My luck, today of all days. Mr. Magner from the grocery store had taken a rare coffee break.

"No, just filling in." I said, pasting a smile on my face, wondering what everyone else in the café was thinking. The closing of the radio station had been front-page news in the *Brewster Banner* last week.

"I can always use an extra checker at the store." Mr. Magner sipped his coffee. "We offer benefits."

All ears in the café were tuned our way. The only benefit Mr. Magner could offer me would be to quit talking.

"Sorry," I replied, "I have some other things lined up."

Like what?

"Like vhat?" Apparently Mrs. Bauer could read my mind.

I smiled enigmatically. I filled her cup without saying a word. Let everyone wonder what I would be doing. It would give them something to think about other than their own boring lives.

And yours is so fascinating?

Just like that it hit me—my life held nothing for anyone to wonder about. I'd spent my whole life in this dumpy little town, imagining a life that didn't exist. A life I'd always known was waiting for me somewhere. Anywhere but here. A life I'd never had and never would have. This was it. This was what my life had come to. Pouring coffee into empty cups at my sister's café. Sudden tears filled my eyes. My throat closed. I hated my life. I hated this town. Hated everything about these people. If it hadn't been for the prison Brewster had become, I would have been out of here ages ago and made something for myself. Now I had nothing. Nothing.

Blinking rapidly I threaded my way through the tables, ignoring Pastor Ammon pointing to his cup for a refill. I had to get out of here. I set the coffeepots onto their warming pad and turned left toward the front door, my line of escape. It swung open, Dan Jordan entering with a wave to the crowd. I turned right and ran into the kitchen, a small sob escaping my throat.

"What's wrong?" Vicky was pulling an order of fries from the deep fryer.

"Something in my eye," I croaked, dashing to the private bathroom behind the kitchen. I knew Vicky wouldn't be fooled by my lie, but she didn't have time to follow me either. I needed to be alone. My sobs echoed against the bathroom walls. It didn't matter if Vicky could hear them or not. I simply had no control over the emotion pouring from my throat.

"Ruthie, are you okay?" Vicky's voice filtered through the door.

I shook my head behind the closed door, but choked out, "Ye-es." I'd lied to myself for twenty years, why stop now? As Vicky's footsteps retreated I sunk my face into my hands and let the tears flow. Gut-wrenching sobs pushed from my throat as I sunk to the floor. Nothing. I really did have nothing. My mind and body felt empty, a vast desert with only one oasis and that was filled with tears. I let them pour out.

I don't know how long I sat there, but eventually the tears stopped. I splashed cold water on my face, hoping to wash away any traces of the hopelessness I felt. Whatever my future held, it wasn't hidden in this small bathroom that smelled of French fries and hamburgers. I opened the door ready to tell Vicky I had a bad case of PMS. Anything but the truth. The kitchen was empty. Only a stockpot of soup simmering on the stove gave indication anyone was here. I didn't hear any voices coming from the front of the café. No spoons clinking in cups, no coffee cups being put into saucers. Slowly, I pushed open the swinging door leading from the kitchen. The coffee crowd had left and it was too early for supper. My eyes did a quick sweep of the café. Six clean tables and twice as many booths sat empty, waiting for diners. The room was deserted; even Vicky was gone. Maybe she'd stepped out to empty the garbage and I could grab my coat and make a clean getaway.

Almost on tiptoe I hurried toward my coat, ready to nab it from its hook and put it on after I got outside. The less explaining I had to do to Vicky, the better.

"Rootie!" Mrs. Bauer's voice caught me like a bullet in the back. Where had she come from? I whipped around. In the back corner of the café she sat, her wrinkled hands wrapped around a coffee cup. "Wicky had to run to Mackner's to get some breadt. I said I'd stay and vatch the café until she got back. Come here." She patted the booth beside her. "Come wisit with me."

I looked at my watch as if I were in a hurry, then remembered I had nowhere to go other than the post office. I could close my box as easily tomorrow as today. Visiting with Mrs. Bauer would give me an excuse to put off thinking about what lay ahead after I stopped at the post office. Slowly, as if I were trying to use up time when in reality that was all I had, I refilled Mrs. Bauer's cup, then poured one for myself. I slid into the booth across from her.

"Mmmm, this tastes good." I gulped half the hot liquid in two large swallows, realizing I was probably dehydrated from all my crying. I took another large gulp then got up to refill my cup.

"Vhat are you running from, Rootie?" Mrs. Bauer's wire-thin voice stopped me in my tracks.

"What do you mean?" I asked, turning back, knowing as I asked the question I was inviting a conversation I didn't want.

"First you run away from the coffee crowdt, then you run avay from talking witt me, and," she paused, lifting her cup for a slow sip, and then nestling it back into its saucer before speaking, "I hear you are maybe going to run away from Brewster."

I had to give her credit; she didn't beat around the bush. "What have you heard?" I slipped into the booth without refilling my cup. I might as well hear what the entire town must be gossiping about.

Mrs. Bauer lifted her cup for another slow sip, then set it down. Her ceramic-warmed hands encircled mine like soft gloves. The café was completely silent as if waiting for her words, and I found myself eager to hear what she had to say, feeling as though she had some sort of message for me. I squeezed her hands, encouragement in my grasp.

"Rootie," she said, her voice sure, "tink of your namesake."

Who was she talking about? I'd never been told I'd been named after anyone in the family. What did Mrs. Bauer know that I didn't? "Namesake?" I asked.

"Yah," she replied, "your namesake. Root, from the Bible."

Inwardly I sagged. Oh great, *that* Ruth. I felt my grip on Mrs. Bauer's hands loosen. I knew the story of that Ruth, and she had nothing to teach me.

"She vas a strong woman," Mrs. Bauer said.

Oh yes, Ruth the follower, as I'd thought of her all these years. So strong. The woman who blindly followed her mother-in-law all over the country.

Mrs. Bauer couldn't hear my mental protest and went on. "She followed her mother-in-law even vhen she didn't haff to. Vhen it wouldt have seemed she wouldt be better off going another vay."

Well, maybe Mrs. Bauer did have a point. I'd done the same thing, followed a man right into financial ruin when certainly another way would have been better. Okay, I'd give her one point. But I knew there were no other lessons here for me to learn. I slipped my hands from hers and picked up my cup. Let the woman talk. I'd sit here until Vicky returned and then pass Mrs. Bauer off to her.

"Vhy, that Root, she vas a hart vorker. Chust like you." Mrs. Bauer was practically spitting her words. "Look at you, running dat radio station all on your own."

Okay, one more point.

"Dat can't be easy." She patted the table where my hand had been. "Vell, neither vas it easy for Root. She hat to go out in the fields and pick up grain *after* the men had harvested it."

Kind of like me trying to pick up the pieces after Jack left? I put down my coffee cup and laid my hands on the table, just in case Mrs. Bauer needed to touch them again.

"How much grain coult haff been left for her to pick up? But Root didn't complain. She chust vent out there and picked up vhat she couldt find." Now Mrs. Bauer reached for my hands, as I'd found myself hoping she would. "Oh, Rootie, don't tink I don't see how hard you vork."

The tears I'd thought I'd left in the bathroom burned my eyes as Mrs. Bauer went on. "And den dat other Root, vhy she lookt after her mother-in-law."

Just when I'd been ready to concede maybe I did have some similarities to the Ruth from the Bible, Mrs. Bauer had to throw that in. The tears that had threatened instantly dried. What kind of parallel could she possibly draw from in-laws? In-laws I'd never had. Even if I'd thought to claim Jack's folks as some sort of pretend-relatives, they had been divorced and gone from Brewster long before I'd paired up with him. I doubted even Jack knew where they were.

My negative thoughts did nothing to stop Mrs. Bauer. "Vell, the way Root looked after her mother-in-law vas chust like you looked after Wicky after your folks were kilt in that terrible accident." She took her hands from mine and pulled a napkin from the holder on the table, wiping at her eyes as if the accident had happened yesterday. "She didn't haff to look after her mother-in-law, chust like you didn't haff to look after Wicky. You chust did what vas right."

Why is it so hard to imagine that you could have something in common with someone from the Bible?

Suddenly I felt like wiping my eyes, too, and reached for a napkin. What was it with my emotions? One minute I was a sarcastic rock, the next a blubbering idiot. Hot tears streamed down my face, a reminder of that time when Vicky and I had been left alone. A reminder now, of how alone I still was. Of the nothingness looming ahead.

Thankfully, Mrs. Bauer didn't notice my Jekyll-and-Hyde turns. She went right on talking through her tears. "And Root, she vas left witt nothing."

Had she just said Ruth had been left with nothing? Had Mrs. Bauer read my mind? Was she talking about the biblical Ruth, or me? Or both of us? It was almost creepy.

Or divine.

I shook off the strange thought, curious as to what Mrs. Bauer might have to say next.

"Root's husbant had died. And back in those times a woman hatt no rights wittout a husbant." Obviously she was talking about the other Ruth. "Oh, Root, you may tink you are wittout hope, but you're not." So she was talking about me again. This was getting weird. Half the time I couldn't figure out which Ruth she meant.

Maybe it doesn't matter which Ruth she's talking about as long as you understand the message.

"Gott has a wonderful plan for you. I chust know He does."

Well, if that's what His message was, it would be nice if He'd clue me in on the specifics. Mrs. Bauer's vague ramblings weren't doing a thing except cooling the little bit of coffee in my cup. I sneaked a peek at my watch. If I hurried I could still make it to the post office and close my box.

Mrs. Bauer patted her hand on the table as if it were a period at the end of a sentence. "...she fount a husbant."

Oh, goodness, in the two seconds I'd been looking at my watch Mrs. Bauer had changed subjects. Someone in town was getting married? Who could that be? There weren't many single people in a town this size, and none I knew were in a serious relationship. If I wanted to know who, I'd have to show my inattention and ask. I dabbed at my dry lips with a napkin, a decoy to make her think I'd been busy swallowing, or something. "Excuse me," I said, "who did you say was getting married?"

"Root!" she said, sounding surprised, as if I were the one getting married and didn't even know it.

"Me?" I said, pointing at myself, wondering if Mrs. Bauer had lost her mind in the last minute.

"Acht!" She laughed, her rounded shoulders shaking, "you're having fun witt me."

Well, I was, but not intentionally. I nodded. Let her think my confusion was a joke.

Mrs. Bauer picked up the conversational ball as if I'd never dropped it. "And it vas after Ruth did all those goot tings, then she fount a husband."

Oh, boy, I should have seen where this was going.

"He vas a goot man too." Mrs. Bauer reached across the table and patted my hand. "I know there iss a goot man chust vaiting for you. Gott has been preparing his heart especially for you. One day you'll see. I'm praying goot tings for you, Rootie."

Inwardly I scoffed. I'd sat here all this time, listening to an old Bible story, only to find out Mrs. Bauer's point was that a man was the answer to my problems? No, she had it all wrong. A man had *been* my problem. Jack.

Jesus.

Under different circumstances I might have thought a swear word had followed Jack's name, but this word had a whole different tone.

Jesus.

Once more, the strange voice that had been interrupting this whole conversation spoke. I felt goose bumps dimple my arms. Was this Mrs. Bauer's message?

Not hers. Mine.

Okay, now I was officially creeped out. I'd been able to pass off the other interruptions as random thoughts popping into my head. But this was no thought of mine. I glanced around the café as if to find an explanation for this strange interference. The room seemed oddly empty. Come to think of it, it was also strange that Vicky had left Mrs. Bauer in charge. That Vicky hadn't returned minutes ago. After all, Magner's was only across the street.

I work in mysterious ways.

Well, that did it. I was out of here. I slid from the booth. "Nice talking to you, Mrs. Bauer, but I need to get to the post office before the window closes." She opened her mouth to reply, but I wasn't about to take a chance on anything more she might have to say. Or what anyone else might have to say. Whoever that voice belonged to. "I need to close my post office box, and tomorrow Ben Pearson is coming to the station to pick up my desk..." I walked backwards towards the café door, talking all the while. "And I'll need to vacuum the floors..." If I sounded like an idiot, I didn't care. Let my babbling fill the void. Better that than thoughts that didn't originate from my mind.

"Sorry. Sorry." Vicky rushed in the door as I slipped one arm into my coat, ready to make my getaway. She waved to Mrs. Bauer. "Thanks for watching the café. No one came in, I see."

"No," Mrs. Bauer said, "it was chust Rootie and me. Ve had a nice wisit."

"I'm glad," Vicky replied as she walked to the kitchen, completely oblivious to that mustard-seed voice I'd been hearing as if it were another customer in her café.

I don't know why I'd thought I was in such a hurry to get to the post office. The building held nothing for me but the final stamp that KBRS was officially closed. The closer I got to the door, the slower my feet moved, the faster my heart beat. This was it. The last thing to do and KBRS would be no more. What was I going to do? No magic answers had appeared in all my wondering. Tomorrow looked as empty as the day after. I felt a rise of panic in my chest. I needed a job, and I needed it yesterday. I wanted to leave Brewster, but now that I had the chance I had no money, and I was scared.

Help! I screamed in my mind to whatever forces heard those sorts of cries. *What am I supposed to do?* I yanked open the post office door.

Do not fear. I am with you.

I stopped in my tracks. I knew the postmaster, Dale Herr, and he'd never say something like that. I stared at Dale, who stood with his mouth unmoving. Again I heard, *I am with you.* "What did you say?"

"I was wondering when you'd be in." Apparently Dale had been monitoring my schedule as closely as the rest of the town. He tossed a handful of mail into a dirty, gray sack. "Figured you'd be in to close your box before now. The mail's been piling up in there. Third-class mostly, but you also have a couple first-class letters." Ah, the privacy of Brewster. "I left them out of the box so they wouldn't get jammed in there with the catalogs and stuff." He walked behind the sorting partition. I could hear him pulling mail from my box. He returned with a jumbled pile of mail. Catalogs, fliers, junk. I sorted through the stack quickly. No need to drag stuff back to the station when I could dump it here.

All that was left of the pile when I was done were the two first-class letters Dale had placed on top of the stack when he'd given it to me. Both of the envelopes had radio station call letters as the return address. Probably asking if KBRS would pick up a program they were offering in syndication. Sorry. I held them over the trash can, then decided if they'd paid first-class postage, the least I could do was open them. I stuffed the letters into my coat pocket, then fumbled with my key ring. How long had this KBRS post box key been on my key chain? Too long to have nothing to show for it. I didn't even want to think about it. I slid the key across the counter, waiting for Dale to offer his condolences on one more business closing in Brewster, one less postal box he had to fill.

"Got the other key?"

"Huh?"

"You got the other key?" Dale pointed at a card he had pulled from a file. "The record shows there were two keys with this box."

"Uh, well," I stammered, surprised at not receiving the sympathy I somehow expected. "I guess Jack took the other one with him."

"I'll have to charge you."

So much for sympathy. I pulled five dollars from my purse and tossed it on the counter. Just like Jack to leave me with one last bill. I turned to leave, ready to march over to the station and use my anger to give the place one last cleaning. I was going to wipe all traces of Jack, and then this town, from my feet.

And how do you plan to do that when you don't have a job? You don't have a college education? You don't have anything to show for all these years? The now familiar panic weighed on my chest.

"What do you want me to do with your mail from now on?" Dale's words caught me as the door was closing.

"Put it in Vicky's box," I called, my voice sounding high and scared. I couldn't imagine there was anyone left in the world who needed to mail me anything.

"That's what I figured." Even though the door between us was closed I could hear Dale's assumption.

I wrapped my coat around myself as the damp early spring wind nipped at my legs. This is what my life had become. So predictable even the postman had me figured out. Pathetic.

Back at the station I threw my coat on the floor, then plopped into the one remaining chair. After today I wouldn't even have this empty office space as refuge. I put my elbows on the desk and sunk my head into my hands. An empty roar filled my brain. The sound of panic.

I'm praying goot tings for you.

Mrs. Bauer's words pushed their way in between the emptiness and fear. Right now I couldn't think of one good thing in my life.

Oh, Mrs. Bauer, pray hard.

In desperation I called to Mrs. Bauer's God. If she had so much faith in Him, maybe He'd listen to me just this once. *Help me. Help me. Help me.* My words were feeble but I had no other prayer. Not even tears came to wash away the hopelessness I felt. *Help me.*

Minutes later I sat back in the chair. No answer had come to my cry. What now? My eyes fell on my rumpled coat at the side of the desk, the two letters poking from the pocket. I grabbed them. Two last pieces of garbage for the bag. I slit the first one open with my thumb and scanned the letter quickly.

> *Dear Ms. Hammond:*
>
> *Thank you for your inquiry about an on-air position at our station. We regret to inform you we are not hiring at this time. We will place your letter in our files, and should we find need of your services in the future we will be sure to contact you...*

A rueful snort of air pushed from my nose. How many months ago had I sent out that request? I remembered what seemed like ages ago. I'd sat on my old bed in Vicky's basement so sure all it would take was a letter from me and I'd have stations across the country begging for my voice to be on their airwaves. All it would take was a letter to transport me out of Brewster. I'd thought I had heard from all the stations I'd sent my résumé and air-check tape to. I'd forgotten about this one. Well, if they were going to put my letter in their files, I'd add theirs to mine. I ripped the paper into tiny pieces and tossed them in the direction of the garbage bag in the outer room. My failure littered the floor. I slit open the second letter, ready to shred it as well. My eyes scanned the letter, then slowed and read the words again. I placed the letter on my lap, my heart hammering in my chest. One minute. I'd wait one minute and then read it again.

I picked up the envelope, studying the call letters on the return address. Funny, I didn't remember ever hearing about this station, much less sending them my air-check tape. But I'd sent out over a dozen résumés so long ago I couldn't remember exactly which stations I'd sent them to. Maybe I had sent one there.

I took a deep breath, sure that a third reading of the letter would reveal something I'd missed the first two times. I lifted the letter and read it again.

> *Dear Ms. Hammond:*
>
> *Your air-check tape was impressive. I have been trying to contact you to set up an interview. Apparently the wrong phone number was on your résumé. Please call me as soon as possible as I am anxious to talk to you about a possible position at our station...*

Automatically my hand reached for the phone. When my hand grabbed air, I remembered I'd had phone service stopped two weeks ago. The phone had been sold at the sale. I jumped from the chair, ready to run to Vicky's house and make the call, then realized it was almost supper time, too late to call any business to set up an interview. I sunk back into the chair, my knees weak. I smoothed the letter on my desktop. Minneapolis. A station in Minneapolis wanted me to work for them.

Oh, Lord, I thought, understanding for the second time this day that I was truly praying. *Thank You.*

As quickly as the prayer went through my mind another thought followed, *Are you sure you still want to leave?*

The Detroit Route

Paul

I didn't realize how much I'd started counting on Ruthie's friendship until she was gone. Life in Brewster seemed somehow dulled without her dropping into my office to say, "Hi!" Walking across the street to Vicky's café wasn't near the adventure it had been when I'd thought I might bump into Ruthie. Stopping off at Vicky and Dave's house wasn't the same either. Sure, Sam and Angie always had something to tell me about school, and Dave was ready to discuss whatever game happened to be on TV, but it was Vicky I really wanted to talk to. She was always eager to fill me in on Ruthie's latest adventures in Minneapolis.

"So," I'd ask, wandering casually into the kitchen, considering myself fortunate to find Vicky at home, "what do you hear from Ruthie?"

"She found an apartment." Vicky stirred a pot of chili on the stove. "And she found a couch at a secondhand store. It's navy." She stopped and laughed. "Oh, I guess you wouldn't care about that."

I did. I found myself caring about everything Ruthie did. "Did she say how work is going?"

"Good."

I couldn't believe Vicky thought "good" was an answer. I was trying to figure out how to get her to say more when she said, "Here, taste this for me."

She held out a spoonful of chili. I blew on it, then stuck it in my mouth. "Good," I said.

She swatted at me. "Good? That's all you can say when I've stood here for an hour adding stuff to this pot? Is it too spicy? Not enough? What?"

There. She didn't like the short version either. "It's good," I reiterated. "Just enough bite to make it challenging." Glancing at my mom's copy of *Cook's Illustrated* magazine had served me well. "Speaking of challenges, did Ruthie say any more about her new job?"

Vicky gave me a sidelong glance. Maybe jumping from spices to Ruthie was a stretch, but if Vicky could pump for information, so could I. "Oh," she said, stirring the chili as if it was more important than my question, "she said there's a lot of new equipment to learn to use. That was about it."

That was about it? About it? I'd learned as much in the brief note Ruthie had tucked in with her loan payment to the bank.

The second week after Ruthie had left, I'd received a letter at the bank. It had already been slit open and my secretary had removed the check Ruthie had enclosed as payment on her loan. The note had been casual. *I found an apartment and bought a couch.* She'd left out the part about it being from the secondhand store and navy. *There's a learning curve on the job, but it's fun.* She didn't say a thing about missing Brewster. But then, knowing Ruthie, I hadn't expected her to. I just wanted her to.

"Oh!" Vicky's exclamation cut into my memory, "I almost forgot. Ruthie wanted me to mail her leather jacket. She forgot it."

Listening to Vicky's report was about as interesting as listening to a shopping list. Either I already had the ingredients or didn't need what was being offered. What I wanted to hear was about Ruthie. What she was thinking. Feeling. If she missed anything about Brewster. For instance, me. Without that information the news seemed somehow lacking. As if the life had been left out. Much like Brewster felt without her.

"Guess I'll be going," I said, knowing there was no more for Vicky to tell. "Tell the kids 'bye.'" I grabbed the coat I'd hung on the kitchen chair when I'd arrived. The phone right by me on the wall rang. "Want me to get it?" I asked.

"Nah, it'll be for Angie. Aren't you going to stay for chili?" Vicky sounded surprised.

"No," I said, not hungry at all. "I'll grab a sandwich later. Mom's at the senior center and I have some work to do."

"Mo-om," Angie called from upstairs, "phone. It's Auntie Ruth."

Vicky smiled at me. "Why don't you pick it up? This chili is about ready to serve, and I'm sure Ruthie would like to hear your voice for a change."

I grabbed at the receiver, a football player catching the perfect pass. "Hi, Ruth? It's Paul."

"Paul?" She paused, a small sigh passing through the line. "It's so good to hear your voice. What's been going on in Brewster? Did Dan get the station building rented out? How's your mom? What about…"

I settled into the kitchen chair, the phone pressed to my ear, not even trying to answer her barrage of questions. Obviously she had been thinking about Brewster. Vicky placed a bowl in front of me, raising her eyebrows my way. *Want to stay?* I nodded, suddenly ravenous. Nothing seemed more satisfying than chili, homemade bread, and Ruthie on the other end of the line.

⌒

I held the *Be a Better Manager* brochure in my hands. Had Nancy placed it on top of my morning mail pile intentionally? It was hard to miss the fact the meeting was being held in Minneapolis, but I highly doubted Nancy knew just how often each day I thought about Ruthie.

Well, I didn't have to decide on attending the meeting today. It wouldn't be held for another month. Maybe I'd come to my senses before then. I set the brochure on a stack of papers on the credenza behind my desk and continued going through the bank mail. My thoughts drifted to the phone conversation I'd had with Ruthie at Vicky's several nights ago.

"It's so good to hear your voice," she'd said.

It was good to hear hers too.

"It was good talking to you," I'd said as Vicky called the family in to eat after the quickest supper preparations I'd ever witnessed.

"I'll talk to you soon," Ruthie said.

When? I'd wanted to ask.

"Take care," she added.

"You too," I replied, wondering if she could hear the questions I hadn't asked. Are you okay? Are you safe walking to and from your car? Has anyone asked you out? Do you miss me?

Even I was baffled by my emotions. I'd been hesitant about committing my heart to anyone after Mia and Jenny had died, but I continued to trust that God had a plan. During the past year I'd found myself longing to have a relationship again but had never felt that sort of chemistry with Corinne. And even though Sam still thought his teacher, Sandy Quinn, and I should get together, I hadn't done much but answer his persistent, "What do you think of my teacher?" questions with one of my own. "What do you think I should think about her?" All I'd get was a sly smile. A fifth grader's crush on his teacher being batted into my ballpark. I hadn't pursued his blatant hints, but now with Ruthie gone, maybe this was God's way of telling me He had other plans.

But it was Ruthie I found myself wanting to see. Ruthie who made me laugh every time we talked, who made me think about her even when she wasn't in Brewster anymore. Ruthie, who didn't seem to care one way or another about her faith.

That was the baffling part. Why would God have me so attracted to someone who didn't believe in Him?

How do you know what Ruthie believes?

How did I know? Was it God's voice that had me continuing to look for some sign of faith in her? Or was it my own stubborn will drawing me to her? Was I simply looking for a reason to justify the attraction? Make it seem like God's will when it was purely mine? Ignoring Sam's prodding toward Sandy when maybe it was God prodding him?

Once again my questions circled about with no answers to stop them. I threw several pieces of mail into the garbage can at my feet, determined to concentrate on work. I ruffled through the rest, finding myself looking for Ruth's printed handwriting. So much for concentration. Why was I so anxious to hear from her? Why did I search the mail each day hoping for another brief note like the ones she included with her loan payments?

The evenings I'd spent at the station, helping her sort through what remained of KBRS, had somehow served to cement the friendship we'd been building. Maneuvering Jack's desk through the doorway had pointed out how alike our minds worked.

"A little to the left," Ruthie had said. I'd known, instinctively, she'd meant *her* left, my right.

"I'm going to bring 'er down," I'd replied, trying to squeeze the desk around the corner without scratching the top. Without a word, in perfect synchronization, Ruthie had raised her end, exactly the move we'd needed to round the corner.

There'd been a closeness between us that felt like something more than mere friendship. Something that didn't need to be put into words but begged to be said anyway. That last night at the station I'd wanted to kiss her. Wanted to tell her what I'd been feeling. But once again, something kept the words inside. I'd held her face in my hands, looked into her eyes, then touched her forehead with mine instead of kissing her lips.

I'd practically run from the station to the Wildlife Club meeting, not sure what I was fleeing. I wasn't sure where Ruthie was with her faith, and that was starting to not matter so much to me. Was that the reason I ran, so I wouldn't say words I'd regret later? Words offering a promise God knew I shouldn't make? Maybe instead of the Wildlife Club meeting I should have run to church.

That night after I left the station having immediate answers to my questions hadn't seemed to matter. I'd thought I would have time to let my relationship with Ruthie grow, letting God reveal His will in His own time, not mine. Instead, any unfolding answers had been cut off with something so simple as a letter.

"Paul, guess what?" Ruthie had dashed into my office late one afternoon, stopping in her tracks when she saw my secretary, Nancy, sitting across from me going over the bank's personnel policy. "Oh, sorry," she'd said, backing up, a video in slow rewind, "I'll come back later. I knocked on the side door and Peggy let me in. I assumed you weren't busy."

"No," I said, motioning to Nancy that we'd finish another time, "come in."

Ruthie danced around Nancy as she left, pulling a letter from her purse as she sat down. "The answer to Mrs. Bauer's prayers," she'd said, smoothing the letter on my desk, then spinning it around and pushing the sheet of paper my way.

Was this letter any answer to prayers by Ruthie? I was still looking for signs of a faith of her own.

I took in the radio call letters at the top of the page, then scanned the letter, wondering what Ruthie was thinking. I knew she needed a job. She'd agonized about that more than once as we organized KBRS for her sale. I also knew she still had dreams of leaving Brewster, but I wondered if our growing friendship had changed her opinion about leaving. I looked up at her. Obviously not. A grin was plastered across her face. I pasted a smile on mine.

"Wow," I said, trying to sound enthusiastic. "Have you called this guy yet?"

"Just a few minutes ago." Ruthie sat straight, a self-satisfied look on her face. "I have an interview at the end of the week." She leaned forward, her grin growing wider. "Can you believe it? I have an interview with a station in Minneapolis." She leaned back in the chair, a queen on her throne, her words coming as quickly as a messenger reporting to the castle. "This is what I've been wishing for for twenty years. I can't believe it's finally happening." She tucked a strand of hair behind her ear. "There's always a chance I won't get the job," she added, as if she didn't believe that for a second, "but the guy sounded so positive, as if he already had his mind made up to hire me. He'd heard a tape of mine and said he was really impressed." Ruthie paused, staring into space for a second, then shook her head. "I still don't understand how they got my tape. I don't remember sending it there. But," she waved a hand in the air, "who knows, maybe I did. I sent out so many. Anyway, it doesn't matter. They're looking for someone to partner with the afternoon drive-time announcer and they're looking at me! That is such a plum spot. I can't believe this is happening to me." The Cheshire cat would have been envious of her grin.

"I can't either," I said, then realized I sounded as though I didn't think she was qualified for the job. "What I mean is, it's a great opportunity and I know how long you've waited. I'm glad you're getting the chance to pursue your career." My words sounded stilted.

The truth of it was, I wasn't glad. Wasn't glad to have this letter sitting on my desk. Wasn't glad to have Ruthie so excited about a job that was going to take her far from here. Far from me. Especially just when I'd thought we'd have time to discover where our relationship was going.

I said a small prayer asking God to forgive me for pretending to be happy for Ruthie. I wasn't about to stomp on her excitement, but I did wonder why God was stomping on mine.

~

"Paul?" A short tap on my office door snapped me into present time. Wayne Jorgenson stood in the doorway. "Do you have time to go over Jason Wynn's loan with me? I have a few questions. I'm still trying to work him out of that hole we...I dug."

"Sure," I answered, glad for a diversion from my fruitless search of the mail and my fruitless thoughts of Ruthie. I cleared a spot on my desk for the Wynn file. Ruthie had an exciting new job to do and I did, too, but the fact was, my job had felt old and unexciting ever since Ruthie left town.

Ruthie

"Okay, I already figured out that when I tap this icon," I'd pointed to the computer screen in the broadcast room, "I'll get a play list for the next hour. But you're saying if I tap this one I'll get a list of the commercials that will air during the broadcast?"

"You got it."

I'd tapped at the screen and sure enough the commercial list popped onto the screen. "Amazing." I had grinned at my on-air partner, Marv.

"That's called an ROS. Run of schedule," he'd explained, tapping at the screen to show me what other marvels the computer held.

Two months later I was still marveling at the technology available in this studio. It made the equipment I'd sold in Brewster seem akin to caveman technology.

Marv held up a finger, paused, then spoke into the mike. "When you hear this sound," he played three measures of an old country song, "the nineteenth caller will get a chance to win this group's new CD."

Nineteen callers? Inside I laughed. If we'd had nineteen *listeners* in Brewster we considered it a KBRS ratings coup.

"Let's have some fun." Marv winked at me. Immediately he played the three measures and the phone started ringing. He picked up the receiver. "One," he called into the mouthpiece. Pushing the line two button he called, "Two." Then, as quickly, he went all the way to, "You're lucky number nineteen. You have a guess?"

"Diamond Rio." The voice was sure.

"Hey," Marv said, "is this Jeffrey?"

"Yep."

Marv punched a button and ta-da music played over the air. He covered the mouthpiece of the phone and whispered my way, "Prize hog." Into the mike he said, "It's one of our favorite fans." Marv rolled his eyes at me, his words a shield of deception for his feelings. "Okay, Jeff, tell our listeners what your favorite station is…"

"K-M-I-N," Jeff intoned. He'd done this before.

"The new Diamond Rio CD will be on its way. Thanks, Jeff." Marv punched at the computer screen. The strains of a song played into the air. "Here's a new one from the Dixie *Chicks*." Marv's subtle inflection was my cue.

"Love this," I said into my mike. Actually, I'd never heard the song before, but that didn't seem to matter. Our job was to push the music.

"I wish Jeffrey wouldn't have won that." Marv gazed at the clock. "It's bad when the same callers win the prizes. Makes it look like we rig the contests. If it had to be a repeater, I wish it'd been Julie." Marv drummed his fingers on the countertop, waiting for the song to be over.

"A fan?" I asked. I'd quickly learned ego feeding was part of my job in getting along with the other deejays.

Marv shrugged a shoulder, one corner of his mouth turning up. "Guess you could say that."

Obviously Julie had never seen Marv. But in this business, looks didn't count. It was all in the voice and the way you used it. On-air Marv sounded like a hip, smooth-throated flirt. Harry Connick Jr. does country. Behind the mike Marv was stretching his extra-large sweatshirt to the max. He ate his insecurity and hid behind a microphone in the broadcast booth, asking after each segment, "What'd you think?" I was learning the more I praised him the better we sounded. Good thing Jack had given me so much practice.

At first everything about this station seemed thrilling. Cutting-edge technology had deejays recording shows that aired when they weren't even in town. Advertisers practically bid on programs to sponsor. *Advertising I didn't have to sell.* They had a whole sales force dedicated to that job. I marveled to think of how many times I had listened to Cal, from the hardware store, tell his championship pen-manship story just to sell a few more minutes of advertising. All I had to do here was show up for my shift, banter on-air with Marv for a few hours, record some voice-overs, then go home. It felt like a part-time job compared to the double time I'd worked in Brewster. Double time? Make that quadruple.

"That'll do it for us today." Marv's smooth voice reminded me we were done. Another day had flown by. "Remind our listeners what the best station in Minneapolis is, Ruthie."

"That's K-B—" After years of repeating the KBRS call sign I was having a hard time wrapping my mouth around these new letters. "Uh, K-M-I-N, Marv."

That's okay, Marv mouthed. "Say so long, Ruthie."

"So long, Ruthie," I repeated. Our take-off of the old George Burns and Gracie Allen joke had become our signature sign-off.

"So," Marv, said, switching off the mike in our broadcast booth as another deejay took over the next shift from another booth, "wanna go get a drink or something?" His voice was full of the inse-curity he exhibited when he wasn't on-air.

I glanced at my watch. The last thing I wanted to do was lead Marv on. To let him think there was something between us I knew would never be. But the thought of going home, if you could call the small studio apartment I was renting home, had no appeal. There was something to be said for all the extra hours I had worked in Brewster; they hadn't left me much time to think. Something I was finding I had way too much time to do here. "Sure," I said, then added, "but I can't stay long. I'm waiting for a call from my boyfriend." An image of Paul came into mind. Where had that excuse come from? Well, he was my friend and he was a boy...okay, *man*. The rest was semantics Marv didn't need to know about. "I'll take my car and meet you at Caribou Coffee." There, that should get the message across.

"Coffee?" Marv asked. "But I don't drin— Oh, sure," he amended, probably hoping for the darkness of a bar to hide his insecurity but then quickly understanding this get-together would only happen in a coffee shop.

"So," he said a half hour later, blowing on the mochachino I'd convinced him to order, "you have a boyfriend?"

"Uh-huh," I replied, blowing on my plain decaf, the image of Paul still there. I wracked my brain for another topic. Apparently I'd used all my words on air. My mind was blank.

"From back home?" he asked, pursuing the only topic on the table. The only thing I didn't want to talk about.

"Mm-hmm," I mumbled vaguely.

"So where is home?" Marv took a gulp of his mocha. I had a feeling small talk away from a microphone wasn't his area of expertise. I'd known him a little over two months, and this was as personal as he'd gotten. Five words at a time were about his limit.

"North Dakota," I said, knowing those two words would bring this line of conversation to a halt. Every time I mentioned my home state to someone they would inevitably say, "Oh, I've heard of the Black Hills."

"That's in *South* Dakota," I'd reply, and they'd shut up like a clam.

"You don't say?" Marv sat up as straight as his belly would allow. "I used to work with a guy from North Dakota. Don't suppose you'd happen to know him. I mean, North Dakota isn't all that big."

I shrugged. What were the chances? "Who was it?" I took a sip of my coffee, waiting to hear a name I could quickly dismiss. Then what would we talk about?

"Jack. Jack Warner."

I had to give myself credit. I didn't spray my mouthful of coffee all over him. Instead, I gulped the hot liquid down while my blood ran cold. I'd read the phrase in countless mystery novels and had never known what it meant. Until now. My blood ran cold. I could feel it.

"Jack Warner?" I asked, my voice sounding much calmer than the earthquake happening on my insides. "From Brewster?"

"Mmmm," Marv replied, "not sure of the town, but it sounds familiar. Skinny guy. Red hair. Talked a lot." He shrugged, adding quickly, "Guess a lot of radio guys do. He used to work at KMIN. Had the shift before mine. That was before I got moved to afternoon drive time. Before you came." Marv gave a low whistle. "Guy knew his music, that's for sure."

That was Jack, all right. I tried to keep my jaw from dropping but it was hard. Jack had worked at KMIN and now I was working there? It hardly seemed possible in a city this size.

Marv continued without prompting. "I used to room with the guy."

I just about blurted, "*So did I*," but managed to simply nod.

"Sad story," Marv added.

I wasn't sure I wanted to hear anything about Jack, but found myself asking, "What happened?"

"Drinking problem," Marv said, shaking his head. "Gambling. Too bad, too. The guy could have written his own ticket in radio if he'd had things together."

"He left, then?" I asked. Marv's clipped style of speaking was starting to rub off.

"Fired," he said. "Least that's what I figure. One day he was working, the next he wasn't. I came home from work and his stuff was gone from the apartment." Marv swirled his coffee drink. "Not that he had much to take. I got moved to his shift at work. That was right around the time we switched formats." Marv gave me a crooked smile. "Who knew country was my thing? Next thing I know I'm being moved to drive time and hooked up with you." He shrugged. "Guess I have Jack to thank for that."

Thanking Jack for something—now that was an oxymoron.

~

"Sure, I can do that." I nodded confidently at Doug Sommers, KMIN's station manager. He'd asked me to deejay on one of KMIN's chain of stations along with my duties at KMIN. I'd been surprised to learn having the same air talent do double duty was common practice in the radio business. Good talent was hard to find, according to Doug, so they used people on staff rather than searching for someone new. I also suspected they saved a bundle on benefits. I'd be prerecording my show from this same studio and then they'd simply feed the broadcast to the sister station.

I was glad for the opportunity. As it was I was having a hard time making ends meet. If it hadn't been for the five hundred dollars Dave had pressed into my hand saying, "For all the times you helped Vicky in the café," I didn't know if I would have even made it out of Brewster. I'd put my first month's rent on my credit card, promising myself it wouldn't happen again. My studio apartment may not have looked like much, but it cost more than anything I'd ever heard of in Brewster. Everything was more expensive here. Even a plain cup of coffee at Caribou was twice as much as Vicky charged. That's why I rarely went out. Economizing had become my middle name. I was determined to send as much as I could spare each month to the bank in Brewster. I might have to live to be a hundred, but I was going to get those loans paid off. Taking on double duty at the station wouldn't double my pay, but it would bring in enough extra that I could already imagine the smile on Paul's face when he saw the check I planned to send. Funny, imagining Paul's face wasn't hard at all. I'd found myself thinking about him a lot. Especially how he looked the night of the going away party Vicky had thrown for me.

"Okay, listen up, everyone." Vicky clapped her hands twice. "Before you go, I want everyone to give Ruthie some advice for the big city."

"Go shopping," Cindy Pearson called out immediately.

"Get renter's insurance." Leave it to Dave to think of that.

"Find a new way to drive to work every week," Vicky said. "That way you'll learn your way around." My practical sister.

I could feel myself flushing. Being the center of attention wasn't my idea of fun. But Vicky meant well and this was supposed to be a party. I pasted a smile on my face.

"Don't forget to check your oil." Sandy Quinn chuckled. "That's what my dad still tells me." Just lately Sandy had started to be included in the circle of friends Vicky and Dave chummed with. She seemed nice enough.

"What about you, Paul?" Vicky asked. "Do you have some advice?"

The air in the room seemed to stop moving as I waited to hear his response. We'd been exchanging glances all night, his blue eyes holding something I couldn't read. I waited.

"Don't…" He cleared his throat. "Don't forget m—us."

"That's sweet," Vicky said, her words filling the space between Paul and me. The space where he'd changed what I was certain would have been the word *me* to *us*. Including the whole group in words meant for me alone.

Don't go. That's what I found myself wanting him to say. Ever since I'd been told, "You're hired," I'd felt as if I'd become two people. The Ruthie who was having a dream come true being hired by a radio station in Minneapolis, and the Ruthie who suddenly wanted nothing more than to stay where Paul was. What was the matter with me? Paul and I had no commitment, not even an understanding of sorts. All I knew was that now that I could leave, I wasn't so sure I wanted to. The fact was I didn't have a choice. I needed a job and now I had one. In Minneapolis. I should have been overjoyed. Instead I was simply pretending I was.

"You'll have to use a different name." Doug's words brought my thoughts back to his office. Back to this job of my dreams. A job that was expanding even if I wasn't so sure it was my dream anymore. "Even though our avid country listeners will rarely listen to our oldies station, if they do, we want them to feel they're getting something different. Any idea what name you might like?"

For a second I felt as though I was being inducted into the witness protection program. If I'd ever wanted an alias, now was the time. I recalled the movie-star names Vicky and I used to take on when we played dress-up. They seemed far too obvious to mention to Doug. "How about Gracie?" I asked.

"No." He shook his head. "Too much like Ruthie. We want something fresh. How about Angela?"

I laughed. "That's my niece's name. Much too confusing. Although I suspect she'd be flattered." I imagined Angie hearing I was calling myself by her name on the air in Minneapolis. I knew she'd be thrilled, but the thought of repeating her name again and again seemed too much like reminding myself how far away I was from her. From Sam. From Vicky and Dave.

And Paul?

And Paul. I felt a sudden pang of loneliness. Why had I thought of him for the second time since I'd been in Doug's office?

Why not? He's been on your mind every minute since you left Brewster

It was true. I had thought of Paul over and over, his name and face popping into my mind at countless unexpected times. I loved exploring Minneapolis. The Mall of America was where I found my very own purple hat. An indulgence to mark the start of my dream. It wasn't soft felt like my Aunt Lillian's; purple straw was the best way to describe it. It didn't matter, I didn't plan to wear the hat, just look at it, to remind myself that dreams did come true. I checked out the boutiques in Uptown, and Nicollet Mall downtown. The fact I didn't feel free to buy anything didn't matter. I'd waited twenty years to live in a place larger than Brewster, and I was determined to enjoy it. I toured the Walker Art Center, splurged on a play at the Guthrie Theatre, and got myself good and lost my first week in town trying to find the Uptown Theatre to catch an indie film I'd seen advertised. The only thing I didn't enjoy was doing it all myself. I'd quickly found out that while attending a play was exciting, talking about it at intermission made it even more fun. Not having anyone to talk to made me feel conspicuous and lonely. Those lonely feelings came over me often, especially when I thought about Vicky and Dave, Angie and Sam.

And Paul?

And Paul.

I squeezed my eyes shut, steeling my reserve. Feeling lonely was okay. I'd expected to feel that way for a while. I'd get over it. I wasn't going to let a few pangs of loneliness chase me back to Brewster. As if that was an option.

"How about Sheila?" I asked, dredging up the name of a childhood playmate. I was determined to make this job work.

"Try it out," Doug said.

My radio-voice kicked in. "This is Sheila at K-M-C-Y." I cleared my throat. "Coming at you from 97.5. It's Sheila and we'll have six in a row after a word from our sponsor." I nodded my head. "It works for me."

"Me too." Doug picked up a pen and tapped it on the Arbitron booklet lying on his desk. The radio ratings for the past three months. "I just got the new numbers in and, let me say, your ratings are way up there. I'm impressed." Doug leaned back in his chair, lacing his fingers behind his head. "It's funny how things work. I had a guy working here a few months ago who had more natural talent in his little finger than most deejays have in their whole bodies after twenty years."

I knew he had to be talking about Jack. I simply listened, curious to hear if Doug knew more about what had happened to Jack than Marv had.

"The guy had an innate sense for music and could talk circles around anyone I'd ever heard on air. He also had some personal vices that cost him his job. It was a shame." Doug shook his head, as if he still couldn't believe Jack had messed up so badly.

I could.

He went on, "I sure hope he gets things straightened around." He paused. "But," he sat up and tapped his hand on the desk, "if it wouldn't have been for him leaving, I may have never found out about you. Not too long after the guy left, I was looking for a new deejay to replace him when your air-check tape showed up on my desk. Perfect timing, I'd say."

"I'd have to say so too," I replied, a strange chill running down my spine. How had my tape gotten on Doug's desk? I *knew* I hadn't sent it here. Could Jack have possibly…? No, that hardly seemed like Jack. But then again, the fact I had Jack's old job was stranger than fiction. Maybe…?

Doug tapped at two cassette tapes lying on his desk. "Someone must have viewed you as competition back there in North Dakota." In response to my puzzled look he added, "In this business it's not uncommon for a radio station manager to make tapes of the competition in their air space. The deejays who are taking away their listeners. They send the tapes to stations outside of their ratings area, hoping the deejay will get hired away. In your case, it worked. I'm sure whoever sent me your tape is delighted to have you out of the area. Just like we're glad to have you here." He pushed himself away from the desk. "Just goes to show," Doug stood, my cue the meeting was over, "that all things do work for good."

My mind felt as if it were being turned inside out. I knew there was no one who wanted me out of Brewster's meager air space. It could have only been the work of Jack.

Or God? Again my mind twisted. Where had that thought come from? I stood, walking slowly as Doug followed me to the door.

Why would he do that?

Jack? Or God? Right now it didn't seem to matter. Either one. Why would they do that? For me?

Doug laid his hand on my shoulder. "You're doing a great job, Ruthie. We're glad we found you. Like I said, all things work together for good."

I'd heard that line before but I was never quite sure about the reasoning that something good could come from something bad. This time it made perfect sense. Jack's problem had solved mine. Strange sense. But perfect. But why?

Paul

It seemed as if my life should be perfect. Bank earnings were up. Charge-offs were down. Wayne had proved a quick learner once he had the information he needed. Banking school only reinforced his dedication to the profession. I had no doubt he'd be made a vice president within a few years. Everything at the bank was running like clockwork.

Even on the home front things were fine. My mother had responded well to her new medication. So well she almost sold her cane at the August city-wide rummage sale. It was only a rainy day the week before the sale that had her knee aching enough to make her decide to hang on to the cane "just in case." Or, "just in *cane*," she joked, tucking the stick behind the utility room door. In fact, she was so much better I'd put the word out to Dan Jordan that I was interested in looking at buying a place for myself. Yes, life seemed as if it should be perfect. Even Dan thought so.

"Got the perfect spot." He threw a three-ring binder over the papers on my desk at the bank. It was open to a small house overlooking Brush Lake, four miles out of Brewster.

"Is that the Brinkman farm?" I leaned in for a closer look at the photo. Obviously it had been taken recently, the trees surrounding the homestead were in full leaf, the house freshly painted. I remembered last fall when Dave and I had hunted that land, I had thought the house could use a paint job. Ed Brinkman must have thought so too.

"Sure is," Dan confirmed. "Eddie's been talking of selling the place ever since his wife died. About five years ago now. His health isn't great anymore, and after last winter when he got socked in during that New Year's blizzard, well, his kids finally talked him into moving into an apartment in town. The place will be available by the end of the month, just in time for hunting season."

I ran my fingers down the specs on the page.

Dan had them memorized. "The house is small, a hair under 1500 square feet, but it's in good condition and should be big enough for you."

I didn't need to be reminded I was alone. I'd found myself brooding about that more than once over the past months. But Dan was right. It was big enough for me. "I know you've hunted that land," he went on, aware of my weak spot. "Eddie's selling the whole section along with the home. Great pheasant country out there."

Dan didn't have to tell me. I knew.

"I've got to tell you, I've got a couple folks that are interested." I shot him a look. He caught it and said, "Hey, that's not a sales line; it's the truth. The thing is, one of the interested parties wants the land so he can parcel it out as lake lots. You know Brush Lake has been built up quite a bit over the past few years. Lake property is getting to be scarce. I'm sure he'd have no problem selling the shoreline property and cash-renting the pastureland behind it. But Eddie's pretty set on keeping the land together. He doesn't want to see his place broken up for 'a bunch of jet-skiers.' "

I laughed—it sounded just like something Ed would say. He could be a stubborn old German when it served his purposes, like keeping out-of-state hunters off his property, but he was a man who loved the land and had always let Dave and me have the run of it all fall. A cleaned bird handed over at the end of a good hunting weekend kept Ed waving us onto his property year after year.

"When can I show it to you?" Dan asked, shoving his hands into his pockets.

"You're pretty sure I want to look at this, huh?"

"Hey, what can I say?" He pulled one hand from his pocket and tugged at his ear. "It's my job to match up property and people. The way I see it, this place has your name written all over it."

I didn't tell Dan then, but I thought so too.

"What do you think?" Dan shifted his new pickup into park and turned off the engine. He and I had just finished a bumpy ride around the extensive fence surrounding the farm. I was sure it wasn't pure coincidence that the pickup was angled so I had a view of the house on my left and the wide expanse of lake on my right.

"Fence needs fixing in a few spots." I doubted Dan would be fooled by my nit-picking. Everyone around here knew Ed Brinkman was a meticulous farmer. It was only because of his bad hip that he couldn't get out to fix fence like he used to. "And the house could use an update."

Dan nodded. "Needs a woman's touch, that's for sure. You got any ideas?"

My head cranked to look at him. Would he be nosy enough to ask if I had a woman in mind to live here with me? Give me decorating ideas? He couldn't possibly know that I'd thought of Ruthie as we toured the farm. How much I found myself missing her, wishing she could share this with me.

"What?" he asked, responding to my wide-eyed gaze.

"Nothing," I said, suddenly embarrassed as it dawned on me he'd simply asked if I had any ideas about fixing up the house. "The house is fine for now." There went that bargaining tool.

"You want to think about it overnight?"

I didn't need to think about it. The place was perfect. A four-mile commute on mostly paved road. Just far enough to cover my day in prayer before work. I might need something besides my VW to get me through the winter, but I'd been eyeing a pickup for hunting even before I'd looked at this place. The pastureland had been rented to the same farmer for the past ten years, and he'd already told Dan he wanted it for another ten. I didn't have to worry about finding a renter. The outbuildings were in good shape; what I didn't need for storage could easily be sold and moved off the land. I already knew the hunting prospects were prime. And the house, while small, certainly had possibilities. The only thing that wasn't perfect was that I had no one to share it with.

No Ruthie?

No Ruthie.

"Yeah, let me think about it," I said to Dan. I didn't need to think about the land deal. I'd already prayed that over several times, feeling assurance each time I did. What I needed to think about was why I saw Ruthie everywhere I looked.

Maybe you should pray about that?

Maybe I should. Or maybe I should stop wishing for what I couldn't have and start being grateful for what I could.

Sandy Quinn?

Sandy Quinn. I hadn't even needed Sam's encouragement after church last Sunday to find myself striking up a conversation with her. We had a lot in common, and before I knew it we were standing by the curb in front of the church.

"Can I drive you home?" The offer was out before I'd thought about it.

"No, I drove myself. But thanks." She looked disappointed.

"Well then," I paused, tongue-tied suddenly and feeling a little as though I were back in junior high. "Have a good day."

"You too." She smiled, wiggling her fingers at me, her eyes crinkled in a way that was cute and…engaging.

Maybe you should pray about that?

Maybe I should.

Ruthie

There's an old phrase, "Be careful what you wish for, you might get it." And I did. For as long as I could remember I'd wished to live in a big city and have a life that was busy and exciting. If I admitted it, I'd even wished for some sort of fame. It wasn't New York or Paris, but Minneapolis held everything I'd ever dreamed about. All of a sudden, I had it all. A studio apartment, two highly rated radio shows, and my face on a billboard with Sunny, the KMIN call letters a mere fraction the size of our photo.

Well, okay, it hadn't happened all of a sudden. It had taken *years* of wishing, but now that I was living it, it seemed like all of a sudden. I had definitely "got" the life I'd wished for.

"Is this Sheila?" The male voice over the station line sounded timid.

"It is. What can I do for you?" I'd just gone off the air after doing the live broadcast with Marv. I had prerecorded my oldies show earlier in the day. I marveled at the fact that *Sheila's Show* aired on another station the same time I was on-air with Marv. I was competing with myself. Go figure. This caller wasn't unusual. Fans often called the station wanting to request a song. Many were savvy enough to understand that my oldies show wasn't broadcast live, even though we made every effort to make it sound that way. If I was free, the receptionist forwarded requests to me. It was habit to hit the record button on the tape machine; if the caller was animated and interesting I'd splice the call into the broadcast when the requested song came up on the computer. I hit the "record" button now.

"Uh, I was wondering if, uh, you could, uh—"

This caller wouldn't make it on-air. I hit the "stop" button.

"Uh, play, like a Beatle's song?"

"Sure thing," I responded. Beatle's songs were always in the computer line-up. "Thanks for calling." I quickly hung up.

Seconds later Jenni interrupted again. "Caller on line two."

"This is Sheila, what can I do for you?"

"You already do lots of things for me." The deep bass voice was slow and unfamiliar.

"You enjoy the songs I play?" He didn't need to know the computer did all of the programming.

"I en-joy wat-ch-ing you." Static broke the words, but I had no trouble filling in the spaces.

A creeping sensation prickled the back of my neck. "Don't you mean listening to me?"

"Oh, no, Shei-la," the voice had taken on a sinister tone, "I en-joy watch-ing you." Static or not, I could sense his innuendo. "You leave work aro-und seven-thir-ty."

I did...and almost always alone. I slammed the phone down, my hands clammy and my heart pounding. My mind raced. The station's address was no secret. All it would take was for someone to look up the call letters in the phone book. The address was right there. Was he out there right now on a cell phone? The fact he'd called me Sheila was my only assurance he didn't really know who I was. Suddenly all I wanted was to get home, but the thought of the dark parking lot outside sent my heart racing again.

"Hey, Ruthie!" Sunny peeked around the doorframe, her bleached-blonde hair perfectly rumpled. "You want to go get a drink?"

"Sure," I said, not one bit thirsty, wanting only an escort through the parking lot.

Minutes later we each had a glass of wine in front of us. Sunny's eyes darted around the bar as she ran her finger around the rim of her glass; I gripped mine as if it could somehow give me courage. I wished now I had ordered coffee. At least the warmth of it would soothe me. I remembered the time not so long ago when Mrs. Bauer sat across the booth from me in Vicky's café, grasping my hands with her coffee-warmed ones. I could almost feel the comfort her hands had given me that day. I longed for that same comfort now. I slid my hands from the wine glass and clasped them together, a poor substitute for Mrs. Bauer's touch. Slowly, I slid my fingers around the glass again, the cool veneer a sharp contrast to the comfort I craved.

Sunny's eyes continued to scan the bar while I tried to shake the sound of the ominous voice that still rang in my mind. Even though noise and people surrounded me, I felt scared and alone. In all my dreaming I'd never imagined this. Right now, Brewster seemed like the safest place in the world.

You can find safety in Me.

I recognized that silent voice. The mustard-seed voice, I'd started calling it. I grasped at it, crying out in my heart as Sunny chatted away, *help me feel safe.*

"I've been wanting to get to know you better." Sunny's modulated tone filtered through my racing thoughts, her eyes continuing to bounce around, scanning the bar.

"Huh?" I responded, obviously not listening, continuing my silent prayer.

Sunny took a sip of her wine. "I thought we should be friends. Since we're KMIN's golden girls and all." She lifted her glass to me in salute.

I lifted my glass, not sure how to respond. I wasn't feeling one bit golden.

"How are you liking this job?" Sunny looked everywhere but at me. If she wanted to get to know me she had a weird way of doing it.

I shrugged one shoulder. "It's good." I paused, not knowing how much to say to Sunny. But then, who else did I have to talk to?

You can talk to Me. That voice again.

I pushed the thought aside as words tumbled from my mouth, answering Sunny's casual question with a barrage I hadn't known was there. "I don't know, in some ways it's way more than I dreamed, but parts of the job, well, it's not quite what I imagined. I mean I hardly even listen to the music anymore. Having two shows is a lot of work. It seems like all I'm doing is punching at the computer or laying down voice tracks."

"Uh-huh," Sunny said, her eyes landing on mine for a second before drifting off.

I could tell she wasn't really listening, but words kept tumbling from my mouth anyway, my loneliness grasping at straws. "The thing that's strange though," I rolled a small corner of napkin into a point, staring at the table, talking as much to myself as to Sunny, "is that I talk to callers all the time, but I don't *know* any of them. Back in Brewster—" I stopped talking, remembering the times I'd wished for strangers on the other end of the line…I had my wish now.

Invisible fingers raised the hair on the back of my neck as I remembered my last caller. I took a big swallow of wine, then cleared my throat, trusting Sunny's attempt at friendship. "Do you ever get any creepy calls at the station?"

A laugh burst from her mouth. "Haaah! All the time." I had her attention now. She leaned forward. "Has DeepVoice called you yet? That's what I call him, anyway. Some guy with a deep bass voice. He calls all the female deejays eventually. Says he's," she lowered her voice so it came out sounding like a bad imitation of Darth Vader, "*watching you.*" She laughed again. "He's harmless. He calls the station all the time. Calls once and requests a song in a wimpy voice, to see if you're there, then calls back and talks low and slow. I figure," she shrugged one shoulder, "he must have a pathetic life if that's his idea of fun."

A wave of relief flooded over me. A harmless prank call, that's all it had been. My prayer for help had already been answered.

Sunny twirled the wine in her glass. "You stay in this business long enough and you'll see all the crazies." Her eyes made a wary appraisal of someone over my shoulder. "Here comes one now."

An okay-looking guy in a business suit approached our table. The top two buttons of his white shirt had been opened, his tie loosened. A gold chain dangled against his neck. "Don't I know you two from somewhere?"

"Did you think that up all by yourself?" Sunny deflected his question with one of her own.

"Did you?" he answered, the glint in his eye showing Sunny he could play the game too. "Can I buy you a drink?" His eyes flitted from Sunny to me, including us both. He turned and began to pull an empty chair towards our table.

Sunny murmured, "*Mr. Originality.*" She smiled up at him. "Thanks, but I don't think so." She slid her hand across the table and put her hand over mine. "My friend and I would like to be alone." Her gesture intimated more than her words.

My heart started a heavy thumping. Sunny didn't really—? She wasn't—? My hand froze under hers.

The guy practically backed over the table behind him. "Sorry," he mumbled, moving quickly toward the bar.

Sunny patted my hand and withdrew hers. "Sorry too," she said, apparently reading my racing thoughts, "that's the quickest way to get rid of those guys. Now if some guy who looked promising happened by…" She took a swallow of wine, appraising someone behind me. "Well, speak of the devil." Sunny half rose, gesturing for the man to join us. "I was hoping to see you." Sunny ran her hand across his forearm. "Al, Ruthie. Ruthie, Al." Her eyes never strayed from his as she made the perfunctory introduction. "Where have you been keeping yourself?" She ran a finger over the back of his hand.

"I was on a business trip." Al crooked a finger at the cocktail waitress, swirling his finger in the air, indicating another round of drinks for the table.

"No," I protested, holding my hand over my glass, as if someone were pouring me a refill. "I've got to be leaving." I could tell Sunny had something in mind that didn't include me.

"Stay," Al said, "any friend of Sunny's is a friend of mine."

"Did you bring my present?" Sunny asked, leaning towards Al.

He reached into his jacket pocket and slipped a small packet into her hands. Abruptly Sunny rose. "Excuse me."

As she headed toward the ladies' room, Al leaned my way. "So, you new around here? I haven't seen you before."

"I work with Sunny. At the station." My mind was a step behind, still wondering what Al had handed Sunny.

"You need a present too?" Al's fingers rubbed together as though he was waiting for me to slip him a tip.

Suddenly it dawned on me why Sunny had been so anxious to go out with me. Get to know me better, my eye. She hadn't wanted to wait here by herself. She had used me as an excuse to come looking for Al. I pushed back my chair. "I need to go. Tell Sunny I had to leave."

"Hey wait." Al held out his hand. He looked worried. Was he afraid I would run and tell the cops? "I didn't mean anything by that."

"By what?" I asked, watching him squirm for an answer.

"Nothing." He looked around nervously. Let him think I was an undercover policewoman. Let his heart pound as hard as mine.

My anger propelled me to my car. I didn't need a drug to get high. My adrenaline was doing a good job of it all by itself. I slammed the car door and cranked the ignition, backing out of the parking space as if I were in hot pursuit of a drug deal. I might have been naïve about Sunny's motives when I came here tonight, but I wasn't anymore.

I turned off the freeway, detouring around the same orange road construction markers that had been there ever since I'd moved to Minneapolis. Embarrassed warmth flooded me as I replayed my conversation with Sunny. If you could call a monologue a conversation. What had ever made me think I could confide in her? She must have thought I walked straight off the farm into KMIN. I had a vision of the rolling hills surrounding Brewster. Funny how I used to see them ringing the town, holding me in. Tonight they seemed like a safe haven, a protection from strange callers and false friendship.

The beep of a car horn behind me startled me from my thoughts, letting me know it had been a millisecond since the stoplight had turned green. I jammed the accelerator, hurrying nowhere. I still had a couple hours to kill before I'd be tired enough to get to sleep, and the creepy sound of that caller's voice nagged at the fringe of my mind. Sunny had said he was harmless, but now I didn't know if I could believe her, and the thought of my empty apartment only freaked me out more. As if on cue my stomach grumbled, and I pulled to the curb in front of a small café. I didn't need atmosphere, just food and something to fill an hour or two.

"I hep you?" A young girl stood at my table with a notepad, her head covering indicating English may not be her native language. "You want order?"

"Uh, ya—I mean, yes." She might be having as hard a time understanding me. "Do you have a menu?"

"Eeess dare." She pointed to a laminated piece of paper stuck between the salt and pepper shakers.

"Thanks," I said, picking up the menu. "Give me a minute, okay?"

"Ho-kaaay." She nodded.

I looked down the menu at the unfamiliar selections. Diet Coke I understood, but little else. The young girl carried a plate of steaming food past my table. It smelled wonderful. When she came back my way I motioned her over. "I'll have that." I pointed to the table where she'd placed the food.

She rattled off a sentence that was totally unintelligible.

Not knowing what else to do I nodded. "And Diet Coke," I added, determined to get one familiar thing.

Around me were people of several nationalities, speaking in dialects I couldn't begin to decipher. I felt out of place, finding myself longing to hear Mrs. Bauer's heavily accented voice. Funny. I understood her plain as day. I'd made fun of the local Brewster dialect all through my teen years, considering the native German accent an indication of poor grammar and lack of education. For the first time it dawned on me that Mrs. Bauer was possibly smarter than me in many ways, and one of them was her ability to speak two languages. Another was her strong faith. I could almost hear what she'd be saying to me, "Oh, Rootie, don't be afrait. Don't vorry about tings like peoples witt accents or prank phone calls. Gott iss vatching out for you. He luffs you. You chust pray and everyting vill be all right."

Oh, if only it were that easy. The fear that had dogged me since the phone call settled around me. I hoped Mrs. Bauer was praying for me.

"Here your food." The waitress placed the steaming plate in front of me, an orange-tinged mixture of chicken, rice, and vegetables. She set a small basket of flattened bread above my plate. "You try," she said, "Ees good."

She was right, it was good, but all I could think of was how badly I wished I were in Vicky's café eating a plate of chicken and dumplings covered with cream gravy. I hurried through my dinner, anxious to get back to my apartment and call Vicky. Maybe listening to her talk about everyday life in Brewster would help me remember how dull things were there, how much better my life was here.

I maneuvered my car into the only parking spot left on the street, at the far end of the block from my apartment. Making sure the car doors were locked, I stepped onto the dark sidewalk gripping the keys in my right hand, my apartment key ready to quickly unlock my door. I glanced over my shoulder, the creepy voice of the caller following me like a shadow. When I turned my head forward, I noticed three young men walking toward me. They were eyeing me and jostling each other as if egging themselves into some sort of action. My heart pounded. In Brewster I could walk any street in town, any time of the day or night, and the only thing I had to fear was a stray dog barking at me. If a group of kids happened my way, I could greet them by name, first and last, and ask about how their parents and grandparents were doing. I'd never felt fear like this in Brewster.

Don't look at them. Don't look at them. I repeated the instruction I'd read about meeting people on the street, fighting against my Brewster-bred instinct to look them in the eye and say, "Hi!" I sidestepped around them, hoping once again Mrs. Bauer was praying.

You can pray too. To Me.

The quiet thought gave me an instant of calm as the boys jostled past. *Keep me safe. Keep me safe.* I repeated the prayer as if it were a mantra as I unlocked the door to my apartment and walked into the small space. After the pounding of adrenaline I'd felt all evening, my apartment was strangely quiet. I lit a candle as much to cover the smoke smell that hung in my hair from the bar as to calm my nerves. I sank onto the couch, my apartment feeling nothing like the safe haven I'd been hoping to find. I dialed Vicky's number only to get a persistent busy sound that scratched at my nerves. Probably Angie on the phone with Steph. I slammed the phone into the cradle, the sharp sound making me jump. Tonight everything felt menacing.

Wherever I am, I am content. Words similar to Vicky's resonated within my swirling emotions. If only that were true. If only I were content. But I wasn't. The prank phone call, Sunny's false attempt at friendship, sitting in the foreign-feeling restaurant, and then being frightened by the young men on the darkened street only served to underline the fact I was alone in a city very far from Brewster. The place I'd wished to leave all my life. The only place in the world where I wished I was right now—if only for a few minutes.

I pushed myself off the couch and walked into the bedroom, making sure the shade was completely closed before changing into my pajamas. I went into the bathroom, checking behind the shower curtain before grabbing a washcloth to scrub the makeup off my face. I wiped my face with the soapy cloth, locking eyes with myself in the mirror.

Wherever I am, I am content.

That was a laugh. I hadn't been content in Brewster, and I sure wasn't content here. I rinsed the washcloth and ran it over my face again, avoiding my gaze in the mirror. Life in Brewster had felt like anything but contentment. It had felt confining. People watching my every move, talking about me to my face and behind my back.

They were concerned about you. They cared about you.

They did not! The automatic rebuttal was right there. I swiped at my face with the cloth. I'd imagined life in the city to be freeing, a place where I could live as I wished without wondering what other people would think or say. Well, that part was true. No one gave a darn what I did here.

Wherever I am, I am content.

I caught my gaze in the mirror again. My face, without makeup, appeared pale and tired. Where was the contentment Vicky had? Mrs. Bauer? Paul? Where was it? Why did contentment seem so easy for them to find and so elusive for me?

Paul

I glanced at my watch. I'd work another hour and then call it a day. I wanted to get out to the farm by five-thirty. I had a pheasant in the slow cooker with potatoes and carrots and a can of mushroom soup I'd mixed with a full can of milk, a recipe Vicky had assured me was *no fail*. I still had to set the table and chop lettuce for a salad. Sandy had said she'd bring dessert. My first dinner party at my new place was making me nervous.

I pulled the last stack of papers on my desk toward me. My secretary had devised a system that seemed to work well. Each day Nancy divided my mail into two piles. Business that needed tending to immediately she put at the top left corner of my desk. Items I could look at later she stacked on the far side of my L-shaped desk to my right. Usually by Friday I could wade my way through to the last pile. I was right on schedule.

I quickly worked through the top third of the stack, tossing most of it. I set aside two banking newsletters and the *The Kiplinger Letter;* I'd take them home to read over the weekend. I recognized the handwriting on the next envelope. Even without a return address I knew immediately it was from Jack. A couple months ago, out of the blue, he'd started sending a check in the mail every two weeks. Sometimes it was for one hundred dollars, sometimes less, but they had come as consistent as the sunrise. Every now and then he'd jot a short note. *Paul, apply this to the KBRS loan. Hope you're doing well. How's the hunting?* I wondered what he'd say this time.

I pulled the small piece of paper from the envelope. Nancy had removed the check, penciling *$150.00* in the upper right-hand corner of the paper.

Paul, I'm moving. New job. Got a raise too, so hopefully I can keep up the larger payment. Might be late though as I'll be on the road and getting settled. Thanks for your patience. Jack

I looked at the postmark on the envelope. The town was smudged but the state was still Minnesota. No clue as to where he was moving, what he'd be doing. He'd left Brewster as quiet as a thief in the night, disappearing with hardly a trace, leaving Ruthie with a huge debt. As suddenly he'd reappeared in a sense, with his twice-monthly checks and short notes. I hadn't mentioned anything to Ruthie about Jack's sudden generosity, not sure how long it would last. I figured anything Jack contributed to the KBRS loan would serve as a pleasant surprise to Ruthie someday.

In the meantime we'd moved the loan into our charged-off loan portfolio and written the loan off the books to satisfy the examiners. Anything we collected now would be returned to the loan loss reserve fund. I could almost imagine how surprised Ruthie would look the day she discovered Jack had contributed to repaying the KBRS debt. I found myself smiling as I shuffled through the next few papers, an image filled my mind of Ruthie's mouth hanging open in surprise when she realized her debt was less than she thought.

It's always been less than she's thought.

I stopped working, lifting my eyes to the colored leaves outside my window. Ruthie might think the burden she carried was made up of money she owed the bank. I knew, as well as God, it wasn't. I just wished Ruthie could see that her debt had already been forgiven. Written off cleaner than the one at the bank. There was no loan loss reserve with God. When He cancelled a debt, it was gone for good. I closed my eyes. *Lord, let Ruthie experience true freedom. Freedom from debt that comes only from You.*

Over the past months I'd felt an increasing urgency to pray for her. I didn't know the foundation of that prod. I just knew if God was poking me, I'd better pray. What for, I wasn't sure. Vicky kept me up-to-date on Ruthie's life, and occasionally I'd be over at Dave's when Ruthie called. Somehow the phone always ended up in my hand, our conversation picking up as though it had never stopped.

Her voice was unfailingly cheerful. Her life "*great, just great!*" But I sensed there was more going on than Ruthie was telling Vicky or me.

Maybe the reason I thought that was because there was more going on in my life than I was sharing with her too.

Most everyone seemed to be hinting, and not so subtly, that Sandy Quinn and I would make a good couple. We'd been the only two singles at the Backyard Olympics party Ben and Cindy Pearson had thrown three months ago on the Fourth of July. Of course, Sandy and I got paired up.

"Okay you two, get a little closer." Cindy was kneeling to tie my leg to Sandy's for the three-legged race. "There." She patted our knees. "Looks good. Oh wait," she said, squatting again and tugging at the rope, "maybe I'd better *tighten the knot*."

Her reference didn't go over my head, and the way Sandy blushed I was sure she caught it too. When we crossed the finish line and Sandy threw her arms around my neck in a quick hug saying, "We won!" it only caused everyone to assume there was more between us than we'd been letting on.

And then there had been the jostling over the seating arrangements at barbeque time. Sandy and I had practically been forced to share a blanket on the ground, rather than sit with some of the kids and parents at a picnic table. Sam had whispered loudly to Vicky as she approached our shady blanket with a full plate, "No! You can't sit with them!" Everyone laughed, which made the setup all the more obvious.

The only thing obvious to everyone was the fact we were both single. What wasn't obvious was that all the arranging in the world couldn't substitute for feelings that were as unsettled as warm Jell-O.

"I suppose I could give you a bite of potato salad off of my fork," Sandy had said, a smile playing on her lips. "That should make them happy." She'd shot a wide smile at Sam, who had been staring at us so hard he had trouble getting his hamburger into his mouth. Sandy took a bite of her hotdog, ketchup dripping onto her navy shorts. "Ooops," she'd said, her words muffled by food, "this is embarrassing."

She'd dabbed at the stain with a napkin. I wasn't sure if she meant the ketchup drip or the way everyone kept glancing our way.

"You've got ketchup—" I motioned to the left of my mouth, noticing more people than Sam had their eyes on us.

Sandy swiped at the right side of her face.

"No, there." I pointed, obviously far off the mark, as she tried to catch the spot with her tongue. I finally leaned forward and wiped the spot with my napkin. "There." I could hear Sam almost choke on a potato chip.

"Thanks." Sandy grinned. I wasn't sure if her smile was in reaction to Sam or me, but I found myself grinning back.

The setups continued through the summer, and while I didn't want to lead Sandy on, I had to admit she was mighty pleasant company. Her presence made me feel less a fifth wheel at the couples get-togethers we were invited to. It was easy enough to swing my VW past her father's house and pick her up. Without my noticing, we had become an unofficial couple. I should have remembered how Brewster operated. I hadn't. Now I found myself in a relationship I hadn't realized I was getting into. Maybe God had a plan I hadn't caught on to yet.

I had a few more papers to wade through, but I leaned over and clicked the "shut down" command on my computer. My mind wasn't on work. I had to admit I was feeling a bit nervous. I'd invited Sandy out to the farm for dinner, her first visit there, along with the Pearsons and Vicky and Dave. Now I was beginning to have second thoughts. If I hadn't invited Sandy, her feelings would have been hurt and the others would have wondered. But would my invitation give Sandy the impression I thought of us as a couple too? Did I? What had I been thinking?

Obviously, I hadn't been.

I pushed the remaining papers into a neat pile and picked them up; they'd go onto my "later" stack. Right now I needed to get home and make dinner for my company. I leaned toward the one remaining stack on my desk, the highest one, the one I never quite got to the bottom of. Nancy often teased me about my method of sorting; she called it "filing by piling." It was true. I did have a habit of making organized piles, but the up side was I knew where to look when I needed something. It worked for me. As I reached for the stack beside my computer, my shirt cuff caught on an edge of paper in the pile, sending the whole thing sliding, my frantic effort to catch the papers only causing more of them to fall to the floor. I walked around my desk, kneeling to restack the documents. If I had followed Nancy's advice and dealt with my incoming mail as it came across my desk, I wouldn't be here now. I'd be on my way to the farm. I pushed the papers back into the semblance of a stack, crouching low to reach for a brochure that had flown under the printer stand. As I picked it up my eyes caught the words on the front of the brochure: *in downtown Minneapolis.*

I could visit Ruthie! My heart did a funny little blip at the thought as I sat in my chair and opened the brochure. I remembered seeing it months ago, advertising a bank meeting in Minneapolis. Something I had put aside for later. Well, it was later all right, the date for the meeting long past. I threw the brochure in the garbage, my hopes dropping along with it. I got up and walked out of my office.

You could go visit Ruthie. You don't need the excuse of a meeting.

When Ruthie had lived in Brewster, I'd worked so hard to keep my feelings for her in check, concerned about falling into a convenient relationship, a partnership God hadn't made. Now that she was gone, I found myself in that exact kind of relationship with Sandy, thoughts of Ruthie never far from mind, still unsure what God's plans were.

Maybe God had a reason to keep Ruthie at the forefront of my mind. She might not need my companionship, but I was fairly certain she could use my prayers. I put on my jacket, started the VW, and prayed for Ruthie as I traveled the four miles to the farm. As I turned onto the gravel road leading to my house, I could see Sandy's car already parked by the garage. I added a prayer for Sandy. It would be a long evening if she had her thoughts on me and I had mine on Ruthie.

Ruthie

Funny how the October air in Minneapolis reminded me so much of Brewster. It smelled like Pumpkin Fest weather as I stepped out of my fourplex. Last year at this time I had been lining up advertisers to sponsor the Pumpkin Fest broadcast, my heart filled with resentment over being stuck in Brewster. Here I was a year later, in Minneapolis, the land of my dreams—or so I'd thought back then.

It was hard to believe I'd been gone from Brewster almost eight months. As I kicked through crunching leaves to my car, I imagined Vicky stocking up on supplies for her pies. Her baking frenzy would start in two weeks. How would she ever get it done this year without my help?

The crisp fall air cut through my leather coat as I jumped in my car for the drive to work. I was running late and knew the traffic this time of day wouldn't help me get to the station any faster. That was one thing I'd never had to worry about in Brewster, commute time. It had never occurred to me how convenient it was to be able to get to work in five minutes flat until I didn't have the option.

There were lots of things that hadn't occurred to me when I'd lived in Brewster. I'd been looking beyond my hometown for so many years I hadn't even seen the good things that were there. Getting to work in minutes. Dropping in at Vicky's café for coffee. Spending time with Angie and Sam. Listening to Mrs. Bauer's accented advice. Even Pumpkin Fest, the celebration I'd made fun of for years, now radiated with charm. Funny how the town seemed so attractive now that I was no longer there. Maybe I could take a couple days off and go back for Pumpkin Fest?

You wanted to be anywhere but there last year. You're living your dream. Remember?

I looked over my left shoulder, tapping between the gas pedal and the brake as I merged onto the freeway. The line of cars had at one time appeared to me as if they were all driving toward some place exciting. Now they were a long line of ants, slowly crawling to work.

And you're one of them.

What could be holding up traffic? I switched radio stations, trying to find a traffic report. What a laugh a traffic report would have been in Brewster, our no-stoplight town.

Just a minute folks while I look out the window. Yup, all clear. Oh, wait, here comes Mr. Ost, cruising down Main at five miles-per-hour. He's scheduled for cataract surgery next week; so until then, watch out for him.

No, traffic was something that wasn't a problem in Brewster. I stepped on the gas, switching lanes, an action I'd found futile, but it made me feel as though at least I was trying to move ahead. The semi in front of me slammed on his brakes. So did I. The traffic in both lanes came to a complete standstill. Some dream. I sucked in a deep breath and let it out slowly.

Calm down. This won't last forever. You have plenty of time to get to work. I closed my eyes, determined to not get stressed over this everyday occurrence. *Open your eyes. Look around. Enjoy the scenery. Think of this stop as a coffee break.*

I opened my eyes and looked around. If I had coffee, the break idea might have worked. As it was, all I saw was an endless line of cars and the back of the semi directly in front of me. The diesel fumes were giving me a headache. I cracked the window and looked to my right, through the windows of the SUV beside me. The man in the vehicle stared straight ahead; beyond him was nothing but trees. Granted the fall leaves were pretty, but that's all I could see. Trees. I switched my eyes to the left, nothing but the cement median, more lines of traffic and trees. Where was the horizon? Where was the expanse of sky that embraced Brewster like a blue ocean? I longed to *see* something. To look into the distance and see rolling hills and sky, not trees, housing developments, and billboards. A stab of longing pierced through me as the traffic began to creep ahead. As hard as it was for me to admit, I missed Brewster.

I shifted into gear and tapped on the gas; it didn't take much concentration to keep up with this ant-like pace. A dirty smudge of diesel fuel blew towards me as the semi shifted gears. Quickly I closed the window. What had happened to the glamour of city life? Ever since the day I'd gotten that creepy telephone call at work, I'd started noticing a side of city life I hadn't seen before. People caught up in their own lives, not having time to even say hello to someone they didn't know. Store clerks so busy with other customers that one more didn't catch their attention. It wasn't like Brewster, where a person was greeted as if they were a long-lost friend whether they were a stranger or a local. It didn't matter if you were walking down the street or walking into Cal's hardware store. There was always someone to notice you there.

Remember when you used to hate that very fact about Brewster?

A lump pushed its way into my throat and I blinked away tears. What was I becoming? Schizophrenic? I hadn't been happy living in Brewster, but now that I was in the city, I wasn't happy here either. If I was honest with myself, I had to admit my dream was not what I'd imagined it would be. Within the months I'd been in Minneapolis, a sense of boredom had already begun to creep into my life. My job was boring. I showed up for work each day, recorded one show, did another one, then went home. The work wasn't challenging or satisfying. I wasn't like Jack. Music didn't fuel my soul as it had his. I'd gotten into the radio business because of the words, the venue it gave me to express myself. I enjoyed talking to people over the air. Knowing my listeners. At KBRS I had often wondered if anyone was listening, but I knew they were. They told me. At KMIN I knew people were listening; I had the numbers and callers to prove it, but I didn't *know* a single one of them. I stayed in the business because it was what I knew. It wasn't what I loved—at least not now.

City life wasn't what I had imagined it to be in my dreams either. I'd thought it would be a whirlwind of events; instead most everyone I knew had a lifestyle like mine. They put in their time, picked up their paycheck, and were anxious to beat the traffic and get home. And they were happy to stay put once there.

The traffic speed picked up and I pushed on the accelerator, the increased pace matching my racing thoughts. I'd thought for certain, happiness existed anywhere outside the Brewster city limits. Now here I was, far, far away from the implement dealership that marked Brewster's edge, cruising along the freeway in a city I'd dreamed of, going absolutely nowhere.

I glanced in the rearview mirror, watching as another semi squeezed in behind me. One in front, one in back, making me into a sandwich that couldn't see a thing.

Kind of like your life. You were so blindly following what you thought was your dream that you never took time to look at what you already had.

I sighed, the air I exhaled coming from a spot deep within my soul. Where was the contentment I longed for? Would I ever find it? I hit the steering wheel with the heel of my hand as I pushed harder at the gas pedal, trying to keep up with the semis pulling and pushing me down the freeway. Trying to keep up with this line of thought. If I could just figure out where I'd gone wrong, maybe then I could find a place where I could finally belong. If it wasn't here, where was it? Chicago? L.A.? New York City? Did Katie Couric need a new cohost? Maybe I should consider a move to TV. Maybe my discontent had more to do with radio than Minneapolis.

Wherever I am, I am content.

Those familiar six words nipped at my questioning. Somehow I sensed my restlessness wouldn't be solved by Katie, TV, or another city—just as it hadn't by my move to Minneapolis—as hard as that was for me to admit. Was contentment even possible for me? Being content wherever I was? I gripped the steering wheel with both hands, needing something to hold on to in my crumbling world.

Hold on to Me.

Hold on! Suddenly the taillights of the semi in front of me lit up like a neon sign. I slammed on my brakes, gripping the steering wheel like a vise, trying not to swerve into the other lane, trying not to plow into the back of the huge truck. It was as though time had slowed into a stop-action movie scene. I pumped at the brakes, gripped the wheel, and watched as the back of the semi came closer and closer. *Dear Jesus, save me.* Brakes squealed from behind. I'd forgotten about the other truck! My eyes flew to the rearview mirror and I watched in horror as the semi behind me closed in—a slow-motion rush as the grill of the huge vehicle loomed in my mirror. Closer and closer. *Oh, Lord, save me!*

Hold on. I cringed, squishing my eyes shut, waiting for the crunch of metal, the pushing sensation I expected to ram me into and under the semi in front of me. My heart was beating so fast I imagined it invisible, the wings of a hummingbird trying to stay aloft. Or alive. Five minutes passed, or was it one second? As quickly as it had all happened, all was quiet. I opened my eyes, looking ahead and then behind. There had to be only a hair's breadth separating my car from the two semis in front and back of me. Only a hair's breadth.

If I have even the hairs of your head numbered...and care for the birds of the air... From somewhere in the depths of my soul, the words of Bible verses I'd memorized in Sunday school flooded my mind, flooded my body with an overwhelming sense of protection. *Think how much more I care for you.*

My arms felt like limp spaghetti, my legs not much firmer, as the traffic slowly started moving again, yet somehow the concerns I had been wrestling earlier no longer gripped my mind. I recalled the words I'd heard when I'd thought for sure I was going to crash into the semi. *Hold on.*

I blinked my eyes for a long second, feeling the peace those words held. *Hold on. Hold on to Me.* Was that peace meant for me? The pastor in Brewster had said if I had faith the size of a mustard seed, even the impossible was possible. Could my speck of faith possibly be enough? It seemed like it just might be. It had been seconds ago. I wanted it to be longer than that. I wanted more than a speck. Much more.

Oh Lord, thank You for holding on to me just now. I began my prayer with my eyes wide open, watching the freeway unfold in front of my petition. *For holding on always. For not letting go. Ever.* I sighed, thinking of all the times God held on while I blindly tried to run my own life. Yet today, He'd been right here when I'd called out. What a mess I'd made of my life and He was still here. Amazing.

Traffic clipped past me. Cars and trucks filled with people I didn't know. Now I knew what the phrase, "a stranger in a strange land," meant. That was me. A stranger here in Minneapolis. A stranger of sorts in Brewster, too, always feeling I wasn't where I belonged. *I hate never feeling as though I'm where I'm supposed to be, always wishing I were somewhere else. I'm tired, Lord. Tired of trying to find my place in this world. Tired of doing it all on my own. I want to be happy. I want to be content...wherever You've put me. Show me how, Lord. Show me how to have the peace that comes from You.* I was ready to let Him be in charge. More than ready. "*I'm ready,*" I whispered softly, somehow hoping He would hear.

There was no miraculous break in traffic. No cop pulled me over to ask what happened. The road continued to unwind beneath my tires, but I could tell I was no longer alone. A peace I had only imagined until this moment seeped from the innermost part of my heart into every fiber of my being. It was a calm of the highest order, releasing the weight that had laid on my chest for years, sending it off as though it were a mere feather in the face of this force. Even my fingers tingled, then relaxed as if warmed by Mrs. Bauer's hands. But I knew this feeling hadn't come from Mrs. Bauer. There was no longer any doubt in my mind where this peace had come from.

"Thank You, God," I whispered into the air. And for the second time in as many minutes I knew He really had heard my prayer. Tears of gratitude, gratefulness, maybe even contentment, blurred my vision. I quickly blinked them away. Having God rescue me once on the freeway today was probably enough. I smiled, and it felt that just possibly, God smiled too.

What had happened to me in those short minutes during my drive to work was unexplainable. And yet it was something I wanted to share. Still, I realized I didn't know these people. I'd worked with them for months and had never gotten to know them. They would never understand what had happened—I wasn't sure I did. The odd looks I got as I greeted everyone in sight, anxious to share the bubbling joy I felt inside, were only fuel to make me want to reach out more.

"Hey, Marv, is that a Packers' sweatshirt? Pretty brave to wear that in Viking country."

Marv shrugged. "Most people don't notice." He pointed a thumb at his chest. "I'm from Wisconsin. Someone's gotta cheer for the home team."

"Depends where home is," Doug Sommers said as he walked by.

Home. One word I'd never associated with this place. Apparently Marv didn't either. Where was home for me?

Brewster.

For once my mind didn't rebel at the thought of the town where I'd grown up. Yes, Brewster was home for me; make that *had been* home for me. Too bad I hadn't realized that fact when I'd lived there. I walked into the broadcast booth and, drumming my fingers on the desktop, pulled up the play list for the first hour of my show. I felt antsy, as though I wanted to move. Run. Jump. Shout for joy. Do something with my new-found attitude.

But running was what I'd been doing all along. Where had it gotten me? Only into more unhappiness. The restlessness I felt now was different from the running I'd done before. It was more of an inner need to search, as opposed to the outward escape I'd always sought. I pulled up the commercial play list on the screen. Funny, other days the list represented things I couldn't have. Today it was simply advertising for business people who were devoting themselves to their work. It gave me a restless feeling. I wanted something to devote my life to as well.

You just did.

Ah, then it wasn't just restlessness I was feeling? It was God working in me? That thought certainly put a different spin on my whirling emotions. It was amazing how different a day looked when I thought of it that way. I slid onto the high-backed stool in front of the computer and glanced over the play list. I thought of the people who would be listening to these songs today. Amazing how I'd never thought of my listeners before, what kind of day they might be having. I'd thought only of myself and the impression I made while on the air.

Today felt different. I leaned into the mike. "Hey there, all you KMIN listeners, I hope you're having a fabulous day!" And, for once, I really did.

Maybe, just maybe, God did have a plan for me. Maybe, just maybe, contentment was waiting for me somewhere. Today it all seemed possible.

∼

I was trying. I really was. But trying to make myself feel at home in the Christian bookstore I'd found was a stretch.

The perfectly-normal-looking clerk smiled at the completely-normal-looking customer in front of me. "Have a blessed day." Her words sent a shot of panic through me. Would I be expected to say the same thing back? I was having enough trouble conjuring up the words to ask for a Bible. Spouting religious-sounding phrases was a step I wasn't ready to take.

"Thanks," said the customer.

I relaxed. "Thanks" I could manage. I don't know what I'd expected to find inside the store. Maybe little old ladies shuffling through the aisles, their lips pursed as tight as their white curls. Instead I'd passed a young man with a pierced eyebrow on the way in.

"Can I help you?" the clerk behind the counter asked.

My turn. "Uh, yes. I was, uh, I am…looking for a Bible." I blurted the last words out. I couldn't believe how vulnerable I felt. As though I was exposing a gaping hole in my soul or something.

Don't be afraid. I will fill it.

The impact of that thought hit me full force. I was no longer alone in my struggle. I wasn't searching alone. I spoke past the tears gathering in my throat. "I, uh, want a Bible I can understand. Do you have one that's not written in Greek?"

The clerk's gentle laugh brushed away my fear. "You've come to the right place," she said, walking around the counter. "Follow me."

Who knew the Bible industry was big business? The clerk led me to an entire wall covered with Bibles. Apparently this club I'd joined was way ahead of the curve when it came to people like me. She pulled out several examples, then handed me a thick navy Bible with silver-trimmed pages. "This is my personal favorite," she said, flipping the book open. She handed it to me, the solid weight of the pages security in my damp palms. "It's a study Bible. It's written in plain English," she explained, "but see this part down here?" She pointed to a smaller-print section on the bottom half of the page. "This part explains the verses up here. I'll leave you alone so that you can look through some of these." She placed her hand on the small stack she'd removed from the shelves. "Pick one that feels right for you." She moved the Bibles to a small table, motioning me to sit in the uphol-stered chair nearby. "Take your time."

I put down the open Bible and thumbed through three of the others she had pulled from the shelves, reading a verse here and there. I was amazed. Bibles had changed a lot since I'd been confirmed as a young teen. I pulled the original opened Bible towards me, my eyes drawn to the page. "*Therefore, if anyone is in Christ, he is a new cre-ation; the old has gone, the new has come!*" A tingle of recognition ran down my spine. Could those words be describing me? My eyes trailed down the page, finding the corresponding explanation. Second Corinthians, chapter five, verse seventeen. *When you make a com-mitment to Christ, your old life is past. You are re-created into a new person.*

A new person. I sat back in the chair, repeating the words in my mind. A new person. I didn't have to be the person I'd always been. Always searching for a way out. Always looking beyond to anywhere but where I was, wishing my life away while I waited for something better. I could be new right now. I was new.

"Having any luck?" The store clerk stood by my elbow.

"This one," I pointed, certain the page she'd opened for me had been no accident.

⌒

I gazed at myself in the bathroom mirror. A week had passed. A week when I'd literally devoured a good portion of my new Bible. I'd even found the words in Philippians that Vicky quoted about being content whatever the circumstances. I was trying my darndest. Trying to like my job, trying to know my coworkers beyond the "Hi, how are you" level. So then why did I feel so unsettled? As though this was not where I was supposed to be? If I was to be content no matter what, why did I still feel as though I'd be happier somewhere else? I splashed water on my face, determined to find something I liked about my job tomorrow.

When I'd read the words about becoming a new person, I'd imagined I'd wake up and look in the mirror and see a whole new me. Not quite new hair color or blue eyes instead of brown, but something almost visible. I was finding out the transformation wasn't quite that simple. I struggled with my old self-talk, words that told me I'd be happier somewhere else. This time though, I knew that thought was false. Been there, done that.

Lord, I prayed, *make me new in You. Help me to be happy where I am...even if it's at KMIN.* In another part of my brain I added, "although I don't see how that could happen." I may not have been visibly changed, but I was certainly seeing my job with new eyes. The insecurities and fragile egos of the people I worked with were wearing thin, no matter how hard I tried to be supportive. It just seemed as though whatever work I did, it should be more purposeful than this job felt. *Show me where it is You want me to be, Lord. What it is You want me to do.* I climbed into bed and switched off the light, pulling the covers up to my chin. *And if You have another plan in mind for me, I wouldn't mind hearing about it soon.*

I addressed the envelope, adding "Attention, Paul" to the bottom left corner of it, my twice monthly attempt to lessen my debt. I licked the flap, wondering if I'd still be paying this loan out of my Social Security check. The pittance I paid each month hardly seemed to make a dent when compared to the total I owed. I laid the envelope by my purse. I'd stick it in the mail when I went to work this afternoon. I imagined Dale, Brewster's postmaster, tossing my envelope into the bank's postal box in a couple days. As curious as he'd always been, he'd probably already figured out I was trying to pay off the debt I'd left behind.

What I'd left behind. I'd left so much more behind than money owed to the bank. I'd left the only family I had. I'd left people who had known me my entire life and accepted me just the way I was, negative attitude and all. I'd left Paul, the man I'd hurt to the core, yet the person who'd forgiven me and offered another chance at friendship.

As ironic as it seemed, all I wanted was to be back in Brewster. I pushed my hair behind my ears, realizing as I did that I'd have to give my hair another shot of spray before I left, but I felt too frustrated to sit still. Why had these things not mattered when I lived in Brewster? They seemed like the only things that mattered now. Now, when I was no longer there.

Could I ever go back? No I couldn't, that's all there was to it. For one thing, I needed a job, and there was nothing for me to do there. And, even if there was work for me, how could I ever swallow my pride and admit Brewster was where I was meant to be? Arrggghh! This line of thinking was getting me nowhere.

If I couldn't *be* there, I could at least talk to Vicky and pretend I was just down the street instead of hundreds of miles away. I looked at my watch. She should be free now in the lull before the lunch rush started. I dialed the café number.

"Wictoria's." I recognized Mrs. Bauer's voice immediately. What was she doing answering the phone? Vicky must be running an errand.

"Mrs. Bauer? It's Ruthie. Is Vicky there?"

"Rootie, hello! Ach, I miss wisiting witt you. How are you doing in dat big city?"

"Great. Just great." It wasn't exactly a lie. My job was going great, Doug Sommers told me almost every day. Mrs. Bauer didn't need to know about the part of my life that wasn't so great. The part that right now had me wishing I were visiting with her in person, in the back corner booth of Vicky's. "Is Vicky there? Or are you holding down the fort while she stepped out for a minute?"

"I'm her new vorker." Mrs. Bauer's voice was touched with pride.

"You're *working* there?" Vicky must have been desperate to hire Mrs. Bauer. The woman was close to eighty.

"Yah, chust until Pumpkin Fest is ofer. Wicky is trying to make pies in between customers. I'm pouring coffee in the mornings and running the cash regchester. That vay she can stay in the kitchen and get someting done. She's in dare now. I'll get her."

"No, no, that's okay," I protested, feeling guilty to be interrupting Vicky's frantic schedule, but Mrs. Bauer was already calling, "Wicky, it's Rootie."

"I could use your help, you know," Vicky deadpanned as Mrs. Bauer hung up the extension. I could imagine Vicky holding the phone to her ear with a cocked shoulder, her floured hands working the rolling pin that clicked softly through the phone line.

"I wish I could be there helping." Little did she know how badly I was wishing I could be there. I could almost feel the warmth of the kitchen. As if I were standing there with her.

"Excuse me, I must have a bad connection." Vicky tapped at the phone with what I could only imagine was a set of measuring spoons. She chuckled. "I thought I heard you say you wish you could be here."

"I do."

"No, you don't," Vicky said. I could hear the mixer being turned on. "It's a madhouse here. The Tastee Freeze closed for the season and that leaves only me. It's been wild, and now I have all these pies to bake before Friday. I had Angie down here with me until midnight last night. She's got a test tomorrow, so I can't ask her to help again tonight. I recruited Mrs. Bauer to take care of the coffee crowd in the morning and afternoon. If no one orders anything off the grill, I can at least get a few more pies in the freezer." The mixing sound stopped. "Who ever started this festival, anyway?"

Vicky complaining? "In all situations I am content," I reminded her.

"Ruthie?" I could tell I had her full attention. "Are you okay?"

"I'm fine," I sighed. "A little homesick, maybe."

"Well, don't be. It's same-old, same-old around here." The water started running in the sink. "Oh, here's something new."

I didn't want to hear something new. It was the same-old, same-old that was comfort to my lonesome ears. What I wouldn't give to be in Vicky's kitchen right now, helping fill piecrusts with pumpkin filling, knowing in two days time we'd be rushing around the old high school gym, serving those handmade pies to all sorts of folks from around the area. Instead, in a few minutes I would be off to work at KMIN, playing songs for people I never saw.

Vicky turned off the water. "Paul and Sandy Quinn are dating. Sam's in his glory. He's convinced it was his introduction at Pumpkin Fest last year that set them up. Who knows, maybe it was." I could hear pie tins rattling as hard as my heart was thudding. "Oh, hey, I've got to go. Mrs. Bauer just brought me an order for the lunch special. The rush is starting early today. Bye. I miss you."

Just like that I was back in my small apartment, far from the place I'd been in my imagination. Far from the changes occurring in Brewster. When I'd lived there, it seemed as if nothing ever happened; now Paul was dating Sandy Quinn? I remembered last year's Pumpkin Fest, watching Sandy and Paul eating pie in the bleachers, feeling a stab of jealousy. I felt the same stab now. Paul had found his way to me that night. Had I somehow thought he'd find me again?

You're being ridiculous. You and Paul had nothing but a good friendship going. Why shouldn't he date Sandy? Did you expect him to stay single the rest of his life just in case you decided you wanted him?

I grabbed my coat and car keys, pulling the door closed behind me. I'd get to work and get my mind out of its nostalgic rut. I had the life I'd always wanted; now I needed to learn to live it.

It was only halfway to KMIN when the traffic came to a near standstill that I remembered the envelope for Paul I'd left lying in my apartment. For a brief second I laid my head on the steering wheel. Why had God put me here when He knew my heart ached for Vicky and Dave? For Angie and Sam? For Paul?

For Brewster?

Paul

"There, that should about do it." Dave gave the nail a final tap. The crossbar holding up the Pumpkin Fest banner was secure. He stood, putting his hands on his hips, surveying the old high school gym. "Tomorrow night this place will be hopping. Too bad we can't have a celebration like this every month; I like it when the place is full. Well, except for…"

"Yeah," I said, my eyes landing on the empty corner of the gym where last year Ruthie's booth had filled the spot. This year the space was vacant. No other business in town had taken its place. Her absence had left more than a gaping spot in the exhibitors' lineup at Pumpkin Fest; I noticed her missing from Brewster every time I turned around. I missed her head popping around the door of my office simply saying, "Hi!" I missed her in Vicky's café, the way she knew everyone in town and greeted them like an old friend. I missed her over at Dave's house, the way her eyes sparkled at the unique things Sam would come up with and how she would get flustered when I stayed for a meal. I hadn't realized how much I'd been watching for her until she wasn't there anymore.

"It's going to be weird this year," Dave said, "not having Ruthie here. She never thought many people listened to KBRS, but you'd be surprised how many people stopped by my booth and said they'd heard Pumpkin Fest advertised on the radio and decided to come. And she's helped Vicky with those pies for…" He paused. "Well, for as long as I can remember." Dave slapped his hands together. "Speaking of pies, I hope you know we're counting on you to help serve this year."

I high-fived Dave. "You bet. I'm ready." My overenthusiasm caused him to give me a puzzled look. He didn't need to know I'd already used Vicky's pie booth as an excuse for not attending Pumpkin Fest with Sandy. I didn't like making excuses, but Sandy had been assuming a familiarity I was still unsure of. I didn't feel ready to flat-out talk to her about it. I didn't know what I'd say. And I guessed that said something too. I needed more time to evaluate our relationship...if you could call it that. And working at Pumpkin Fest seemed like a good enough excuse. Not that working in the pie booth would give me time to think, but it wouldn't give Sandy the impression that we were going to do everything together. At least not yet.

"See you tomorrow," I called to Dave as I opened the door of my VW. Tomorrow night I wouldn't have a chance at this parking spot near the gym door. The gym would be packed with people, just not the one person I really wanted to be there. I could already imagine Sandy hovering around Vicky's booth, waiting for a lull in the pie business for the slim "*maybe I'll have time for coffee*" promise I'd given her.

I should have remembered how these things worked in Brewster. All it took was a couple unofficial pairings at a ball game, a dinner party, or an offer of a ride home, and all of a sudden the folks in Brewster had you linked together. The fact that Sandy was part of the group Vicky and Dave hung around with made it easy for people to assume we were a couple. We weren't. Not yet, anyway. At least not in my mind. I had a feeling Sandy might be viewing things a bit differently. Her disappointment had been visible when I'd told her I'd committed Pumpkin Fest night to helping in Vicky's booth.

"If she needs help," Sandy said, "I sure don't mind pitching in."

That's all I needed, Sandy and me working together in Vicky's popular pie stand. Not only would the folks of Brewster have us paired up, the whole tri-county region would. "Thanks," I replied, my mind scrambling for words, "but I think she has the schedule made up. With Angie and Sam, Mrs. Bauer, and me, she should have the bases covered. Oh, Dave too," I added in case five of us, including

Vicky, weren't enough to squeeze behind the small space of the booth. "And my mom's serving coffee." Insurance.

"Well then, I guess I'll just have to wave to you from the line." Sandy sighed, her eyes avoiding mine.

"Maybe," I said, feeling my stomach plummet as I spoke, "if I have some downtime, we can squeeze in a cup of coffee."

"That would be nice," she said, her eyes rising to meet mine.

I felt like a cad. Sandy was a wonderful person, but just because we were almost the only two single people in our age group in town did not mean we were meant to be together. Did it? Lately, I'd started wondering what *was* meant for me.

I'd been certain God had led me back to Brewster for a reason. A new outlook on work. A job where I could directly see the difference I was making in people's lives. The mentorship I'd developed with Wayne and my mom's health improving, then finding the farm, had seemed like a pure gift on top of my work at the bank.

I didn't like to question my blessings, but I was having a hard time understanding why God would lead me back to Brewster only to stick me out on a farm all by myself.

I was looking forward to Pumpkin Fest if only for an evening surrounded by people. I hadn't needed the reminder in my devotional time today: "It is not good for man to be alone." The cold October wind whistling around my farmhouse only served to emphasize how alone I felt. I was sure God was well aware of that lonely place inside of me. After all, I'd been talking to Him about it a lot lately. And somehow Ruthie's name always seemed to come up.

Ruthie

The dead-air alarm at the station was ringing! Where was Doug? He was supposed to know how to turn it off. I slapped at the wall, certain the off switch must be somewhere near. My hand hit air, then mattress, the sudden movement jerking me awake. The sound continued until I realized my bedside phone was ringing. I fumbled with the receiver. My voice crackled with sleep. "Hull-o-o?"

"Auntie Ruth, youhavetocomehomerightnow." I understood the Auntie Ruth part, but everything after that was beyond understanding by my sleep-filled brain.

"Angie?" I swung my legs over the side of the bed and switched on my lamp. The sharp brightness caused an instant ache behind my eyes. "Slow down. What's going on? Where's your mom?"

"Inthehospital." She drew in a deep breath, then repeated, "She's in the hospital. You have to come home right now."

I glanced at my digital clock. Three-forty-two. Why in the world was Angie calling me at this hour? Why would Vicky be in the hospital? She wasn't sick. "Angie," I said, straightening my back, readying myself for whatever she would say, "tell me what happened."

"Mom had an accident. She's in the hospital. Dad went to check on her and—" The sound of sobbing filled the phone line. "Oh, he's here. Here-re." I could hear the receiver being jostled as Angie handed over the phone.

"Hello?" A voice that wasn't Dave's came on the line. "I'm sorry, I'm not sure whom I'm speaking to."

It took me a second to realize it was Paul on the other end of the line and not Dave. "Hold on a minute," I said, holding out my palm as if he could see me, shaking my head to clear any remaining sleepiness. "Paul? What are you doing at Vicky's?"

"Ruthie?" Paul sounded as surprised as I was.

I could hear Angie sniffing in the background, saying, "I called her."

"I suppose you're wondering what's going on," Paul said, adding, "I'm afraid I can't tell you a whole lot. Dave called me about twenty minutes ago from the café and said he'd found Vicky there on the floor, unconscious. He'd called the ambulance. I offered to come in and stay with the kids until he got back. That's all I know. I was going to call the hospital when I got here."

"Unconscious?" I whispered the word, staring at my bedroom floor as if Vicky were lying there. "What was she doing at the café this time of the morning?"

"I'm guessing she was baking pies for Pumpkin Fest. It's tomorrow—no," Paul interrupted himself, "actually it's today."

"Pumpkin Fest is today?" Even though I'd been dreaming about it for the past two weeks as if counting the days until Christmas, hearing the words "it's today" was like having a bucket of cold water thrown at me. "What's Vicky going to do? What if she's…" I was pacing by the bed, the phone tucked between my cheek and shoulder, my hands waving in the air. "I'm on my way," I said, already moving toward my closet. The phone slipped off my nightstand, pulling the receiver from my shoulder.

"Ruthie?" Paul's worried voice traveled from somewhere under my bed. "Ruthie! Are you okay?"

I spoke to him from my hands and knees, "I'm fine. I dropped the phone. I'll be there as soon as I can." Already I was mentally packing for my trip. My black slacks, a pair of jeans, my blue sweater. "I'll call you from Fergus Falls." I stood up, slipping one arm out of the T-shirt I slept in. No use wishing for a cell phone now. I'd long ago decided the money I saved was better used to pay my loan. "I'll stop there to fill up on gas."

"Maybe you should wait until it's light," Paul said. "Until we find out for sure what's going on with Vicky." He sounded as if he knew I wouldn't listen. He blew a puff of air into the phone. "I don't want to have to worry about you too."

"Don't worry," I said. "Pray. I'll call you in a couple hours."

Paul

Pray? I looked at the phone receiver, the steady rhythm of the cut-off signal a reminder of Ruthie's word…pray…pray…pray. *Ruthie* had told *me* to pray? Slowly I placed the phone into its cradle, wondering where her instruction had come from. Had she been caught up in Vicky's situation and responded with the first thought that came to mind, or was there something deeper behind Ruthie's command? I wasn't sure, but either way, Ruthie had instructed me to pray. I didn't have time to breathe more than a sentence before Angie was urging me to call the hospital.

"Mrs. Johnson has been transferred to Carlton," was all I could get out of the nurse who answered the phone. That fact alone let me know whatever had happened to Vicky was not good. If she'd been fine, they would have kept her in the small Brewster hospital. Other than hopping in the car and following Dave to Carlton, there wasn't anything more I could do at this hour of the morning, and if I did drive to Carlton, Ruthie would have no way of knowing what was going on when she called.

"What are we going to do?" Angie was still sniffling, wiping at her eyes with the sleeve of her pajama top.

"We're going to pray," I told her, not sure why I felt so confident everything was going to be all right. "Then you're going to get some sleep while I try to get ahold of your dad in Carlton. By the time you wake up, we'll know exactly what happened to your mom."

But three hours later, as I stared at the clock willing Ruthie to call, I didn't know much more. I'd talked to Dave at the Carlton hospital. All he could tell me was that Vicky had been staying late at the café, trying to finish the pies for Pumpkin Fest. He'd helped her until ten, calling home occasionally to check on the kids. Vicky had finally chased him home to make sure the kids got to bed since Angie had a big test the next day. He'd fallen asleep in the recliner and woke up about three amazed he hadn't heard Vicky come home. When he'd wandered into the bedroom and had seen the untouched bed, he knew right away something was wrong.

"I jumped in the car and drove like a wild man to the café," Dave had told me over the phone. "I could smell overcooked pie the minute I opened the back door. There lay Vicky, out cold on the floor, the oven door open, the pies half in and half out of the oven. There was a spot on the floor, a piece of pumpkin shell that had dropped earlier, I'm guessing. All I can think is that she slipped on it and hit her head. I called the ambulance and, I know it sounds dumb, but after I made sure Vicky was breathing and had a steady pulse, well, I know how much those pies mean to her, so I turned off the oven and put the pies on the counter to cool. There I was standing in the café kitchen with potholders on my hands when the paramedics rushed in. They must have thought I was nuts. Baking pies while my wife was passed out at my feet." Dave gave a wry chuckle. "I guess I wasn't thinking about what it looked like. I was just thinking how important all that stuff is to Vick-y." His voice cracked. He sucked in a deep breath, releasing it into the phone. "You can hardly imagine what it's like to see your wife lying there like she's—" He stopped talking. "Oh man, I'm sorry, Paul. I didn't mean—I don't even know what I'm saying anymore."

I knew exactly what he'd almost said... *to see your wife lying there like she's dead.* Like I'd seen Mia. The sudden vision sent a stab of recognition through me. I knew exactly how Dave was feeling. I pushed the image from my mind, realizing as I did that God was using my tragedy for His good purpose. "I'm right here for you, buddy."

Dave didn't answer. His uneven breathing spoke for him.

"As soon as Ruthie calls I'm packing up the kids and coming to Carlton. Hang in there. We'll be there soon."

From the way I jumped when the phone finally rang you'd think I hadn't been expecting it to ring. Hadn't been staring at it for half the night. "Ruthie?" Her name was out before the receiver was near my mouth.

"You must have been sitting on the phone," she said. "What's wrong?"

"Nothing. Well, not exactly nothing." I scrubbed at my face, early morning stubble scraping my fingertips. "It's just that we don't know much more. When I talked to Dave he said they were going to be running some tests. They'd take time. Vicky was still unconscious but she had a strong pulse. I told Dave I'd bring the kids to Carlton as soon as you called back."

"I'll head straight to Carlton," Ruthie said, her voice sure. "Keep praying."

Ruthie

I cracked open the car window, considering fresh air a weak substitute for my morning coffee. I didn't know why I wasn't panicking. Why I wasn't falling apart as I pushed the speed limit to the max, watching the miles pass by in a dusky haze as the highway between Vicky and me rolled beneath my car. All I did know was that I needed to be with her, and until I could get there, talking to God was the next best thing. At least praying made me feel as though I were doing something instead of simply wishing Vicky was alive. It was as if my thoughts formed a three-way connection between God, Vicky, and me, bringing about a kind of healing that was comforting me as much as I hoped it was her.

This new-found faith of yours is nothing but a crutch. Whatever happens to Vicky is going to happen whether you are praying or not. I shook my head as the thought threaded its way into my road-numb brain. My old way of thinking felt almost as out of place as my renewed faith did at times. Funny, though, how my old thoughts gave no comfort and my prayers did. I continued to pray my way to Carlton, adding prayers for Dave and the kids and for Paul too. His night had been just as long as mine.

I entered the city limits of Carlton around ten o'clock. It felt as though I'd already put in a full day of work, driving six hours through the night and morning. Only then did it dawn on me I'd never even thought to call the station and tell them I'd had a family emergency. A half smile crept over my face as I understood the lesson in my rush to be with Vicky. Sure I needed my work, but without people in my life, work meant nothing. I glanced at my watch, the clock in my car long past trusting with the time. Even though it felt like afternoon, there were several hours until I was expected at the station. Time enough for Doug to arrange for Marv to do our show solo and to have another deejay take "Sheila's" place. I'd call in as soon as I found out how Vicky was doing. Maybe then I'd have a better idea how long I'd be gone.

Funny how the idea of missing work didn't bother me a bit. At one time my job had been my whole life. Now it seemed a mere blip on life's radar when compared to the thought of what Vicky was going through.

I pulled into the visitor's parking lot at the hospital, grabbed my purse, and jumped out of the car. Halfway through the parking lot I was wishing I'd thought to grab my winter coat from my apartment. This North Dakota morning was much colder than the Minnesota mornings I'd left behind. I wrapped my arms around myself as I approached the information desk.

"Cold?" Paul's voice was an electric blanket tossed around my shoulders. The timbre of his word sent a warm shiver down my spine, comforting and disquieting all at once.

"Kind of," I said, even though the sound of Paul's voice had pushed the cold right out of me. I was supposed to be worrying about my sister and yet simply seeing him made me feel assured.

"I thought you'd be getting here about now," he said. "I left Dave and the kids with Vicky and came down here to wait. She started coming around about an hour ago."

"She did?" Another glad flush of warmth rushed over me. *Thank You, God*, I mouthed, closing my eyes for a second. It felt good to have Someone to thank beyond mere coincidence. I opened my eyes. "Let me just call the station and let Doug know I won't be in today, or maybe for a few days," I added. Now that I knew Vicky would be okay, waiting one extra minute to see her didn't seem that long. My eyes searched for a pay phone.

"Use this." Paul handed me his cell phone. Our hands briefly clasped as he placed the phone in my hand, his fingers lingering a moment longer than necessary, which was fine by me.

Quickly I dialed the station, Paul's eyes glued to mine as I waited for the call to connect. That was fine too. Doug was more than sympathetic and quickly agreed to rearrange my schedule when he'd heard what had happened. I handed the phone back to Paul. "Thanks. Lead the way." I was anxious to see Vicky with my own eyes.

Paul rubbed his hand across my back. "She's going to be glad to see you," he said. He didn't even have to add, "I am too." I could tell that by the silly grin plastered across his face. "What's so funny?" he asked.

Apparently the same silly grin was on my face too. "I'm just glad to be here," I said, marveling at how a hospital lobby could feel so much like home.

～

"I'm going home right now and that's all there is to it." I could hear the stubborn tone in Vicky's voice from the hall. "I feel fine…whoa." She fell back against the raised bed as I walked into the room. "Okay, so I'm a little dizzy…Ruthie?…What are you doing here?" Vicky didn't give me a chance to open my mouth before she turned to Dave. "Did you call and tell Ruthie to come here?"

"No, I did!" Angie spoke from her cross-legged position on the end of Vicky's bed, ducking her head when she caught the chastising look Vicky shot her way. "I thought you'd want her here," she mumbled, picking at an invisible spot on the blanket.

"Glad to see you too," I added pointedly.

"Sorry." Vicky gave me a sheepish smile, rolling her eyes and lifting the cast on her right arm in a half-baked wave. "You guys are making way too big a deal out of this. All I did was slip in the kitchen, and everyone is acting like I'm on my deathbed." As if to emphasize her point, Vicky flopped her head against the pillow. "Yeow-ouch!" She rubbed the back of her head with her left hand. "Wow," she said, pulling her fingers from her head and staring at her cupped hand, the perfect imitation of a goose egg. "I didn't feel *that* before."

"Vicky," Dave said, sounding more like a stern father than a husband, "the doctor said you have a concussion. You're going to have to stay here for obser—"

"Kids have concussions all the time," Vicky interrupted, "and they get sent home with their parents."

"Well, those kids might not have been unconscious for six hours." Dave pressed at his temples with his fingertips. "You had us really worried, honey. Just cooperate, okay? I don't want to go through this again. Ever."

Vicky closed her eyes and slumped into the pillow, silent for a moment. "But what about my pies?" She opened her eyes, speaking to Dave, "It's Pumpkin Fest and I—"

"Forget about the pies, okay?" Dave stuffed both hands into the pockets of his jeans as if trying to keep his exasperation in check. "Even when you were out of it, you were mumbling about those stupid pies. You knock yourself out over them every year." He paused, then added, "And not just figuratively. This year you literally knocked yourself out *and* broke your arm." Sam snickered as the play on words sunk in. Dave didn't think it one bit funny. "Brewster will survive Pumpkin Fest for one year without pies. I don't want to hear one more word about it."

"But—" Vicky's eyelids were beginning to droop, the fight going out of her like a slow leak in a balloon. "What will I do with all of them? I'll never be able to sell that many slices at the café."

"We'll give them away if we have to." Dave pulled his hand out of his pocket and stroked Vicky's arm. "Right now I really don't care. I just want you better."

Once again Vicky tried to protest, "I can pour coffee with my left hand and—" Dave put a finger over her lips silencing her.

Vicky sighed her surrender.

"Paul and I can do it." The words were out of my mouth before I realized I'd said them. Regrouping I added, "I'm not driving all this way to watch you sleep, you know. And besides, we practically ran the show last year. It'll be fun. Like playing 'café.' " I was sounding like a bad actress from a 1950s "B" movie. Paul was nodding his head as though he were my leading man.

Sam decided to join the act. "I can help!"

"Me too," Angie chimed in.

"Listen, young lady," Vicky wasn't about to totally cave in to our barrage. "If I remember right, you have a big test today. Skipping school is one thing if your mom is unconscious, but I'm not anymore. You studied hard for that test. You go take it and then you can help at Pumpkin Fest." Vicky shifted her gaze to me. "Could you drive the kids back to Brewster? Drop them off at school?" She sleepily blinked her eyes. "I think I'm going to rest for a minute. You know where everything is in the café, right?"

"No problem," I said, sounding as if I'd done this before. My mind was racing, realizing there was probably much more to this pie business than cutting the slices and putting them on paper plates. Where were the plastic forks? And what about making the coffee? I had no idea who had ever been in charge of that. And coffee cups? And napkins? And a cash box? Not to mention the fact that Pumpkin Fest would start within the hour and we weren't even in Brewster. My heart began trying to keep up with my thoughts. Whenever I'd helped Vicky before, I'd always shown up after KBRS had gone off the air at sunset. Vicky already had her crew working like clockwork and I was simply a second hand, sweeping in, fitting in with ease, mainly because all I had to do was lay plates on a counter. Now I had volunteered to do a job I had no idea how to begin. "I suppose we should go," I said to the kids, my voice not near as confident as it had been when I'd said, "*I can do it!*"

Paul led the way out, the kids giving their mom a quick kiss before they pushed their arms into their coats. Vicky reached out and grabbed my hand. "If you have any questions, ask Mrs. Bauer. She knows how it all works." Her eyelids fluttered as she fought sleep. "Remember," she half whispered, "be content."

I remembered a year ago, almost to the day, when I had complained to Vicky about everything having to do with Pumpkin Fest and with Brewster, she had uttered those same words...*I have learned wherever I am to be content.* Words that had dogged me for almost a year. Words that had started my search for a different path.

Now I was on it.

I squeezed Vicky's hand. "I am," I said, realizing, surprisingly, I was.

⌒

"Keep the change." Mr. Meier slid a ten-dollar bill across the table in exchange for one slice of pie and a cup of coffee.

"That's way too much," I protested, knowing my words would do no good. All afternoon people had been paying for their pie with fives and tens as word spread about Vicky's accident.

"Having that café open is worth a lot more than ten dollars." Mr. Meier blew on his coffee, then cleared his throat. "You tell that sister of yours to get home real quick, okay?"

I nodded as for the umpteenth time that day I swallowed at the lump in my throat. "Thanks," I said, stuffing the bill into my bulging apron pocket. We'd given up using the cash box three hours ago. "I'll give Vicky your message."

Mr. Meier gave a sharp nod. "You do that."

"How's your sister?" Delores Wahl was next in line, a five-dollar bill hanging from her fingers. "It was so strange driving into town today and seeing a 'closed' sign on the café. I mean, I know Vicky usually closes the café for Pumpkin Fest, but knowing it was closed because she was in the hospital..." Delores wrinkled her nose and wiggled her shoulders. "Well, I don't know. It gave me a funny feeling."

I knew just what she meant. Paul had dropped Angie and Sam at school while I left my car at Vicky's house. He had picked me up in his Bug and then headed to the café, coming at the building from Main Street. The curtains were pulled shut, the white shade on the door down, the "closed" sign almost seeming to blink as we drove past the locked door. Even on Pumpkin Fest Vicky always had the curtains open. Not today. Today it had all seemed different as we entered the quiet café through the back door. Several pies stood sentry on the kitchen counter, their spicy scent a counterpoint to the mixing bowl on the counter, waiting for another batch of pie filling. The spot where Vicky had slipped was obvious in the daylight, a glob of cooked pumpkin smeared into a foot-long streak and dried onto the floor near the oven. It wasn't hard to imagine how, in her rush to get all the pies done, she'd ignored a chunk of pumpkin that had fallen on the floor. Had more than likely stepped on it, then flung her arm out to break her fall, hitting her arm on the oven door, her head on the floor. The only thing I couldn't imagine was why she didn't get burned too.

My first urge had been to clean up the mess, as if wiping away the spilled food would help heal Vicky. But there would be time enough for cleaning later. Right then Paul and I needed to get into high gear. Pumpkin Fest had started without the pumpkin pies or the coffee that was IV fluid to the folks around Brewster.

"You stack the pies," I ordered Paul, swinging open the freezer door and motioning to the counter. "I'll scrounge up the rest of the stuff." I shouldered my way through the swinging door into the main part of the café, heading for the cupboard I knew held a one-hundred-cup percolator. My mind was spinning as I grabbed at Styrofoam cups, plastic forks, and paper napkins. What else would we need? Oh! I laughed to myself as I grabbed the coffee grounds. Hard to make coffee without coffee.

By the time we arrived at the gym, Pumpkin Fest was in full swing, the high school band playing polka music, people browsing the makeshift aisles visiting local merchants at their booths. The scene reminded me of every Pumpkin Fest in the past with three exceptions. The first was that Dave's insurance booth sat empty, Dave choosing to stay with Vicky in spite of her protests. Somehow I envisioned Sam more than willing to hand out brochures when school was out for the day. The second difference was the front half of the gym, the spot where in the past pumpkin pie slices had been lined up like chess pieces waiting to make their move into waiting mouths. Today the spot was barren, an empty desert of tabletops. No coffee-perking sound or smell filled the gym either.

The second difference got solved in a hurry as Kenny and Ben Pearson helped Paul unload the pies and other folks pulled plates, forks, and the large coffee pot from the back of Paul's car. Several ladies from Vicky's church covered the tables with white paper as I took up a post behind the tables, ordering my makeshift troops into action. Within a half hour we had last night's pies ready to serve, a new batch thawing in the gym kitchen's ovens. The first few cups of coffee were weak, but no one seemed to mind.

"It's hot and that's all they care about," quipped Paul's mom, who had miraculously appeared to man the coffeepots.

From the moment I cut into the first pie, Vicky's pie booth was swamped, the line snaking halfway through the gym. As fast as a pie tin was emptied, Paul would slide another one under my knife. It wasn't until Angie came puffing in, having run the several blocks from the school building to Brewster's old gym, that I stopped long enough to flex my fingers.

"How'd your test go?" I asked, my fingers imitating a deformed sort of wave.

"Great!" Angie said, stuffing her coat and books into a corner of the kitchen. "I got done early and my teacher let me leave right away." She glanced around the kitchen, eyeing the long line of people waiting for pies. "What should I do?"

"Let's get two lines going," Paul said, picking up the knife I'd set down. "I'll cut pies. Angie, you carry them out to the table and Ruthie, you start serving."

And that's what we did, the third difference of this Pumpkin Fest occurring so subtly I almost didn't notice. It was after we'd turned away the last of the folks hoping for pie. After we'd torn paper from the tables and scrubbed the insides of the coffeepots. After Dave had collected the kids, Sam proudly announcing he'd handed out every brochure in the insurance booth. Angie had picked her coat off the floor, uncovering the whole pumpkin pie she'd stashed away for her dad to share with Vicky. It was after all of that, when Paul and I were the only two people left in the pie stand, when we were tying garbage bags and filling our arms with empty pie tins to haul back to the café, that the third difference crept into my being. I had loved this whole day.

Not once had I thought about how silly a festival celebrating pumpkins seemed. Not once had I begrudgingly pretended I was having fun. Not once had I wished I were anywhere but right here.

Is this what it feels like to be content, Lord? Is this it?

I didn't need an answer to my prayer. I felt it deep in my being. This was contentment…being surrounded by people who cared about me, doing work that served others in a place that felt like home. This feeling felt like a precious gift. It *was* a gift. But how could I keep it?

As I placed the stack of pie tins onto the backseat of Paul's car, a sense of peace flowed through me, quickly followed by a sense of panic. I no longer lived here. This job wasn't mine. If this was contentment, how could I possibly have it? My brain tumbled with questions that had no answers as we carried the pie tins, coffeepots, and percolator into the café.

I climbed into the bucket seat beside Paul, glad for the silence between us, the kind of silence that comes from working hard together at a job well done. I leaned my head against the headrest, closing my eyes as if tired. Instead my mind was trying desperately to cling to the peace I'd felt all evening. The sense that this was where I was meant to be. Right here. Right now.

Oh, Lord, I don't know what You want me to do. Where You want me to be. All I ever dreamed about was leaving this place, and You know that dream didn't bring happiness. Now I'm back and for once in my life I feel content. Why now? What's going on? I can't come back. People would laugh at me. Say I couldn't make it in the city. You know that's not it, Lord. I am making it. It's that the things I'd imagined would bring contentment…don't.

I'm so confused, Lord. For the past eight hours I didn't once wonder where contentment was. I was living it. You wouldn't finally show me this feeling of peace only to take it away, would You? Show me what it is You want me to do. Where it is You want me to be. Whatever it is, wherever it is, Lord, help me find my home in You. Show me clearly. Show me… Show me…

"Ruthie?" Paul gently nudged my arm. "Are you sleeping?" The car was idling quietly in front of Vicky and Dave's house. The porch light was on.

"I guess I was." I rubbed my eyes, my mind still half-praying, half-dreaming. "It's been a long day. And night," I added.

"It has." Paul nodded.

"Sorry I conked out. I can't believe I couldn't say awake for four blocks."

"That's okay, you're home now. Go in and get some rest." He leaned over me and pushed open the car door, his spicy cologne brushing past, an invisible caress.

He looked at me and I smiled up at him. "Thanks," I said, "for helping, and all."

He smiled back, staring into my eyes for a silent moment as if he might say something very important. Instead he raised his hand to my cheek, tilted my head back every so slightly, then placed the softest kiss I'd ever felt on my waiting lips. If there was anything in creation softer than feather down, it was this. If there was anything I wanted more of, it was this. He pulled away, staring into my eyes with a longing that made me ache. A soft sigh escaped my lips. "Go home," he said softly.

It seemed I'd been waiting for that kiss for twenty years. I got out of the car, not sure if I should laugh or cry. I watched as Paul drove down the street, a smile on my face, a lump in my throat. Had that kiss meant welcome or goodbye? I closed my eyes, imagining the soft brush of his lips. Somehow I hoped it had meant more than farewell. Slowly I breathed deeply, filling my lungs with Brewster's crystal-clear air, reliving the past moments.

Home. I loved the sound of that word coming from Paul's lips. Home. Paul's last word of the night. I doubted that was the important thing I'd thought he might say, but for some reason I had no doubt his word might be part of what God wanted me to hear.

Home.

I looked up at the clear night sky, the streetlight at the end of the block not nearly bright enough to dim the stars over Brewster. They floated above my head in a glad array, as if thrown into the sky like sparkler sparks to celebrate the night. I reached inside the door of the house and turned off the porch light. I didn't want to go in just yet. I stood outside breathing in the cool night air, the peace I'd felt earlier wrapping itself around me.

Home. If this is what it felt like, I wanted it. I tilted my head into the night and whispered my prayer, "If this is my home, Lord, show me the way to get back."

Paul

The crunch of gravel under my tires signaled I was almost home. The short drive from Brewster had given me time to think about this long day, but I wanted more time to think about this night. I downshifted as I neared my farmhouse, stopping outside the garage. I got out of the car and leaned against the door, my head tilted back as if nudged by God. *Look at these stars,* He seemed to say, *I put them here for you.*

The night sky was filled with hundreds of thousands of stars. The Milky Way a brilliant patch of gauze. Northern lights dancing to a tune from heaven.

Did You put Ruthie here for me too? Having her in Brewster and working with her all day had felt so right. Kissing her tonight had felt like a kind of completion. The end of a journey that had started eons ago. Or was it a beginning?

I'd kissed her, then told her to go home, the only way I knew to make sure she left before I said the words that had been pushing at my heart. *Stay. I love you. Stay.* Words I wanted to say so badly, words I still wasn't sure God wanted me to say. If God had something planned, I certainly wanted to know what it was.

Look at the stars.

I was, and all it was doing was making me wish Ruthie were here beside me. I picked up a rock and threw it into the night sky, trying to throw my loneliness far away. Today, for the first time since I'd known Ruthie, she had appeared utterly content. All those years in school, she'd always seemed restless, waiting for something else…whatever that might be. I didn't think even Ruthie knew what that something was. But today, whether she was cutting pies, putting slices on plates, starting a new urn of coffee, or bantering with old Mr.

Feist, Ruthie exuded a peace I'd never seen before. If at one time I'd found her attractive for her exuberance, now I was attracted to her calm. What had changed in the months she'd been gone? Had her job in Minneapolis been what she had longed for all these years?

I kicked at loose gravel under my feet. *Why are You showing this side of her to me now? If You don't mean for us to be together, take these feelings away. Take her away.* I heaved another rock into the sky, then another and another, anger and frustration mingled with loneliness as I flung it all up to God. *You said it's not good for man to be alone, so then why am I?*

I knew I could be with Sandy, but she wasn't who I wanted. I recalled how Sandy had looked at me when she'd stopped by the pie booth after school, offering her help. Her eyes had turned first to me, then Ruthie, and then back to me. A question there I didn't need to answer. She knew just by looking. I knew too. It was Ruthie who had my heart. Sandy was probably asking God the same questions I was tonight. *What is Your plan for me? Why am I alone?*

Look at the stars. If I could put them so carefully in the sky, don't you think I can take care of you? Be patient. I have a plan for you. A plan for good and not for harm.

The familiar bit of Scripture drained the questions from me, and the fight. God did have a plan for me; of that I was certain. It wasn't fair for me to put so much weight on this one area of my life when all the other parts were so blessed. When I'd been looking for change, He'd moved me back to Brewster. He formed an unlikely bond between Wayne Jorgenson and me, and He brought enough relief to my mother's arthritis so that I'd been able to move to this farmstead. I just didn't want to be alone on it.

I dropped the two stones I had left in my hand and rested my arms on the top of my VW, settling my chin on my arms. I gazed at the dark horizon, moonlight and starlight creating shadows in the cool night. If only Ruthie were here to share this view.

A falling star caught my eye, and I followed it during the second it took to burn itself out. *Make a wish.* The old childhood chant ran through my head. I stood up, stretching my arms into the sky. I didn't believe in wishes, only prayer, and God knew very well what was in my heart. I was confident He had a plan for me. Apparently I would just have to wait to see what it was.

～

The Sunday school kids came racing up the church basement steps as I made my way across the foyer into the sanctuary. I stood for a moment surveying the backs of people's heads already in their pews. The Brewster church pews were a bit like cattle stalls; everyone had their own spot and sat there like well-trained animals. My mother was in her pew, sitting beside Irene Bitz. They'd been widowed the same year and had become fast friends, Irene picking my mother up for church each Sunday, Mom treating her to a light lunch after church. They fended off my offer to drive them both, saying they were perfectly happy with the arrangement they had. I noticed Mom had left a spot in the pew for me, her one Sunday concession to a change in her routine.

The pew where Dave, Vicky, and the kids sat was empty, as I'd known it would be. Dave had taken the kids to Carlton to visit their mom. He was hoping she'd be released later in the morning, and if she felt up to it, they were going to take the kids to a matinee before returning to Brewster. "We could use some fun time," Dave had said.

I walked down the side aisle and slid into the pew beside my mother as the Sunday school kids scurried among the congregation finding their parents. Two young candlelighters made their way up the three steps to the altar and lit the candles while the organist held the last notes of her prelude. Pastor Ammon walked to the lectern and said, "Good morning!"

"Good morning!" All around me familiar voices chimed in.

"Let's take a moment to greet our neighbors." Pastor Ammon strode down from the lectern, hand outstretched.

My mother turned and gave me a quick hug, then greeted Irene as if they hadn't already chatted for twenty minutes. Little Erica Frank, sitting in front of me turned and stuck out her left hand. "I'm three," she said in greeting. I shook her tiny hand, then those of her parents. Irene reached over and squeezed my hand. I turned to the folks behind me, their faces familiar but not their names. Pastor Ammon was heading back to the pulpit so there was no time for anything other than a quick handshake and smile. The congregation rustled back into place, a last "good morning" echoing from somewhere in the back before quiet settled over us.

"Please turn in your hymnals to hymn number seventy-two."

I waited while my mother opened the hymnal, licking her fingers as she fumbled with two sticky pages. The organ music swelled, our cue to sing. I waited for Mom to find the page, letting the familiar music surround me. Sometimes listening was worshiping too. I closed my eyes. Mom nudged me with her elbow, my half of the book now ready for me to hold. I scanned the page, finding the spot as the congregation started in on the familiar chorus. I didn't need the book for this part. I opened my mouth, ready to sing, my eyes lifting from the words I knew by heart. Just as quickly the words disappeared from my throat. Where had Ruthie come from?

There she stood, all alone, two rows in front of me, in the pew where Vicky and Dave usually sat. When had she come in? Why hadn't I seen her? My mom nudged me again, looking at me out of the corner of her eye. She loved to sing and thought everyone else should too. The fact I wasn't didn't escape her.

By the time I found my voice, the congregation was back at the chorus again. This time I sang out strongly. It didn't matter when Ruthie had come into church. All that mattered was she was here.

Ruthie

I'd almost talked myself out of coming. On the short drive from Vicky's to the church I'd almost turned around twice. I knew how people in Brewster talked, and I could almost hear the things they'd say when they saw me in church.

Oh sure, now that her sister is in the hospital she feels the need for church.

Big-city girl showing off her new coat.

Look at her all alone there. Too bad she never got married.

I'd lived here long enough to know exactly what some of them would think. I'd also lived here long enough to know what the others would say.

Isn't that Ruthie Hammond? I'll bet she's here to pray for her sister.

Lucky girl, getting that good job in Minneapolis. I bet she's great at it.

Too bad she never got married.

I knew all the things they might think but I went anyway. To be truthful, I really didn't care what any of the people were thinking. What I did care about was trying to find out what God had in mind for me. If it wasn't Minneapolis, then where?

I thought I'd feel weird walking into church all by myself, but I didn't. Organ music greeted me even before I opened the door. An usher slipped me a bulletin and didn't even raise his eyebrows at my coming in a minute late. Instead he winked and seemed glad I was there. Just as I stepped into the back of the church, Pastor Ammon invited the congregation to greet each other, the perfect foil for me to slip down the side aisle and into a seat. Out of long-ingrained habit, I gravitated to the pew where my family had sat all those years ago. Those years when church on Sunday wasn't an option.

Yesterday, after spending the morning at the hospital in Carlton visiting Vicky, I'd driven back to Brewster with my thoughts in a jumble. Even though Vicky might be released soon, it was obvious she wasn't going to be able to head back to the café full-time. Bouts of dizziness from any sudden movement left her grabbing for support. Not to mention her broken right arm. The arm she'd probably slammed against the oven as her feet flew from under her. It made me shudder to think of it.

I'd dropped my car at the house, then took off on foot for a walk around town. The two-mile square that formed the perimeter of Brewster wasn't nearly long enough to sort out my thoughts. I'd cut to the center of town, walking past the KBRS building, the call letters still hanging outside as if ready for business. The bank building stood quiet. There was not enough Saturday business in Brewster to warrant opening on the weekend. I cut across the street, past Cal's Hardware Store, the old wooden door still creaking as a customer stepped inside. I walked halfway past the café, then stopped, staring at the sign hanging inside the door. I knew there hadn't been many days over the years that sign had stated "closed" during daylight hours.

As I'd stood there, Mrs. Bauer stepped out of the hardware store. "Yah, see, vhat did I tell you," she said, as if we'd been having a conversation all along, "dat sign looks terrible dere, chust terrible." She put her hand on my arm. "You shoult tink about moving back and helping Wicky. Dis place coult use the two uff you."

Often in the past I'd made secret fun of Mrs. Bauer's accent, but yesterday her speech had not only planted a seed, it also made me know that Brewster and its people were what meant home to me.

I closed the hymnal and sat down in the pew. I didn't care what anyone thought. I'd come to church looking for guidance, but I doubted I'd find any in the announcements Pastor Ammon started giving. I tuned out, my mind replaying the joy I'd felt serving pie at Pumpkin Fest, the dread I felt when I thought about returning to Minneapolis. Nothing waited for me there. What was I going to do? I couldn't very well barge into the café and tell Vicky I was going to take over. Silently I prayed, *Lord, show me what to do.*

I highly doubted I'd find any guidance in the offering either, but I dug to the bottom of my purse. Four quarters. They'd have to do. As the plates began to pass through the aisles, the simple notes of an old children's song began to play. *Jesus loves me, this I know.* One by one, the notes tinkled out the tune. I didn't need words to sing along in my mind. Soon the simple melody had turned into chords and arpeggios that transformed the familiar tune into something completely new. A song that seemed to seep into my heart, softening it in a way digging for quarters hadn't done. Suddenly I wished I'd given more. I found myself closing my eyes, letting the music wash over me, ministering to me in a way the songs I played on the radio never did. *Yes, Jesus loves me...* As the song came to an end, a reverent silence filled the church, replaced by exuberant clapping. Who in Brewster could play the piano so tenderly it caused these conservative Germans to clap in church? I looked at the bulletin. *Offertory music played by Emily Marsden in memory of Anne Abbot, a former church member whose birthday would have been this past week.* Emily Marsden. She couldn't be more than sixteen. God had certainly given her a gift. I was glad I'd been here to share in it. I settled back, even more sure now that God had brought me here for a reason. I was waiting.

"I'd like to invite all the children up for the children's message," Pastor Ammon said as he clipped a portable microphone onto his robe.

Kids stampeded the stage, surrounding Pastor Ammon as though he were a children's magnet. Little Erica Frank was shouting, "I know! I know!" even though he hadn't asked a question yet. I couldn't help but smile. I had to admit she was pretty cute.

"Have you ever wanted to do something a whole lot?" Pastor Ammon began. "I mean, so bad that all you could do was think about it? You think about it in the morning when you get up. And you think about it when you're eating a snack. And then you think about it when you go to bed at night. Have you ever wanted something that bad?"

Well, sure, to move out of Brewster. Oh wait, this sermon was for the children...not for me.

Mike Jangula was waving his hand in the air. You could tell the kids who were in school or had siblings who were—they were the ones who raised their hands. The other kids simply shouted out answers. The pastor nodded at Mike. "I want to go to Disneyland!" A couple other kids chimed in with "me too's!" Another little boy chattered until the others went quiet and he could be heard. "Once I wanted a Champion game really bad, but then I got it and it wasn't that much fun."

Like my big-city dreams. The pit that formed each time I thought of returning to Minneapolis took its place in my stomach, pressing there like a heavy weight.

Pastor Ammon snapped his fingers. "That is exactly what happened to the young man in our Bible story today. He wanted something really bad, but when he got it...Well, let's read and find out what happened."

I sat up straight, curious. Someone in the Bible knew how I felt?

Pastor Ammon opened his Bible, then turned to the congregation. "This is the Scripture reading for today from an unconventional pulpit, the feet of children. Somehow I have a feeling God would approve." A low chuckle swept through the congregation. "For those of you who want to follow along, you can find the reading in Luke fifteen, starting with verse eleven." He adjusted his glasses. "I have to warn you, though, I may take a few liberties." He cleared his throat. "Once upon a time, in a faraway land there lived a rancher with two sons." The congregation chuckled again, catching on quickly that this wasn't an ordinary reading. The kids leaned forward, Mike Jangula flopping on the floor and resting his head in his hands as if he were watching a fascinating movie. I found myself leaning forward too.

"Now both sons—the older and the younger have interesting stories to tell—but today I want us to think about the younger son's story. This younger son dreamed of a life that was more fun than tending sheep and feeding pigs like he had to do at his dad's ranch. He wanted to go to Disneyplace." Pastor Ammon looked out at the congregation over the top of his glasses and said, sotto voce, "Or someplace like that." I couldn't help but join in the laughter. "The young brother asked his dad for a lot of money and went off to have fun. And for a while he did."

Me in Minneapolis.

"But one day he woke up. He didn't have any money left and he didn't have any food. Disneyplace wasn't much fun anymore. All of a sudden the home he'd left looked like a much better place than where he was."

Just like Brewster.

"But how could he go home?"

How could I? Suddenly, I knew exactly how that young man had felt. The longing I was experiencing was almost tangible. I just wanted someplace to call home.

"He'd already spent everything his dad had given him."

The same way I did, squandering my inheritance on a radio station that failed.

"He didn't have a job."

Okay, so I was one step ahead. Somehow it didn't seem to matter. I leaned forward, eager to hear more. I'd heard this story before, but it hadn't been *my* story then.

"And since he'd left home telling everyone he was glad to be leaving, he didn't think anyone back home would be very happy to see him again. But, oh, he was sooooo hungry." Pastor Ammon clutched his stomach with his free hand as if it was one big ache. "The only thing he could think to do was to go home and ask his dad if he could work for him like a hired hand. He knew he didn't deserve to be treated like a son after what he'd done. All he wanted now was a place to sleep, eat, and work. The young man was really scared; he thought his dad might not let him come home. That he might yell at him and tell him…" The pastor lowered his voice and spoke loudly, "Go away! You don't belong here anymore." Little Erica Frank clapped her hands over her ears. "But the young man really wanted to go home, even if it was just to live with his father's other workers.

So, even though he was afraid, he started walking to his father's house. Do you want to know what happened?"

The kids shouted, "Yes!" I wanted to know too.

"When the young man was still a long way off, the father came running down the road to meet him. He threw his arms around his son and gave him a big kiss. And when the son tried to apologize to his father for how foolish he'd been, the father wouldn't even listen. Instead he said, 'We're going to have a big party! I thought you were lost, but now you are home.'"

I sat back in the pew, the knot that had pressed at my stomach lighter somehow. It was strange. When Pastor Ammon had been telling the story of the son returning home, I hadn't seen a young man walking down that road...I'd seen myself. Scared and uncertain as to what waited ahead. And it hadn't been his father who had run out to greet me. It had been Vicky and Dave, Angie and Sam. Paul, who wrapped me in the biggest hug.

"The young man was finally *home*," Pastor Ammon concluded, satisfaction filling his voice.

The kids clapped, and a sigh of satisfaction left my lips as well. Home. There was that word again. The only place I wanted to be. The place where I was.

Pastor Ammon stood and faced the congregation. "I want to make clear that this isn't simply a children's story. There is forgiveness and redemption for everyone who has made a bad choice. All you have to do is ask, and God, your heavenly Father, will hold out His arms, wrap them around you, and welcome you home."

Funny, I had no trouble imagining that part at all. God wrapping His arms around me. It was complete forgiveness, total acceptance, unconditional love in one giant embrace. The knot came completely undone, and warmth, gratitude, and a gentle knowing flooded that spot of release, filling a part of me that had been empty all these years.

What had been so murky to me before was suddenly so clear. Not only had God been waiting for me to come home all along, but so had Vicky, so had Paul. The people of Brewster too. Like the father in the Bible, people here weren't judging me; they weren't going to reject me because I'd left. They were simply waiting with arms open wide for me to come home. And here I was. Finally.

Vicky had asked me countless times to help her in the café. All it would take was a single word from me and I'd be welcomed with open arms, a coffeepot in each hand. I was completely ready to say that word.

Paul might not have said anything, but it didn't take a rocket scientist to pick up the signals he'd been sending. I was ready for that too.

And the people of Brewster? I didn't think they'd ever really let me go in the first place.

While Pastor Ammon held hands in a circle with the kids, I bowed my head and said my own prayer, thanking God for bringing me home. Home to Brewster, where everything important had been all along. Home to Him, where everything important would always be.

Home from Detroit

Epilogue

Paul

I rearranged the pillow Ruthie had brought along, wedging my shoulder into the crook between the seat and the door. Snug as a bug in an Explorer. I'd fought sleep for a half hour before we'd stopped outside Denver for supper, and now that Ruthie was driving and I was free to snooze I couldn't doze off. Ah, the mysteries of life.

I closed my eyes. Maybe if I pretended I was asleep I could fool my weary body into it. No, that wasn't working. I let my gaze wander out the side window of our vehicle, the stars over Colorado as steady as those over Brewster. Talk about mysteries, who would've guessed that six months after I threw rocks towards heaven, throwing all my longing up to God, I'd be walking down the aisle, married to Ruthie?

People in Brewster didn't even bother to whisper about the fact Ruthie and I got engaged so quickly—they just flat-out asked.

"Isn't it kind of quick?" Ed Brinkman had limped into my office and settled himself into a chair. I didn't have to guess at what he meant; Kenny Pearson had asked me the same thing when I'd stopped for gas the morning the news of our engagement hit Brewster.

I'd put down the past-due loan report I'd been studying and looked Ed in the eye. "Some people might think it's quick, but what can I do?" A stupid grin replaced any look I might have had. "I'm in love." I didn't add that part of my heart had always stayed with Ruthie. Our getting married simply felt like I was getting it back.

Ed nodded his head slowly. "Can't fight that." His old eyes crinkled. "Marie and me had many happy years on that old farm. It'll be good for you to have a woman in the house. I wish you the best." He pushed himself out of the chair. "See any pheasants out there yet?"

One thing about folks in Brewster, once they had their question answered they moved right on. No pretense there.

"You bet I've seen 'em. You keep your oven on this fall and I'll bring you a couple."

Ed turned towards the door. "I'd like that." He lifted the back of his hand over his shoulder in goodbye.

I almost lifted my arm right back remembering the scene. I stretched my legs as far as the leg space in the Explorer would allow, then flipped the pillow over to the cool side and rearranged my head on it, closing my eyes. Looking back, I could see how Ed would think our marriage had happened fast, but to me it seemed it had somehow been pending for twenty years. I didn't mean to discount any of my time with Mia. I had truly loved her, and if I hadn't, I wouldn't have become the person I was now. No, I'd long ago learned God uses *all* things for good. Even events that are bad. Ruthie turning down my first proposal. Mia and Jenny dying. Somehow God had knit them all into something good. Our delayed honeymoon celebrated that fact.

I shifted position again. I really needed to get some sleep; Ruthie would want me to take over the driving at some point. My mind drifted to the conversation Dave had had with me before Ruthie and I had left on our trip.

"Now that Vicky and Ruthie are working together in the café, what would you think about buying into half of the business?" We'd been sitting in a boat in the middle of Brush Lake, trying to get our money's worth out of our fishing licenses.

I'd cast my line far out into the water, then reeled it in slowly. "What brought that on?" I'd asked. "I thought you had the café paid for already."

"We do," Dave had replied, tugging at his line, checking for a bite. No go. He reeled it in quickly, then tossed the line back in. "We just thought if you guys owned part of it, Vicky and I might feel we could take off now and then. We haven't been able to do much of that these past years."

I knew they hadn't. Between Dave's insurance business and Vicky running the café practically single-handed some days, they were overdue for a vacation. "Has Vicky said anything to Ruthie about it?"

"Yeah, but Ruthie told her with all the debt left on the station, she didn't want to bring it up to you." One corner of Dave's mouth turned up. "She didn't say I couldn't. And besides," he'd added before I'd had a chance to reply, "Vicky has an idea for another business she'd like to start. We could use the money for that."

Investing in Brewster. I liked that idea. I planned to tell Ruthie I thought it would be a good investment for both of us as soon as we got back from our trip.

Static from the Explorer's radio worked its way into my thoughts. The announcer's voice crackled over the airwaves, "Stay tuned for 'Brown Eyed Girl,' coming up next after this station break." Ah, our song. I was sure I'd have no trouble staying awake to hear it.

I'd made sure Ruthie and I had danced together to that song at our wedding reception, no cutting in allowed. I'd wanted to hold her in my arms for the whole song and I did. As I cradled her head against my shoulder, our feet moving together as if we'd danced together for years, I wondered if Van Morrison had ever thought of doing the song as a ballad, the slowed-down version the band played at my request was perfect. Curt Sailer, one of Brewster's better farmers, had tapped on my shoulder as the first verse ended. "Dance with the bride?"

"Sorry, Curt," I smiled, "this one's ours." I pulled Ruthie close. He backed away. "Got it," he said, giving me a sly wink.

I winked right back, knowing he'd be making a beeline to Sandy Quinn. I had a feeling she was going to remember this night. Even though Sandy and I had never had a real relationship, I knew she had probably hoped we would. I'd tried my best not to lead her on as I'd tried my hardest to discover God's will. When Ruthie had returned for Pumpkin Fest all thoughts having anything to do with Sandy had floated right out of my head. I would have wished her well, if I'd even thought to think of her. To call Ruthie's and my romance a whirlwind might make a hurricane sound slow. It had blown both of us right into each other's arms.

I watched as Curt threaded his way through the crowd on the dance floor. Sure enough, there stood Sandy grinning him over to her. He'd come into my office last week on the pretense of reviewing his operating loan. It was only after I'd told him everything looked good that he'd casually asked, "Any idea how much engagement rings cost? I'm thinking of asking Sandy to marry me."

I had to admit I'd felt some sort of giddy-laughter bubble near the back of my throat as I replied, "As a matter of fact, I do." The idea of Sandy and Curt had never occurred to me; maybe because she was a couple years older than him. But who was counting at this stage of the game? They'd make a perfect couple. During the short time I'd dated her, she'd often commented about missing life on the farm she'd grown up on outside of Brewster. At the time I'd thought she'd been hinting that my farmstead looked okay. I guess it turned out Curt's looked even better. I was happy for both of them. And even happier for me.

As the dance neared its end, Ruthie reached up and put her hand on my cheek, gently turning my face towards hers. "Penny for your thoughts? Or do bankers charge more for theirs?" she asked, laying her head once again on my shoulder.

"You don't have to pay a thing," I chuckled, nuzzling my face against her hair. "I was just thinking how much I love you. How much I love this town. How I'm so glad God is in charge because somehow His plans always turn out much better than mine."

Ruthie nodded into my shoulder. I pulled her even closer, if that was possible.

God had done for Ruthie what KBRS, Minneapolis, or even I, couldn't do. Ruthie told it best one evening as we sat on my front porch watching the moon rise over Brush Lake. We'd returned from Minneapolis late that afternoon, a U-haul in tow. I'd driven her there in my new Explorer, the hitch installed just so I could move Ruthie back to Brewster. I'd told the mechanic, "Put on the best you've got." I considered it an investment in my future. On our way out of Minneapolis we merged onto Interstate 94, passing a billboard where Ruthie smiled down on us, larger than life. I tried to keep my jaw from dropping. I'd never seen anyone I knew on a billboard before. Only then did I realize what she was giving up.

"Are you sure about this?" I asked, forcing the words past the logjam in my throat.

"I've never been more sure about anything in my life," she answered. "Keep driving."

I did. Happily. All the way to Brewster.

Ruthie would be living in Vicky's basement, at least until Vicky's cast was removed, so we'd stacked Ruthie's furniture in one of my nearly-empty outbuildings. Ruthie would be returning the U-haul to Carlton in the morning.

As we stacked the last of her belongings in the shed, Ruthie sighed.

"There, that's done." She threw a blanket over her television set, clapped dust from her hands, and declared "I'm starving!"

Just what I liked, a woman with an appetite.

"Let's see what I've got in the fridge," I offered.

"Race you to the house," she said. I took up a stance, waiting for her cue to start the race.

Ruthie poised herself beside me, arms bent to race. "One… two…GO!" she yelled, taking off one count before I was ready. I was laughing too hard to even try and keep up.

"You win," I conceded, walking into the kitchen in time to see the four thick sandwiches stacked inside my fridge, Vicky's note leaned against the plastic wrap.

Thank you for bringing my sister home.

"Another reason I love Brewster," Ruthie said, "you don't have to lock your doors, and look—people put things *into* your house!"

We carried our makeshift picnic to the table, devouring the sandwiches, chips, and Cokes like starving college kids, home on semester break.

When the last crumb was gone we slipped into coats and walked outside, the front steps a perfect theatre to watch the giant harvest moon that was rising above the lake. Ruthie wrapped her arms around her bent knees, resting her chin on crossed arms. The shadows of dusk formed a room around us. She sighed deeply, then spoke. "I feel like I've been...been *found*." She gazed across the lake, then turned to me, eyes glistening. "I don't know if this is going to make any sense," she said softly. Her eyes focused on the orange moon for a moment, then she continued. "I spent all those years searching for what I thought would bring me happiness. A certain job. A bigger town. Anything but what I had. I look back, and now I can see what I'd thought was searching, was *wandering*. I was lost and He found me." She slipped her hand into mine. "And then, there's you." Her breath formed tiny, white clouds in the cold, fall air. "It seems like too much."

I took my hand from hers and put my arm around her shoulder, pulling her into my chest. "I know," I said, remembering that certain Sunday—the Sunday Vicky got out of the hospital after her accident. The day Ruthie came to church alone. I'd looked up from the hymnal I was sharing with my mother to see Ruthie standing a few pews in front of me. My impluse had been to leave my spot and sit by her side, but something kept me rooted where I stood. This was time between Ruthie and God. I didn't hear much of the service that Sunday. I was too busy praying. But I had a feeling that was okay with God.

After church Ruthie said two words to me I'll never forget. *"I'm home."* She didn't have to say more, the look on her face said it all. If hearts can dance, mine did that day. It hadn't stopped since.

Oh! I startled out of the sleep I'd finally fallen into. It was the seatbelt I was hugging, not Ruthie. I looked to my left. There she was, driving us northeast, the direction of home. I reached out and squeezed her hand. I should have known by now that God would take all my frustration and fear, all my unspoken longing, and toss it all back to me as one big blessing.

I should have known.

Jack

"That was the latest from Hitch and just about wraps things up for my show tonight. Two more tunes and then Jason will be behind the mike. I've saved my two favorites for last, so listen up." I punched at the screen, cueing up the second-to-last tune of my shift. As always I spoke into the mike, "This one's for anyone out there who's still searching. Keep on looking. He's there." I started the mega-hit, "Shout to the Lord." Sometimes I thought maybe it wasn't one of my favorites anymore, the beginning was too slow. But just about the time I'd have my mind changed, that chorus would kick in and I'd close my eyes and let the song take me away. I leaned back in my chair, hooking my hands behind my head, letting the music do its thing.

The music. I had followed it my whole life. Who knew the music would lead me here? First Brewster, then Minneapolis, and now Colorado. It blew my mind when I thought about it. Blew my mind how God could still use my love of music, after all I'd done to ruin my life.

I wasn't proud of the person I used to be. To put it bluntly, I was a jerk. A first-class jerk. But I'd changed, and I had God and Doug Sommers to thank for that. If Doug hadn't slipped me that card that day...who knows where I'd be now?

I reached out and nudged up the volume control in the studio, bouncing my head in time to the soaring notes, singing along for a bit. I'd spent the past two years trying to make up for who I used to be. I'd reconnected with my mother. Paid my bills. Gone to church. I also joined an accountability group. They helped make sure all areas of my life jived with who I was now.

There was one thing I had left to do. Apologize to Ruthie for all the things I dumped on her. My drinking. My gambling. Running away from my debts. She'd seen the worst of me, that was for sure. Someday, when the KBRS debt was paid, the part that was repayable with money, that is, I planned to let her know how sorry I was. Until then all I could do was send my twice-monthly payments to Paul and grow into the man God was shaping me to be.

I'd lost a lot of things over the years, including my integrity. I was working hard to get that back. But the one thing that never changed was my sense for the music. God had let me keep that.

I sat back up, leaning into the mike. I turned down the studio volume and cued up the last song. "Here it is folks, my last song of the night." I let the first strains of music drift out over the airwaves before I spoke into the mike, "This one's for you, babe." I cued up the volume, then spoke again, "It's an oldie. My wife's favorite. Ginny Owens singing 'Springs of Life.'" I let the music wash over me. A spring of life that had stayed with me through it all. I let the last tender note die out then spoke my signature sign off, "Hug our little guy…"

Ruthie

Vicky was calling this trip Paul and I were taking our maternitymoon. A combination honeymoon and maternity leave.

Six months after Pumpkin Fest, Paul and I were married, two weeks after Easter. It seemed a good time to be starting a new life. The ceremony was small, neither of us needing a crowd to seal our marriage vows. Dave stood up for Paul, Sam, too, handsome in his first tuxedo. Vicky was my matron of honor, Angie a junior bridesmaid. The silver-glittered headband she'd insisted on wearing was a pale glimmer compared to the platinum-set diamond Paul had given me one night as we walked near Brush Lake by his farm.

It had been Christmas Eve. The café and bank closed early, as did most of the town businesses. It was a time when most families gathered in the evening for church Christmas programs, then gift opening. Paul had invited me out to his farm for chili and homemade bread before we attended Angie and Sam's Christmas program. I knew he'd taken an interest in cooking since he'd moved to the farm, but I'd raised my eyebrows about the homemade bread.

Okay," he'd laughed, "I confess, my mom told me to stop by her house after work and pick up a loaf. But I am making the chili myself. In the Crock-Pot." He nodded, very proud of himself.

I lowered my eyebrows, no longer able to hide my grin. He was just so pleased about his new hobby, he reminded me of a little boy. A very cute boy. "I'm beginning to think you might be a good fill-in cook at the café if this bank job doesn't work out," I teased.

"I'll pick you up after I clear my desk at the bank. Around four-thirty? Then we can drive out to the farm and come back in for the program together." We'd be joining Vicky and Dave at their house, where I was once again living, for punch and gifts after church. Paul's mom was invited too.

I'd dressed for the program, my five-year-old black velvet pantsuit getting its annual wearing. What I hadn't planned on was the walk Paul suggested we take before dinner. Outside. By the lake.

"But it's snowing," I'd protested, thinking about my hair. "And I didn't bring boots." I looked down at my black heels. "And it's cold." The satin lining of my dress coat would not do a thing against the North Dakota prairie wind.

"No problem." Paul pulled a gigantic parka out of the hall closet, helping me into it as though it were mink. He flopped up the huge hood, any illusions of fancy fur disappearing. I certainly didn't need to worry about my hair; I couldn't even see. I rolled back the edge of the hood just in time to see him set a pair of old work boots by my feet. He knelt, slipping my heels from my feet and guiding first my left foot, then my right, into the way-too-big boots as though I were Cinderella and he was the Prince.

Paul walked out of the house. I clomped, lifting my knees over small drifts in the yard, sure the boots would fall off any second. They didn't. The crisp winter air bit into my cheeks. Paul pushed up the sleeve of the coat and took my hand. Between long sleeves and Paul's warm hand I didn't need mittens. Light snowflakes fell as we made our way down to the frozen lake, our breaths like little clouds in the night air. When we reached the shoreline, Paul stopped, turning me to face him. He put his fingers under my chin, nudging it up. My hood fell off, but suddenly my hairdo didn't seem important after all.

"Merry Christmas," he said softly, the corners of his eyes crinkling as he bent to kiss me.

I was going to answer back but his lips were on mine. I kissed him back, an answer of its own sort, I guessed.

He straightened, turning my back to his chest, wrapping his arms around me so we both faced the lake. Dark comes early to North Dakota in December, but a hazy moon backlit the clouds. Snowflakes glittered as they floated down. Silent night. How could I have ever wished to be anywhere but right here? Tears of joy filled my eyes. My body relaxed into Paul's, our heavy coats a conduit for the warmth between us. *Two shall become one.* This was what that felt like.

"Look at the stars," Paul said.

I tilted my head to look up. Snowflakes fell into my eyes. "There aren't any stars," I said, "it's snowing."

"Yes, there are. Look harder." He stepped back as I searched the sky, looking for the stars he claimed were there. "Here," he said, his voice coming from behind me. I turned. Paul was on one knee in the snow, holding a star that looked awfully similar to a diamond ring in the palm of his hand. "Marry me?"

I dropped to my knees in front of him, not giving one thought to what snow might do to black velvet. I was crying, laughing, rejoicing as I threw my arms around his neck.

"Careful," Paul laughed, returning my hug. "A star might be hard to find in a snowbank." He took the ring and slipped it on my finger. "Is that a yes?"

I nodded through tears, my throat too full to add any words.

Pastor Ammon officiated at the ceremony, closing the service by removing the stole from his neck and binding Paul's and my left hands together, saying, "A strand of three chords is not easily broken. Go with God."

The small congregation clapped as we kissed, then laughed when Paul asked the pastor if we had to keep our hands knotted forever. Pastor Ammon quickly undid the binding, then invited our guests to the old gym for a reception. The same gym where I had hurt Paul so many years ago. It seemed we'd come full circle, a binding up of hurts and dreams that had somehow brought us to that joyous day.

A crowd waited for us at the gym, which had been decorated in pastel colors, mostly by Vicky and me. We'd achieved a spring garden look. Sort of. We'd dragged big old branches out of the shelter belt on Paul's farm, spray painted them white, then stood our makeshift trees upright in buckets of cement, weaving silk flowers and lights among the branches. Paul and Dave had thought we were nuts, but I knew we'd achieved the effect I'd been looking for when I overheard Mrs. Bauer say, "Chust beautiful," as we walked into the gym.

It had been too hard to decide who to, or not to, invite to the reception. Between us Paul and I knew practically everybody in town. We finally took out a notice in the *Brewster Banner* inviting anyone who wanted to share our day to come. No gifts, we'd said, all we asked was that folks bring a donation of food for the Brewster Food Pantry. Paul and Dave had scrounged up an old farm wagon to set inside the gym for donations. The guys thought it was fine, slivers and all. Vicky and I knew better. We'd sanded it down, then painted it a soft shade of Martha Stewart green, fastening to the corners garlands of white silk morning glories. Little Mike Jangula had commandeered the wagon, accepting donations as though they were cargo for an upcoming adventure.

Paul and I stayed to the very end of the reception, dancing and visiting, sharing one large piece of cake as though it were a slice of pumpkin pie and we were the only two people in the room. After we'd shaken the last hand, received the last hug, and were finally alone, Paul had taken me into his arms, cupped my face in his hands, then kissed me softly. "Let's go home," he'd whispered.

"Let's go home," I whispered back.

~

We'd planned to take a honeymoon in May after we got settled at the farm, but I'd forgotten, or rather at that point I didn't know, about Vicky and me having to cater the senior prom banquet. Vicky couldn't understand how she'd ever run the café without my help, and I couldn't either. I also couldn't understand why it had taken me so long to realize how much I enjoyed the people in Brewster. Visiting with them every day was a gift that came along with serving.

Mrs. Bauer was in the café kitchen, helping Vicky and me get organized for serving the prom banquet. She said it gave her "pocket monies." I had a feeling she liked feeling needed. She was.

"Ida, how are you?" I filled a coffee cup to the top, just the way she liked it, patting at a chair to get her off her feet for a few minutes. I was still getting used to calling Mrs. Bauer by her first name, but as she'd said, "Frients shoult call each other by dare front names." I bit the insides of my cheeks, then grinned anyway. Why not? She was a joy. "You're right, we are friends. Ida it is." She grinned right back.

The day after the prom banquet, when Paul and I had thought we'd be able to take off, Wayne Jorgenson's mother-in-law died and he needed some time off to help settle her estate. Paul couldn't leave the bank. Then it was June and we had two weddings to cater. In July I got pregnant. A bad case of morning sickness put me out of the mood for just about everything but naps and saltine crackers. Most days I managed to drag myself to the café by the crack of ten, in time to help with the thick of the coffee crowd. Paul and I gave up the idea of a honeymoon and concentrated on outfitting a nursery.

Two days before her due date little Naomi decided to show up.

"Are you sure?" Paul questioned when I'd called him at work to tell him I was in labor. "I have a board meeting this after—" My panting through a contraction changed his tune. "I'll be right there."

Thrilled doesn't begin to describe how Paul looked when the doctor said, "You have a healthy baby girl."

One day, a month after Naomi was born, Vicky stopped by the house and said, "Just go already."

"I thought you were coming to tell me how much you needed me back at the café," I said, expertly swiping Naomi's behind with a baby wipe.

"I do need you. But you need a honeymoon first." Vicky fastened the last snap on Naomi's sleeper, then scooped her into her arms. "I don't want to hear you telling this kid twenty years from now that you never got a honeymoon because of me. Consider it part of your maternity leave."

So there we were, two weeks later, Paul, Naomi, and I, on our maternitymoon. Naomi was asleep in her infant seat in the back, and Paul dozed in the passenger seat beside me. We'd planned to stop hours ago, our route back from seeing the ocean in California flexing to accommodate a baby's schedule. But Naomi was having an exceptional day, content to ride the time away. We'd switched drivers after supper outside of Denver, Paul and the baby asleep within minutes. I didn't mind the time by myself. The stretch of road was lightly traveled late at night, and it provided an opportunity to think about how quickly my life had changed. How God had known, even better than I, what would bring me back to Brewster, back to Him. Bring me to a place of contentment I hadn't known to ask for.

The radio played softly as I drove through the night, my mind free to go far beyond the confines of our Explorer. We'd quickly discovered the VW was best for Paul's short commute to and from work. I'd doubted we'd ever part with the car; it held too many memories for both of us. We'd be two old fogies lurching through the streets of Brewster some day. I smiled at the image, then frowned at the fading signal coming from the oldies station I'd found. It couldn't fade out now. The deejay had said our song would be played soon. I left it a bit longer and crossed my fingers.

One time Angie asked if I ever wished I still lived in Minneapolis. Her eyes held a wanderlust that looked familiar. "Tell the truth," she'd said.

I did. I told her sometimes I missed going to the theater. Sometimes I wished I could be at the Mall of America, touching what I saw in magazines for myself. I also told her I loved the city for what it taught me...that Brewster was home. For me, anyway. "Besides," I said, holding her close, "if I still lived in Minneapolis, you wouldn't have Naomi to baby-sit." It was a small bribe that worked, for now.

For a moment I was back in Brewster with Angie, the next moment static from the fading radio station brought me back to a road in Colorado. I punched at the button, sending the radio into a search for a clearer signal. Not in the mood for country, I pushed the button again. Ah, there, one of my favorite songs, "Springs of Life." I turned up the volume, just enough to sing along, not enough to wake anyone.

I tapped at the steering wheel, feeling the bluesy notes of the music. For just a second I missed the days when music made up my life, but I didn't, however, miss the mess that came of it. I glanced over at Paul, remembering the afternoon he'd told me that Jack had been sending payments on the KBRS loan for over a year.

"You can close your mouth now," Paul had said, grinning. I'd stood in his office that day, mouth gaping like a landed trout at the news. Jack? Making payments?

"What? Where? When?" I sounded like a stunned newspaper reporter. Paul didn't have any information other than that the payments were as regular as the calendar. I'd told him before we were married that I intended to pay off that loan all by myself. I still planned to give all of my tip money and part of my paycheck to the bank, but his news was another unexpected gift. One of the many God seemed to be piling on my lap these days.

I tapped out the last few measures of the song on the steering wheel, wishing I could hear it one more time. I reached for the volume knob; better turn it down before some deejay broke in loud enough to wake the dead or my sleeping family. My fingers paused, frozen in midair as an oh-so-familiar voice said softly, "Hug our little guy for me, babe. Light the fireplace, too. I'm on my way home."

Could it be...? Could it? It had to be. I left the station on, but when the deejay returned another voice had taken the place of the person I knew had been Jack. Jack on a *Christian* radio station? I threw back my head and softly laughed. Another surprise from God. Wherever Jack was, I prayed he was well. He'd been part of my journey too. Who could have guessed God would reweave even that part of my life into something so good?

I often marveled at the long road I'd taken just to get back to Brewster. The "Detroit Route" as our family called any path that took you completely out of your way, only to end up right back where you'd started. It had begun in Brewster with Paul so many years ago, detoured to my time with Jack and the radio station, then turned into a freeway through Minneapolis, a road which had, miraculously, led me back to Brewster, back to Paul. I wondered what *that* map looked like? Obviously, God could read it all along.

I'd been looking, forever it seemed, for somewhere to call home. A place where I belonged. Always certain that place was anywhere besides Brewster. I'd been so busy imagining life somewhere else, I almost missed the life I had. Almost missed the fact that my certain somewhere had been with me all along. Whether I'd been in Brewster, Minneapolis, or anywhere in between, there was a certain Someone who made everywhere feel like home.

My eyes swept down the dark road, far past the stars that were shining over Colorado, the same stars that were waiting for us in Brewster. "Thank You, thank You, thank You," my heart seemed to breathe.

Paul stirred in his seat. "How're you doing? Getting tired?"

"Nah, I'm okay." I reached out and patted his hand. "You can sleep some more."

"Okay," he said, turning his hand, squeezing mine. "Take us on home."

"I plan to," I replied. My eyes traveled over Paul and glanced into the backseat at our sleeping little girl as I whispered into the night, "I already am home."

A Note from
Roxanne Sayler Henke

I would love to hear about the certain somewhere you call home. You can write to me at:

Roxanne Henke
c/o Harvest House Publishers
990 Owen Loop North
Eugene, Oregon 97402

Or you can reach me via e-mail at
roxannehenke@yahoo.com

Finding Ruth
Conversation Questions

A note from the author:

Like Ruthie Hammond, I have lived almost my whole life in a small, Brewster-like town in rural North Dakota. At times I, too, struggled with living out my dream of writing novels from a location far from publishing houses, editors, or agents.

The very things that can make a place seem attractive—quiet, remoteness, a close-knit community—can also make it feel confining, especially when you are dreaming of something different. It's taken awhile, but God has shown me that nothing is impossible for Him. He has brought me to a place of contentment, and it's right where I've been all along. Amazing how He works!

I hope this book and these questions will help lead you to a place of contentment too.

1. Whether you live in New York City, rural North Dakota, or somewhere in between, you have your own "small town" of people with whom you live and work. Describe your "town." Do you have someone you can confide in? A caring older person in your life? A friend who has known you since childhood? What about the daily contact you have with office workers, in the coffee shop, at the grocery store? How do these people affect your life? Do you allow them to?

2. What dreams have you had for your life? Have you ever felt like Ruthie, having unfulfilled dreams of your own? Discuss how Ruthie felt trapped by her circumstances. What could she have done to change them? Why didn't she?

3. Mrs. Bauer is a minor character in the book and yet Ruthie finds herself thinking about Mrs. Bauer's words often. Talk about how Mrs. Bauer affected Ruthie and about seemingly minor people in your own life who have had a major impact.

4. Have you known anyone like Jack? Someone who only thinks of himself or herself? Why might it be hard for a person like this to come to faith?

5. What role did Doug Sommers (the radio station manager) play in Jack's life? What might have happened to Jack if it hadn't been for Doug? Has anyone ever been helpful to you in a similar manner, nonjudgmental, yet willing to help? Have you ever done this for someone else?

6. The theme of the book is contentment. Do you think it is possible for someone to be content in *all* circumstances?

7. Discuss the difference between contentment and complacency. How might this have affected Ruthie?

8. Talk about the aspects of living in a small town. Can you see why Ruthie would feel confined in Brewster? What are some of the advantages of small-town living that Ruthie could not see while she was there? Discuss advantages of large towns. Where would you prefer to live? Why?

9. How does a person's viewpoint affect their outlook on a situation? Caring versus snooping...what defines the difference?

10. Do you think people ever outgrow their dreams? What happens when you have to give up a dream? What can take its place? Was Ruthie foolish to cling to her dream for so long? What did holding on to her dream for so long do to her?

11. Discuss how God worked in Paul's life...his work, his friendship with Dave, his relationship with Ruthie. Can you see God working in similar ways in your own life?

12. Why was Ruthie so discontented with her life? What could she have done to be happier? Did she have to experience discontentment in order to know contentment?

13. Over the years Brewster remained a haven in Paul's heart. Do you have a place like that? Why was Brewster so different for Ruthie? How, or why, did it finally change for her? Have you ever changed your feelings about a place you lived in?

14. Ruthie talks about taking the "Detroit Route." Have you ever gone far afield from your plans only to end up back where you started? What did you learn from the detour? Are there advantages and disadvantages that come from taking "the long way" home? Do you think God *sends* us on a winding path, or is it us seeking to do things our way?

Harvest House Publishers

For the Best in Inspirational Fiction

～

Roxanne Henke

COMING HOME TO BREWSTER

After Anne
Finding Ruth

Melody Carlson

Blood Sisters

Linda Chaikin

A DAY TO REMEMBER

Monday's Child
Wednesday's Child
Thursday's Child
Friday's Child

Mindy Starns Clark

THE MILLION DOLLAR MYSTERIES

A Penny for Your Thoughts
Don't Take Any Wooden Nickels

Sally John

THE OTHER WAY HOME

A Journey by Chance
After All These Years
Just to See You Smile

Craig Parshall

CHAMBERS OF JUSTICE

The Resurrection File
Custody of the State

Debra White Smith

Second Chances
The Awakening
A Shelter in the Storm
To Rome with Love
For Your Heart Only
This Time Around

Lori Wick

THE YELLOW ROSE TRILOGY

Every Little Thing About You
A Texas Sky
City Girl

CONTEMPORARY FICTION

Sophie's Heart
Beyond the Picket Fence
Pretense
The Princess
Bamboo & Lace

THE ENGLISH GARDEN

The Proposal
The Rescue
The Visitor

Roxanne Henke lives in rural North Dakota with her husband, Lorren, and their dog, Gunner. They have two very cool young adult daughters, Rachael and Tegan. As a family they enjoy spending time at their lake cabin in northern Minnesota. Roxanne has a degree in behavioral and social science from the University of Mary and for many years was a newspaper humor columnist. She has also written and recorded radio commercials, written for and performed in a comedy duo, and cowritten school lyceums. *Finding Ruth* is Roxanne's second novel in the Coming Home to Brewster series, following *After Anne*.